ROOK

The first

Gra

PAN BOOKS

ROOK

PAN BOOKS

This edition published 1999 by Pan Books
an imprint of Macmillan Publishers Ltd,
25 Eccleston Place, London, SW1W 9NF
Associated companies throughout the world
www.macmillan.co.uk

This first world edition published in Great Britain 1996 by
SEVERN HOUSE PUBLISHERS LTD of
9-15 High Street, Sutton, Surrey SM1 1DF.
First published in the USA 1997 by
SEVERN HOUSE PUBLISHERS INC., of
595 Madison Avenue, New York, NY 10022.

British Library Cataloguing in Publication Data

Masterton, Graham, 1946-
Rook. – (Rook; bk. 1)
1. English Fiction – 20th century
1. Title
823.9'14 [F]

ISBN 0 330 396536

Typeset by Palimpsest Book Production Limited,
Polmont, Stirlingshire, Scotland.
Printed and bound in Great Britain by
Mackays of Chatham plc, Chatham, Kent

WEST GROVE COMMUNITY COLLEGE

SPECIAL CLASS II

Greg Lake	Amanda Zaparelli	Sue-Robin Caufield	Seymour Williams
Sherma Feldstein	empty desk	Russell Gloach	Sharon X
Beattie McCordic	Ray Vito	Elvin Clay	John Ng
Mark Foley	Ricky Herman	Muffy Brown	Tee Jay Jones
David Littwin	Rita Munoz	Titus Greenspan III	Jane Firman

Jim Rook
English
and Special Needs

Chapter One

He heard shouting and whooping in the corridor a second before Muffy came bursting into the classroom, her eyes wild, saying, "They're killing each other! Mr Rook! They're killing each other!"

Jim dropped his felt-tip pen and threw back his chair. He strode to the door and Muffy clutched hold of his sleeve. "You have to stop them, Mr Rook! They're going crazy!"

He ran down the corridor, past the lockers to the boys' washrooms. A crowd of twenty or thirty pupils had gathered outside, chanting and yelling and beating on the locker doors with their fists. "Tee *Jay*! Tee *Jay*!"

Jim yelled, "Get out of the way!" and pushed past them into the toilets.

At the far end of the washroom, two seventeen–year-old black boys were fighting. One of them – tall, and heavily built – had forced the other right back against the basins, and was knocking his head against the mirrors. Both of them had nosebleeds, and blood was spraying up the walls like graffiti.

Jim grabbed the bigger boy by the scruff of his T-shirt, and swung him around.

The boy's face was like a mask: sweaty, spattered with blood, with bulging eyes. He was so hyped up that he couldn't speak anything but gibberish. "Let go of me, man – I gotta – let *go* of me, man, I'm going to kill him – he diss me so bad – you don't even—"

"*Tee Jay*!" Jim yelled at him. Tee Jay tried to wrench himself free, but Jim twisted the neck of his T-shirt even tighter so that it was almost throttling him. Jim forced him back against the tiles and stared into his face with all the ferocity that he could muster. "Tee Jay, what in God's name has gotten into you?"

"He diss me – he *diss* me – I'm going to kill him for that – I'm going to murder that mother – don't try to stop me – 'cause you can't – you *can't*, you hear me?"

Jim kept Tee Jay pinned back against the wall. He turned to the other boy, Elvin, who was leaning over the basins with blood streaming from his mouth and nose. "Elvin, you okay? Elvin, can you hear me? You okay?"

Elvin coughed and nodded. Jim pointed to a tall fair-haired boy standing by the washroom door. "Jason! You and Philip take Elvin along to the infirmary! The rest of you, get the hell out of here! This isn't a goddamned cabaret!"

He turned back to Tee Jay. Tee Jay was still quaking with adrenaline, and he didn't take his eyes off Jim for a second, sniffing and shuffling and twitching his head. Jim could hardly recognise him. He was usually so quiet, and together, and funny, too. He was the tallest boy in the class, good-looking apart from a smattering of acne scars on his cheeks; a great basketball player. He wasn't especially bright, because none of the students in Jim Rook's class were especially bright. But he was always willing to learn – and he had never been obsessed with 'disrespect'. Not until now, anyway.

"All right," Jim demanded. "Are you going to chill out, or what?"

Tee Jay tried to pull himself away again, and the seam

of his T-shirt tore. "I'm never going to – *never*! – that mother—"

"Tee Jay, for Christ's sake! Listen to me, will you? I could have you arrested!"

Tee Jay quietened down. He attempted to jerk himself free one more time, but then he turned his face away and obstinately stared at the toilet doors.

Jim said, "Tee Jay? Come on, Tee Jay?" and when Tee Jay looked back again his eyes were crowded with tears.

"I'm sorry," he said. "It was just what Elvin said to me, man. I couldn't—"

"What *did* Elvin say?" Jim demanded. "What could anybody say to you that provokes you into attacking them like that?"

"Nothing, man. He didn't say nothing."

"So you just started beating up on him for the hell of it?"

Tee Jay wiped the blood away from his nose with the back of his hand. "Look, I've said I'm sorry, okay?"

"You think it's okay? *I* don't think it's okay. I think it stinks. I have enough of a hard job defending you guys without you behaving like mad dogs. I'm going to have to haul your ass up in front of Dr Ehrlichman when he comes back this afternoon; and Dr Ehrlichman will have to decide whether we're going to allow you to stay on here, or whether we're going to ask you to leave."

"It was a *fight*, man, that's all."

"You don't solve any problem by fighting, Tee Jay. I thought you had enough brains to know that."

"If I had any brains I wouldn't be in Special II, would I?"

Jim let go of his T-shirt and stepped away from him. "There," he said. "You're free to go. You think it's demeaning to be in Special II, then clear out your locker and go home. I don't want anybody in my class who thinks that arguments are settled by hitting people. And I don't want anybody in my class who isn't proud to be in it."

He waited, and watched Tee Jay sniffing. Then he furiously banged his fist against the toilet door. "Jesus, Tee Jay! Think what you're risking! Elvin dissed you? So what? Don't tell me you're *that* goddamned sensitive. You want to sit with the girls?"

"You can't talk to me like that, man!" Tee Jay warned.

"Oh, no? So what the hell's going on? You've made more progress this semester than anybody else in the class. When you came to me, you didn't even know who Shakespeare was. You could hardly read. You couldn't add up. Christ, you thought that President Washington's first name was Denzel. Think how far you've come. But now you're ready to throw away everything you've done, *snap*, just like that, for the sake of what? Your *vanity*? And you think you deserve respect?"

Tee Jay instantly flared up again. "That's it! You *always* doing that! Bringing people down! Making them look like a fool when they ain't! You walk around your schoolroom pretending to be friends but all the time you laughing behind your hand, man. You *laughing*!"

"I'm not laughing now, Tee Jay. Get yourself cleaned up. Then report back to class."

Tee Jay shuffled over and stood over him. "I could take you, man."

"Is this the first time that's occurred to you?" Jim asked him. He held his ground. He couldn't count how many times a rebellious teenager had loomed over him and warned him that, "I could take you, man," or words to that effect. In seven years of remedial teaching he had suffered one stab wound (screwdriver, upper shoulder muscle) and two missing teeth. But since he had taught over two-and-a-half thousand disturbed, disruptive and dyslexic boys and girls, he reckoned that he had probably gotten off lightly. His predecessor had been shot in the lung.

There was a moment of extreme tension – made all the tenser because Tee Jay had never challenged him like this before, and there was no predictable agenda.

But then Tee Jay said, "Ah, shit," and shook his head as if he couldn't be bothered, and slouched out of the washrooms with his hands in his pockets.

Jim watched him go, and then looked around at the blood-spattered mirrors. Behind the loops and squiggles of crimson, he could see himself, standing alone. A lean, dark-haired man of thirty-four, with eyes the colour of hazy green glass pebbles and a six-o'-clock shadow (even though it was only 9.20 in the morning.) His features were angular, slightly haunted-looking, as if he slept badly and never got quite enough to eat. He wore a short-sleeved denim shirt and a red-and-green necktie with palm trees and hula girls on it. His arms were thin and his wrist-watch looked too big for him.

Sometimes he looked at himself and wondered what the hell he was doing, trying to teach the unteachable, especially when it came to violence, like today. You could work for months on a student like Tee Jay – months of inch-by-inch progress, months of sweat and stuttering and tightly-clutched pencils – and then it could all explode, in an instant, for the stupidest of reasons, and you would be back with the swaggering, bad-mouthing streetwise numbskull that you first started out with.

Respect, he thought. *Don't make me laugh.*

Just as he was about to leave the washrooms he thought

he saw a very tall man passing the entrance. It was only a fleeting glimpse, like a shadow crossing a wall, because the man was walking along the corridor very quickly and very quietly, even though the floor was covered in polished thermoplastic tiles, which usually set up a hard rapping (stiletto heels) or a tortured squeaking (sneakers.)

Jim came out of the washrooms and looked down the corridor after him. The man was silhouetted against the sun-bright windows at the far end – even taller than he had seemed at first glance, wearing a baggy black suit with flapping trousers and a black, wide-brimmed hat, low in the crown like an old-fashioned preacher's hat, the sort that Elmer Gantry wore.

"Hey, can I help you?" he called out, but the man took no notice. "Pardon me, sir, can I help you?" he repeated. Still the man ignored him, and turned the bend at the end of the corridor and disappeared.

Jim went jogging after him. As he reached the corner, however, he almost collided with Susan Randall, the geography teacher, carrying a huge disorderly heap of books. She tipped most of them on to the floor in a flapping, slapping cascade.

"What are you doing, rushing about like a pig in a china shop?" she shrilled at him.

"Hey, Susan, I'm real sorry," he said. What made their collision all the more embarrassing was that he liked her, a lot; although she was still very suspicious of him. She had short brunette hair and pouty lips and a figure that could have won her a walk-by rôle in *Baywatch*, and today she was wearing his favourite yellow ribbed sweater. Even the boys used to whistle at her.

He knelt down and helped her to gather up the books, very conscious of the way her putty-coloured skirt had ridden up as she hunkered down next to him. He looked over her shoulder but the corridor was empty now. No sign of the man in the Elmer Gantry hat.

"Did you, uh, *see* anybody, just before we bumped into each other?" he asked.

"What do you mean *see* anybody? Who?"

God, that perfume. He had taken the trouble to find out what it was: *Je Reviens*; pretty expensive for a woman on a teacher's salary. "There was a tall guy in a black suit and a big hat. You couldn't have missed him."

"I didn't see any tall guy in a black suit and a big hat. I didn't see any guy at all."

"You must have done."

"Well, I'm sorry, Jim, but I didn't. Now do you mind if I get back to my class? I'm ten minutes late already. They'll be trashing the place."

He caught her arm, and frowned at her. "You really didn't see anybody? For real?"

"No, Jim. I really for real didn't. Now, please."

"Okay, then," he said, genuinely mystified. He stood and watched her as she tap-tapped her way toward her classroom. "By the way," he called after her. "It's bull."

She stopped in her tracks. "What do you mean? It wasn't bull at all. I really didn't see anybody. For real."

"I meant in a china shop. It isn't pig. It's bull."

She laughed; and Jim smiled, too. But when she had gone he couldn't stop himself from looking along the empty corridor, and wondering how the man in the Elmer Gantry hat had managed to disappear. It seemed *cold* in the corridor, although he couldn't think why; and there was a strange aromatic smell that wasn't *Je Reviens*. It was more like incense.

He gave an involuntary shiver, and then went to tell the janitor to clean up the blood.

* * *

By the time he returned to Special Class II, both Tee Jay and Elvin were back in their places, looking sullen and bruised. Elvin's lip was split and Tee Jay's left eye was beginning to close. The rest of the class were buzzing and twittering with curiosity and excitement, like a murmuration of starlings on a rooftop. When Jim walked in they all stood up, but the gossiping continued. Jim ignored them. Without a word, he went to the window, hoisted up a window-pole, and noisily opened it. Then he went to his desk and sat down, tilting his chair back, and clasping his hands behind his head.

He sat looking at them for a long time, and still he said nothing.

Little by little, the class began to quieten down. His silence was making them uneasy. Usually he came storming into the room and started talking right away – posturing, dramatising, gesticulating – working his class like an actor working his audience. This morning, though, he sat silent, in the same posture that *they* always adopted, chair tilted back, hands laced behind his head, eyes heavily lidded in a deliberate attempt to look disinterested and totally cool.

After two or three minutes there was complete silence. Mark Foley giggled; and his buddy Ricky Herman gave an adenoidal snort, but otherwise everybody was quiet.

Jim got up at last and walked around his desk. He looked at Tee Jay and he looked at Elvin, and then he looked at each one of his class in turn, slowly and deliberately studying their faces. There were nineteen of them in all: from Titus Greenspan III in the front, with his fishbowl glasses and his freckles, to Sue-Robin Caufield in the back with her mountains of blonde hair and her tight cerise T-shirt. There was John Ng from South Viet Nam – polite, shy and barely able to understand a word that anybody said to him; Beattie McCordic with her cropped hair and her tattoo and her fierce feminist agenda, not to mention her anomia, a chronic inability to remember what things were called. She couldn't say "hammer". She couldn't remember it. She'd have to say, "that piece of metal on a stick you use for hitting nails."

There was David Littwin, who was stringy and tall and almost handsome, apart from his protruding ears, but who stuttered so badly that every sentence seemed to take forever, and the rest of the class would start making loud snoring noises and look at their watches. Rita Munoz, dark-eyed and dark-haired, with lips as scarlet as a blossoming tropical flower. Rita argued with everything her teachers said to her, simply to disguise the fact that she didn't really know what they meant.

All of the students in Jim's class were the students who couldn't fit in anywhere else. Too slow, too aggressive, too vain, too stupid, too immature; or else they had chronic learning difficulties. Some of them he knew for sure had very high IQs. But a high IQ means nothing if you can't apply it; or don't want to apply it; or if you want to apply it only to activities that are either irrelevant or anti-social.

Jim walked right up to Tee Jay's desk and laid his fingers on it. "This morning," he said, "I want to talk about respect. Do any of you have any opinions about respect?"

Beattie McCordic's arm shot up.

"All right, Beattie. Tell us about respect."

"Respect is when people give other people their own space. Like when a woman's sitting in one of those places where they serve those mixed drinks and a man comes up to her and starts hitting on her to go to bed with him, right? And she says no. So he stops hitting on her. That's respect."

"Okay, that's a reasonable definition of respect. Anybody else?"

John Ng put up his hand. "Respect is to say a prayer to ancestors."

"That's good, yes. Acknowledging the debt you owe to your fathers and grandfathers."

"And your mothers and grandmothers," Beattie interjected.

"Yes, Beattie. Can we just take it as read that every time we mention men we mean women as well, and the other way about?"

Ricky Herman called out, "Respect is when you don't eat your food off of your knife."

"Yeah and don't say 'shit' in front of your grandma," put in Mark Foley.

"And don't go around belching and scratching your ass in public," added Ricky.

"That's right. And no farting at table. That's what my dad says: 'Did you just fart?' That's what he says, and I say, 'I hope so. 'Cause if it's the dinner that smells like this, then I ain't eating it.'"

Jim looked down at Tee Jay – looked him steadily in the eye. "How about you, Tee Jay? You tell us all about respect."

Tee Jay lowered his head and shuffled his feet.

"Come on, Tee Jay. I thought you were the class expert." He waited, smiling a little, waiting for Tee Jay to say something, but when he didn't, he backed off, and returned to his desk. Beattie had been right, in her own way. Respect is when people give other people their own space, and Tee Jay needed his.

He continued on a different tack. "There was a French

writer in the 18th century called Voltaire. And he said, 'One owes respect to the living; but to the dead one owes nothing but the truth.' Well, I don't agree with that at all. Because the dead – they've done all that they're ever going to do. We can respect their achievements, but there's no point in criticising what they failed to do, because they'll never have the chance to say sorry, or to put it right.

"But the living – they have the chance to put things right, and that's why we owe them the truth, rather than respect. If one of your friends acts mean, or bad. If one of your friends starts badmouthing their parents, or beating up on younger kids and stealing their lunch money, or smoking crack, and you say to them, 'You're an idiot. You're absurd. You're wasting your life,' then that's the truth. And they don't deserve any respect until they change their ways because respect has to be earned."

Tee Jay slowly turned his head and looked across the classroom at Elvin and there was sheer malevolence in his eyes.

"Tee Jay," Jim warned him, and Tee Jay turned back. "Tee Jay, I want you to open your book at page 37 and read the second paragraph."

Tee Jay opened his English Primer and sat for a moment in silence.

"Well?" Jim asked.

"I just read it. All the way through."

"I meant *out loud*, Tee Jay. Out loud, so that we can *all* hear it."

Haltingly, Tee Jay read the paragraph, his fingertip crawling from one word to the next. His left eye was completely closed now so he had to cock his head to one side. "The season – demands – that America learn – to better duh-wuh – duh-wuh—"

"Dwell. To better dwell," Jim prompted him.

"To better dwell on her – choice – choicest possession—"

Jim picked up Tee Jay's book and finished it for him. "The legacy of her good and faithful men that she well preserve their fame, or, if need be, that she fail not to dissipate what clouds have intruded on that fame, and burnish it newer, truer and brighter, continually."

He put the book down. "That was Walt Whitman, talking about Thomas Paine; and if ever a man deserved respect, it was Thomas Paine. Like he *deserved* respect, because he risked his life fighting for equality and justice and what he believed to be right."

He paused, and then he added, looking straight at Tee Jay, "The day you do that, that's the day that you'll start earning *your* respect."

Jim spent the rest of the time until recess going over yesterday's homework, which had been to write a 300–word appreciation of *Rip Van Winkle*. He never set his class essays longer than 300 words; some of them had to struggle for an hour to write twenty: 'Rip van Winkles old lady was always giving him a hard time so he went to the wood and drank some stuff and woke up twenty years later and she was dead by then so that was cool.'

Others wrote 600 words of incomprehensible nonsense: 'People said that thunderstorms were thunderstorms but they werent they were all these real miserable goblin-type guys playing ninepins and Rip van Winkles knees were smoting.'

And Beattie McCordic, of course, turned Rip van Winkle's nagging wife into a feminist icon: 'He was a typical man with nothing going for him . . . who took the world easy, would eat white bread or brown, whatever was less trouble . . . would rather starve on a penny than work for a pound . . . and the whole story like blames his *wife* for nagging him to try to get his act together. Like even his dog thinks he leads a dogs life but what do dogs know and anyhow the dog was male and what do *they* know (males I mean.)'

In spite of all of his students' shortcomings, however, Jim could feel a real yearning for understanding in everything they wrote. Even in some of the most laboured essays, heavy with crossings-out and misspellings, there was a strenuous groping for knowledge, a genuine struggle to find the key to literacy. Young people in a darkened room, trying to feel their way towards the door. There were times when he could have cried over what they had written; not for himself, but for them.

'Rip van Winkle let his childrin run wile they never wore no shos and his suns pants was alus fallin down.' That was Mark Foley's essay in its entirety. But Jim could see what it was about the story that had caught Mark's attention: the careless, lazy father who never took care of his children, so that his son had to troop after his mother wearing his ragged hand-me-down galligaskins – 'which he had much ado to hold up with one hand, as a fine lady does her train in bad weather.'

In his own way, at home, Mark had suffered the same kind of experience, with a beer-gut father who owned a run-down automobile body shop in Santa Monica, so the story of Rip van Winkle was much more to Mark than just a legend. Mark had lived it; and now he had taken the first step toward expressing himself through fiction.

Who knows, thought Jim wryly, as he closed Mark's book and dropped it into his 'Out' tray. Maybe Mark was destined to be a latter-day Washington Irving.

He was turning to Rita Munoz's essay (printed in

capital letters, as usual, in multi-coloured felt-tip pens), when he happened to turn towards the window. It was dazzlingly bright outside, but he could see all the way across the schoolyard to the boiler-house. A group of boys were playing basketball right outside the boiler-house door; and Sue-Robin Caufield was leaning against a railing talking to Jeff Griglak, captain of the school athletics team and one of the brightest students at Westwood Community College for years. John Ng was sitting on the other end of the bench, eating something indescribable out a box and reading *Treasure Island*.

It was no more than a flicker; a dark shadow passing over his eye. But the door of the boiler-room suddenly opened, and the tall dark man in the Elmer Gantry hat appeared. He hesitated for a moment, looking right and left, with one hand raised to shield his eyes from the sunlight. Then he hurried diagonally across the schoolyard, and disappeared behind the science block.

He left the boiler-room door ajar. But, strangely, it seemed as if none of the students in the playground had noticed him. None of the boys playing basketball had stopped for a moment, and Sue-Robin had carried on flirting with Jeff Griglak without pausing for breath. Her hair bounced and shone in the mid-morning sunlight.

Jim frowned. He got up from his desk and walked up to the window, cupping his hands around his face to cut out any reflection. Apart from the half-open boiler-house door, everything else appeared to be normal. And yet . . .

And yet he had a gut feeling that something was badly wrong. He felt as if he had been shown a picture that had been deliberately designed to confuse him: like a painting by Rene Magritte, or one of M.C. Escher's drawings of never-ending staircases. He left the classroom and walked quickly along the corridor until he reached the swing doors that led outside.

There was laughter and chatter and shouting in the schoolyard but Jim didn't hear it. He was making his way toward the boiler-house door. He cut right through the middle of the basketball game, and smacked away the ball as it came bouncing toward him.

He reached the boiler-house and peered inside. He could see the handrail and the concrete steps that led down to the boilers themselves; but the rest was in darkness. He called out, "Hallo! Is there anybody in there?"

He listened, but there was no answer, only the deep whistling noise of the gas-fired burners. He called out again, and there was still no reply. He guessed that the man in the Elmer Gantry hat must have gone down there to steal something; or maybe to do some damage. There had been several incidents of former students coming back to take their revenge on the college which they thought had failed them. They had to blame somebody or something for their inability to make it in the world outside.

Jim switched on the overhead lights and looked down over the railings. The boiler-room smelled strongly of heat and gas, but the two large grey-painted boilers appeared to be undamaged. No broken gauges; no pipes sabotaged; nothing like that. Jim was about to switch off the light and go back outside when he glimpsed something glistening in the shadows between the boilers. A black, viscous trickle making its way across the floor. It looked like an oil leak, quite a bad one. He went down the steps, his shoes chuffing on the concrete, approached the boilers and hunkered down so that he could see between them.

The glistening fluid had crept so far across the floor that it was almost touching his toe. He dipped his finger into it and held it up; and it was then that he felt a chilly, tingling feeling all the way down his back. This wasn't an oil-leak. The liquid had looked black against the concrete, but on his fingertip it was dark, congealed crimson.

Jim strained his eyes to see into the shadows. He fumbled in his pocket and found half a book of matches from the El Torito Mexican Restaurant. He struck one, and it flared up briefly, but it did little more than burn his thumb. He wished to hell he had a flashlight. There was *something* there – a dark, lumpy shape – but that was all that he could make out.

With his knees bent, he edged his way between the boilers, feeling his way with his hands. It was so hot in there that sweat was dripping from his forehead before he had even managed to shuffle six feet forward, and his shirt was clinging to his back.

He thought he heard a bubbling, groaning noise, and he stopped and listened, although the sound of the boilers was deafening.

He struck another match, and shouted, "Anybody there? This is Mr Rook! Is there anybody there?"

Again, that agonised, bubbling noise. It sounded like somebody trying to talk while they were drinking a glass of water.

Jim inched forward a little more, and suddenly he was touching something heavy and warm and wet. He shouted out, "*Ah*!" and recoiled violently.

Shaking, he struck another match; and used it to ignite the last few remaining matches in the book, to give himself a brief flare of bright light. Lying on the concrete in front of him was Elvin, recognisable only by his Dodgers T-shirt, plastered in blood. He had wounds everywhere: all over his arms, all over his face, all over his body, as if somebody had been determined to stab every inch of him. They looked like the gaping mouths of a shoal of stranded fish.

Sensing the heat from the matches, Elvin tried to lift his hand up. He let out another groaning sound; but it was the last gargling exhalation of air and blood from punctured lungs. As the matches burned down, and the light died, so Elvin died, too, and Jim was left in darkness, with the boilers roaring on either side of him.

He took hold of Elvin's sticky hand, and squeezed it, and whispered, "God be with you, Elvin. So goddamned young," and that was all he could manage to say.

Chapter Two

Lieutenant Harris knocked on the open classroom door, and stepped inside. He was short and stocky, built like a hefty little linen-chest, with a snub nose and a scrub of sandy hair and a livid red scar on his chin. He wore a sandy-coloured polyester suit with sweat marks under the armpits.

"Mr Rook?" he said. His voice was a soft, congested rasp.

Jim had been standing by the window, looking out. On his desk was the single page of Elvin's last essay, *My Best Poem*. He had taken it out of his file, with the intention of giving it to Elvin's parents. It was *Three* by Gregory Corso: three short verses, and the last verse read,

> '*Death weeps because Death is human*
> *spending all day in a movie when a child dies.*'

Jim turned around. He didn't know whether to smile or cry. The red-and-blue police lights were still flashing outside, although the ambulance and the coroner's station wagon had left about ten minutes before. Special Class II had been excused college for the rest of the day, and they didn't have to come back tomorrow if they were still too upset. Three grief counsellors had been called in, to help the students to cope with what had happened. After all, Elvin had been everybody's friend. Slow, very slow; but endlessly patient; and willing to help anybody if they needed help – fixing the transmissions on their automobiles, putting up shelves, wiring plugs, running errands. Nothing had ever been too much trouble, because the best way in which Elvin had been able to communicate with people was not through words but through practical actions.

Jim had recognised that, and had let him help around the school – mending fences, draining the swimming-pool, and repairing damaged lockers. Elvin used to sing, when he was working. He loved it.

And now, at the age of seventeen years and four months, he was dead.

Lieutenant Harris prowled about the classroom. "What can you tell me about Thomas J. Jones?"

"Tee Jay? What do you want to know? That he's black? That he's not very clever? That he comes from a broken home?"

"I want to know if you think that's he capable of homicide in the first degree."

Jim turned around and looked at him. "What can I say? I guess we're all capable of homicide in the first degree, if you give us enough provocation."

"Come on, Mr Rook. You saw Elvin's body. You saw what his assailant did to him. One hundred and twelve stab wounds, that's what the medical examiner counted. Most of us would stop feeling provoked after we'd inflicted just one."

"I don't know what you're trying to say."

"I'm trying to find out from people who knew him well whether Thomas J. Jones had the motive or the psychological characteristics to murder Elvin P. Clay.

You're his teacher. You probably know him better than anybody; his mother excepted."

"I don't think he's a killer," said Jim.

"He sure isn't a babe in arms."

"Listen, he finds it difficult to read. He can't manage anything more than basic maths. His mother has three daughters and four other sons, and they all live together in a three-bedroom house in the shabbiest part of Westwood. He's intelligent and energetic, but he's also dysfunctional and deeply frustrated, like most of the kids in my class. If it hadn't have been for a garbled set of genes, he probably could have been somebody very special."

"But you caught him fighting Elvin this morning, didn't you? A pretty damned serious fight, from what I've heard about it so far. And from what I've heard about it so far, Thomas J. Jones made specific and unambiguous threats to kill Elvin, in front of several witnesses."

He took out his notebook and flipped it open. "His actual words were, 'I'm going to kill him – I'm going to kill him for that – I'm going to murder that mother.'"

Jim said, "Yes. That's exactly what he said. But he was angry. Elvin said something to upset him, I don't know what. But in my opinion Tee Jay's threats didn't really mean anything."

Lieutenant Harris gave Jim a long, pained look, as if he were feeling the first pangs of chronic indigestion. "They didn't really *mean* anything? Yet less than two hours later, you found Elvin fatally wounded in the college boiler-room, with more holes in him than a chickenwire fence."

"But Tee Jay didn't do it, did he? I talked to him already. He spent the whole of recess talking to his friends on the basketball team; and they vouched for that, too."

"Well, that's right. Except that we have a ten-minute

window. Tee Jay left his friends at approximately 11:05 and said that he needed to call his uncle. He was seen going into the main college building and he wasn't seen again until 11:15 or thereabouts."

"Did anybody see him going to the boiler-room?" asked Jim.

"No, sir. But that isn't really the point. The point is that he had just enough time to go to the boiler-room and perpetrate an act of homicide. He had the motive, and he had the opportunity. What's more, he has a considerable amount of blood on his clothing, which he freely admits is Elvin's."

"Blood from the fight in the washroom. That doesn't prove anything."

"Maybe not. But we'll be running some tests."

Jim said, "What about the man in black?"

"Excuse me?"

"The man in black. Black suit, black wide-brimmed hat. I was marking books. I looked up and saw him coming out of the boiler-room. He stopped, and took a look around, as if he didn't want anybody to see him, and then he went off."

"He was acting suspicious?"

"Well, *furtive*. That's the word. Furtive."

Lieutenant Harris tapped his pencil against his puckered lips. "He must have been. In fact he was so darn furtive that nobody else saw him. There were seventy-nine students out on that playlot this morning – *seventy-nine* – and not one of them saw anybody unfamiliar."

"You're kidding me," said Jim, in disbelief. "He walked out of the boiler-room in open view of everybody. He opened the door, looked around, and just went marching off, right through a whole crowd of kids. *One* of them must have seen him."

"Black suit? Black wide-brimmed hat?" Lieutenant Harris flicked all the way through his notebook and shook his head. "None of your students saw anybody like that."

"All right. Maybe not. But I sure did."

Lieutenant Harris tucked his notebook into his pocket. "So . . . do you want to give me a description?"

"You're not going to take a note?"

"It's all right, Mr Rook. I can remember it. How tall would you say he was?"

"Hard to tell, with that hat on. Six feet plus. Not heavily built. One hundred and ninety max."

"And a black suit?"

"That's right. Baggy, flappy, unconstructed."

"And what would you say was his ethnic origin?"

"Couldn't tell, exactly. The sun was against me."

"You don't even know if he was black or white?"

Jim thought for a moment, trying to remember what the man had looked like; but then he said, "No." He hadn't glimpsed anything which would have conclusively shown him whether the man in the Elmer Gantry hat was Caucasian or Afro-American or even Oriental for that matter. Both times the man's face had been turned away, or shielded by the brim of his hat, as if he hadn't wanted Jim to see what he looked like. But the mystery was, how come nobody else had seen him? Sue-Robin Caufield couldn't have been standing more than fifteen feet away from him when he came out of the boiler-room door; and Jeff Griglak had actually been facing him.

"Okay, Mr Rook." Lieutenant Harris took out his notebook again and went through a whole list of procedural questions. How old Jim was. Whether he was married or divorced. Where he lived. His telephone number and his e.mail domain name. Then he said, "Fine . . . thanks for your time."

"What happens now?" Jim asked him.

"Thomas J. Jones has been arrested on suspicion of murder in the first degree. We'll be taking him back to headquarters for questioning."

"You've arrested Tee Jay already? What about the guy in the black hat and the black suit?"

Lieutenant Harris made a complicated face, half apologetic and half dismissive. "We'll be keeping an open mind, Mr Rook."

"You mean you won't be making any effort to look for him?"

"Well . . . I have to say that your description's pretty sketchy. Quite apart from the fact that nobody else saw him, except you. I know you mean well, sir. I know that you have quite a reputation for protecting your students. That's admirable. But I have to consider the facts."

"The facts? The fact is that a guy in a black suit and a black hat came out of that boiler-room just before I went in there and found Elvin dying on the floor."

"We couldn't find any footprints, Mr Rook, except yours."

"You didn't have Tee Jay's footprints, then?"

"No. But then we didn't find Elvin's, neither. The only person who trod in Elvin's blood was you."

Jim tiredly ran his hand through his hair. "I don't know, Lieutenant. I can't believe that Tee Jay would have done anything like that. It just wasn't in his nature."

Lieutenant Harris gave a dry, thumping sniff. "In my experience, Mr Rook, it's the people we think we know the best who give us the nastiest surprises."

Jim packed up and was on his way out of the building

when he heard somebody calling his name. He turned around and saw Ellie Fox hurrying toward him. Ellie was head of the college Art Department: a petite woman with a little snubby nose and straight toffee-coloured hair held back in a band. She always wore voluminous denim smocks, jeans and sandals, and more often than not she was carrying a pencil or a paintbrush behind her ear, just in case people didn't get the message that she was an artist.

"Jim! I wanted to talk to you last week, but I was always missing you!"

"Listen, Ellie, I'm sorry – what with everything that happened today – can't we talk tomorrow?"

"But, Jim, this is important. Really."

"I'll look into the Art Department first thing tomorrow. I promise."

"It's something to do with Tee Jay. I thought you'd want to see it."

"Tee Jay? What?"

She took him by the arm, and led him back up the steps. "Come look. Tell me what you think."

He followed her along the echoing hallway until they reached the Art Department. For Special Class II, the Art Department was especially important. It was here that they could learn to express themselves in colour and light and shape. If they couldn't write, they could still tell stories – in crayons and paint. If they couldn't add or divide or multiply, they could still make necklaces of glittering beads. They could model with clay; they could paint with their fingers. Ellie Fox was an almost obsessive believer in art of all kinds. "Most of the reason people kill themselves is because they never look at pictures; or sculptures; or anything. Art brings you out. Art makes you regular, body and spirit both."

A modelling class was in progress: eight girls and three boys trying to make animals out of clay. As Jim crossed the studio, several of the students looked up from their work in curiosity, and Jim could hear a vibrant whisper travel around the room: ". . . says that Tee Jay didn't do it . . ." ". . . saw some guy all dressed in black . . ." ". . . what, The Shadow? What's he on?" ". . . well, do *you* think Tee Jay could've done it?" ". . . maybe it was a one-armed man . . ."

Ellie stopped in front of a large grey plan-chest. She opened the top drawer, and said, "I have all of their recent work in here. Anything that's creative, anything that's strong, anything that's different." Now she raised her voice so that the whole class could hear. "Provided, of course, it isn't obscene, or defamatory toward West Grove Community College or any of its faculty."

There was a burst of giggling over in one corner of the art studio, and Jim saw Jane Fidaccio quickly knock an immense clay penis off the rhinoceros that she was modelling.

Ellie drew out three large sheets of paper and spread them on top of the plan chest. They were all painted in reds and oranges and blacks. One showed a man being burned alive on top of a funeral pyre. Another showed a procession of men walking through a jungle. Jim didn't immediately find it horrifying until he realised that they were walking in line because a long stake had been driven through their stomachs and out through their backs, keeping them together like a human kebab. The third picture showed a naked woman lying on her back, eating her newborn baby even before she had passed the afterbirth.

"Tee Jay's work," she said.

"Jesus," Jim acknowledged. "These are pretty strong."

"I was going to destroy them, but I thought you'd better take a look at them first."

"Did Tee Jay ever do anything like this before?"

Ellie shook her head. "Only in the last two weeks. I asked him what they meant, and he said they were something to do with his ethnic heritage, but that was all."

"His *heritage*? He was born in Huntington Park, so far as I know. Then his father got a job as a chauffeur and the family moved to Santa Monica. What kind of ethnic heritage is that?"

"Well, I don't know," said Ellie. "But it seems to me that he's been very disturbed."

Jim picked up the painting of the men in the jungle. "You see these letters here? V – O – D – U – N. Do you have any idea what these could mean?"

"No idea at all. Tee Jay wouldn't say. He said the pictures spoke for themselves."

"Not to me they don't," said Jim. "Look . . . what's he written down the side here? S – A – M – E. Same? What does that mean? Same as what? Or maybe it's an acronym . . . Skewer All Men Equally, or something. Or an anagram. Who knows?"

"Maybe you could ask him?" Ellie suggested.

Jim nodded. She was a wise woman, Ellie; tender and wise. He said, "Can I keep these?"

She said, "For sure . . . I don't want any of my freshman students seeing them. They might get ideas."

Jim rolled up the paintings and twisted an elastic band around them. "I owe you one," he told Ellie, as she showed him to the door. "Maybe that special Rook pizza I keep on promising to make you. The one with the smoked ricotta."

"Not just yet," she said. "Let's wait till some of this dust has settled."

"Sure, Ellie. I didn't mean now."

"No," she said, as if none of the men she met ever meant now.

He went home first, to his second-storey apartment in a pink-painted concrete block just off Electric Avenue, in Venice. There was a small blue pool in the courtyard, around which the residents relaxed in the evening on rusty half-collapsed sun-loungers, drinking warm wine and reading thick blockbuster novels. This evening it was so warm that even Mrs Vaizey was outside, seventy-six years old, in a huge pair of black silk shorts and a shrivelled tube top, and one of those SpaceFace lobster visors that were thought to be such a scream about 15 years ago.

"You're looking grim, Jim," said Mrs Vaizey, shielding her eyes against the sun. "Bad day at Black Rock?"

Jim nodded. "One of our students was killed today. It's been pretty heavy all round."

"Killed? That's awful! How did that happen?"

"We're not entirely sure. But so far it seems like another student stabbed him."

"The world isn't what it was, Jim. In my day you went to school to get yourself educated, not to kill other students, or to get yourself killed."

"Well, that's right, Mrs Vaizey. But I'm not so sure that this killing is quite so simple as it looks."

The pale pink lobster on top of her head gave him a beady-eyed look and dangled its plastic claws. "You think different, do you? That's because you *are* different."

"Don't start giving me that mystical stuff, Mrs Vaizey. I respect your gifts, and I respect what you believe in, but one of my favourite students died today, and this isn't the time."

"Nonsense," she said. The skin on the back of her hand was like crumpled tissue-paper. "This is exactly the time. You tell me *why* you think different."

Jim glanced over at Myrlin Buffield, from Apartment no. 201, who was pretending to read *Primary Colors* but who was listening to their conversation intently. Myrlin was ninety pounds overweight, with black slashed-back hair, and bosoms, and a gold earring in the shape of a dagger; and skin as white and luminous as a freshly-caught pollock. Nobody knew what Myrlin did for a living. Nobody liked to guess.

"Why don't you come up for a drink, Mrs Vaizey?" asked Jim. "Then we can talk in private."

"Beer?" asked Mrs Vaizey, suspiciously.

"What do you think I am? Bourbon."

"In that case, Jim, I'd be happy to join you."

He picked up her newspaper and her glasses and her sewing-bag and helped her up the steps to his apartment. He didn't speak to her very often; mainly because she was always trying to persuade him to have his palms read; or his Tarot cards interpreted; or his tea-leaves scrutinised. He believed in a whole lot of odd things, but he didn't believe in fortune-telling, or Ouija boards, or ghosts. He believed that the future was unpredictable, and that when you died, you died. *Click*. The light was switched off, and that was it.

Jim unlocked the door of his apartment and ushered Mrs Vaizey inside. The calico blinds were drawn down, and it was dim and warm. It wasn't untidy, but there were several tell-tale signs that a single man lived here, and that nobody had cleaned up during the day. The cushions on the couch were still crumpled. There were dead sweet peas in the vase on the windowsill. Yesterday's paper still lay where Jim had dropped it, as well a single slipper.

Mrs Vaizey cautiously sniffed. She could smell it, too. Nothing unpleasant – just stuffy, motionless air that nobody had breathed all day.

"Where's your cat?" she wanted to know.

"The feline formerly known as Tibbles? He'll be back, once he knows that I'm here. I never let him in during the day. I'm allergic to the smell of litter-trays."

Mrs Vaizey sat down on the couch and Jim went through to the kitchen to find his bottle of Jim Beam. He sploshed out two generous glasses for both of them, and knocked his glass against hers, in salute, and to frighten away the devil. "Here's to Elvin, who died today. And here's to justice, and sense, and respect."

"I'll drink to that," said Mrs Vaizey. "Whatever the hell you're talking about."

Jim said, "I'm talking about young people who die too young, Mrs Vaizey. Elvin, you know – he didn't have much of a chance to begin with. He was so damned slow he couldn't catch a cold. His father was an invalid and his mother could never cope. But he was always so cheerful. He always made the best of what he had."

"So who killed him?"

"One of his classmates. A boy called Tee Jay. That's what the police think, anyway."

"But you think elsewise?"

"I'm not sure. Tee Jay and Elvin were having a fight, earlier on; and when the fight was over I saw a man walking down the corridor. Tall, with a black suit and a wide black hat. He disappeared before I could find out who he was. But I saw him again, coming out of the school boiler-room; and that's where Elvin was stabbed to death. I saw him, as clear as I can see you; but the trouble was that nobody else saw him. Nobody."

Mrs Vaizey knocked back her bourbon and wiped her

mouth with the back of her hand. "I think I should look at the palm of your hand, Jim."

"Mrs Vaizey, with all due respect, that's not going to answer anything."

"Jim . . . there's something different about you. I always knew there was. You got the aura."

"The aura? What's that?"

Mrs Vaizey made a circular motion with her hands. "It's a kind of a *glow* that some people have around them. Sometimes a happy person can shine like a light. But most people have more like a *mottled* effect, different colours for different parts of their psyche, if you get my meaning."

"So what colour is mine?" asked Jim. He poured her another drink.

"Yours is different. Yours scarcely glows at all. Yours is more like a shadow than a shine."

"What does that mean? That I'm depressed?"

Mrs Vaizey shook her head. "Nothing like that. It means that you're in touch with the world beyond. There's a part of you that can see *through* this everyday world right into the next, same as looking through a store window on a sunny day. You have to cup your hands around your eyes, and press your face close, but you can always see *something*."

Jim gave an amused grunt, but Mrs Vaizey took hold of his hand between her claw-like fingers with all her knobbly silver rings and clutched it tight. "What do you think you saw today, Jim? You saw a man that nobody else could see. Now, was that man alive, do you suppose, or could that man have been something else?"

"I don't know what you mean by 'something else'. What are you talking about, a ghost?"

"Maybe a ghost. Who knows? It isn't just the spirits of

dead people who wander through the world. Sometimes the living can do it, too."

"What, like an out-of-body experience?"

"That's one of the ways," said Mrs Vaizey, looking down at the palm of his hand. Her sharp orange-lacquered nail probed his heartline, his headline and his lifeline.

"You're very bright," she told him. "The trouble is, you're stubborn, too. You don't like taking advice from other people. You always think that you have a better way of doing things. On the other hand, you have moments of great self-doubt, when you feel that you might have taken the wrong fork in the forest. At times like these you feel that the trees are closing in on you, and that you can hear strange growlings in the undergrowth."

She looked up, and knocked back her second glass of bourbon. "Metaphor-orically speaking, of course."

Jim watched her, the way her silver hoop earrings dangled in the sunlight. He should have been sceptical but somehow he wasn't. After today's murder, he was prepared to consider almost any explanation for what had happened. If God could allow a young man like Elvin to die; then obviously they were living in a universe in which nothing was logical, and nothing was fair.

"You're very emotional, and capable of very great love," Mrs Vaizey continued. "You had a love once who let you down, and it took you a long time to get over it. But another love will appear when you're least expecting it – quite soon, by the looks of it – and this relationship will endure, on and off, for the rest of your life."

"On and off? I'm not sure I like the sound of that."

"Everybody has quarrels, Jim, especially people who really love each other."

"Well, I guess."

Mrs Vaizey probed his lifeline. He wished she wouldn't

dig her nail in quite so deeply. But then she looked up at him again and there was the most extraordinary expression on her face. She was staring at him as if she couldn't believe that he was real. She probed it some more, peering at it intently; and then she said, "I don't understand this at all."

"What's the matter?" he asked her.

"It's very strange. Normally, if somebody's lifeline is broken, you can predict when they're going to die. You know, almost to the *year*."

"And, what? Is my lifeline broken?"

Mrs Vaizey nodded. "You see here . . . way down at the bottom. It breaks up and goes every which way."

"So what does that mean? You're not telling me that I'm not going to die young, are you? My dad and my mom are both still alive."

"Jim, this break happens very, very early in your life. It means that, by rights, you should be dead already."

"What?"

"There's no mistaking it. It's very clear. It means that you died when you were eleven or twelve."

Jim laughed. "I died when I was eleven or twelve? That doesn't say much for palmistry, does it? I mean, how dead do I look?"

"There's no mistake," said Mrs Vaizey, and her voice was completely serious.

"So I'm supposed to believe that I'm dead, is that it?"

"You're not dead now; but you were once. Just for a moment, perhaps. But dead."

Jim took his hand away, and held it against his chest, as if it were injured. "Listen," he said. "This doesn't make any sense."

"I don't know, Jim," said Mrs Vaizey. "Maybe it could.

Were you ever sick, when you were a child? I mean seriously sick?"

"I went down with pneumonia once, when I was ten or eleven."

"Can you remember what happened?"

"Not very clearly . . . I was always pretty skinny and weedy when I was a kid. I went down with the grippe and the grippe turned into pneumonia. My dad and mom took me to hospital and there were all these people in white, looking after me. They were great. They took me for walks and they talked to me, and in the end they brought me back to my bed and I was cured."

"What do they look like, these people in white?"

"I don't know. I guess they were doctors and nurses. But there were dozens of them . . . all talking to me, all trying to make me feel better. And in the end, yes. I felt better."

Mrs Vaizey held out her glass and Jim filled it again. The sun had fallen, and there were wide stripes of light across the only picture which Jim had hung on the wall: a large reproduction of *The Surrender of Breda* by Veláquez, Dutch soldiers handing over the keys of the city to Spanish lancers. Jim had always taken a particular kind of strength from it, because it showed sworn enemies behaving toward each other with courtesy and understanding – two qualities which he had always tried to instil in the students of Special Class II.

Mrs Vaizey said, "Has it ever occurred to you that those people in white might *not* have been doctors and nurses?"

"I don't follow you."

"You were very young, and close to death. Clinically, perhaps, you *did* die. But, believe me, there are many kind spirits on the other side who do their best to turn back young souls before it's too late."

Jim shook his head. "I'm sorry, Mrs Vaizey. I don't believe in life after death."

"Even though you probably saw some spirits for yourself?"

"I was very young. I was probably dreaming."

Mrs Vaizey took hold of his hand again, and ran her fingernail up and down his lifeline, again and again. "The point I'm trying to make to you, Jim, is that if you've seen spirits once, you can see them again. Coming close to death, that gives you a *facility*, if you understand what I mean. An extra sense that you never lose."

Jim said nothing, but watched and winced as Mrs Vaizey pored over his palm. After a few moments, she frowned, and peered even more closely at his lifeline.

"Something wrong?" he asked her.

"I don't know . . . I can't understand what this means. You have a double break and then a loop, almost, like an oxbow. You're going to have a strange meeting, unlike anything you've ever experienced before. Then something very frightening is going to happen. But that's all that I can decipher." She drew her fingernail along his lifeline yet again, and as she did so, Jim felt a searing pain. Her fingernail scratched against his skin like a safety-match, and flames sprang up behind it, right out of the palm of his hand.

"Jesus!" he shouted, and instantly clamped his hand shut. But flames burst out from between his fingers and engulfed his whole fist.

He tried to jump up, but Mrs Vaizey shouted, "No!" She snatched a cushion from the couch and pressed it over Jim's hand. She held it down for a long, long moment, and then she cautiously lifted it up again to make sure that the flames had been extinguished. Slowly, Jim opened his fingers. The fire had vanished, leaving nothing but a pattern of faint red marks.

"Does it hurt?" Mrs Vaizey asked him.

Jim raised his hand and turned it this way and that. "Not really. There's a dull kind of a burning sensation . . . but I guess that's all. What the hell happened?"

"It's a warning," said Mrs Vaizey. She was so shaken that her hands were trembling. "I've heard about it but I've never seen it, not for real, not right in front of my eyes."

"A warning? A warning about what?"

"I can't tell you. There are some things that people shouldn't know."

"Come on, Mrs Vaizey. My goddamned hand just caught light. You have to tell me."

She pressed her hand over her mouth for a while, thinking. Then she said, "All right . . . I suppose you have the right. Sometimes, when the danger of death is very close, people show signs of it on their bodies. The more sensitive a person is, the clearer the signs. I knew a woman in Santa Barbara whose lips went blue; and three weeks later she was dead of cyanide poisoning. Then there was a movie producer in Westwood who kept getting these red bite marks on his arms. Before the year was out, he was attacked by two Dobermanns when he was visiting one of his friends. They practically tore off his face."

She paused for a moment, and then she said, "I've seen burns before, too, on people who have died by fire. Arm burns, facial burns. But I never saw actual *flames* before. Never. You must be even closer to the spirit world than anyone I ever met."

"But what are you saying?" Jim asked her. "You're saying that I'm going to be burned to death?"

Mrs Vaizey didn't answer. All she could do was to stare at him in sorrow.

"It's not inevitable, though, is it?" Jim demanded. "I mean, I can change my own destiny, can't I, now that I know?"

"I never heard of anybody managing to change their destiny before," said Mrs Vaizey, laying her hand on top of his. "Maybe *you* can. Who knows?"

Jim said shakily, "How about another drink?"

Chapter Three

Back at college the next morning the students of Special Class II were quiet and subdued, but nobody was absent, with the exception of Amanda Zaparelli who was having her braces removed. Jim wasn't surprised that they had all shown up. They badly needed to share their grief; and they needed to come to college to see for themselves that Elvin's desk was empty, and that he really had left them for ever. Jim knew that during the college semester, a class can be closer than a family, and to lose a classmate can hurt even more than losing an uncle or a cousin.

Jim came into the room tucking his blue denim shirt into his chinos. He looked and felt particularly bleary. He hadn't slept well. He had dreamed all night of shadowy figures in wide-brimmed hats, and fire; and of voices that whispered in languages he didn't understand. He had switched on the light several times to look at the marks on his hand. He had made himself a mug of hot chocolate and had stirred it and stared at it for half an hour before emptying it, undrunk, down the sink.

"*I never heard of anybody managing to change their destiny before*," Mrs Vaizey had told him. "*Maybe* you *can. Who knows*?"

"Okay," he said. "This is going to be a special day and a very difficult day. Yesterday we lost Elvin but we also lost Tee Jay, too. The police have charged him with murder in the first degree, and so far as I understand it, they're not looking for anybody else."

He walked through the lines of desks to the back of the class, so that he was standing next to Sue-Robin Caufield. Sue-Robin was wearing a very tight black V-neck T-shirt, and a thin black ribbon around her neck. Tiredly, Jim thought: trust her to make mourning look sexy. In the far corner, Greg Lake was frowning fiercely and blinking as if he were riding a motorcycle in a high wind. Greg suffered from a lack of co-ordination, and every facial expression was a deep struggle. If anybody told a joke, the rest of the class had finished laughing for at least a minute before Greg managed to arrange his face into a smile.

Jim said, "I want you all to remember one thing. As sad as we are that Elvin has gone – as *angry* as we are – and let's not make any bones about this, anger is as much an ingredient of grief as sadness – the justice system says that nobody is guilty until they are *proved* to be guilty. Tee Jay has been charged, but he hasn't been tried. So let's be mature, and wait for a jury to decide whether Tee Jay was really responsible."

"Oh, sure," said Ray Vito, turning around in his seat. Ray had a shiny black pompadour, a pasty, triangular face, and a narrow, eagle-like nose. "And I suppose OJ Simpson was innocent, too?"

"A jury found OJ Simpson innocent. Whatever I think about it, that's good enough for me."

"Oh, come on, Mr Rook. We all watched the trial. There was no way."

"You watched the trial but you weren't presented with the facts in the same way that the jury was. They listened to the facts, and they ended up with reasonable doubt. I have reasonable doubt that Tee Jay didn't kill Elvin. I saw somebody leave the boiler-room just before I found Elvin dead. I don't know who he was, or what he was doing there. I can't understand why nobody else saw him. But he must have been the last person to see Elvin alive; and he wasn't Tee Jay; so let's at least keep and open mind."

Russell Gloach put up his hand. Russell had black short-cropped hair and eyeglasses so thick they must have been bulletproof. He weighed 215 pounds and had an eating disorder which had severely disrupted his schoolwork. He couldn't sit through a forty-five minute lesson without a cake or a candy-bar or a sandwich. In spite of his size, however, his mind was quick, and he could be very irreverent. "I don't believe you saw nobody," he said. "I think you're covering for Tee Jay . . . trying to make people think that maybe he didn't do it, just maybe . . . so they'll have to let him off."

"Why would I do that?" Jim asked him.

Russell shrugged. "Tee Jay belongs to Special Class II, doesn't he? Whatever he's done. He *belongs*."

Jim looked at Russell for a long time, and then he nodded. "Sure," he said. "Tee Jay belongs."

"The point is, though, Tee Jay's been acting real weird lately," said Muffy. Muffy was small and pretty, with one of the most complicated braids that Jim had ever seen. It was looped and butterfly-bowed and decorated with ribbons and beads. She must have woken up at about five in the morning to get it right in time for college. Tee Jay and Muffy had dated for two or three weeks, but Tee Jay had been quiet and laconic while Muffy was like an explosion in a firecracker factory.

Up until yesterday, of course, when Tee Jay had exploded, too.

"What do you mean by *weird*?" Jim asked Muffy.

"Well, he was always so cool, wasn't he?" said Muffy.

"Like nothing ever fazed him, ever. But in the last two or three weeks, he went right into himself. He didn't hardly speak to nobody. You must have noticed in class."

Jim said, "I didn't notice at the time, no. But now you come to mention it." And he thought of the paintings that Ellie had shown him, the skewered men walking through the jungle, the woman devouring her new-born baby.

"I think he had some kind of trouble at home," said Muffy. "He wouldn't talk about it, but I know for a fact that he slept in his car one time; and another time he called me up at two in the morning and asked if he could crash at my place. I mean, I couldn't. My parents would've wigged."

Jim walked slowly to the front of the class. "Did anybody else notice that Tee Jay was acting strange?"

"He started bringing me down for being Jewish," said Sherma Feldstein – a dark, plump, pretty girl with a beauty spot and thick black eyebrows. "He kept saying there was only one religion and that was his. He said that all Jews were – well, he used a rude word."

"Did he tell you what his religion was?" asked Jim.

Sherma shook her head. "He tried to explain it. He kept on talking about crows and mirrors and candles; and there was something about dust, too. Breathing in dust."

"Could you make any sense of that?"

"Unh-unh," said Sherma. "And he wouldn't explain himself, either. He said if I didn't understand it now I never would."

"I noticed something else, too," put in Beattie McCordic. "He was out playing that game where you throw one of those round things over a net. It was hot and he stripped off the thing he was wearing on his top. He had all these marks on his back."

"You mean a tattoo?" Jim asked her.

"No, no. Like lumps, when you cut yourself. What do you call them?"

"You're talking about scars?"

"That's right, scars. In all these kind of like circles."

"Well, I guess if anybody wants to have circles on their back, who are we to say that they can't? He's probably had them for years."

"No, he hasn't. They're really new. Like they're still red-raw and all."

Sharon Mitchell put up her hand. Sharon was as militant about black rights as Beattie was for women's rights. She was strikingly pretty, but she was very tall, almost 6ft 1ins, and she had suffered all of her life for being gawky, and black, and a girl. She always signed her essays 'Sharon X', in honour of the Black Muslims, and Jim never called her anything else. This was a time in their lives when his students needed to be taken seriously, no matter how rebellious and irrational they seemed to be. They felt bad enough about themselves as it was. They didn't need anybody else making fun of them.

Sharon said, "Some people in Africa do that. It's a manhood thing. It's supposed to show that a boy can put up with pain; but also it shows what spirit you belong to."

"I don't follow you."

"Well, some tribes have these guardian spirits who are supposed to look after them all of their lives. The same as godparents, you know. When a boy reaches manhood, the elders choose a spirit for him, and that spirit is supposed to protect him and give him good advice and kill his enemies for him."

Kill his enemies? thought Jim, remembering the dark-suited figure coming out of the boiler-house. He said, "That's interesting, Sharon. I'd like to know some more about that."

"I've got plenty of books at home. I'll bring them to college and you can read them for yourself."

Jim looked around the class. "I'll be going to see Elvin's parents later today, and I'm sure that you'd all like me to take a message of condolence. Tomorrow I'd like you all to pool your efforts and make a sympathy card, so that you can all sign it.

"I've been thinking all night of what I could say to you today about Elvin. But I believe the best I can do is read you these words by Emily Dickinson."

He picked up a book and opened it. The class was so quiet that he could hear them breathing.

"'*Because I could not stop for Death,*
He kindly stopped for me;
The carriage held but just ourselves
And Immortality.

"'*We passed the school, where children strove*
At recess, in the ring;
We passed the fields of gazing grain
We passed the setting sun.

"'*Since then 'tis centuries, and yet*
Feels shorter than the day
I first surmised the horses' heads
Were toward eternity."

He lowered the book. Sitting right in front of him, Jane Firman had tears trickling down her cheeks. She and Elvin had both suffered from dyslexia, and they had spent hours together, struggling to make sense of their books. Elvin's sudden absence was more than she could bear.

Even Ricky Herman was wiping his eyes with his sleeve, and Sherma had her face covered by her hands.

"Okay," said Jim, gently. "Let's have a minute's silence, shall we, so that we can all say our own private prayers."

The class sat with bowed heads. For the first time ever, Mark and Ricky weren't giggling and shuffling. Russell's stomach rumbled, but nobody laughed. It just seemed to make the silence even more poignant. Life was going on as normal and Elvin wasn't here.

The minute was almost over when Jim's attention was caught by a flickering shadow on the other side of the yard. It was a bright day, and the porch that led to the main building was deep in darkness. But Jim was sure he had seen something moving. He walked slowly over to the window and peered out. At first he couldn't see what it was, but gradually he was able to make out the figure of a man, standing close to one of the supporting pillars. He was dressed in black, and against his chest he was holding a black wide-brimmed hat.

Jim beckoned to Titus Greenspan III. Titus was wearing a T-shirt with bright pink stripes across it. With his bulgy black eyes and his nervous, querulous manner, he looked like an oversized prawn. "Titus . . . come here. That's it, get out of your desk and come over here. Now I want you to look out of the window . . . over there. You see where the porch is? You see the right-hand pillar?"

"Which one is that?" asked Titus, blinking.

"It's the pillar on the same side as your right hand. No, *this* hand. Now, can you see anybody standing beside that pillar? It's pretty shadowy, but look hard. A man in a black suit holding a hat."

Titus stared and stared, but in the end he slowly shook his head.

"Is this some kind of intelligence test?" he wanted to know.

Jim looked back at the porch and the man was still clearly in sight. In fact he had taken a step forward so that he was easier to see.

"You can't see a man standing beside that right-hand pillar, with a hat in his hand? Come on, look again." (For a split-second, Jim was tempted to add, 'What are you, for Christ's sake, blind?' but he managed to bite his tongue.)

Titus stared across the yard for over half a minute, the tip of his tongue gripped between his teeth. At last, he said, "Nope. I'm sorry, Mr Rook. Hff. No can see."

"Ricky, come here," Jim beckoned him; and then he pointed. "Look over there. You see that man, standing in the porch? Just left of that pillar."

Ricky stared across the yard, but then he let out a whinnying noise and said, "No. Sorry, Mr Rook. I don't see nobody."

"All right," Jim told him. "Go back to your seat. Wait here everybody. Take out your poetry readers and see what you can make of page 26 . . . *Dead Boy*, by John Crowe Ransom. And don't just read it, *think* when you read it, think what it means. I'll be back in a minute."

He left the classroom and hurried along the floor-waxed corridor. He pushed open the swing door with its wire-glazed windows, into the sunshine. He ran across the tarmac yard, toward the porch. And the man was still there. The man in the black suit, holding his wide black hat over his heart. But as soon as he saw Jim running toward him, he rolled away from the pillar in a brief kerfuffle of black, and then he was gone. By the time that Jim reached the porch, panting, the door to the main building was slowly easing its way closed with a quiet pneumatic *pifff*! and the man had vanished.

Jim wrenched open the door and stepped inside. He

listened for the sound of running, but the building echoed with nothing more than the voices of teachers and the slow, plangent echoing of a piano lesson. *Für Elise* played note by hesitant note.

He walked half-way down the main corridor, looking into every classroom window. His footsteps echoed and re-echoed. This was where the most promising students were taught: the students who would graduate with honours, and find themselves a well-paying job. Very few of them would ever be really famous, or really rich. But the college had taught them to work hard, and to apply themselves; and in return most of them had realised that we can't all be Michael Jackson, or Demi Moore.

Jim's class hadn't learned that yet, and maybe they never would. But that was what made them Special Class II.

Jim stopped; and he was about to turn back; when the tall man in the black suit appeared at the very far end of the corridor, half-blurred by the sunlight, and started to tug off his gloves, finger by finger. Jim said nothing for a while, but watched him, his heart beating like an overwound wrist-watch. The man's face was so overshadowed by the brim of his hat that it was still impossible to tell if he was black or white. His head was slightly lowered and he appeared to be waiting. Jim couldn't make up his mind if he was waiting for him, or not. He certainly wasn't going to approach him until he knew for sure that he was unarmed; and even then he was going to be cautious. The man must have been at least six inches taller than Jim: square-shouldered, and brooding, and *shadowy*. Now he knew what Mrs Vaizey meant by an aura. This man carried with him a smoldering, dangerous atmosphere of his own like a thick cloud of volcanic ash. No brilliance here. No rainbow. Not even any mottled colours. He was burning up as darkly as Mount St Helen's.

It sounded as if he were *humming*, too, a strange monotonous drone interspersed with occasional growls deep down in his throat.

"I don't know who you are," Jim called out, trying to sound authoritative, "but this is college property and you're trespassing!"

There was a silence as long as the end of a tape-cassette, before it starts playing Side Two.

Then – "You can *see* me, can you?" the man replied. His voice sounded like somebody dragging a wet sack across a concrete floor.

"If I couldn't see you, I wouldn't be telling you to leave, would I?"

"Of course you wouldn't, no." The man paused again, and thought about that, and then he said, "I suspected that you could see me, the way you came rushing out of that schoolroom yesterday, before nothing had happened. There aren't too many like you, I'm happy to say. People who can *see*."

"I think you and me had better talk to the police, don't you, sir?" said Jim.

"The police? What would be the point of that? They wouldn't be able to see me."

"A boy was killed in that boiler-house, and you were the last person to leave it."

"You mean Elvin. Alas poor Elvin. I didn't know him too well."

The man was paraphrasing *Hamlet*. "Don't mock him," said Jim, although the man was probably mocking *him*, too, the English teacher.

"I don't need to mock him," the man replied. "He mocked himself. He mocked his own race."

"And that's why you murdered him?"

The man said nothing for a while. Then he held out both of his hands. "Do you know something, you and me ought to be friends. I could use a friend with the gift of sight; a friend who can actually see me. I've had friends before, for sure."

"What the hell are you talking about?" Jim demanded.

"Oh, come on, now, Jim; you know what I'm talking about. People who can *see*. Kids who were dropped on their heads. Men who were cut out of automobile wrecks. Women who tried to give birth in toilets, and almost bled to death. They could *see*, those people, but most of the time they were pretty slow on the uptake – even if they hadn't been brain-damaged. Unlike *you*, Mr Rook. You can see; but you're clever, too. I could sure use a friend like you."

"Who are you?" said Jim. He was quaking with rage, but he didn't dare to step any closer.

There was another long silence, but then the man said, "Somebody has to keep the faith, Mr Rook. Somebody has to keep the lamps lit. Some people say we should forgive and forget, but I can't do neither, and I never will."

The man's image seemed to shudder. Then, quite silently, he turned away, and opened up the door to the geography room. He disappeared inside and quickly closed the door behind him.

Jim ran to the geography room and peered in through the window. It was empty apart from the man making his way between the desks, with his back turned. Where the hell was he going? This was the only door, and for safety's sake the windows couldn't be opened up wide enough for anybody to climb out. Jim twisted the handle, but the door wouldn't open. He rattled it, and banged on the window with his fist, but the man kept walking across the room toward the opposite corner.

But the further away he walked, the taller he seemed to be. He grew, *stretched*, as if the room's perspective had been reversed. By the time he was half-way across the room he must have been seven or eight feet tall; and when he reached the wall and turned around, he was standing higher than the picture-rail.

Jim stopped rattling the doorhandle and stared at the man in total dread. This time he could see his face, grinning at him from the top of his dark, attenuated body. It was the face of a black man, his eyes yellow, his cheeks marked with scars. The skin around his mouth was deeply lined, so that it looked as if his lips had been sewn together, like a shrunken head.

But it was his height that unnerved Jim the most. His hat almost touched the ceiling, and his arms were so long that they could reach half-way along the walls.

Für Elise continued to echo along the corridor: a plonking, mundane counterpoint to the horror inside the geography room.

Jim looked at the man for one more hair-prickling moment. Then he turned and ran to the principal's office, beside the entrance-hall. Dr Ehrlichman's secretary was arranging some flowers on the windowsill when Jim came skidding in. She had big ash-blonde hair and oversized spectacles, and she always wore fussy blouses with lacy collars and cuffs.

"Sylvia – call the cops!" Jim told her.

"Mr Rook! The police? What on earth for?"

"There's a man – it's the same guy I saw yesterday – he's locked himself in the geography room. Now, please, will you call the cops!"

Sylvia dithered, so Jim picked up the phone himself

and punched out 911. "Yes – West Grove College – will you please dispatch somebody fast before he gets away. And if you can get a message to Lieutenant Harris – that's right, he's been handling the whole investigation. Yes."

He put down the phone just as Dr Ehrlichman came out of his office. Dr Ehrlichman was small and neat, with a bald suntanned head and a voice like Micky Rooney. He always wore grey Sta-Prest slacks and a crisp short-sleeved white shirt and his favourite word was 'businesslike'. "Jim – what's going on here?"

"It's the same guy that I saw yesterday," said Jim. "The one who was coming out of the boiler-house when Elvin got stabbed. He's here. He's right here in the building."

"You've called Mr Wallechinsky?"

"I've called the police."

"Jim, listen to me. We pay good money for Mr Wallechinsky and there's a reason for that. He's an ex-cop. He knows how to deal with security problems. And you know college policy, don't you? Nobody calls the police to this college without my say-so. Can you imagine the kind of reputation we're going to get? Yesterday's incident was serious enough, without compounding it."

Jim pointed toward the geography room, his arm rigid. "Dr Ehrlichman, there's a guy in this building who stabbed one of our students so many times that even the medical examiner could hardly count how many holes he had in him. And you think Wallechinsky could deal with somebody like that?"

Dr Ehrlichman said, "Mr Wallechinsky is a good man. Sylvia – do you mind giving him a call? Let's see if we can deal with this problem in-house."

"I'm warning you," Jim told him. "This guy is not an ordinary guy. Not by any stretch of the imagination."

Dr Ehrlichman took off his spectacles and looked at Jim

bulgy-eyed. "I don't think you're the one who ought to be talking about stretches of the imagination, Jim. Nobody else saw your man in black yesterday, and so far nobody's seen him today."

"Then come look," Jim urged him.

"When Mr Wallechinsky's here – then, yes, I will."

Jim said, "I was talking to a woman last night. She's kind of an expert when it comes to things like this. She said that it's possible for some people to leave their bodies and walk around. They don't have to be dead or anything. But the whole point is, only certain people can see them. People who have come within a whisker of dying. That near-death experience gives them an ability to see things that most people can't. Dr Ehrlichman, we have invisible spirits walking among us, all the time. But the trouble is, we simply don't have the eyes to see."

Dr Ehrlichman replaced his glasses and stared at him as if he was having an afternoon off from the madhouse. "You haven't been drinking, Jim, have you?"

"Of course not. What do you want to do, smell my breath?"

"You haven't been smoking? Or snorting? Or whatever it is you people do these days?"

"I'm a teacher, Dr Ehrlichman. I don't come to college stoned or drunk or even impatient."

Dr Ehrlichman looked unconvinced, but at that moment George Wallechinsky arrived, six feet five inches of lumpy human tissue in a tight brown uniform. His face was broad, with two tiny expressionless eyes, buried in his flesh like two sultanas buried in a bread pudding.

"George," said Dr Ehrlichman, briskly, "it seems like we've got ourselves an intruder. Mr Rook says that he's locked himself into the geography room."

Wallechinsky sniffed, and cleared his throat. "How long ago was this?"

"Five minutes; not more."

"Did you ever see the individual before?"

"Sure. I saw him yesterday, coming out the boiler-house, just before Elvin was killed. In fact he was the only reason I went over there, to see what was going on."

"You sure it's the same individual?"

"Believe me, Mr Wallechinsky, there's only one guy like this."

"Okay, then. Let's go take a look. You're sure he's not a college inspector? Sometimes they send inspectors by surprise."

Wallechinsky waddled steadfastly in front of them, all the way down the corridor, his keys jingling on his belt. "This it?" He stopped outside the door of the geography room and looked inside, stooping down so that he could see the ceiling, then angling his head close to the glass so that he could see the floors and corners.

"This room is empty, so far as I can see," he reported. He tried the handle, rattling and shaking it, but it was still locked, or jammed, and he gave it up.

"Did he have any kind of weapon?" he asked Jim.

"Is he there?" Dr Ehrlichman demanded.

"Well, I can't see anything, Mr Principal, sir; but that doesn't necessarily mean that there's nothing there. He could be pressing himself flat against the wall here; or behind this here bookcase; or even under the teacher's desk."

Dr Ehrlichman pressed his nose flat against the window. "No," he said. "He's gone. That's if he ever existed at all."

Jim said, "He was there, Dr Ehrlichman. He even spoke to me."

"I'd like a talk with you later, Jim," Dr Ehrlichman told him. "Mr Wallechinsky, you'd better call the police and tell them it was a false alarm."

"I'd like to check the room first, Dr Ehrlichman," said Wallechinsky. He lifted his keyring, heavy with all kinds of keys, and picked out the one which would open the geography-room door. He inserted it, and turned.

"It's not locked," he said, in surprise.

"What do you mean it's not locked?" Dr Ehrlichman demanded. He seized the handle and shook it until he almost pulled it off.

"No disrespect, Dr Ehrlichman, sir. But I mean it's not locked."

"Then open it."

Wallechinsky reached out for the handle, but Jim lifted his hand and stopped him. "Let me," he said. He hesitated for a moment, and then he opened the door with no trouble at all. He pushed it, and it swung open, so that sunlight fell across the corridor and illuminated their shoes. Dr Ehrlichman's brown rubber-soled lace-ups; Wallechinsky's highly-polished black boots; and Jim's balding blue suede sneakers.

Wallechinsky tried to push his way his inside, but Jim held out his arm to stop him. If Mrs Vaizey was right, then Wallechinsky wouldn't be able to see the man in black anyway. Jim stepped into the classroom, looking right and left, ducking down so that he could check under the desk, then turning around to make sure that the man in black wasn't hiding behind the bookcase.

It was then that he saw him. He was no longer dressed in black, but all in white, and even his face was white, although it was still the face of an Afro-American. He looked as if he had been rolling in flour, or ashes. Even the pupils of his eyes were white, like lychees.

He was up on the ceiling, lying horizontally against the cornice, his hands crossed over his chest as if he had been laid out in a funeral parlour. He wasn't dead, though: he was staring at Jim with those milky white eyes and he was grinning in triumph.

Wallechinsky came into the classroom and circled around it with the clumsiness of a purblind bear, peering behind bookcases and wallcharts as if a man could hide in a space less than an inch wide. He turned to Jim and saw that he was staring at the ceiling, and he stared up at it, too.

"You want to tell me what you're looking at?" he asked. "You don't expect the guy to be up on the ceiling, do you?"

Jim whispered, "You can't see him, can you? You really can't see him."

"See who?"

"The intruder, that's who. He's there. Look. Use your imagination."

"You're not trying to tell me he's invisible? He's up on the ceiling and he's invisible? Come on, Mr Rook. Is this some kind of a practical joke?"

Up above them, the man grinned even more widely. Jim couldn't take his eyes away from him. He felt so terrified that he couldn't speak; but what was worse than his terror was his sense of helplessness. In all his years as a remedial teacher, he had always been able to cope. But he couldn't cope with this. Not logically, or emotionally, or any way at all. He had to stand in the middle of the geography room and admit to himself that there was nothing he could do, and that was the most horrifying feeling of all.

Testily, Dr Ehrlichman said, "Are we done now? I'm extremely busy."

"Ain't nobody here but us chickens, Mr Principal,"

said Wallechinsky, giving Jim an exasperated shake of his head.

"All right, then. You'd better call the police and tell them it was a false alarm."

He turned away. As he did so, the door slammed shut with such violence that the glass cracked and plaster dropped from the architrave. Dr Ehrlichman's face immediately reappeared in the window, and he was shouting something, but Jim couldn't hear what.

Wallechinsky went for the door-handle and tried to pull it open, but it was stuck just as fast as it had been before.

"Give me a hand here!" he called. But Jim could see what he couldn't see; and that was the white-faced man slowly sinking from the ceiling, slowly turning around, so that he landed feet-first on the floor only four or five feet away from them. His shoes touched the floor completely silently, and with exaggerated grace. Jim backed away, colliding with one of the desks. The white-faced man lifted his hat and dust fell off it and sifted to the floor.

"Will you please give me a hand here, *sir*?" Wallechinsky repeated. Outside the room, Dr Ehrlichman hammered on the door with his fist and shouted, "What's going on? Will somebody tell me what the *hell* is going on?"

The white-faced man was gliding toward Wallechinsky, smiling and gliding. When he was only two feet away, he stopped. He grasped his right wrist with his left hand, and twisted; and to Jim's horror, his right hand rotated, around and around, until it came off altogether. A false hand, carved out of ebony and smothered with ash. But the white-faced man was left with more than a stump. Out of his right wrist protruded a long, wide-bladed knife, which looked as if it had been grafted into his bones. It gleamed in the sunlight, wickedly sharp; and the white-faced man mockingly waved it from side to side in front of Wallechinsky's face, because he knew that Wallechinsky couldn't see it.

Jim said, "George, I want you to step back from the door."

"Trying to get the damn thing open," Wallechinsky protested. "There's no reason why it shoulda jammed."

"George! Get away from the door! Now! Quick! As fast as you can!"

"Why? Do you think there's some kinda—"

Jim lunged forward and shoulder-tackled the white-faced man as hard as he could. He went right through him, as if he didn't exist, and collided with the door, splitting the wood and hurting his shoulder so badly that he spun around, saying, "Shit, shit, shit," over and over. He had felt the briefest of draughts when he passed through the white-faced man, like a fridge door opened and shut, but that was all.

The white-faced man silently laughed, and circled his arm around and around, so that his knife actually whistled.

"Don't touch him," Jim warned him. "You've done enough goddamned damage already."

"I haven't done anything," Wallechinsky complained. "Begging your pardon, sir, it's *you* that broke the goddamned door."

"Just stay back," Jim warned the white-faced man, edging away.

"I don't know what you're talking about," said Wallechinsky. "Stay back from what?"

But the white-faced man had made his way behind him, and was grinning at Jim over his shoulder, and there was something in those milk-white eyes that told Jim what he was going to do.

"Listen," he said. "You want me to be your friend? I'll be your friend. I'll do anything you want."

Wallechinsky looked deeply uneasy. "Listen, Mr Rook, I'm a married man. Three kids. A wife who's put up with me for twenty-eight years."

"I don't care what it is, I'll do it," said Jim.

"Mr Rook, sir—"

At that instant, with a sharp racketing noise, the door was kicked open from the outside, and two police officers came bursting into the geography room. Instantly, the white-faced man whipped up his knife and drew a line of blood down Wallechinsky's right cheek, a razor-thin cut that Wallechinsky could have scarcely felt, because he didn't even flinch. The white-faced man turned to Jim and said, "You've made me a promise, Mr Rook. I expect you to keep it. Otherwise, I'll be back for this fellow, and *then* you'll see what a knife can do."

He turned around and flowed out of the room as if he were no more substantial than a cloud of smoke from a summer bonfire. Jim was about to call out after him, but now he had two sceptical-looking cops in the room, as well as Wallechinsky and Dr Ehrlichman, and he decided it would be wiser for him to keep his mouth shut.

"You hurt there, buddy?" asked one of the cops, pointing to Wallechinsky's cheek. A thin scarlet stream of blood was running into his uniform collar.

"What? Hurt?" said Wallechinsky, in bewilderment; and then he dabbed at his cheek with his fingers. "Hey. What the hell happened? I'm bleeding."

Dr Ehrlichman took a clean squared handkerchief out of his breast pocket. "Here, use this. You'd better have it seen to."

"How the hell did I cut myself like that?" asked Wallechinsky. "Mr Rook, did you see what happened?"

Jim shook his head. "I don't have any idea," he lied. "It just – *happened* – just like that."

"So who are we supposed to be looking for?" asked one of the cops.

"I'm sorry," Jim told him. "I must have made a mistake. I saw somebody suspicious in the building, and I thought he came in here."

"Can you give us some idea of what he looked like?"

"Hard to say. Tall, dark, dressed all in black."

The second cop turned to Wallechinsky. "You see anybody like that?"

"I didn't see nobody. Only Mr Rook."

"Have you *any* idea how you could have gotten that cut?"

"I told you. It just happened."

"Mr Rook didn't cut you? Maybe by accident?"

"Mr Rook wasn't nowhere near me."

"Okay," said the cop. "Why don't you get your face cleaned up, and maybe we'll talk to you later."

Wallechinsky left, clutching Dr Ehrlichman's blood-sodden handkerchief against his cheek. As he did so, Lieutenant Harris arrived, wearing a lurid purple necktie and perspiring furiously.

"So what's going on here?" he wanted to know.

Jim said, "I'm sorry . . . this is all a misunderstanding. I thought I saw the same man in black that I saw yesterday outside the boiler-house."

"The same man in black that nobody else could see?"

Jim grimaced. He couldn't tell Lieutenant Harris how shocked he was; and how much the white-faced man had unnerved him. If he could hover on the ceiling and change his colour like a chameleon and cut people who couldn't even see him, God alone knew what he else he was capable of. Besides, even if Jim explained everything, there was no chance whatsoever that Lieutenant Harris would believe him.

Lieutenant Harris said, "Have you thought of talking to somebody about this guy that you've been seeing?"

"What do you mean?"

"Well—" clearing his throat, embarrassed, "—I mean like a counsellor; or maybe a psychiatrist."

"You think this is some kind of hallucination?"

"I don't know what to think, Mr Rook. You're a college teacher and from what I've gathered from most of the other members of the faculty you're a very well-respected college teacher. But you teach a difficult class, don't you? Maybe you've been suffering from stress. When people are stressed, you know, they sometimes get their heads filled up with some pretty wacky ideas."

"I'm not under stress, believe me. My class is fine. I'm fine. Everything's fine."

Lieutenant Harris shrugged. "Okay, you're fine. So you won't mind my asking you if you indulge in recreational substances of any kind."

"I smoke now and then."

"Did you smoke yesterday?"

"Unh-hunh. I never do it at school. Evenings and weekends only; and then only once or twice a month."

"So you didn't smoke today, either?"

"Absolutely not."

"You know I could easily check that out."

"Listen, Lieutenant," Jim told him, "I'm not under the influence of stress or drugs or anything else. Yesterday I saw what I told you I saw. Today . . . well, let's just say that I was a little confused."

Lieutenant Harris stared at him for a very long time without saying anything. A bead of sweat ran down his cheek and he wiped it with the back of his hand.

"Okay, then, Mr Rook. Maybe I'll talk to you later."

Jim's class reconvened after the lunch recess for a session of reading and word-recognition. Unusually for him, Jim went to the classroom early so that he was waiting for them when they arrived. No dramatic entrance this afternoon.

After they had settled down, he stood up and paced to the back of the room. "Before we start reading," he said, "I want to know if any of you believe in ghosts."

John Ng's hand shot up. "My grandfather is a ghost."

There was a loud hooting of derision from the rest of the class, mingled with spooky whistles and moans of "*woooooooooo*!" but Jim remained serious. "You've actually seen your grandfather for yourself?"

"No, but my father said that he visited him when he was in a time of trouble, and stood at the end of the bed, and told him the proverb of the golden carp always trying to swim upstream. He was all dressed in orange and he wore an orange mask, so that only his eyes peeked out."

"I believe in ghosts," said Rita. "*And* I saw one, too."

"Go on," Jim encouraged her.

"Well, we used to use this beach-house on Santa Monica beach when we were kids and every time we went there we used to see a kid with a surfboard under his arm coming out the door. Always the same kid. Then he used to disappear in the crowd and we'd never see him again till next time. We asked the lifeguard about him and like described what he looked like and the lifeguard said it was a kid who got drowned about seven years before. He came out of the beach-house and went into the sea and like two days later they found his body under the pier."

"That's *scary*," said Sherma.

"I think that's great," said Ricky. "I mean the kid

may be dead, right, but he gets to go surfing every day."

"I d-d-don't b-b-believe in g-g-g-g—" David Littwin began. Immediately a loud chorus of snoring started up, but Jim raised his hand and the class could tell by the look in his eye that he wasn't going to tolerate any teasing, not today. "I think that when you d-die your spirit g-g-g-gets reborn in somebody else. Or s-s-something else."

"Hey, Littwin, just so long as you don't get yourself reborn as a sports commentator," Mark put in.

Jim said, "Shut up, Mark. A whole lot of people believe in reincarnation – the Buddhists in particular. Now let's take it a step further. Does anybody believe that some people can see ghosts when maybe other people can't?"

Russell said, "Are you trying to tell us the guy you saw yesterday was a *ghost*?"

"I'm not sure what he was. But I think I saw him again today, and believe me, he doesn't act like a human at all."

"Mr Rook's finally flipped," said Ricky. "Guess you've been teaching us dummies for too long, sir."

Jim smiled, but then he said, "Let me tell you what happened, and then judge for yourselves."

He walked back to the front of the class, and went up to the blackboard, with the intention of drawing a picture of the black-suited man floating on the ceiling. As he picked up the chalk, however, he saw something moving in the small window in the classroom door.

He turned and stared, and he felt that terrible cold prickling sensation up his back, like centipedes walking down his spine. In the window he saw the face of the black-suited man – black now, as he had been the first time that Jim had seen him. His fingertip was held to his lips, and his yellow eyes were as threatening as a poisonous snake.

Jim hesitated, and then flipped the chalk back into the tin. "Let's forget it," he said. "It's not your problem. Let's get down to some reading, shall we? Russell, how about you? *On The Road*, from the beginning of chapter ten."

He didn't look at the window again, although he was conscious that the man was still there, watching him.

After a few minutes, however, he disappeared. Jim immediately went to the door and opened it, and looked out, but the corridor was empty in both directions, except for a lanky boy leaning over the water-fountain.

Chapter Four

He let class out an hour earlier than usual, and left the college on his way to see Elvin's parents. He was crossing the faculty parking-lot when Dr Ehrlichman called out to him.

"Jim! Are you leaving already?"

"I'm going to see Elvin's parents. You know, to give them the class's condolences."

Dr Ehrlichman laid a hand on his shoulder. "Jim . . . I know you've been through a tragic experience, but I think it's essential that you keep your grip on reality. It's going to be very disturbing for your students if you don't."

Jim said, "I guess it depends on what you mean by reality, Dr Ehrlichman. There's one reality for each of us, and sometimes those realities don't exactly match. Sometimes it's hard to know which one you ought to be keeping a grip on."

"I'm sorry, Jim. I'm not here to get involved in a philosophical discussion. I just have to tell you that if we have any further incidents like today's, I'm going to have to consider putting you on suspension and requiring you to undergo – well, a psychiatric evaluation."

Jim had reached his car, a '69 Rebel SST in its original screaming orange. "I see. We can't have the staff being as nutty as the students, can we?"

"'Nutty' is not a word we use in association with West Grove College, Jim . . . even for Special Class II. I simply want to make sure that you're mentally stable and that you're able to carry out your professional duties without you seeing phantom prowlers everywhere you look and calling the police out willy-nilly. The students come first, Jim, every single time. The students, and West Grove's good name."

Jim replied, "I'm aware of that, sir. You won't hear any more about men in black." And he meant it. His new-found friend had made it chillingly clear that he didn't want Jim talking about him to anybody.

Dr Ehrlichman seemed to be satisfied with that. He slapped Jim on the back and walked off with his bald head shining in the sunlight. Just then Susan Randall appeared, carrying an armful of books. She had her hair pinned back and she was wearing a white sleeveless blouse with pointed lapels.

"You're not headed anywhere south of Santa Monica Boulevard, are you?" she asked him.

"Sure. Do you need a ride?"

"If it's not too far out of your way. My car's in the shop and I don't relish the idea of carrying all these books on the bus."

Jim opened the door for her and she climbed in. He had never noticed before that she wore a gold ankle chain. He said, "Watch your skirt . . . I mean you don't want to get it caught in the door."

They drove out through the college gates and headed southward on Westwood Boulevard.

"Great car," said Susan. "I really love classics."

"This car's classic all right. It was crap when it was new and it's still crap."

"It's a terrific colour, though, isn't it?"

Jim shrugged. He wasn't in the mood for talking about cars. Susan watched him for a moment, and then she said, "You must be feeling pretty bad about Elvin."

"I'm feeling bad about both of them, Elvin and Tee Jay."

"You really believe that Tee Jay wasn't responsible?"

"I don't know. He *could* have done it. He had the time and he had some kind of motive. But I really don't believe that he did."

"Because of this man you saw? The man in black?"

"I'm sorry, Susan. I can't talk about it any more. I have to get a few things straight first."

"Okay, whatever. It's just that yesterday you seemed so sure."

Jim didn't answer. They had stopped at the traffic lights at Wilshire and all he could think of was the man in black glaring at him through the classroom window, his finger pressed to his lips.

As the signals turned to green, Susan said, "We've never really had the chance to get to know each other, have we?"

"I guess not. Always busy, busy, busy."

"Ron Philips said you were something of an expert on antique maps."

Jim turned and stared at her. "Ron Philips said that?"

"Sure. He said you had one of the finest collections of antique maps he'd ever seen."

Shit, thought Jim. Ron Philips, the faculty smartass. I'll garotte him next time I see him. The only antique map I'm an expert on is the well-worn Chek-Chart of Central Los Angeles in the glovebox.

"I'm totally *fascinated* by antique maps," Susan continued. "I bought a 16th-century map of the Huguenot settlement in Carolina last year, but it's only a reproduction. Authentic maps are so expensive, aren't they? Ron said you have hundreds."

"Well, not quite hundreds. In fact, to tell you the truth—"

"I'd love to see them," she said, touching his arm. "Maybe I could come round sometime."

It was the touch that did it. "That would be great," he said, thinking: of all the luck in the world, the most attractive woman in the whole school has just invited herself around to my apartment, and it's all because of some stupid dumbass joke.

"Maybe Saturday?" Susan urged him. "I could bring around some Chinese food."

"Saturday? Like, this coming Saturday? The day after tomorrow? I don't know. I'll have to check my diary. And you'll have to remember that I keep all the really valuable maps in a safe-deposit box."

"Do you have anything extra-special?" she said, her eyes bright. "Go on, give me a for-instance."

"I don't know. There are just so many."

"Tell me just one."

"Well . . ." he said. "I have a chart of Martin Frobisher's voyage to Greenland in 1577, when he was trying to find a way through to China." Thinking: thank God I know some history.

"Oh, I *have* to see that," said Susan. "That must have cost you a fortune."

"Yes, well. It's pretty rare. There are only three copies in existence, and one of those is supposed to be a fake. Trouble is, nobody can decide which one." You're getting in deep here, Jim. Don't say any more.

He stopped outside Susan's neat white house on Almato Avenue and helped her to carry her books to the door. The sprinklers had just finished and the concrete path was still wet. "Time for a drink?" she asked him.

"No . . . I'm sorry. I promised Mr and Mrs Clay I'd be there by four."

"All right, then," she smiled. "I'll see you tomorrow."

With that, she kissed him on the cheek. He stood staring at her as if he had forgotten his lines. This wasn't a play, and he wasn't an actor, but he simply didn't know what to say next.

"Tomorrow, then?" Susan prompted him.

"Oh, sure, tomorrow." He turned off-balance and brushed against a wet bush. "That'll save me taking a shower." Brushing the droplets off his shirt and pants, he walked back to his car. Before he climbed in, he raised his arm in a goodbye wave and Susan waved back. He felt extraordinary. It was just as if his lungs couldn't remember how to breathe. He hadn't felt this way for such a long time that he had to pull down the sun-visor and stare at himself in the vanity-mirror to make sure that it was really him.

He looked back toward Susan's house but she had gone inside now and closed the door. "Maps," he said. "Where do I get some goddamned maps?"

Inside Mr and Mrs Clay's second-storey apartment the drapes were half-drawn and Grant and Elisabeth Clay were sitting in the shadows. Jim was let in by a solemn nine-year-old girl with cornrows and white satin ribbons and a very white dress. There were other relatives in the kitchen, drinking coffee and talking in low, respectful voices. A large photograph of Elvin hung above the couch, draped in a black cloth. Beside it hung a crucifix and a 3–D picture of The Last Supper.

Jim went over and gave Mrs Clay a long, sorrowful hug.

He felt her tears through the shoulder of his shirt. Then he turned to Mr Clay and held his hand in both of his.

"We're going to miss Elvin so much," he said. "All of his classmates send you their love; and they all want you to know that they're thinking of you."

"You found him, didn't you?" said Grant. He was a short, stocky man with wire-grey hair. He was wearing a formal white shirt and a black bowtie. He spoke well, and he carried himself with supreme dignity. He could have been mistaken for a judge.

"Yes, I found him," said Jim.

"He was alive, wasn't he? That's what the police lieutenant told me."

"Only barely, Mr Clay. He died just as soon as I reached him."

"And he didn't say nothing? No last words?"

Jim shook his head. Elisabeth Clay took hold of his hand and looked up at him in tearful incomprehension. "Why did this have to happen, Mr Rook? What did Elvin do? He wasn't smart, I know that, but he always worked hard. He was always good, and kind, and Christian."

"I don't know why it happened, Mrs Clay. Every time a young man dies, I guess that every grieving mother and father ask themselves the same question. And I guess that they always come up with the same answer. Wrong place, wrong time; wrong friends, wrong situation. Sometimes I think that God turns his back, and doesn't see what's happening, not until it's too late."

Grant said, "Elvin and Tee Jay were such good friends, that's what I can't understand. And I used to like Tee Jay. He was always polite, and called us 'sir' and 'ma'am', and once he took Elvira to the beach. She's our young one. Eleven now; and all we have left. Elisabeth can't have no more children. Not that any child could ever replace our Elvin."

"Do you believe that Tee Jay did it, Mr Rook?" asked Elisabeth.

Jim said, "Let's put it this way. I have my doubts. But I can't say too much about it right now – not while the police are still looking into it."

A wide, pretty woman in a black dress and a black pillbox hat came out of the kitchen and said, "Would you care for some coffee, and a piece of fruit pie?"

"Coffee would be great," said Jim.

Grant went up to Elvin's portrait and stared at it, as if he were willing it to speak. "Elvin didn't see too much of Tee Jay these past three months. Elvin didn't know too much about it, but it seemed like Tee Jay was having trouble at home. I can't tell you much more than that, because it was one of those things that you don't put a mind to, till something tragic happens, and then you look back."

"Do you have any idea what kind of trouble Tee Jay was having?" asked Jim.

"The police asked me that, but I don't have any idea at all. What kind of trouble does a seventeen-year-old boy usually have with his parents? He wants to party; he wants to stay out late; he doesn't want to do what he's told. He wants to experiment with alcohol and drugs. I don't know. All I know is that Elvin stopped hanging out with Tee Jay so much as he used to."

A young girl in a black-and-white gingham blouse was standing by the door, listening. She said, "Elvin told me that Tee Jay was getting too religious."

Elisabeth held out her hand. "Come here, honey. Mr Rook – this is Elvira, Elvin's sister. Elvira, this is Elvin's teacher, Mr Rook."

Jim said, "Good to know you, Elvira. I came here to tell your folks how sorry we are about Elvin."

"Elvin talked about you a whole lot," said Elvira. "He said you were crazy sometimes, but you always taught him more than anybody else."

"What was that you were saying about Tee Jay getting too religious?" asked Jim.

"I didn't understand that, either," put in Grant. "How anybody be *too* religious? Elvin was religious. The whole family, we go to church regular, always have. Elvin sang in the choir before."

"But it wasn't that kind of religion," said Elvira.

"What do you mean?" Jim asked her.

"I heard Elvin and Tee Jay arguing once. Tee Jay was trying to get Elvin to bite the head off a chicken. He said they should drink its blood, and say some prayers, and then they would never die."

"You didn't tell us this before," said Elisabeth.

"I couldn't. Elvin and Tee Jay caught me listening and they said I had to swear not to tell, otherwise the smoke would come and get me."

"The smoke? What smoke?"

"I don't know. But the way Tee Jay said it, I was frightened; so that's why I didn't say anything."

"Okay," said Jim. "You did good to tell us. Now why don't you cut me a piece of that pie?"

Elvira went back into the kitchen. Jim turned to Grant and said, "Does any of this mean anything to you? Killing chickens? Or smoke?" He paused, and then continued, "How about crows and mirrors and candles? Or breathing in dust?"

Grant glanced uneasily at his wife. "This isn't the time to talk about things like that. Nor the place, neither. We're devout people, Mr Rook. We don't hold with blasphemy."

"Then you know what I'm talking about?"

Elisabeth looked up at him and Jim couldn't understand the expression on her face at all. But Grant said, "Yes. I know what you're talking about. You're talking about killing chickens, to please the spirits. You're talking about crows, which are sometimes crows and sometimes men. You're talking about mirrors . . . the kind of mirrors that don't reflect your own face."

"Hush," Elisabeth interrupted him. "You shouldn't be saying such things . . . not now, not in front of Elvin's picture."

"Maybe there's somewhere else we can talk," Jim suggested. Grant hesitated, but Jim said, "I think it's important, Mr Clay. It may be too late for Elvin but it's not too late for Tee Jay."

"Come out on the balcony," Grant suggested; and so they did, and slid the doors shut behind them. Grant leaned on the railings and looked down at the small concrete yard where children were playing in a sandpit and a group of teenagers were hanging around smoking and playing techno-rock on a huge ghetto-blaster. "Kids," said Grant. There was no pity in his voice, but there was no judgement, either. "What do they have to look forward to, but this?"

"You were telling me about Tee Jay's religion," said Jim.

"I don't know too much about it, but it's like voodoo. My grandfather used to tell me stories about it to frighten me, when I was a boy. He told me all about the goofer dust which the priests blow into your face to make you seem like you're dead, although you're not. They can stick pins into you and you can feel them but you can't cry out. Then they bury you, even though you're still awake."

"Do you believe in any of that?"

Grant's eyes gave nothing away. "I'm just telling you what my grandfather told me."

"All right, then. What about the smoke that Elvira was talking about?"

"My grandfather used to mention the smoke, too, but I could never understand what it was. He used to say, 'The smoke can always find you; and the smoke can always do you harm; like real smoke can choke you to death. But what can you do to the smoke? You can't do nothing. It's there, but it isn't there. You can smell it,' that's what he used to say, 'but you can't touch it. You can see it, but you can't feel it. Watch out for the smoke', that's what he used to say."

"But you don't know what the smoke actually is."

"No, Mr Rook, I don't. And to tell you the God's-honest truth, I believe I'd rather not."

"Well, I appreciate your telling me," said Jim. "I was beginning to think that I was going crazy."

Grant looked at him narrowly. "You know something about Elvin's killing, don't you? Something connected with this voodoo stuff. You want to tell me what it is?"

"I'm sorry. I can't, just at the moment."

"You can't, or you won't? Which is it?"

"Mr Clay . . . I don't know very much more than you do. But I've seen some things that aren't normal at all, and I think they could be connected with Elvin's death. You've done the best thing possible: you've put me on the right track. I promise you, if I can find out who killed your Elvin, then you'll be the very first person to know."

Grant said, "Thanks," and relaxed.

The doors slid open and Elvira smiled, "Your pie's ready for you, Mr Rook."

"Thanks, Elvira," said Jim, and followed Grant inside. As he glanced over the balcony, however, he was sure that he could glimpse a shadow in the trash-crowded corner between the swings and garages. He tried to focus, but the garages were too far away. Besides, Grant was taking his arm and ushering him inside to finish his coffee.

Chapter Five

It took him over twenty minutes to find the Jones house, in a tatty triangle of scrubby hinterland right next to the freeway. It was so noisy that you had to shout at yourself to find out what you were thinking; and the air was yellow with photochemical smog.

There was a scrubby patch of grass outside the house, on which a derelict bronze Buick Riviera with no wheels was supported on cinderblocks. A small black boy with no pants on was furiously tricycling up and down the sidewalk. Glistening snot poured from each nostril and he intermittently stopped to lick it. Jim was almost tempted to give him his handkerchief, but one handkerchief wouldn't do much to solve the problem of child neglect. He had seen kids of seven and eight, openly smoking cigarettes that their parents had given them. What was a little snot?

Jim went up to the front porch and rang the doorbell, although the door was already half-open. The green paint was faded and flaking and one of the windows was cracked. From inside the house came the smell of chicken frying and the monotonous thumping of garage music.

After a while, Jim stepped inside. The house was shabby but well-kept, with lace doilies on all of the side-tables and antimacassars on the backs of the armchairs. The walls were crowded with colour photographs of aunts and uncles and cousins, as well as a garish painting of wild animals coming down to an African waterhole to drink.

He made his way along the corridor to the kitchen, where a thin bespectacled woman in a green dress was chopping peppers. He rapped lightly on the open door, and she looked up, flustered. She was obviously Tee Jay's mother: he had inherited her eyes and her nose and her firm, determined jawline.

"Mr Rook!" she said. "What brings you here?"

"How are you, Mrs Jones? I just came by to make sure that everything was okay at home."

"As good as it can be, with my son accused of killing his best friend."

"Have you seen him yet?"

"Saw him this morning, over at the police headquarters. They were fixing to find him a lawyer."

"How is he?"

"Not much different from always," said Mrs Jones, scraping the chopped-up peppers into a saucepan. "He hardly said more than two words strung together."

"Mrs Jones, I want you to know that I don't think Tee Jay did it."

"Huh!" she said, wryly. "Looks like you're the only one who does."

"I'm not so sure. Most of his classmates don't think he did it, either; although some of them said that he'd been acting kind of weird lately."

"Acting kind of weird is the understatement of the century," said Mrs Jones. "For the past three or four months, Tee Jay has been just impossible to live with. Staying out till all hours, giving me mouth. Hanging out with all kinds of low-life."

"You mean he's been behaving like any normal eighteen-year-old?"

"Maybe so. But I'm trying to keep this family together all on my own, working every hour that God sends me; and the last thing I need is rebellion and bad language and slamming of doors. I just don't need it."

She suddenly turned to Jim, and her eyes were crowded with tears. "And I don't need my son in jail, accused of first-degree murder."

"Mrs Jones—" Jim began, "if you don't want to talk right now—" But then the garage music stopped and Tee Jay's older brother Anthony appeared, wearing a Dodgers T-shirt and a baggy pair of Bermuda shorts. He was even taller and broader than Tee Jay, and he put a large, protective arm around his mother's shoulders.

"Hi, Anthony," said Jim. "I just came round to make sure that your mom was okay. You found yourself a job yet?"

"Start Monday, Mr Rook, working for Santa Monica 'Vette. The money ain't great but I'll be doing what I'm good at."

"Hope you're still reading . . . keeping your brain in shape."

"Oh, sure thing. I just finished *Native Son.*"

"Have you been to see Tee Jay too?"

Anthony shook his head, and gave his mother a comforting squeeze. "Tee Jay and me haven't been getting along too good lately. Tee Jay hasn't been getting along too good with anybody, as a matter of fact. That's why he left."

Jim frowned. "You mean he doesn't live here any more?"

"Uhn-hunh. Not for three months now."

"So where *does* he live?"

"Down near Venice Boulevard. He's staying with his uncle, Dad's big brother. That was another reason we were arguing so much. His uncle's been away for years and years, right, working in Nigeria and Sierra Leone and places like that; and all of a sudden he turns up and pays us a visit. Me and mom and the rest of the family really dislike him, you know, but for some reason Tee Jay takes a shine to him. He starts visiting him two or three times a week and that was when the trouble really starts. In the end the rows get so bad that Mom tells Tee Jay to pack his bag and get the hell out. So of course, where does he go? Straight to Uncle Umber."

Jim thought for a moment, and then he said, "This Uncle Umber. Tell me about him. Why didn't you and the rest of the family like him?"

"You ought to meet the guy, then you'd know. He's, like, really heavy, if you know what I mean. He walks in through the door and he fills up the whole house. And he's full of all this stuff about racial heritage and African tradition. Real mumbo-jumbo, you know; but if you try to disagree with him he gets totally aggressive, and treats you like you're some kind of traitor to your race."

Jim said, "I think I'd like to meet this Uncle Umber of yours."

"Believe me, Mr Rook," said Mrs Jones, "you wouldn't. If I were you, I'd leave well enough alone."

"All the same, do you have his address?"

Anthony tore the corner off a piece of kitchen-towel and wrote it down. "He's a blowhard, okay? So don't take him too serious."

"*Ly*," Jim corrected him. "It's 'serious*ly*'."

"Right, well, that too," said Anthony.

Uncle Umber's address near Venice Boulevard turned

out to be one of four apartments over Dollars&Sense, a small cut-price supermarket in a scabby street lined with ten-year-old automobiles and overflowing trash cans. The upper part of the building was painted white, but at one time it must have been light green, because the paint was scaling off like skin-disease.

There was an intercom speaker and three doorbells, one without any identifying card, one saying Puchowski, and the other 'U.M. Jones'. Jim pressed it and waited.

Nobody answered, so he pressed it again, and then again. At last a deep, crackly voice said, "*Who is it*?"

"Mr Jones? My name's Rook, Jim Rook. I'm Tee Jay's teacher. I wonder if I could have a word with you."

"*You'd better come on up, Mr Rook. I've been expecting you. It's Apartment 1.*"

The buzzer sounded and the door unlocked, but Jim hesitated. *I've been expecting you*? He didn't like the sound of that. Maybe he should back off, and leave Mr U.M. Jones for Lieutenant Harris to interview.

The buzzer sounded again. "*Are you coming on up, Mr Rook, or is there something that's bothering you*?"

"I'm coming."

He pushed open the door and found himself in a gloomy, airless hallway with a single fluorescent tube dangling from the ceiling by its wires. He climbed the concrete steps until he reached the first landing. Then he went up to the black-painted door marked '1' and knocked.

The door was opened almost instantly – and there, to Jim's horror, stood the tall dark man from college, hatless now and dressed in a long black kaftan. He was grinning at Jim with a gleeful ferocity, baring his teeth.

"It's *you*," Jim whispered. He wished to God he had

a crucifix or a vial of holy water or whatever it was that kept supernatural creatures at bay.

"Yes, Mr Rook, it's me. But don't look so shaken. I'm only Tee Jay's uncle, after all."

"Oh, no. You're a hell of a lot more than that. I don't know what you are or who you are, but don't try to tell me that you're 'only Tee Jay's uncle'. You murdered Elvin Clay."

Uncle Umber gave a light, dismissive shrug. "So what do you propose to do about it? Call the police? Make a citizen's arrest?"

"There's no point in that if nobody else can see you. You said so yourself."

Uncle Umber's brow furrowed. For the first time, Jim noticed that he had a pattern of cicatrices on his forehead, tiny self-inflicted scars in an arrow-pattern that met between his eyes. "Nobody else can see me? What are you talking about?"

"Don't play games," Jim told him. "Nobody can see you but me, and even I can't feel you. But you murdered Elvin Clay and by God I'm going to find some way to make you pay for it."

Without a word, Uncle Umber stepped out of his apartment and swept past Jim to the opposite door, Apartment 2. Jim felt his silky kaftan sliding against him, and he could *smell* him, too: that distinctive incense aroma that had been left in the college corridor the first time that Jim had encountered him. He stood back while Uncle Umber knocked at the apartment door; and then knocked again.

The door opened and an elderly man in a grey short-sleeved shirt appeared, with a checkered napkin tucked into the collar. His face was grey and his hair was grey and even though it was thinning it stuck up at the back like a cockatoo's crest.

"What is it?" he demanded, querulously. "I'm trying to eat my supper here."

"Zygmunt," said Uncle Umber, with all the showy patience of a stage magician, "can you see me?"

The elderly man stared at him as if he were mad. "What the hell do you mean, Umber? Of course I can see you. I just don't happen to *want* to see you, that's all. I'm trying to eat my supper."

"Zygmunt," said Uncle Umber, "before you go . . . can you tell this gentleman where I was yesterday morning round about eleven o'clock a.m.?"

"You was in your apartment, wasn't you?" said the elderly man. "I saw you going in round about quarter after ten and I saw you coming out again just before two."

"You're sure of that?" asked Uncle Umber.

"Of course I'm sure. You couldn't have left without closing the street door, and when I hear that street door shut, I always look out to see what's what."

"There," said Uncle Umber, in triumph. "I don't appear to be the man that you say I am, do I? Other people can see me; and I couldn't have possibly killed Elvin, because I was here; and I have a witness to prove it. Even if I *had* managed to leave without Zygmunt hearing me go, I could never have reached West Grove College in time to do the dirty deed – now, could I?"

He came up to Jim and stood right over him; and this time Jim could actually *feel* his aura, vibrant and dark. His eyes were yellowish, with bloodshot rims, like the yolks of fertilised eggs. He laid his hands on Jim's shoulders and gripped him hard. It hurt, but Jim did his best not to wince.

"You said you could see me but you couldn't feel me?" Uncle Umber growled. "How does this feel?"

Jim said, "You don't frighten me, Mr Jones. I know what I saw and I know what I felt. Or rather, what I *didn't* feel."

"So call the police," Uncle Umber suggested, lifting his hands away from Jim's shoulders and holding them up wrist-to-wrist as if he were waiting for handcuffs.

"I came here because of Tee Jay," said Jim. "Not because of you. All right, you can prove to the police that you didn't do it. But what about Tee Jay? No matter what else you are – if you're his uncle, how can you let him take the rap for a crime that *you* committed?"

"He won't," said Uncle Umber. "The police don't have any witnesses. They don't have any forensic evidence. They don't have anything but circumstantial evidence – except, of course, *your* story that you saw me leaving the boiler-house, and they won't believe that for a moment. Plus, one more thing."

"What's that?" asked Jim.

"One of your class will suddenly remember that he saw Tee Jay at the very time that he was supposed to be stabbing Elvin Clay."

"What the hell do you mean?"

"He saw him smoking behind the science block, that's what I mean."

"But the cops have talked to every student in the school. Nobody saw him doing that."

Uncle Umber tapped his forehead with a long, dry finger. "They will, Mr Rook. They will." He held out his hand in front of his face, palm uppermost, and gently blew. "All you have to is to puff a little dust their way, Mr Rook, and they will remember anything you want them to remember, forever. Polygraph proof."

He beckoned Jim toward his apartment. Inside, it smelled even more strongly of incense, and Jim sneezed three times before he could go any further. There was a dark hallway, its window shuttered, its walls painted oxblood red. Three skulls were hung in a triangle. They had twisted horns and pointed noses, and they were probably nothing more bizarre than oryx, but Jim was beginning to think that anything was possible. Standing in one corner, half-hidden by the thick black velvet drapes, was an ebony statue of a beautiful naked woman with the head of a snarling dog.

Uncle Umber led Jim into a large living-room, whose walls were entirely lined with black-and-red fabric. It was furnished with two leather sofas the colour of clotted blood, a black carpet, and a huge coffee-table strewn with books and magazines and strings of beads and all kinds of other bizarre detritus, such as bones and feathers and wedding-veils. One side of the room was taken up with charts and diagrams and something that looked like an astrological map, although it was covered with drawings of scorpions and beetles and oddly-deformed children.

In the opposite corner stood a wooden carving of seven naked men, all joined together with the same long spear.

Jim said, "I've seen that before."

Uncle Umber looked at him in surprise. "You've seen the piercing ceremony? Where?"

"I mean I've seen the same image. Tee Jay drew it in his art lesson."

"Tee Jay is very expressive, Mr Rook. Very creative. He is also very proud. He finds it difficult to do what he's told."

"There are times, Mr Jones, when, for the common good, everybody has to do what they're told."

Uncle Umber went across to a small antique desk, pulled open the drawer, and rummaged around inside.

A few moments later, he reappeared, carrying a small linen bag tied with thin black string and sealed with black sealing-wax. He grinned, and held up the bag between finger and thumb, and shook it. "Do you know what this is? This is memory powder, the people in Dahomey used to call it *loa* powder, because they thought it was made by the lesser spirits, so that they could see Vodun."

"Vodun?"

"That's right, Mr Rook. Vodun, the greatest god in Dahomey Fon folk belief. It was after Vodun that voodoo was named."

He held it out and Jim took it. He sniffed it, and it had the strangest smell, a smell that reminded him of dreams and drying grass and some long-lost flickering picture of his mother, turning around in front of a sunlit window to say—

He looked up, and Uncle Umber was smiling at him. "Memory powder," said Uncle Umber. "But you never know if the memories are true; or if they're false. I could give you a memory with memory powder, and even a lie-detector wouldn't be able to show if you were telling the truth."

"So what am I supposed to do with this?"

"It's very easy, Mr Rook. All you have to do is to blow the powder over one of your students, and then tell him or her that – why, didn't they see Tee Jay smoking behind the science block at the time when he was supposed to be stabbing his friend?"

"That's it?"

"That's it, Mr Rook. The memory powder will do the rest."

Jim offered him the bag back. "I can't do anything like that, Mr Jones. All of my students are my own personal responsibility. If any one of them should come to any harm—"

Uncle Umber flared his nostrils. "Don't try to be pious with me, Mr Rook. You promised that you were going to be my friend. Unless you do this thing, your class will suffer a tragedy like nothing they have ever experienced before."

"Listen, Mr Jones, if you touch any one of them—"

"You'll do *what*, Mr Rook? You'll kill me, and spend the rest of your life in jail? You said you came here for Tee Jay's sake, didn't you? *This* is for Tee Jay's sake."

Jim said, "If Tee Jay *wasn't* smoking behind the science block, then where was he? If he didn't have anything to do with Elvin's death, then why do you have to cook up this cockamamie alibi?"

"You don't understand. Tee Jay had to be there when Elvin died, to see."

"You mean he *was* in the boiler-house, after all? He stood there and watched you cut Elvin to pieces? You're sick, Mr Jones. You're very, very sick."

"I'm just keeping the lamps lit, Mr Rook. Far more terrible things have been done in the name of Christianity."

Jim said, "Forget it. I'm not going to poison any of my students. No way."

Uncle Umber gave him another grin. "Then try it on yourself first. Go home, and tell yourself one thing that never happened to you, and then sniff a pinch of the powder, and see what happens. It won't kill you, I promise. It's only made of roots and hair and ground-up bones. I wouldn't hurt you, Mr Rook. Like I said to you before, I need a friend."

Jim looked Uncle Umber in the eyes, trying to challenge him, trying to show him that he couldn't play with children's lives. But there was no feeling at all in Uncle Umber's eyes, nothing but cold-blooded indifference, that in the end he had to turn away.

"All right," he said. "I'll do it. But only for Tee Jay's sake. And when Tee Jay's free, I want you to send him home to his family, where he belongs."

"Tee Jay will only go where he wants to go, Mr Rook. He's an independent spirit."

Jim had hardly been home five minutes when there was a knock on the door and Mrs Vaizey came in, wearing a wide floppy straw hat, a pink bikini with a lobster motif on it, and a white nylon cardigan. "Jim! I was hoping to catch you!"

He quickly opened one of the kitchen cupboards, took down the china jar in which he usually kept his snipped-out shopping premiums, and dropped the bag of memory powder into it. He didn't want Mrs Vaizey to get wind of what he was doing. "How're you doing, Mrs Vaizey? Haven't run out of bourbon, have you?"

"No – no – nothing like that, sugar. I've been doing a little research today, on your behalf, and I've found out some *very* interesting things."

"Oh, yes?" said Jim. He went to the fridge, took out a can of Coors and popped the top, noisily sucking up the froth.

"How long have you had that cheese?" asked Mrs Vaizey, peering into the dairy shelf. "It looks like it's ready to run the 200 metres."

"It's gorgonzola, Mrs Vaizey. It's supposed to look like that. Now what are these very interesting things you found out? I'm kind of bushed."

"Oh, yes . . . well, I looked it up in *The Occult Review*. In the past ten years, there have been fifteen recorded cases of people who claim that they have seen other people when nobody else can – just like you and your man in black."

"Are these ghosts we're talking about here?"

"Ohhh, no. Not ghosts. Not ghosts at all. Every one of those manifestations was the image of somebody who was actually living at the time. But here's the interesting bit: they *all* emphatically denied being at the locations at the time they were seen."

Jim thought of Uncle Umber, with his eye-witness evidence that he had been back at home when Elvin was killed. Jim had seen him at the college, and yet all the time he had been back at his apartment near Venice Boulevard. "So what's your conclusion?" he asked Mrs Vaizey.

"I think my first hunch was absolutely right. The man you saw was having an out-of-body experience. His physical body was lying somewhere else, in a state of trance, while his spirit went out walking."

"I saw him again this morning," said Jim. "He came to the college and confronted me. He said he wanted me to be his friend."

"Well, he would. Spirits have only limited powers, outside of the body; and out-of-body experiences are very taxing. If he were to stay out too long, his physical body would be at risk of a stroke or a heart-attack."

"What I don't understand is how he can be nothing but a spirit and at the same time be able to hurt people. He was floating on the goddamned ceiling, for God's sake, and when I tried to push him he just wasn't there. Yet he cut our security guard's face, right in front of me; and of course he stabbed Elvin, too."

Mrs Vaizey said, "Spirits have been known to bruise people. You can wake up in the morning and find purple fingermarks all over your body. They've strangled people, too. A force doesn't have to be visible or touchable to do you harm. You can't see the wind but it can blow you over. You can't touch smoke but it can make your eyes water."

"Smoke . . . that's it," said Jim. "That's just what Elvin's sister was talking about. She overheard Elvin and Tee Jay talking about sacrificing a chicken, biting its head off, and they told her to keep quiet about it or else the smoke would get her. Elvin's father said his grandfather used to give him the same warning, when he was a little boy. If he didn't behave himself, the smoke would come to get him."

"It's not just 'smoke'," said Mrs Vaizey. "It's '*The* Smoke'. It's what they call out-of-body experiences in Haiti. A man can rise from his body in the night to steal things that he wouldn't be able to take in his physical form; or to make love to a woman who would never normally let him touch her; or to take revenge on his enemies."

"Voodoo," said Jim. "He said so himself."

"You mean you *talked* to him?"

Jim nodded. "I talked to him in his spirit form, at the college, and I talked to him in the flesh. He wasn't difficult to find. He's Tee Jay's uncle, his father's brother, a guy called Umber Jones. He virtually admitted what he's done; but then there's absolutely no way of proving it, is there? The guy was at home, and he's got himself a witness who's prepared to back him up."

"And he wants you to be his friend?" asked Mrs Vaizey.

"He's threatened to hurt some of my students if I don't."

"Oh, yes; and he would, too. What does he want you to do?"

"I don't think I ought to tell you. I don't want any one of my students put at risk."

"I can't help you if you don't confide in me, Jim."

Jim shook his head. "I can't. I'd never forgive myself if anything happened to any of those kids."

Mrs Vaizey pressed her hand over her mouth and stood thinking for well over a minute. Jim stood watching her, feeling as if he had been riding on a rollercoaster all afternoon, shaken and tired and slightly sick.

At last Mrs Vaizey lifted one finger. "There's only one thing we can do," she said. "It won't be easy, but I don't see any alternative."

"Any alternative to what?" asked Jim.

"Give me a drink," said Mrs Vaizey, and she waited while Jim poured her the last of the bourbon. She swallowed a large mouthful, and then she ran her tongue around her teeth. "If you want to use The Smoke, you have to have a *loa* stick, a spirit stick. Every *houngan* has one, so that he can draw symbols in ashes to summon the spirits. I guess you could say that it's the voodoo equivalent to a magician's wand. It has to be carved from a ghost oak, from Western Africa, and it has to be carved from a ghost oak which grows in a cemetery . . . a tree that's been nourished on human flesh.

"Without his *loa* stick, your new friend will still be able to leave his body, as we *all* can, but he won't be able to call on the spirits to help him, which means that he won't have the power to hurt anybody in the physical world."

"So what do you suggest we do?"

"As I say, there's no alternative. We have to take it away from him."

"But how the hell do we do that? We can't exactly break into his apartment and go rummaging through his closets, can we?"

Mrs Vaizey looked up at him and her expression was deadly serious. "Not in the flesh," she said. "But we can do as he does, and leave our bodies, and visit him as ghosts."

Jim said, "Come on, Mrs Vaizey. This is beginning to leave the ground."

"But it's true. Everybody can leave their body, if they wish. You did, when you nearly died, and you almost didn't come back."

"All right, let's say for the sake of argument that it's possible. But even if it's possible, how do you do it?"

"I'll teach you, if you like. But you won't have to, not this time. If you tell me exactly where this Umber Jones man lives, *I'll* do it."

"Is it dangerous? I can't let you do it if it's dangerous."

Mrs Vaizey gave him the briefest flicker of a smile. "Yes, Jim, it's dangerous. But life is dangerous, and we don't stay in bed all day, frightened to go out, just in case an airplane falls on our head, or the ground opens up underneath our feet."

"Look, if there's any risk at all, I'd rather do it myself."

"*No,*" she said, with surprising firmness. "If your friend were to find you when you were out of your body, you wouldn't stand a chance. You don't try to do your own wiring, do you? You call an electrician. This is one job that you ought to leave to a professional."

"Well . . . if you say so," said Jim. "But I can't say that I'm too happy about it. When do you want to do it? Tomorrow maybe?"

"Tonight. *Now*. The sooner the better."

Chapter Six

Mrs Vaizey prowled around Jim's apartment, sniffing the air and rearranging books and ornaments.

"Which way's east?" she asked.

"Er . . . that way."

"East is very important. All evil spirits come from the east. You don't mind if I use your couch, do you?"

"Of course not."

"Then go down to my apartment, go into the kitchen, and open up the left-hand cupboard. You'll find two brass incense-burners inside, and a pack of incense. Bring them up here, and we'll see what we can do for you."

Jim said, "How do you know all of this voodoo stuff? I knew you read horoscopes, but I never realised that you were into black magic, too."

Mrs Vaizey went over to the couch, picked up a newspaper that was sprawled across it, and rearranged the cushions. "I wasn't always an old lady living in a low-rent apartment block in Venice, you know. My father used to work for the State Department. I spent most of my girlhood in France and Morocco, and a year-and-a-half in Haiti. We had a Haitian housemaid who taught me all about the *loa*. There is Legba, who seduces women; and Ogoun Ferraille, who looks after men when they are fighting; and Erzulie, the spirit of purity and love. Then of course there is Baron Samedi, who devours the dead.

"By the way," Mrs Vaizey admonished him, "you mustn't call it 'black magic'. It has some of the same rituals as black magic, like sacrificing chickens. But it's a mixture of Fon culture and Roman Catholicism, and it has the power of both."

Jim said, "I'll go find your incense, okay?"

In less than twenty minutes, his apartment was thick with incense smoke. The only light came from a single table-lamp with a nut-brown shade. Mrs Vaizey was lying full-length on the couch with her eyes closed, her cardigan drawn around her wrinkled brown stomach. She had spread a sheet of newspaper on the rug and drawn a complicated design with white ash that Jim had brought her from the barbecue. "Any ash that has been used to burn flesh will do," she had told him, and he just hoped that Oscar Mayer wieners counted as flesh.

Now she was muttering a long, droning incantation which seemed to Jim to be a mixture of Latin, French and some other language which he couldn't understand. He recognised fragments of it, bits and pieces of the Catholic mass, and something to do with '*sang impur*', or bad blood, and and '*la mort et la folie*' – death and madness.

She had allowed Jim to sit and watch her, but she had made him promise not to move and not to say a word. He stayed in his armchair in the darkest corner of the room, while the incense-smoke eddied all around him. He coughed twice, and she opened her eyes and gave him a disapproving look, but it was obvious that she was entering into some kind of a trance, because her pupils were unfocused and her eyelids were trembling. He had opened another can of beer but so far he had left it untouched. Mrs Vaizey's droning was so hypnotic that he was practically falling into a trancelike state himself.

"*Libera nos a malo*," she mumbled. "*Panem nostrum quotidianum da nobis hodie*."

Without warning, it suddenly felt as if the air in Jim's apartment were under intense pressure. He went momentarily deaf, as if he had closed a car window at high speed. Mrs Vaizey shuddered, and her left hand fell sideways across the couch. Her mouth was open but she had stopped chanting, and her face was the colour of cheap newsprint. She let out a reedy little gasp, and then another one, and then her head dropped back and she looked as if she were dead.

She had warned him about this; but he was anxious, all the same. He got out of his chair and walked across the room and crouched down next to her, taking her hand. Her fingers were very dry and very cold, like a lizard with silver rings around its legs. He felt her pulse and it was so weak that it was barely detectable, but this was another aspect of out-of-body adventures that she had warned him about. "The body can't live for very long without a soul. That's what makes humans what they are."

He hesitated for a second or two, but then he reached his hand over her face and lifted her eyelid. Her pupils were totally white, as if she had suffered a heavy concussion. "Mrs Vaizey?" he said, quietly. Then, louder, "Mrs Vaizey! This is Jim Rook! Can you hear me, Mrs Vaizey?"

He shook her shoulders, but all that happened was that her head lolled from side to side. She felt as if she were dead – and not only that, she felt as if she had been dead for two or three days. "Mrs Vaizey? Mrs Vaizey? Can you hear me, Mrs Vaizey?"

The pressure in the room gradually eased. Jim continued to hold Mrs Vaizey's hand, but he sat back, more relaxed. Her pulse may have been faint but it was regular, and showed no signs of faltering; and she was breathing distinctly, with her mouth open, like someone involved in a very deep dream.

He looked up, and it was then that he felt the ice-bath sensation of total shock. Here he was, holding Mrs Vaizey's hand while she lay on the couch. But Mrs Vaizey was also standing by the front door, staring at him.

At first he couldn't speak. His throat was completely constricted with fear. But then he managed to say, "You've done it. My God, you've done it."

She made a complicated sign in the air with her hand; like a benediction. Then she spoke, and her voice sounded reedy and distant, as if she were speaking on an answerphone in an empty office, with nobody to hear her. "*I'm going now, Jim . . . I'll bring back the loa stick . . . and then you can . . . mmmmmllllooowwaaaaahhh . . .*" Her words trailed away into a long, echoing distortion.

She waited for a long, long moment, still staring at him. Then, abruptly, she turned, and walked through the door. It was open only a half-inch, but she seemed to flow through it in the same way that Uncle Umber had flowed through the door of the geography room, like a shadow, like smoke.

After she had gone, Jim looked down and realised that he was still holding Mrs Vaizey's hand. That is, he was still holding the hand of Mrs Vaizey's *body*, but this was a body without a soul, not dead, but not capable of life. He let go, and folded her arm over her cardigan. Then he sat back and watched her in the way that people at airports watch the arrival gates, waiting for their friends and their loved ones to reappear.

He checked his watch. He still hadn't touched his beer. It was 7:06 precisely.

At seven forty-five he got up and went to the window. Over Venice, the sky was the colour of a bruised cheek. He hadn't smoked in years but he felt like smoking now. He glanced back at the couch. Mrs Vaizey hadn't moved, although she had whispered once or twice, nothing that Jim had been able to follow. It was strange, standing over another human being who was so utterly helpless. He couldn't tell where she was or what she was doing. He began to wish that he had prevented her from going. The incense was all burned out now, but his apartment still smelled like a church.

All of a sudden, Mrs Vaizey's right arm flapped up. She twitched on the couch as if she were falling asleep, and her reflexes had tried to jerk her awake. She said something like, "*Agnus—*" but then she fell back into her coma.

Jim knelt down beside her and felt her forehead. She was cold, desperately cold, and her pulse-rate seemed fainter than ever. *Oh Christ*, he thought, what's going to happen if she dies? How am I going to explain the presence of a dead seventy-five-year-old woman on my couch, wearing nothing but a bikini and a cardigan?

He thought of dialing 911. After all, Mrs Vaizey's life was worth more than his reputation. But then Mrs Vaizey appeared to settle again, and breathe more evenly, although her fingers kept on trembling, and her head flopped from side to side, as if she were searching for something.

Maybe she was. Maybe she was searching for the loa stick.

It was almost eight o'clock. Jim sat on the end of the couch, worriedly drumming his fingers against his half-empty beer can. Mrs Vaizey's condition hadn't changed, but now and again she had whispered a few words, and once she had almost sat up. He wished to God that he had a way of knowing where her soul was, and what she was doing. She had said that Umber Jones would probably keep his *loa* stick well-hidden. What if she couldn't find it? What if Umber Jones found her first?

Eight-fifteen came and went. Mrs Vaizey was still breathing and her heart was still beating, but she felt as cold as if she were dead. Every now and then her fingers jumped or her feet shifted, but it seemed to Jim as if she were further and further away. This was a body that had no soul, and somewhere near Venice Boulevard there was a soul that had no body – a whole personality, disassembled.

Jim took hold of her left hand and chafed it between his, in an effort to warm it up. "Mrs Vaizey, come on. It's time you came back. Forget the spirit stick. It isn't worth it. We'll find some other way of dealing with Uncle Umber."

Mrs Vaizey murmured, "*Monstre* . . ."

"Come on, Mrs Vaizey," Jim urged her. "Just come back. You said it yourself: your soul can't stay outside of your body for too long."

"*Monstre* . . ." Mrs Vaizey repeated. "*Monstre* . . ."

"Please, Mrs Vaizey, you don't have to do this. You'd be better off coming back and then we can work out some different way of doing it. Come on, you know all about voodoo. There must be *some* way of getting rid of Uncle Umber without risking your life to do it."

At that instant, Mrs Vaizey's eyes opened. She stared up at Jim, and her expression was one of total desperation. Not fear. It was that stage beyond fear, when people have given up hope that they're going to survive, and simply want to die with the least pain possible.

"Mrs Vaizey!" said Jim, and clutched both of her hands, tight. "For God's sake, Mrs Vaizey, hang on in there!"

"*Monstre*!" she screamed, her mouth opening so wide that she almost dislocated her jaw. "*Monstre*!"

Jim slapped her. He didn't really know why. Maybe it would shock her into waking up. Maybe it would bring her soul back.

She started to shudder, gently at first, but then faster and harder, until the whole couch was jostling and the cushions dropped onto the floor. She flung her head from side to side, and thick white foam began to boil out of her mouth. Jim gripped her wrists and tried to keep her still, hoping that she was going to tire, but she kept on thrashing and shuddering so violently that he could scarcely hold her.

Suddenly she stopped, and glared into his face. He had never seen so much concentrated fury and contempt, and he was so alarmed that he almost let go of her. "You bastard!" she spat at him. "You liar! You told him you were going to be honourable! You told him you were going to be his friend! A fine friend you turned out to be!"

Then, right in front of his eyes, something terrible began to happen. Mrs Vaizey's mouth puckered inward, as if her face were nothing more than an empty rubber mask. Her nose collapsed into her mouth, and then her cheeks were drawn in, too. Her eyes stared at him mutely, as glutinous as oysters, before they, too, were sucked down into the crumpled hole where her mouth had once been. She was literally consuming herself – disappearing down her own throat.

Her head unrolled into her neck with a sticky, slithery sound unlike anything that Jim had ever heard before. It was Mrs Vaizey's brain-tissue, sliding down inside her.

She was still tense, still quivering, even though she had no head. Jim let go of her wrists, and stood up. Her shoulders were beginning to be dragged into her neck now, as well as her cardigan. Her arms were pulled in, right up to the elbows, and for a moment the two of them protruded from her neck, jostling together as if they were waving. Her hands were pressed together in a momentary mockery of prayer, and then they disappeared, too.

Jim backed further and further away, but he couldn't keep his eyes away from her. Her collarbone stuck up beneath her skin in a V-shape before it was dragged inward. Her ribcage dropped inward, rib by rib, and Jim heard her lungs collapse with a punctured sigh. She was only two-thirds of a woman – headless and armless, yet her stomach continued to swell, and swell, and her flesh and bones and gristle and fat continued to pour into it.

Her legs doubled back under her, and her feet were drawn into her stomach first, before her shins and her knees. For a moment there was nothing on the couch but a grossly-distended stomach with two suntanned thighs on either side of it, and Jim was horribly reminded of a giant Thanksgiving turkey. Then there was a last crackling noise, as her thighbones were drawn in, and all that remained was a lumpy, bloody stomach-lining, as big as a garbage sack filled to bursting with offal and bones and connective tissue. It was stretched so thin that

Jim could see Mrs Vaizey's right hand pressing against it, with all her silver rings.

Shaking uncontrollably, he managed to walk stiff-legged to the kitchen, where he vomited warm beer into the sink. He was cold and sweating and he couldn't even begin to think straight. He couldn't understand what he had seen, or how it had happened. However, he was sure that Umber Jones had done it. What had Mrs Vaizey said? *It's a mixture of Fon culture and Catholicism, and it has the power of both.*

After a long while he rinsed out the sink with a sharp blast of cold water, and then splashed water in his face. It was no good him falling to pieces. Mrs Vaizey must have been aware of the danger of what she was doing, and yet she had volunteered to do it, anyway. Maybe she had wanted to end her life doing something strange and spectacular, instead of slowly ebbing away in a sunset home.

Now he knew why Mrs Vaizey hadn't allowed him to come along with her. Sending your soul out to burgle a man like Uncle Umber wasn't a game for novices. God alone knew what kind of spell he had worked on her, to force her to devour herself.

He went back to the living-room and confronted the terrible thing on the couch. Somehow he was going to have to dispose of it, without anybody finding out. Fortunately, nobody had seen Mrs Vaizey come up to his apartment, as far as he knew. But it would be madness to call the police. What would he say to them? "She just sort of imploded"? "She ate herself"? "Her soul was out burgling this voodoo *houngan* and he got real angry and turned her inside out"?

He went to the bedroom and dragged the quilted

cotton cover off the bed. It was bright red, which would help, in case Mrs Vaizey's stomach-lining burst. There were maroon pools of blood inside it, as well as viscous yellowish fluids and a half-digested spaghetti bolognaise.

He spread the bedcover on the floor next to the couch. Then he laid his hands on Mrs Vaizey's remains, and gently rolled them toward the edge. They were so disgusting to touch that he had to stop for a moment, and close his eyes, and take five or six really deep breaths. He hadn't realised that they would still be warm, and how much all of her limbs and organs would roll and slither together when he started to move her.

But, mercifully, the stomach remained intact, even when it dropped on to the floor with a dull, soggy thump.

He rolled the bedcover around it, and tied each end with cord. Then he went back to the kitchen and scrubbed his hands until they were sore. He could see himself in the mirror next to the telephone, but he thought he looked like a stranger. *He* didn't dispose of dead bodies, not Jim Rook, the teacher. He spent his evenings marking papers or going to concerts or meeting his friends – not trussing up the mutilated remains of old ladies.

He called his father in Santa Barbara. "Dad? It's Jim. Yes, I know, I meant to call you back but everything's been so hectic since yesterday. No – well, the police have one boy in custody, but I'm not at all sure he's the one who did it. No."

He paused, and then he said, "Listen, Dad, is it okay if I borrow the boat tomorrow evening? Well, just for three or four hours. Well, I've met this girl and I thought it might be romantic to take her out for a picnic on the ocean. I think I need to take my mind off things. Okay. Fine. No, that'll be fine."

He hung up. He hated involving his father in getting rid of Mrs Vaizey's body, but he couldn't see any other way out. If he tried to bury her, there was always a chance that somebody would dig her up, and he wouldn't be able to feel safe for the rest of his life. But scattered in the ocean, her remains would be lost forever; and he thought that somehow it would give her back the dignity and peace that Umber Jones had so savagely stripped away from her.

For now, he dragged Mrs Vaizey's remains into his small spare bedroom and pushed them under the bed. In the small hours of the morning, he would carry them down to his car and lock them in his trunk.

He took the cushion covers off the couch and took them down to the laundry in the basement. They weren't badly stained, but even the smallest trace of Mrs Vaizey's DNA could prove fatal. As he switched on the machine, Myrlin Buffield came in, from Apartment 201, carrying under his arm a purple plastic basket crammed with withered shorts and misshapen T-shirts.

"Hi Myrlin," said Jim, attempting a grin.

"Hi yourself," he replied. He began to stuff his clothes into the next machine, but every now and then he gave Jim a sneaky little sideways glance.

"What?" asked Jim, after a while.

Myrlin shut the washing-machine door. "Was your apartment on fire before?"

"On fire? Of course not. What do you mean?"

"I happened to be passing and I smelled this strange like *burning* smell."

"Oh, that! *That* burning smell! I was burning some incense, that's all."

"Incense?" said Myrlin, darkly, as if to say, "Everybody knows why people burn incense."

"I'm into this meditation thing," Jim told him. "Tibetan transcendental yogarology. You have to burn incense to get into the mood."

Myrlin slowly scratched his behind and continued to stare at Jim like a baleful child. "You know that there are *rules* in this apartment block?"

"Against Tibetan transcendental yogarology?"

Myrlin lifted an imaginary roach to his lips and deeply inhaled.

"Against drawing in your breath?"

"You know what I'm talking about," said Myrlin.

"I wish I did, Myrlin. I really wish I did."

He went back to his apartment with his damp cushion-covers. He locked and chained the door behind him and stood for a moment with his back against it. The shock of what had happened to Mrs Vaizey had left him feeling exhausted, and his hands were still trembling. He went into the kitchen and poured himself a large whiskey, which he drank without taking a breath.

He poured himself another one, but he didn't drink it immediately. Instead, he opened up the kitchen cabinet and took down the bag of memory powder that Uncle Umber had given him. He found a small knife and cut the hairy, waxy cord that fastened it. Inside, when he unfolded it, there was about a tablespoonful of fine brownish dust, as soft as ground cinnamon, with a pungent aroma that reminded Jim fleetingly of something from his childhood. He tried to focus on it, but it was gone, and he was left with an unexpected sense of loss.

He pinched a little of the powder between his finger

and thumb. So this was the drug that could enable you to remember people and events and places that you had never known. He wondered what it would be like if he could remember being wealthy, with a twenty-bedroom house in Bel Air and a pair of matching Maseratis; or his affair with a ravishing French movie actress in Provence, days of sun and kisses and chilled rosé wine. Or if he could remember seeing his dead brother Paul only last weekend, for a game of tennis and a long walk along the shoreline.

If you could remember it, did it matter that it hadn't happened?

He drew out a chair and sat down. He decided to remember something comparatively modest – something which could be easily tested. He decided to remember that Susan Randall had kissed him and told him that she had fallen in love with him the moment she first saw him. I mean, that would be harmless, right, because she obviously quite liked him anyway.

He held the dust up under his nostrils and cautiously sniffed. Then he sniffed again, more sharply this time. He sneezed, and sneezed again, and then he clamped his hands over his face. He felt as if he had breathed in spice-flavoured fire. It burned his sinuses and made his eyes feel as if they had swollen up to three times their normal size. He sneezed yet again, and stood up to get himself a glass of water from the sink.

He saw the sink. He reached out for the tap. But then suddenly the world was at a different angle, and the floor was tilting. He tumbled over sideways, hitting his shoulder against the table, and lay on his back sweating and trembling. He thought he could hear voices. He thought that there were other people in the room, people with dark faces and dark suits and sunglasses. He thought that he could hear drums; or maybe he could only *feel* them, throbbing through the floor.

He was aware of a sudden wind, blowing through the room, and a whispering voice that said, "*Ah, oui . . . il est triste . . . il est solitaire . . . ha-ha-ha . . . un spectre qui se glisse le long des allées ses pas l'ont conduit . . . de son vivant, ha-ha-ha . . .*"

He thought that there was somebody crouched down next to him, staring him right in the face. A black man, with pitted cheeks and a high sheen on his forehead. A black man with eyes that were filled with blood.

He heard a bell ringing, shrill and urgent. He sat up, shocked. At first he didn't know where he was. He felt as if he had been away for years. But then he managed to grab hold of his chair, and ease himself up. The bell was still ringing and it was his doorbell.

For a moment the bell stopped, and somebody started knocking. Then the knocking stopped and the bell started again. Then there was ringing and knocking together.

With his arms held out on either side to balance himself, he made his way to the front door and opened it.

It was Mrs Vaizey's son Geraint, a short bullet-shaped man with greasy black curls and a bright red face. He was wearing a jungle-patterned shirt and huge Bermuda shorts. "Hey, I've been ringing for five minutes," he protested.

"How did you know I was in?"

"That Myrlin geezer told me. He said to keep on trying on account of you might be taking some kind of trip or something."

"That Myrlin geezer should keep his nose out of other people's business."

"I'm looking for my old lady," said Geraint, trying to

peer past Jim's shoulder into his apartment. "You seen her, or what?"

Jim could never understand how a civilised, well-educated woman like Mrs Vaizey could possibly have given birth to a coarse, overweight loudmouth like Geraint. Geraint ran a video rental store, with a big line in horror and violence.

Jim shook his head. "I haven't seen her since yesterday – sorry."

"Myrlin said she might of come up here."

"Well, Myrlin's wrong, I'm afraid."

"I don't know . . . she's not in her apartment and look at the time. Add to that her door wasn't locked. She never goes out late."

"Maybe she went to the 7–11."

"Yeah, right, and maybe she went on a six-week hiking tour to Guatemala. She left her door unlocked, for Christ's sake, and a salad on the table."

"If you're worried, why don't you call the police? She could have had a memory lapse or something . . . she could be wandering around anywhere."

There were beads of clear perspiration on Geraint's upper lip. "I don't know . . . maybe I should just go look for her. What can the cops do that I can't?"

"Well . . . I hope you find her. She's probably okay."

"What are you, Mr Blue Sky or something? She's probably lying battered to death in a stormdrain."

Jim closed the door, and made sure that he put on the security-chain. He gingerly touched the tip of his nose and it was still a little tender, but his eyes weren't so swollen and he was able to walk back across the living-room without overbalancing. He went into the spare bedroom, and stood for a long time without switching on the light, because he didn't want to see what was lying under the bed. But then he had the idea that Mrs Vaizey's remains might start shuffling out from under the bed on their own, waggling from side to side in his blood-red bedcover like a giant maggot, and he switched on the light instantly.

The bedcover was still there, motionless. He hunkered down next to the bed and prodded it, just make sure, and all he could feel was softness and heaviness.

He left the room and switched off the light. He crossed the corridor to his own bedroom, but then he stopped. He hesitated for a few seconds. Then he went back and turned the key in the spare bedroom door. He didn't believe in life after death, especially a death as grisly and complete as Mrs Vaizey's, but then what was the point in taking chances?

He hadn't meant to sleep. He had meant to wait until there was nobody around, and then take Mrs Vaizey's remains down to the parking lot. But Geraint was coming and going for hour after hour, and Tina Henstell had some noisy friends in for drinks, and Myrlin didn't switch off his bedroom light until well past one o'clock, and even then he was probably watching his neighbours from his darkened window.

Jim slept badly and went through hours of frightening dreams. He kept hearing those muffled drums, beating through the house in a rhythm that became increasingly reckless. He felt that he was in the grip of a power that was beyond understanding: a huge malevolence. He saw fretwork balconies and thunderous skies. He heard feet flying through the rainswept grass.

He heard somebody running and jumping close behind him. "*Ha-ha-ha*! *Ha-ha-ha*!"

He woke up just after seven. A big grey quail was

sitting on the rail outside his window, tapping with its beak on the glass. His sheet was all sweaty and wrinkled, and he had been sleeping at the wrong end of the bed.

"Go on, scram," he said to the quail, and knocked on the window with his knuckle. But the quail stayed where it was, cocking its head to one side.

He climbed out of bed and shuffled out of the room, stretching and yawning. His nostrils still felt a little sore and his mouth was as dry as a sheet of Grade 2 glasspaper. He went through to the kitchen and opened the fridge, taking out a quart of orange juice and drinking it straight from the bottle until it ran down his chin and soaked the neck of his T-shirt.

Wiping his mouth, he saw the little bag of memory powder on the table. He knew that he had tried it last night, but he couldn't think what false memory he had tried to lodge in his brain. Maybe it didn't work. If he couldn't even remember what memory he had wanted to remember, what kind of memory powder was that?

All the same, he tied up the bag and put it on the kitchen counter next to his wallet and his keys and his mobile phone. He had seen what Umber Jones could do when he tried to double-cross him. He didn't want anybody else to end up devouring themselves; not for his sake, anyway.

Besides, he knew for sure now that Tee Jay was innocent, and if it took one of Uncle Umber's spells to get him free, then so be it.

He showered and dressed and made himself a cup of what railroad workers used to call 'horseshoe' coffee – coffee so strong that a horseshoe would float in it. He wondered if he ought to check on Mrs Vaizey's remains, but what was the point? She wouldn't have *moved*, would she? All the same, he thought he ought to drape the spare bed with a double bedcover, so that nobody could see that there was anything underneath it. Juanita wouldn't be back to clean up until Monday, but you never knew. The building super might come in for some reason or another. Jim was quite sure that he wouldn't, but he *might*; and Jim didn't want to be sitting in college all day fretting about that million-to-one chance of discovery.

He unlocked the bedroom door and cautiously opened it. The red bedcover was hunched under the bed, just where he had left it. He approached it as if he expected it suddenly to move, even though he knew what was in it, and that it would never move again. He sniffed the air two or three times to make sure that it wasn't smelling. He had smelled a dead body only once before – when an elderly man had died all alone in the next apartment, but he had never forgotten it. It had been a stomach-churning reminder of what he, too, would one day become.

He went to the closet on the far side of the room and took down a large white woollen bedcover that he occasionally used in the winter. He unfolded it, and he was about to spread it right over the spare bed when he noticed something.

A greyish dust had leaked out of the side of the bedcover in which Mrs Vaizey's remains were wrapped.

Hesitantly, Jim prodded the bedcover with his foot. More dust trickled out, almost as fine as talcum powder. He knelt down and laid his hand flat on top of the bedcover, trying to feel what was inside it. Immediately, it collapsed, and he jumped back in fright, ricking his ankle.

He waited for a moment, panting, wondering what to do. He didn't want to open up the bedcover to see what had happened to Mrs Vaizey's remains, but he knew that he would have to. He approached it again, and very carefully took hold of one corner between finger and thumb, and drew it back. A small landslide of dust fell out on to the floor.

Bolder now, he dragged the whole bedcover out from under the bed, untied the string that held it together, and opened it out. Inside there was nothing but a heap of thick dust, with one or two small bones in it, fingers and toes and the curve of a rib.

He tried to pick up the rib but that, too, fell into dust. Mrs Vaizey's remains had been reduced to ashes just as effectively as if she had been cremated. Jim could see now that he was facing a man of extraordinary supernatural powers, and the problem was that they were like nothing he had ever heard or read about before. The way in which Mrs Vaizey had consumed herself had no parallel in American or European culture – none that Jim had ever heard of, anyhow – and the way that she had crumbled into dust bore no resemblance to any Western phenomenon, such as instant mummification or spontaneous combustion. This was African magic – strange and strong.

He went to the kitchen and came back with a black plastic bag. He lifted up the bedcover and sifted all the dust into the bag, and then knotted it. Mrs Vaizey's remains weighed no more than a heavy cat. Any dust that he had spilled he sucked up with his vacuum-cleaner. At least the poor woman's body was going to be easier to dispose of.

Half-way down the steps he met Myrlin again, who was wearing an olive-green nylon shirt and a nasty look. "There's still no sign of Mrs Vaizey, you know," he said, accusingly.

Jim said, "Maybe she just got tired of living here, that's all."

"What you got in there?" Myrlin asked him, nodding toward the bag.

"Just memories," said Jim. He went to the parking-lot, opened his car, and put the bag into the trunk. "Just memories," he repeated to himself, so quietly that Myrlin couldn't hear him.

Chapter Seven

This morning, in English, they discussed *Dead Boy* by John Crowe Ransom.

"'*A boy not beautiful, nor good, nor clever,*
black cloud full of storms too hot for keeping,
A sword beneath his mother's heart – yet never
Woman bewept her babe as this is weeping.

"'*He was pale and little, the foolish neighbors say*
The first-fruits, saith the Preacher, the Lord hath taken
But this was the old tree's late branch wrenched away.
Grieving the sapless limbs, the shorn and shaken.'"

Jim sat on the edge of his desk swinging his leg as he listened to the class stumble out the poem line by line. He wore his reading glasses perched on the end of his nose. When they had finished, he said, "He didn't sound like much, this kid, did he? So why were his mother and the elder men so hurt that he was dead?"

Titus Greenspan III put up his hand and said, "I don't get this stuff about the tree."

"Ah, yes, but the tree is the whole point. Greg – why do you think the tree is the whole point?"

Greg Lake's face went through a slow series of incredible distortions as he tried to think. He took so long that it gave David Littwin the opportunity to put up his hand and say, "It w-w-w—"

"Okay, David, take it easy," Jim encouraged him.

"It w-wasn't a real t-t-tree he was t-talking about, it w-was a fuh. A fuh. A family tree."

"That's exactly right. The mother and the elder men were grieving because their old Virginia heritage had been put at risk by this one boy's death. No matter how stupid he was, no matter how badly-behaved, he was one of them, one of their line."

He walked up and down between the desks. "Your heritage is something more than you are . . . something to cherish and be proud of. John here honours his ancestors . . . Rita here celebrates the Day of the Dead . . . Sharon has traced her ancestry right back to Sierra Leone."

He reached the end of the room, and turned around, and as he did so he froze. Umber Jones was standing in the corner, next to the flag, his eyes concealed behind tiny black-lensed spectacles. He was watching Jim and his teeth were exposed in a lipless smile.

Jim had a good idea why he had come. He wanted to make sure that Jim made use of the memory powder, so that Tee Jay could be released. Jim stayed where he was, right at the back of the class, while Umber Jones continued to stare at him, and grin.

Russell Gloach said, "What if you don't have no ancestry? Like, I was adopted. What are you supposed to celebrate then?"

Jim didn't take his eyes off Uncle Umber. "You can celebrate the fact that your mom and your dad both wanted you enough to call you their own. It's just like a new branch being grafted on to a tree. It came from another tree, sure; but now it's an integral part of the tree that accepted it. You're part of the Gloach heritage now, no matter where you came from; and I happen to know that your mom and dad are very proud of you."

As he was speaking, Umber Jones began to glide toward him, without even moving his feet. He came right up close, so that Jim could see every pockmark in his face, and every white whisker that protruded from his night-black skin.

"You're not going to let me down, are you, Jim?" he asked, in his harsh, heavy whisper.

"Seems to me like the elder men were more worried about their heritage than they were about the dead boy," put in Amanda Zaparelli. She spoke with hugely-renewed confidence now that her braces had been taken out.

"No," said Jim.

Amanda frowned. "I just thought – you see here where it says about the elder men looking at the casket—"

"You saw what happened to your friend, didn't you?" breathed Umber Jones. "You sent her looking where she wasn't welcome. The same thing could happen to you."

"What the hell are you harassing me for?" Jim demanded.

Amanda turned around at looked at Sue-Robin Caulfield in astonishment. The rest of the class twisted in their seats and stared at Jim with expressions that showed they were deeply impressed. Jim had always been outspoken, but never *this* outspoken.

Jim jabbed his finger at Umber Jones and said, "I don't know what you're trying to do, but by God I'm going to find a way to stop you."

"Way to go, Mr Rook!" called out Ricky Herman. "Let's shut Amanda up for good and all!"

"I hope you're not going to be rash, Mr Rook," said Umber Jones. "Before you could say the Lord's Prayer,

I could leave this whole class dead and dying." He looked around at the walls. "This room could use some redecoration, don't you think? How about a nice shiny red?"

"I'll do it," Jim promised him. "Just wait until recess, and I'll do it."

"Hear that, Amanda?" laughed Mark. "If I was you, the minute I heard that recess bell, I'd run like fun."

Uncle Umber laid his hand on Jim's shoulder. "I'm pleased to hear it. Believe me, Mr Rook, you're going to be the best friend I ever had. You and me, we're going to go far together."

Jim was aware that the class were all staring at him. He lowered his arms and stood with them rigidly by his side. "Get the hell out of my class," he told Umber Jones, between tightly-clenched teeth.

"What's that, now?" asked Umber Jones. "Wasn't sure that I heard you too good."

"Get the hell out of my class," said Jim, much louder. His students started swivelling around and staring at each other and saying, "Me? What, me? He wants *me* to get the hell out? Hey, Mr Rook, is it *me* you want to get the hell out?"

"Couldn't hear you," Umber Jones taunted him.

Jim lost his temper. "This is my class and these are my students and I'm responsible for every one of them. You've already caused enough grief, so help me. I'll do what you want me to do. But get out of my class before I do something that both of us are going to regret."

"Oh, no," grinned Umber Jones. "Only *you* are going to regret it."

With that, he folded his arms and glided backward across the classroom, until he reached the chalkboard.

"I'm keeping my eye on you, Mr Rook," he said. "And

don't you forget it." With that, his outline appeared to waver, as he were no more substantial than smoke, and of course he wasn't. His darkness blew sideways, and curled around, and funnelled itself into the surface of the chalkboard. Jim heard a deep, soft rumbling sound, and then he was gone.

Jim walked stiffly toward the chalkboard and touched it with his fingertips. Its surface was hard and cool and perfectly normal. But as he stood there, a curved white line appeared on the board, drawn in chalk; and then another. With a drawn-out squeaking noise that set his teeth on edge, a picture of an eye appeared, almost three feet across; and underneath it, the words VODUN VIVE.

The class was totally silent. Jim turned around and looked at them and didn't know what to say. It was only when Mark said, "Sheesh, that was so *cool*!" that they suddenly started talking and bantering again.

"How did you do that, Mr Rook?" asked Ricky. "Like, you didn't even use your hands."

"Not like you, Ricky," said Jane Firman. "You're *all* hands, you are."

Jim lifted his hand for silence, and then he said, "It was a trick, okay? Nothing but a trick. At the end of the semester, if you all pass with better-than-average grades, I'll show you how it's done."

He couldn't tell them about Umber Jones. If he did, there was no knowing what Umber Jones would do. But it was becoming increasingly difficult for Jim to keep his presence a secret, and Jim was beginning to feel that he was doing it on purpose: taunting him, provoking him, so that Jim would really snap and Umber Jones would have an excuse to slaughter the whole class.

It was interesting, though: Umber Jones could have

slaughtered them anyway, without an excuse. He was invisible, to everybody except Jim. Nobody believed in his existence, which made him uncatchable. Jim wondered if there were some restraints on his behaviour – if, like vampires, he needed to sleep in a coffin filled with his native soil, or if he couldn't endure crucifixes, or garlic-flowers, or if he had to stay out of the sunlight.

The recess bell rang. The class gathered up their books, laughing and chattering. Jim stood by the window with his back to them, just to make sure that Uncle Umber wasn't out there somewhere, just waiting to do them harm.

Six years ago, Jim had married quickly and misguidedly, and he had never had children. But then he didn't need children of his own; he had them already. Beattie and Muffy and Titus and Ray. During college hours, they were his family. Out of hours, as he sat marking their essays, they were still with him, because each essay was like a letter, trying to explain what they thought he had taught them . . .

'Mark Twain says about Huck Finn that "there were things he stretched but mainly he told the truth" but when you think about it whole of *Huckleberry Finn* is "stretched" because it's a story. Stretching is a way of saying something in a way which people are going to remember.'

He was still standing by the window when Sharon X came up to him, carrying three books. Today she had decorated her hair with dozens of tiny beads and she looked especially pretty. "I brought you those books I was talking about," she told him. "This is the best one. *Voodoo Ritual*. It tells you just about everything you need to know about voodoo."

"Thanks," he said. "That's kind of you."

He thought she would go then, but she didn't. She stood beside him as if she wanted to say something more.

"I'll take care of them, I promise," he said.

"You saw him just now, didn't you?" Sharon asked him.

He put the books down on his desk and didn't answer.

"He was here, wasn't he? *That* was who you were talking to, not Amanda at all. I watched you, and you weren't even looking at Amanda, you were looking right in front of you, like there was somebody standing there. And there *was*, wasn't there?"

Jim looked at her seriously. "Let me just put it this way, Sharon. You're in danger, all of you, if I say one single word."

"But he drew that eye on the chalkboard, didn't he? You weren't standing anywhere near it."

"Sharon, let's forget about it, okay? You know what they mean when they say that even walls have ears."

"That's an evil eye," said Sharon. "And Vodun, he's the head spirit of voodoo. That means 'Vodun Lives'. You only see that eye when Vodun's watching you, to make sure you don't take his name in vain, or do nothing to displease him."

"Sharon, thanks for the books . . . but I'm not going to say any more."

But Sharon was persistent. She picked up *Voodoo Ritual*, licked her finger, and quickly leafed through it. "You're talking about seeing a person when nobody else can, aren't you? Like you can really *see* this dude, can't you, when the rest of us can't? But there's a way that you can show him up, so that everybody else can see him, too."

"Oh, yes?" Jim was growing impatient. He would

rather have studied Sharon's books at leisure; and besides, he needed to get out into the yard and see if he could persuade Ricky Herman to breathe in some of the memory powder. It wouldn't work, he was sure of it. *He* wasn't aware of remembering anything that had never actually happened to him. But it was what Umber Jones wanted him to do, and he would do it.

"Here, look," said Sharon. "Death dust."

"Death dust?" asked Jim, abstractedly. He was still looking out of the window, spooked by every shadow. Was that the oak trees dipping in the breeze, or was it a man in an Elmer Gantry hat, walking across the grass?

"Sure, look. 'Spirits can only be seen by *houngans* and people with special gifts. Otherwise they are invisible. But spirit-hunters used to take bags of death dust with them when they went to exorcise huts and houses. They would toss the dust around the room, and if there was a spirit present, the dust would cling to them, making them momentarily visible.'"

Jim said, "Let me take a look at that." He flicked back and read the two preceding pages while Sharon watched him, fiddling with her beads.

"'A *houngan* has many ways of disabling or killing his opponents. If they use The Smoke to leave their physical bodies and to visit his dwelling-house, he can cast a spell on their body while they are away, when the body will be unconscious and defenceless. There are many spells he can cast. He can put the body into a deep sleep which may last for days or even years. He may cause it to choke; or to suffer a stroke. He may paralyse it, or set fire to it. One of the most gruesome spells is *Se Manger*, when the victim literally devours himself.

"'If the physical body is killed, the spirit will be forced to wander for ever in the Half-World. The physical body itself will decompose very quickly into death dust. Death dust is still remembered in the Christian funeral ritual 'ashes to ashes, dust to dust.'"

"Does that help?" asked Sharon.

Jim closed the book and nodded. "It makes sense out of something that didn't make sense. I'm very glad you brought it in."

"It's my ancestry," said Sharon, with pride.

Jim went out into the yard and wandered around, talking to some of the students. He was conscious that – whatever they were talking about – they always changed the subject as soon as he approached, but then he always used to do the same thing when *he* was a student. The age gap between seventeen-year-olds and thirty-four-year-olds is about 4 million light-years. Jim was patient with them, though. He knew a secret which they didn't know: in another seventeen years, *they* would be thirty-four, too.

He was just about to stroll across to the bench where Ricky was telling a group of girls about the night he had raced his Camaro at 95 mph along Mulholland Drive when John Ng approached him.

"Mr Rook . . . something weird happened in class this morning."

He was obviously embarrassed, but Jim shrugged and said, "Sure. What was it?"

"That time you were talking strangely."

"Yes, what about it?"

John took a silver neck-chain out of his T-shirt. On the end of it dangled a dull black stone. "Look," he said.

Jim held it in the palm of his hand. "Great. Nice-looking stone. Now, John, if you'll excuse me—"

But John clutched his sleeve to stop him. "This is not a stone, Mr Rook. This is a crystal. It comes from a *dzong*, a sacred Buddhist temple. It is supposed to protect me from evil."

"And?"

"It's supposed to be clear, and sparkling. It only turns dark when something is troubling me. It has never turned as dark as this before."

"So what does it mean, when it goes as dark as this?"

"It means that a very great evil has come close to me. It happened at the same time that you were talking strangely."

Jim hesitated, but he knew that he couldn't lie. John was clinging on to his sleeve so tightly and there was such a worried look on his face that he would have to tell him the truth – or part of the truth, at least.

"Somebody was there, in the classroom," John insisted.

"Well . . ."

"Mr Rook, we have spirit-walkers in my religion, too. Monks who can leave their bodies and visit the sick and the dying."

Jim glanced around to make sure that the man in black was nowhere in sight. "Yes," he said, "I did see somebody. The same man I saw when Elvin was murdered. I could see him, but none of the rest of you could. I could hear him, too, and talk to him."

"He is very evil," said John, emphatically.

"Well, that's why I don't want to tell you too much about him. The less you know, the safer you'll be."

"Who is he?" John asked him.

"I think it's better if I don't tell you. Not just yet."

"But what does he want? Why has he come here to West Grove College?"

"I'm sorry, I can't tell you that, either. But I'm doing everything I can to get rid of him."

John took his hand away, and then said, with great simplicity, "You're frightened, aren't you?"

Jim nodded. "Yes, I'm frightened. Not for myself. But I don't want this character hurting my class."

John said, "With respect, Mr Rook, if we are in any kind of danger, wouldn't it be better if we knew about it, all of us? On your own, you may find it a hard fight to get rid of this spirit. Together, we would be strong. My father says that evil loves the darkness; but shrivels up when you shine a light on it."

"Your father's a thoughtful man."

John went off to join his friends, leaving Jim standing alone, thinking. Maybe he was right, and the Smoke spirit of Umber Jones *should* be dragged out into the open. But then he thought of Elvin, bleeding from scores of stab-wounds; and Mrs Vaizey, disappearing into her own mouth; and he knew that if any one of his students was killed or injured, he would never able to forgive himself.

Half-way across the wide, parched lawn that ran all along the east side of the college buildings, he saw Ricky sitting crosslegged, talking and laughing with Muffy and Rita and Seymour Williams, a spotty, friendly boy with heavy-rimmed Clark Kent glasses. Jim felt in his pocket for the bag of memory powder and loosened the ties around it. Then he approached the group at what he hoped was a casual stroll, even though he was so tense that his teeth were clenched.

Ricky looked up and shielded his eyes against the sun. "Hi, Mr Rook. What's happening?"

"I, er, found something in the boys' locker-room."

Ricky immediately blushed scarlet with guilt.

"No, no," said Jim. "It isn't anything that belongs to you." He took the bag of memory powder out of his pocket and held it up. "It's some kind of powder. I didn't want to turn it in to Mr Wallechinsky, though, until I knew what it was. No point in making a fuss if it's harmless."

Ricky said, "Let's take a look at that, Mr Rook. I'm the class expert on suspicious substances." He winked at Seymour and Seymour gave a goofy laugh. Jim had a strong suspicion that Ricky and Seymour and some of the other boys had occasionally smoked grass in the boys' washrooms, but he had never been able to catch them at it. He handed him the bag and watched as Ricky opened it and peered inside.

"Doesn't look like nothing that *I* ever saw before," he remarked.

"Anything," Jim corrected him.

Ricky wet the tip of his little finger and dipped it into the powder and tasted it. He wrinkled his nose up and said, "Urgh. Doesn't *taste* like nothing I ever saw before, neither. Tastes like – herbs, and leaves, and kind of . . ." He paused, his eyes suddenly unfocused. "Kind of – *yesterday*."

"It tastes like *yesterday*?" scoffed Seymour. "What does yesterday taste like? Your old gym socks?"

"Sniff it," Jim coaxed him. He had never felt so guilty and irresponsible in the whole of his teaching career, but he didn't dare to think of the alternative.

Ricky took a pinch of the powder and snorted it up his nose, in the same way that Jim had. Immediately he let out an explosive sneeze and then another. "Jesus Christ!" he swore. "What the hell *is* this stuff?"

"Maybe it's the same stuff that Tee Jay was smoking," said Jim, hunkering down close beside him. Ricky stared at him with watering eyes. "You know . . . when you saw him behind the science block, the time that Elvin was killed. That's where he went, didn't he, at five after eleven? So he couldn't have gone to the boiler-house."

"Unh?" said Ricky and then promptly fell backward on to the grass, knocking his head.

"Hey, is he all *right*?" said Jane, leaning over him.

"Ricky?" said Seymour, crawling over toward him on all fours and staring into his face. "Ricky, can you hear me, man?"

Jim picked up the memory powder and pocketed it. "It's all right . . . he's hyperventilated, that's all." He knelt next to him and gently patted his cheek. "Ricky . . . come on, Ricky, you're fine. Come on, Ricky, wake up now." Thinking: my God, I hope I haven't done him any harm . . .

Ricky said something blurry and then he opened his eyes. He looked at the four faces peering down at him and said, "What?"

"You fainted," said Jim. "You must have breathed in too deeply."

Ricky sat up, smearing his nose with the back of his hand. "Jesus, that stuff *smarts*, Mr Rook. I don't know what it is but it sure ain't coke."

"I'm sorry," said Jim. "I didn't mean for you to get hurt."

Ricky sneezed again. "Doesn't matter," he said. "My sinus hasn't been this clear all summer."

"I think I'll just drop the bag in the trash and forget all about it," Jim told him. "Whatever it is, I don't think it's the kind of stuff that anybody would voluntarily put up their nose."

He was about to leave when Seymour said, "Hey, Mr Rook . . . what was that about Tee Jay? You know, smoking behind the science block."

"What about it?"

Seymour blinked. Jim could almost hear the cogs whirring inside his brain. "Well . . . if he was smoking behind the science block, then he couldn't have killed Elvin, could he? He couldn't have been in two places at the same time."

"The trouble was, nobody actually saw him," said Jim. "He *said* that he was smoking behind the science block but the police couldn't find any witnesses."

Ricky said, "Wait a minute. *I* saw him."

"You're putting me on," said Jim. "Why didn't you tell Lieutenant Harris?"

"I don't know. I just – I don't know. I just didn't."

"You definitely saw Tee Jay smoking behind the science block between five after and a quarter after?"

"Sure. I'd swear to it. He left the other guys, then he went behind the science block and lit up. I could see him all the time. I guess I didn't say anything because I thought he was going to get into trouble for smoking."

"Ricky," said Jim, taking hold of his shoulders. "Tee Jay is facing a charge of murder one. That's a whole lot more serious than smoking."

Ricky pressed the heel of his hand against his forehead. "I don't know why I didn't say anything before. It's like it must have slipped my mind or something."

"Well, now that it's *unslipped* your mind, maybe we'd better talk to Lieutenant Harris and see what we can do to get Tee Jay free."

"Sure. Sure thing." Ricky kept shaking his head, like a confused dog. Seymour and Muffy and Jane looked at each other in bewilderment. It seemed so unlikely that Ricky had taken two days to remember that he had seen Tee Jay smoking at the time of the murder. On the other hand, if he could get Tee Jay released, what did it matter?

Jim said, "Come with me. Let's go tell Dr Ehrlichman. Then we can call the police."

They walked across the grass together. Ricky said, "This is incredible, isn't it? I mean, because of me, Tee Jay's going to go free."

"Lieutenant Harris will give you a pretty thorough grilling. Be prepared for that."

"I'll tell you something, Mr Rook. He can grill me till I'm well done. I saw Tee Jay smoking. I swear it. I saw him with my own eyes."

They had almost reached the main administration block when Susan Randall came out of the main entrance, talking to George Babouris, the physics teacher. She was wearing a blue checkered blouse with the collar turned up, like Doris Day, and a short navy-blue skirt. Jim slowed down as he approached her and a wide smile came across his face. He was beginning to think that she must have been avoiding him this morning, for some reason. Maybe she was teasing him. After all, hadn't she kissed him and told him how attractive she had always found him – how masterful?

He walked straight up the steps, put his arm around her waist, and kissed her on the lips. "Hi, sweetheart. I've got some good news."

Susan smacked at his arm and took two steps back. "Jim!" she protested. George Babouris, big-bellied and black-bearded, stared at both of them in total astonishment.

Jim raised both of his hands in mock-surrender. "What's wrong?" he asked her. "I just came to tell you that—"

"You *kissed* me, that's what's wrong. You kissed me right on the mouth."

Jim was bewildered. Yesterday she had been so

passionate, and now she was treating him as if he were some kind of sex molester. "Listen," he said, "you don't have to blow so goddamned hot and cold."

"What are you talking about? When have I ever been hot?"

"You didn't exactly behave like the Snow Queen yesterday afternoon."

"I said I was interested in seeing your maps, that's all. That's hardly a proposition."

Jim turned to George and gave him one of those oh-ho-ho man-to-man looks. "She's only interested in seeing my maps!" he grinned.

This time, Susan slapped his face, so hard that it stung.

"What the hell was that for?" he protested.

"What the hell do you think it was for? Do you want me to report you to Dr Ehrlichman for sexual harassment?"

"Now, wait a minute," said Jim. "Yesterday afternoon it was 'Jim, I fell in love with you the second I saw you.' Now it's assault and battery. What's going on?"

Susan stared at him in disbelief. "Are you some kind of psychopath, or what?"

Jim looked around. George Babouris was giving him a very odd, old-fashioned kind of look; and even Ricky was keeping his distance. He began to get the feeling that something was very badly wrong and that he was seriously out of kilter with everybody else. He said, "Okay . . . maybe there's been a misunderstanding," and he backed away. "Come on, Ricky, we've got something more important to worry about."

Chapter Eight

Tee Jay was released at ten o'clock that evening, after Lieutenant Harris had interviewed Ricky for over four hours. Ricky offered to take a polygraph test but Lieutenant Harris knew that he couldn't take Tee Jay in front of a jury with no murder weapon, no fingerprints or footprints, and an independent witness whose testimony seemed to be so sincere.

Jim waited at police headquarters all that time, sustained by three cups of wishy-washy coffee and three sugared doughnuts. Tee Jay's mother hadn't been able to come, although Jim had phoned her and told her to expect some good news. Tee Jay's brother hadn't wanted to come and so far there was no sign of Uncle Umber.

Lieutenant Harris came out into the reception area in his shirtsleeves, dabbing at his forehead with a balled-up handkerchief. Tee Jay came up close behind, accompanied by his attorney and two uniformed officers. He stared at Jim as if he didn't recognise him.

"Okay," said Lieutenant Harris. "He's free to go. I just wish his friend had come up with this information the first time I asked him. The first twenty-four hours of any investigation are always the most important. Now he's put us back forty-eight."

"Come on, Lieutenant. At least you haven't charged an innocent man."

Lieutenant Harris pressed his handkerchief against the back of his neck and looked at Jim as if innocence had about as much to do with criminal justice as the price of fish.

Tee Jay's attorney came up to Jim and shook his hand. He was a barrel-chested Afro-American with immaculately-topiarised hair and a silk necktie with hot-air balloons on it. "Assume you're Tee Jay's teacher?" he asked. "You did a great job, bringing Ricky in. Tee Jay would've been real hard to defend, otherwise." He paused, and then he put his arm around Jim's shoulders and said confidentially, "Be a good idea to keep an eye on Tee Jay, though. That boy has some attitude problem. Keeps banging on about African culture and the power of the spirits and all kinds of stuff like that. Told me I was selling out, working for white men. And this is not your average Black Power thing, either. He was chanting and singing. Practically drove everybody nuts."

"Thanks," said Jim. "I think I have a handle on this thing."

"Oh, yes?" The attorney waited expectantly, and then he said, "You're not going to tell me what it is?"

"Sorry, no. I've been told to keep my mouth shut."

"You can't even give me a clue? I mean, I like to keep abreast of what the kids on the streets are into. Helps me with my job."

At that moment, the swing doors opened and Umber Jones walked in, still wearing his Elmer Gantry hat. The reception area immediately seemed to shrink, and even the tallest cops looked as if they were undersized.

"Here's your clue," said Jim, stepping away. The attorney gave him a baffled frown, but then he stepped back, too. Uncle Umber's sheer size and presence were overwhelming. His skin gleamed uner the fluorescent lights like polished black wood. He went up to Lieutenant Harris and said, "My nephew free to leave, officer?"

"For now, yes," said Lieutenant Harris. "We may want to talk to him again. Meantime, I'd appreciate it if he stays in the Greater Los Angeles area and stays out of trouble. I trust you may have some influence in that direction."

"Oh, I've got influence," grinned Umber Jones. He cracked all of his knuckles, one by one, waiting for Tee Jay to sign his release papers and collect his watch and his money and his leather belt. As soon as Tee Jay was finished, he took hold of his arm and guided him toward the door. On the way, he stopped beside Jim and said, "You did what you were told, Mr Rook, and I'm pleased about that. Now there's something else I want you to do for me."

Jim shook his head. "No way, Mr Jones. This is where you and I stop being friends. There's nothing I can do to prove that you stabbed Elvin and that you killed Mrs Vaizey, but I don't want to see you or hear from you ever again."

"I'm sorry you feel that way," said Umber Jones. "I really thought that you and me were going to be bosom friends for the rest of our lives. Still – even if you don't want to be my friend, you can still run a couple of errands for me, now can't you?"

"Forget it. I'm doing nothing for you, ever again."

"You sure are eager to see your children suffer, aren't you?"

"I warned you before. You leave my students alone."

"You *warned* me? Ha-ha-ha-ha-ha. And what are you going to do if I maybe just cut them a little? Give them some nasty scars? Or what if I burst their eardrums and turn them all stone-deaf? Or poke out their eyes? Or give them the fire sickness so that they feel like they've been doused in blazing gasoline?"

"I told you to leave them alone. If you hurt them, by God I'll find a way to bring you down."

"No you won't, Mr Rook, because there is no way. Now . . . stop your blustering, it doesn't suit a man in your profession. All you have to do is wait and I'll send you a messenger, telling you what to do."

"Go eat yourself," Jim suggested, bitterly. "Go turn yourself to dust."

Uncle Umber ushered Tee Jay to the doors. In all the time that they had been talking, Tee Jay had glanced at Jim only once, and his expression had been very difficult to read. All the same, Jim was sure that he had seen a glimmer of the old Tee Jay, somewhere behind those indifferent eyes – a flicker of his eyelids to show that he wasn't totally under Uncle Umber's influence.

Then they were gone, and the swing door briefly showed Jim a reflection of himself, standing with his hands in his pockets, looking tired.

Lieutenant Harris came up to him and sniffed. "What was all that about?"

"Just a word of thanks from a grateful uncle."

"You can't kid me, Mr Rook. I know my body language. That looked more like a toe-to-toe confrontation to me."

"Mr Jones has a forceful way of demonstrating his indebtedness, that's all."

"You intellectuals," said Lieutenant Harris. "What would you call it if the guy hit you in the beezer? A palpable expression of discontent?"

Driving west on Santa Monica Boulevard, Jim couldn't help smiling at Lieutenant Harris's remark. He had never thought of himself as an intellectual. He certainly hadn't come from an intellectual family. His father had sold earthquake insurance, and when Jim was born he had just lost his job. Jim had been brought up in a house where T-shirts were worn until they had holes in them and it was always meatloaf on Sundays and water to drink instead of Coke. He had never had many friends because none of his classmates wanted to come back to his place and eat plain bread-and-butter and watch television in black-and-white.

Jim's first ambition had been to make a name for himself as a Western movie star, like Clint Eastwood. Then he wanted to be a secret agent, like Napoleon Solo. Later, he changed his mind and decided to be an architect. But more than anything else he wanted to be wealthy. He wanted to give *his* children peanut butter on their bread, and Dr Pepper to drink on Sundays.

While he was still at high school, however, his father started his own marine insurance business, and it instantly flourished. By the time he graduated, his parents had moved to a large, comfortable house in Santa Barbara, and Jim was able to take English at UCLA, with the half-formed ambition of being a famous writer. He had a car. He had a generous allowance. He thought he was happy at last.

But while he was still in his freshman year, his cousin Laura came to stay and his cousin Laura changed his life overnight. Jim had last seen her when she was only six years old. Now she was eighteen – a startlingly pretty blonde with long shiny hair that she could sit on and blue eyes that absolutely mesmerised him. What he couldn't understand, however, was why she acted so shy. She seemed to have no confidence in herself whatsoever, and she always seemed to prefer to stay inside and watch television rather than go out and have fun.

Jim appointed himself her unofficial cheerer-upper. He took her swimming, he took her dancing, he took her to parties. He was so breathlessly infatuated with her that he felt as if he were drowning; and it was plain that she liked him too.

He wrote her a love poem, embarrassingly titled *My Golden Girl*. He gave it to her while they were sitting on the beach. She studied it for a moment and then handed it back to him and smiled and said nothing at all.

"You don't like it?" he asked her.

"I don't know," she admitted. "I can't really read it."

That was the first time Jim encountered dyslexia. Laura had no verbal thoughts at all. Everything went through her head like a movie without a soundtrack, and she simply couldn't connect printed words to objects or actions or ideas. At school, both her teachers and her classmates had treated her as if she were ignorant or stupid, and once a teacher had ripped up her work in front of the whole class.

She had often been punished for being late, too, because dyslexics have no sense of time.

The next day Jim went to the university's psychology department and took out nine books on dyslexia and reading dysfunction. He studied them all and then he contacted one of the authors, Professor Myron Davies at Boston University. With Professor Davies' help, he devised a way of teaching Laura to recognise words, using charts and diagrams and pictures.

He taught her the sentence, 'I can jump' by holding a can of baked beans and jumping off a kitchen chair.

Laura stayed with the Rook family all the way through

the summer vacation and slowly Jim taught her to read stories and poems and magazine articles. She became bolder, and more confident, and by the time she was ready to go home, she was able to read whole pages of text, even if it did take her more than a quarter of an hour.

But he never made love to her; not once. And in December she wrote him a Christmas letter saying that she had found a new boyfriend and that she was 'crazy in love'. But she also said that Jim had given her, 'a miracel, a whol new life.'

It had taken Jim almost six months to get over her, and he had never really gotten over her, not really. He would die remembering what she looked like, on the beach, those fine grains of sand on her skin. But at least he knew what he wanted to do. He didn't want to be a movie cowboy or an architect or a novelist. He wanted to save those children to whom reading and writing and mathematics were all incomprehensible. He didn't care what was wrong with them: whether they stammered or whether they suffered from problems at home or whether they had the attention-span of a gnat. They all deserved to be rescued; and Jim studied for four years to give himself the ability to do it.

He reached the beach. He parked, and he lifted Mrs Vaizey's dust from the trunk. He went down the steps and walked across the sand. The ocean sounded uncomfortable tonight, and the surf was surging fretful and luminous all the way from Palisades Park to the Municipal Pier.

He went to the shoreline and the sea drew back as if it were afraid of him. Then, as he lifted up his plastic bag, it came flooding back in again, and warmly filled his shoes. He tipped the neck of the bag and the dust came flying out, into the wind, into the darkness, and blew across the water.

He had almost emptied it all when he remembered what Sharon had told him, after class. *"There's a way that you can show him up, so that everybody else can see him, too."*

The death dust: that was it. *'The physical body will decompose very quickly into death dust.'* Jim stopped pouring out Mrs Vaizey's remains and angled the bag toward the lights on the pier to see how much dust he had left. Enough to fill a coffee-mug, not much more. But he screwed the bag up tight, and carried it back to his car. He had a feeling that it might come in useful. He had dealt with Laura's dyslexia through research, and by talking to experts. He could deal with Uncle Umber in the same way. He was fighting against somebody who was practised in magic, and so he needed to equip himself with magic knowledge and magic skill and magic artefacts. Sharon had lent him her books; and now he had death dust, too. Maybe he could find himself a *loa* stick, if he tried hard enough.

He climbed back into his car and started the engine.

"Do you know what you are?" he asked himself. "You're a lunatic, that's what you are."

When he returned to his apartment, he found a message from Susan on the answerphone. "I'm sorry if I over-reacted, but I couldn't believe what you did. I like you, Jim, and if I gave you the impression that it was more than just a friendship, then all I can do is apologise. But I think maybe that we'd better keep our distance from now on, don't you?"

He listened to the message three times. He simply couldn't understand what had happened today. Yesterday,

Susan had seemed so eager. She had cuddled right up to him and told him how special he was and kissed him with her mouth open. Today, he was supposed to keep his distance. He had heard of fickle, but this was ridiculous.

Oh well, he thought, resignedly. At least he wouldn't have to rush around acquiring a whole lot of maps to show her.

There was another message, from Tee Jay's mother. "I just called to say how much I appreciate what you did, Mr Rook. You saved my boy. He's still with his Uncle Umber, but at least he's cleared of any blame for killing poor Elvin; and that's what means the most to me."

And the last message came from somebody who had a thick, gravelly, uncompromising voice. "Remember what you solemnly promised me, Mr Rook, and don't you go backing down on no solemn promises. My messenger will come to see you soon and tell you what to do. You make sure that you listen to what he has to say, and listen good."

Jim went through to the kitchen. He was suddenly feeling ravenously hungry. He opened the icebox and stared at his old piece of gorgonzola for a while. Then he opened the kitchen cupboard and stared at an out-of-date carton of Golden Grahams and at three cans of red salmon. Then he went to the phone and punched out the number of Pizza Express. "Thin and crispy, with extra pepperami, chillies and anchovies."

He showered and changed into a purple polo shirt and chino pants. He sat back on the couch and switched on the television. He had never felt so disoriented in his life. The way that Elvin had been killed; the way that Mrs Vaizey had died; the smoke and the spirits and the warnings of terrible tragedies – they had all completely undermined every belief that he had ever held about life and death and the supernatural. He had been certain that death was the end. Now he had been shown – in the most violent and extravagant way possible – that death was just a different state of being.

Restless, he went back to the kitchen to find himself a beer. On the floor, in the corner, was the bag containing Mrs Vaizey's death dust. He hesitated for a moment, then he took a blue china mug out of the cupboard, set it down in the middle of the floor and poured the dust directly into it. Then he covered the mug with clingfilm. Pretty damned funny way to end up, he thought. One minute you're sunbathing and drinking whiskey, the next you're a little heap of powder in somebody's coffee mug.

"'A heap of dust alone remains of thee,'" he quoted. "''Tis all thou art, and all the proud shall be!'" He smiled, and then he said to himself, "*Elegy to the Memory of an Unfortunate Lady*. How true."

He drank beer and channel-surfed; and he was still flicking from one programme to another when the doorbell rang. Great – pizza at last. He went across to the side-table and picked up his billfold. The doorbell rang again and he called out, "Okay – okay! I'm coming, don't worry about it!" He licked his thumb and counted out twenty dollars as he approached the door. He was still counting as he opened up the door and there he was.

Elvin.

He was standing right outside the door, wearing a smart dark suit, as if he had dressed up to pay his college teacher a last respectful visit. But his face was distorted with twenty or thirty stab-wounds, his ears were gone, and his eyes were as blind as pebbles. His wounds had mostly healed, but his starched white shirt-collar was stained with a few cranberry-coloured spots of blood and his eyes were still weeping.

Jim held on to the door and didn't know what to say. He was so frightened that he felt as if his skin had shrunk, and all of his insides had suddenly dropped out, leaving nothing in his stomach but a chilly vacuum of fear.

"Hello, Mr Rook," said Elvin. His voice sounded terrible, all foggy and bruised, as if his tongue were too big for his mouth. He stepped forward with an awkward, unbalanced shuffle, his feet dragging on the floor, and as he did so his wounds gaped open, so that Jim could actually see his bright white cheekbones.

"You're dead, Elvin," said Jim, retreating across the living-room. He stumbled against a chair but managed to right himself. "Umber Jones killed you. You're dead. You have the right to some peace, don't you?"

Elvin gave a tilted smile, and swivelled his head around as much as his wounds would allow. "I'm not going to hurt you, Mr Rook. I brought you a message, that's all."

"I don't want to hear it, Elvin. I want you to go."

Elvin stayed where he was. It was his blinded eyes that disturbed Jim the most, slit in half from top to bottom, so that his irises were split like cut-up mushrooms.

"I want you to go, Elvin," Jim repeated. "I don't want to have anything more to do with Umber Jones, and you can tell him that from me."

"You have to hear his message," Elvin insisted.

"I told him back at police headquarters, it's over."

"He says you're his friend, Mr Rook. He says you're the only friend he's got. But he said something else, too. He said that every time you say 'no' to him, one of your class is going to die, the same way that I died."

Jim said nothing, but licked his lips. His mouth

was so dry he felt as if he hadn't drunk anything in a year.

Elvin said, "There's a bar on Vernon called Sly's. There's a guy who hangs out in this bar called Chill. His real name's Charles Gillespie but he doesn't like nobody to call him that. All you got to do is to go see Chill and tell him that you work for Umber Jones and that Umber Jones knows that he's just taken delivery of two kilos of best Colombian nose candy. Then tell him that from now on *he's* going to be working for Umber Jones, too, and that he'd better make sure that he pays over ninety per cent of his profits. Tell him you'll let him know later how and where and when he can make his payment. And if he shows any sign that he doesn't want to co-operate, tell him that Umber Jones is going to be watching him, night and day, and give him this."

Elvin put one mutilated hand into his coat pocket and took out a small fragment of black cloth. He held it out but Jim wouldn't take it.

He laid it carefully on the table instead. "Tell Chill that times have changed. Tell him that he'd better change with them, if he values his life." With that, Elvin turned around and shuffled toward the door, groping and feeling his way between the chairs.

He opened the door but then he hesitated for a moment. "You'd better go tonight, Mr Rook," he suggested. "Umber Jones is a very impatient man." He walked through the door and closed it very, very quietly behind him, which Jim found much more frightening than if he had slammed it.

For a long time he couldn't move, but held on to the back of the couch, his head bent forward, taking deep, steadying breaths. He had read articles about the so-called 'walking dead', but he had always accepted the historical explanation rather than the magical myth. Zombies were the victims of unscrupulous sugar-plantation owners during Haiti's great labour shortage in 1918. The owners were said to have hired voodoo sorcerers to administer soporific drugs to any likely-looking worker – probably a cocktail of tetrodotoxin, from the puffer fish; datura, a powerful hallucinogenic; and an extract from the toad *Bufo marinus*, which gives extraordinary strength. These drugs lowered the pulse-rate and gave the appearance of death – so much so that the zombie-to-be could be buried, and could remain in the cemetery in a trance-like stupor for days.

The sorcerer would then exhume them, revive them and take them to the sugar plantations to work – but not before taking the precaution of cutting out their tongues, so that they would never be able to protest or to explain what had happened to them.

But Elvin – Elvin was different. Elvin had been repeatedly stabbed all over. His heart and his lungs and his liver had been pierced. His body had undergone a full post-mortem, which would have killed him even if he hadn't already been dead. Yet he had walked into Jim's apartment tonight and spoken.

At last, however, Jim began to pull himself together. The first thing he did was go to the door and put on the chain. Then he went to the kitchen and poured himself another drink. His hands were shaking so much that the neck of the whiskey-bottle clattered against the glass. He drank, swallowed, and half-choked himself.

Eventually he went back into the living-room. He sniffed. Elvin had left behind him a curious and distinctive smell, spicy and dry, like Uncle Umber's, but mingled with the underlying sweetness of decaying flesh. The small piece of cloth that Elvin had tried to give him was still lying on the table. He picked it up, and turned it over. It was coarse and very black, as if it had been cut from a priest's cassock. There were some signs and words written on it in dull red, scarcely visible in artificial light. He didn't know what effect this would have on the man who called himself Chill, but it didn't look very threatening to him.

Now he had to decide if he was going to talk to Chill or not. He had never been a coward, but the prospect of going to meet a drug dealer on his own turf and demanding ninety per cent of his income seemed to be tempting fate, to say the least. On the other hand, what if he didn't? He was quite sure that Umber Jones wouldn't hesitate to wipe his class out, one after another.

He checked his watch. A few minutes after midnight. He took his blue linen coat off the peg by the door and shrugged it on. He had never been so reluctant to do anything in his life, but he simply didn't have any choice. He took a quick look around the apartment and then he switched off the lights and opened the door. A tall black figure was standing outside, its head silhouetted by the glass globe light on the balcony. Moths fluttered and whacked around it, so that it looked like the lord of the flies.

Jim couldn't say anything else but "*Ah*!" He stumbled back into the apartment and stood staring at the figure with his mouth open.

The figure stepped forward. It was holding something in its arms, a book or a box. "Brought your pizza, man," it said, worriedly.

Jim switched on the light, and there was a lanky youth with a wispy little beard and an earring and a red-and-black Pizza Hut T-shirt, holding out his supper. "Twenty dollars, man," he asked, holding on tight to the box. Then – as Jim opened his billfold and counted out the money, "You look like you just seen a ghost."

Jim handed him the money, all crumpled up, and a $5 tip. "Yes," he said. "Got it in one."

It took him over 20 minutes to find Sly's. It was a basement bar, reached from the street by a single dark doorway with the name *Sly* flickering in purple neon over the canopy. He managed to park around the corner and then he walked back to Sly's along a sidewalk still crowded with aimlessly-milling young people and watchful, hard-looking men. There were plenty of hookers around, too, in hotpants and short skirts and storebought hair of every conceivable colour.

Sly's doorway was guarded by a short, broad black man who looked like Mike Tyson after having an eight-ton block of concrete dropped on his head. "Sorry guy. Bar's closed," he said, as Jim approached, holding up the flat of his hand.

"I've got a message," Jim told him.

"Oh, yes? So where's your Western Union uniform?"

"Is Chill still here? Charles Gillespie? He's the one I've got the message for."

The doorman eyed him with piggy, glittering-eyed suspicion. "Don't nobody call him Charles Gillespie, excepting his mother. So you better not, white man, otherwise you know what they say about shooting the messenger, bad news or good."

"I have a message for Chill," Jim repeated, in the same tone that he used for his English comprehension class, very slow and very clear. "If Chill is here, I would very much like to speak to him."

"Okay, what's your name?" the doorman asked him.

"That doesn't matter. The message is all that matters. Don't tell me you don't know Marshall McLuhan?"

"Marshall McLuhan? He ain't never been in here," the doorman replied, suspiciously.

He picked a phone off the wall and spoke into it with his hand covering his mouth so that Jim couldn't hear what he was saying. After a few nods and grunts he hung up and said, "Okay, then, you can go on up. C'mere." He gave Jim a quick frisking and then he opened the door. "A word to the wise," he said, as Jim went down the first two steps. "Chill isn't feeling too happy tonight. He just had a root canal job. So, you know, don't like provoke him."

Jim didn't reply, but descended the narrow, black-carpeted staircase with growing trepidation. The walls on either side were covered in dark mirrors and he could see himself going down and down like a man on his way to hell. Another huge minder was waiting at the bottom, with sunglasses and an electric-blue suit. He let Jim pass through a swing door into the bar itself, which was ferociously air-conditioned and lit up in red and blue. A white man with an acne-scarred face was sitting at a black piano playing *I Will Always Love You* as if he were making it up as he was going along, and a large black girl in a small white dress was standing on a podium the size of a hatbox shrieking out the words.

In the darkest corner of the bar, in a semi-circular booth, sat a big black man with bleached hair, surrounded by five other black men with a variety of pompadours and crops and pigtails. They all wore black leather and heavy gold rings. The black man with the bleached hair was strikingly handsome, in a rough, unfinished way, as if he were a sculpture that had hurriedly been chiselled out of ebony, and then abandoned.

Jim went up to his table, drew out a chair and sat down. The six men looked at him like six cobras, ready to strike him dead. "Which one of you is Chill?" Jim asked, quite aware how close he was to committing the ultimate insult of disrespect.

"I'm Chill," said the man with the bleached hair, in a surprisingly high, carefully-enunciated voice. "You got a message for me, messenger boy?"

Jim's heart was beating so hard and so slow that he thought he was about to have a heart-attack on the spot. "I've got a message from Umber Jones," he said, unsteadily.

"Who the hell is Umber Jones? I don't know no Umber Jones."

"Well . . . this is just a message," said Jim. "Umber Jones says he knows that you recently took delivery of two kilos of Colombian cocaine."

Chill leaned forward in a menacing way, lacing his fingers together and looking Jim straight in the eye. "I told you, man. I don't know no Umber Jones. So how come this Umber Jones know so much about me?"

"He has – what can I call them? Very special abilities."

"Like what? To tap my phones? To pay off my runners? What? This Umber Jones wouldn't be the man, by any chance, would he? This wouldn't be no bust? Because if it is, messenger boy, you don't get out of here with two legs."

"Please, listen to me," said Jim. "Umber Jones says that times have changed. He says that he's taking over now and that he wants ninety per cent of everything you make out of this shipment. He says that he's willing to let you carry on, provided that you work for him, and provided that you don't give him any trouble."

Chill was staring at Jim in almost comical disbelief. One of his aides stood up, his earrings swinging, and reached inside his leather coat; but Chill snapped, "Siddown, Newton!" and the man reluctantly sat down again.

Jim continued, "Umber Jones will let you know later where you can pay him the money. He also said that if you lay one finger on me; or if you don't agree to do what he says; there's going to be trouble."

Chill slowly shook his head. "Never in the whole of my life, man, have I come across anybody with the nerve of you. Or this Umber Jones dude, if he really exists. I mean, let me get this right: he wants me to pay him ninety per cent of everything I make? He gets ninety per cent and I get ten percent, is that it?"

Jim nodded dumbly. The singer was approaching the climax of *I Will Always Love You* and her voice had risen to an hysterical screech.

"And if I *don't* give him the money, there's going to be . . . *trouble*?"

"Yes."

"Yes, what?"

"Yes, there is going to be trouble."

"You mean yes sir, Mr Chill sir, there is going to be trouble, sir. So what kind of trouble are we talking about here?"

Jim reached into his pocket and took out the small piece of black cloth. Now his heart was beating so slowly that it had almost stopped and he felt as if he could easily turn into a zombie himself. He laid the piece of cloth on the table and Chill pushed aside a heaped ashtray full of pistachio shells so that he could look at it. He picked it up. He turned it this way and that. He leaned back under a spotlight so that he could see what was written on it.

He looked at Jim with a wary expression on his face. "Where did you get this?" he asked.

"Umber Jones gave it to me, to give to you. I don't even know what it is."

"You don't know what it is? You bring me a voodoo curse and you don't know what it is?"

"Listen – I'm only the messenger here. I'm not a Catholic and I'm not black. I'm a college teacher. All I know about voodoo is what I've read in books and magazines."

Chill banged the table with his fist so that pistachio shells went dancing in all directions. "You brought me a voodoo curse!" he roared. He held the piece of cloth up in front of Jim's face and his eyes were bulging with rage. "You know what this is? This has been cut from the cloth of a murdered Roman Catholic priest and the warning has been written in his own blood! You know what this says? Here, look – *jama ebya ozias* – and here, the mark of Baron Samedi, the lord of the cemeteries! You dare to bring me this? You *dare* to bring me this?"

"I was – I was asked to, that's all. I didn't have any choice in the matter. I owe Umber Jones a kind of a favour, that's all. Don't ask me about voodoo. Don't ask me about narcotics. I'm just trying to stay alive and I'm just trying to protect some people who are very precious to me, okay?"

Chill looked down at him for a very long time. It seemed like hours. Then he reached into his coat and took out a pack of cigarettes. He tucked one into his mouth and instantly four lighters clicked into action. He ignored them all and lit his cigarette himself. "Who is he, this Umber Jones? He tired of living or something?"

"I wouldn't underestimate him if I were you."

Chill rolled the piece of cassock between finger and

thumb. "He knows his voodoo, I'll give him that. Sometimes somebody might take a splinter from the altar; or the communion host; and they'll dip it in chicken's blood, and that's enough of a warning. But this – this is like a death threat. Ain't nobody gives no death threat to Chill, believe me."

"I didn't know," said Jim. "He told me to bring it to you and I brought it."

Chill grinned, and smoke leaked out from between his teeth. "I don't know what somebody like you is doing mixed up in a business like this. But if I were you, I'd forget about this Umber Jones, whoever he is, and put as much distance between you and LA as you possibly can. Like I hear that Nome, Alaska, is pretty nice at this time of year."

"So what do you want me to tell him?"

"Tell him I'll see him in hell."

He said it as coolly as he could; as befitted a man with a name like Chill; but Jim detected an inflection in his voice that betrayed a deep underlying uncertainty. He had heard the same slightly-strangulated talk from countless college bullies. Chill had been seriously disturbed by Uncle Umber's patch of cloth. It was like Billy Bones in *Treasure Island*, being tipped with the black spot.

Jim waited for a moment, but Chill crushed out his cigarette and his minders began to shrug their shoulders and look threatening and the audience was obviously over. Jim got up and left the bar, just as the singer was launching into *You're Simply The Best*, wildly off-key. Quite honestly, thought Jim, if Chill was going to shoot anybody, he ought to shoot her.

Chapter Nine

To Jim's surprise, Tee Jay was back in class the next morning, wearing a Snoop Doggy Dogg sweatshirt and a strange, evasive look on his face. Jim came into the room with a bulging folder under his arm, dropped it on to his desk and stood for a while, taking in everybody's faces – Sue-Robin Caufield, flirting and chatting; David Littwin, frowning at his desk as if he couldn't understand why it was there; Muffy Brown, her head thrown back in laughter; Ray Vito, his eyes half-closed in a smooth Latin flirt with Amanda Zaparelli – he had taken a sudden interest in her now that her teeth were fixed.

Jim rubbed the back of his hand against his chin. He had been plagued by nightmares all night and he hadn't shaved very well this morning. His hair had refused to do what he wanted it to do and there had been no clean shirts in his drawer. He had discovered a blue checkered shirt that he usually used for working on the car. Two buttons were missing but at least it was pressed.

"Okay, class . . . this morning I'm pleased to welcome Tee Jay back to college and I'm sure that the rest of you are, too. What happened to Elvin was a terrible tragedy but in a way it makes it a little easier to bear knowing that the perpetrator wasn't one of us."

As he said "one of us" he turned and fixed his eyes on Tee Jay. He and Tee Jay were the only ones who knew that Tee Jay *had* been involved – and that even if he hadn't killed Elvin himself, he had stood by while Umber Jones had stabbed his best friend more than a hundred times. But Jim still wanted him to feel that he was part of the class – that he had a family to turn to. It was the only possible way of setting him free from his uncle's influence.

"Today we're going to read *Why He Stroked the Cats* by Merrill Moore. Page 128 in your *Modern American Verse*. I want you to read it silently to yourselves first of all, to see what you make of it. It's a difficult poem, strange. But I'd like to hear what each of you think it means."

'He stroked the cats on account of a specific cause,
Namely, when he entered the house he felt
That the floor might split and the four walls suddenly melt
In strict accord with certain magic laws
That, it seemed, the carving over the front door meant,
Laws violated when men like himself stepped in,

But he had nothing to lose and nothing to win,
So in he always stepped—'

He was still reading the poem to himself when he saw what looked like black smoke pouring over the windowsill. It rose, and softly whirled, and eddied around, and gradually the shape of Umber Jones materialised, shadowy and distorted at first, but then quite clearly.

Jim tried not to look at him, but it was impossible, because Umber Jones came right up to his desk and stood in front of him. His face looked as if it had been powdered with ash and his eyes were glittering red. He looked like a zombie himself, but he spoke with his usual thick, threatening aplomb. "You did what I asked, and talked to the man called Chill?"

Jim nodded. He could see that Sharon had looked up from her poem and was frowning at him, as if she suspected that something strange was happening. He didn't want Umber Jones to think that any of his class were aware of his presence. But then he glanced at Tee Jay and it was quite obvious that Tee Jay could see his uncle as clearly as he could. He was giving Jim a small, mocking smile, as if daring him to speak.

"Okay, Mr Rook . . . and what did Chill have to say for himself?"

Jim said nothing. Umber Jones stepped closer to his desk and held up his right hand. "I didn't quite hear that, Mr Rook. Maybe you better speak a little louder."

Jim continued to stare at him and say nothing.

Umber Jones stared back at him for a while, and then he started to rotate his right hand, around and around, and take it off, exposing the blade that was concealed inside it. "You see this knife, Mr Rook? This knife has the power of Ghede, who is Baron Samedi's closest assistant. When Baron Samedi wants bodies, it is Ghede who provides them. Now, you wouldn't want to be one of those bodies, would you?" He held the knife right in front of Jim's face until the point almost touched his chin. "How about you telling me what Chill said to you last night?"

"He said he'd see you in hell."

"Well of course he did," said Umber Jones. "You didn't seriously think that he was going to give up ninety per cent of his income, did you, just because some college teacher told him to?"

"No, quite frankly, I didn't." Two or three more members of the class looked up.

"But you gave him the message, didn't you? And you warned him what would happen if he didn't do what he was told?"

"Yes, I did."

"So next time, when you go to see him, he'll be more amenable, won't he?"

"What do you mean? What are you going to do?"

"I'm going to *persuade* him, Mr Rook, in the time-honoured fashion."

"If anybody else gets hurt—" Jim began. But at that moment John Ng stood up, with an expression of panic on his face.

"Mr Rook!" he said, and held up his necklet. "Mr Rook, he's here now, isn't he? That's who you're talking to! Look at my stone! Look at it! It's turned completely black!"

Sharon stood up, too. "I can *feel* him, Mr Rook! You can't pretend he's not here!"

The other members of the class turned this way and that in confusion. "Who's here? . . . What are they talking about?"

"It's the man in black!" John shouted. "It's the man who killed Elvin! Nobody can see him, only Mr Rook, but he's here! He's here right now, in the classroom!"

Tee Jay twisted around in his seat. "Shut up, you Viet Namese loony! What the hell you say, man in black?"

Sharon said, "He *is* here! I know he's here!"

"You shut up too, bitch," Tee Jay snapped at her. "What are you crazy or something?"

"Tee Jay!" said Jim. And it was then that he felt a cold flick across his face, and the poetry book in front of him was abruptly spattered with a fine spray of blood.

He clapped his hand against his cheek, shocked. Umber Jones was glaring at him with his amber-coloured teeth clenched in a grotesque snarl. "I told you not to tell them but you told them, didn't you? You disobeyed me!"

The classroom was suddenly silent. All of the students stared at Jim wide-eyed. Blood ran down between his fingers and dripped off his elbow. "I didn't tell them anything," he said. "They were sensitive enough and intelligent enough to work it out for themselves."

Umber Jones seemed to rise and swell, so that he was nearly seven feet tall. His suit was black, with a black buttoned-up vest which Jim could clearly see, yet there was a shadowy transparency about it. He could faintly distinguish the faces of some of his students through it, Ricky and Beattie and Sherma Feldstein.

Umber Jones said, "Now they know about me, maybe they need a little lesson on what will happen if they talk about me to anybody else."

"Don't you touch them, not one of them!" Jim retorted.

"And who's going to stop me?"

"Listen, I'll do anything you want! You want me to go back and talk to Chill? Fine, I'll do it. But just don't touch my students!"

"You'll do anything I want, whether I touch them or not. You're my friend, Mr Rook, remember?"

Jim jumped up, knocking his chair over, and made a grab for Umber Jones' arm. His hand passed through it as if it were smoke. Umber Jones swished his hand down and cut Jim's left sleeve open. Then he swished it sideways, nicking the tip of Jim's nose. If he hadn't dodged his head back in time, Umber Jones would have sliced his entire nostril open.

All that his class could see was Jim dancing and

whirling on his own, his sleeve ripped open and blood flying in all directions. Muffy began to scream, and then Jim staggered against Jane Firman's desk and she began to scream too. The boys shouted in alarm. "Hold him! Somebody hold him! Go get Mr Wallechinsky! Don't let him fall!"

But Tee Jay suddenly stood up and shouted, "No! You hear me? Don't call nobody! Shut the hell up and stay where you are!"

There was a sudden hush, all except for Muffy, who kept up a monotonous self-pitying sniff. Umber Jones stepped away from Jim, holding his blade up high, his eyes almost crimson with cruelty. Jim pulled a bunch of Kleenex out of the box on his desk and pressed them against his cheek. He felt shocked and hurt but worst of all, he felt that he was weak. He was supposed to protect his students, but he couldn't.

Tee Jay said, "You listen to me good. You're all going to walk out of here today and you're not going to say one word about what you saw. Because the man in black that Mr Rook here was talking about, he's *real*, even if you can't see him for yourselves. I seen him. I seen him that day when Elvin died and I can see him now, as plain as day."

He stood in the centre of the class, looking at every one of them. "Maybe you didn't believe in him before, but take a look at those cuts on Mr Rook's cheek and tell me where they come from. If you don't want that to happen to you, keep your mouth shut and you don't say nothing to nobody. And if you need any further persuading, go to the funeral home and ask to take a look at Elvin."

"So who is this man in black?" Russell Gloach challenged him.

"He's like a ghost, that's all."

"A ghost?" said Ray. "There's no such thing as ghosts."

"Well, he's more like a spirit. He isn't dead . . . he's just walking around outside of his body."

"How come you know so much about him?" asked Sue-Robin.

"He's the spirit of somebody I know. That's why he's here."

"Can't you tell him to leave us alone?" said Jane, miserably. Her eyes were filled with tears and she was deeply distressed.

Tee Jay emphatically shook his head. "This spirit isn't the kind of spirit you can give any kind of orders to. You want to live a long, peaceful life? You give this spirit respect, and you give him plenty of space. You understand that?"

Jim came forward. He didn't look at Tee Jay, but he said, "Tee Jay's right, everybody. It's in your own interest if you don't tell anybody what happened here today. Even your family, or your closest friend."

"But what can we *do* about it, this spirit?" asked Beattie, looking nervously around the classroom. "Can't we do what they did in that movie when the girl's head went round and round?"

Jim looked at Umber Jones but Umber Jones kept his head lowered so that his face was obscured by the brim of his Elmer Gantry hat. "We can't do anything," said Jim. The class could sense the defeat in his voice and they quietened down.

Jim dabbed at his face. It had stopped bleeding, but it still needed cleaning up. He would have gone straight to the infirmary, but he wasn't going to leave his class alone with Umber Jones.

"Let's get back to the poem," he said. "Tee Jay – you want to return to your seat?"

Tee Jay gave him a shrug and sprawled back into his chair. Jim returned to his desk, picked up his chair, and sat down in front of his blood-stained poetry book. He glanced up at Umber Jones, but Umber Jones remained where he was, silently smoldering, his face still concealed.

The class whispered and shuffled their feet, half-bewildered and half-fearful. "Come on," said Jim. "Let's get back to the poem. He won't do you any harm if you do what he says, will he, Tee Jay?"

"If you say so, Mr Rook."

Jim said, "I want you all to think what the poet was trying to explain. I mean – is this real, the floor splitting and the walls melting, or is it an allegory? If so, what kind of an allegory? And what does he mean by 'certain magic laws'?"

The class remained silent. They knew that Umber Jones was still there, whether they could see him or not. But after a few moments, Umber Jones took off his hat, and ran his hand through his ash-powdered hair, and looked up at Jim with a sloping smile. "Chill frightened you, didn't he?" he said, in that sack-dragging voice of his.

Jim ignored him, but pointed to Greg, over in the corner, and said, "Greg – what did you think he meant by 'certain magic laws'?"

Greg squeezed his face into ten different expressions before he managed to say, "Superstitions . . . you know what I mean? Like spilling salt or walking under a ladder."

"That's very good, Greg. Taboos, that's what he was talking about. That comes from the Polynesian word 'tabu', meaning a sacred or significant object."

Umber Jones said, "You should have someone look at your cheek. Nasty cut, that."

"Don't interrupt," Jim told him, even though he was still shaking. "No matter what you do, these children still deserve their education."

They locked eyes for a moment. Then Umber Jones said, "Okay. I'll send you a messenger."

"Not Elvin, please. Let Elvin rest in peace."

"Elvin? Elvin doesn't want to rest in peace. Elvin's glad to be out and about."

Jim couldn't think what to say. But Umber Jones began to shudder and fade, and in a few moments his smoke had disassembled itself, and blown away, as if he had never been there at all.

"He's gone," said John Ng. "Look at my crystal. It's clear."

"Is he really gone?" asked Rita.

Jim said, "Yes. I think we can all breathe a little more easy."

"But what does he *want*?" Sherma insisted.

"Nothing that has to worry you," Jim told her. "I'm just sorry that you've all gotten involved."

"Come on, Tee Jay, tell us what he wants," demanded Russell. "I mean you seem to be such buddies with him."

Tee Jay said, "You heard Mr Rook. He doesn't want nothing that has to bother you. All he wants is space and respect." He put his fingertip to his lips, in the same way that Umber Jones had done when he looked through the classroom window. "And silence."

He turned to Jim and said, "You need to get that cut fixed, Mr Rook. How about I take you down to the nurse?"

There was something in his tone of voice that made

Jim immediately put down his bloodstained poetry book and say, "All right, Tee Jay. The rest of you . . . I won't be too long. Why don't you write me a poem of your own about your own superstitions . . . anything that frightens you. Breaking a mirror, treading on the cracks in the sidewalk, the number thirteen . . ."

The class looked up at him, still confused and upset. He left his desk and walked up and down the aisles between them, touching their shoulders, squeezing their hands. "Listen," he said, "something very strange and dangerous has happened here. But so long as we don't lose our nerve . . . so long as we all stick together, everything's going to work out fine."

Tee Jay stood up and took hold of his elbow. "Come on, Mr Rook. Let's get that face seen to."

They left the classroom and walked along the corridor. Mr Wallechinsky walked past, his cheek still covered in sticking-plaster, and Jim covered his own face with his hand. "How's it going, Mr R?" said Mr Wallechinsky, and Jim said, "Great."

They rounded the corner at the end of the corridor and Tee Jay stopped. "Mr Rook . . . I got something to say to you. I know you hate me. I know you think that I helped my Uncle Umber when Elvin got killed, but it wasn't that way at all."

Jim stood with his back against the wall. In the distance, he could hear the persistent squeaking of basketball boots on a polished wood floor. He wasn't feeling particularly friendly or amenable. His collar was sticky with blood and he was still trembling with shock. But all the same, Tee Jay was looking deadly serious, and much more like he used to be, instead of the furious swearing hoodlum who had beaten up on Elvin in the washroom.

"All right," he said. "What way was it?"

"It started six months ago, when my Uncle Umber turned up at the door without no warning at all. He said he was back from travelling all around Europe and Africa or wherever, and that he wanted to get to know us again. I didn't remember him. Like I was about two when he first left LA. Mom didn't seem to like him too much, but he was Dad's brother after all and what could she do? I thought he was great. He was funny and he was full of these wild stories about voodoo ceremonies and altars made out of human bones, and priestesses who could speak in languages that nobody had ever heard of.

"He taught me all about it. He *showed* me. He made me see that voodoo is the one true religion, you know what I mean? And it has to be, because it's the only religion that's real. It's the only religion with *evidence* for what you believe in."

"Well, I'll give you that," said Jim, taking his hand away from his face and showing Tee Jay the blood on his fingers.

Tee Jay said, "I'm sorry about that, Mr Rook. I wouldn't have had that happen for the world."

"And Elvin? What about Elvin? I suppose you wouldn't have had *that* happen for the world, either. But Elvin's dead; or what passes for dead."

"That's why I'm talking to you now, Mr Rook. When Uncle Umber killed Elvin, that was when I first found out just how far he was prepared to go. He said he was going to make Elvin show some respect. I never knew that he was going to *kill* him. I swear it."

"You were there when it happened. Why didn't you try to stop him?"

Tee Jay shook his head. "You can't do nothing to stop him, Mr Rook. He can call on all the strength of Vodun and Baron Samedi and every spirit you never heard of. See – when he lived in Venice in the 'seventies, he was scratching for a living washing white peoples' cars and looking for handouts. He promised himself he wasn't never going to demean himself like that again. He was going to find the real black power. Not the political black power, but the *magical* black power. And he promised himself that he was going to come back to LA one day and take over everything, and be respected and rich, so that there wasn't one single white man who would ever be able to pop his fingers at him and call him boy. He wasn't going to let nobody show disrespect to him or his."

"And that's why he killed Elvin?"

Tee Jay swallowed and nodded. "Elvin was always laughing about voodoo. I tried to tell him that it was the only religion that a black man could proudly have. But all he did was diss me, on and on. I could take it for myself, but when he started dissing Baron Samedi, that was something else. He said, you going to start biting the heads off of poultry and strutting up and down with your face all white and your high black hat on? That's when I hit him. I'm sorry I hit him. But he shouldn't of said that. Not about something I truly believe in."

"Then what happened?" Jim asked him. "Your uncle came to college? How did he know you were feeling so upset?"

"I called him at home, because I was afraid that Dr Ehrlichman was going to can me. He asked me what had happened and I told him. He said he was going to fix it, and of course he did. Or his Smoke did, anyways."

Tee Jay took a deep breath and Jim could tell by the thistle in his throat that he was close to tears. "Uncle Umber told me to call Elvin into the boiler-house. I told Elvin I was packing some speed. He walked in and Uncle Umber blew the goofer dust on him and he was paralysed just like he was dead. He couldn't move. He couldn't speak. But all the time his eyes were staring at me, like pleading, you know? Uncle Umber said that in Haiti they cut blasphemers one hundred and twelve times, one for each of the *loa*, to punish them for what they've done."

Tee Jay paused for a long, emotional moment. Then he said, "That's what he did to Elvin, right in front of me. I was scared, Mr Rook. I was so damned scared. I knew that if I tried to stop him, he would do the same to me. He'll kill anybody, Mr Rook, if they stand in the way of what he wants to do."

Jim said, "Why don't you leave him, if you're so damned scared? Why don't you go back home?"

Tee Jay looked down at the floor. "He won't let me."

"That's it? That's the only reason? He simply won't let you? Come on, Tee Jay, I know you better than that."

"That's part of the reason. But the other part is . . . I *believe* in voodoo, Mr Rook. I really believe in it. It gives you power, and I can feel that power for myself. In my hands. In my mind. I never felt so strong. I never felt so confident. For the first time in my life, I feel like I'm somebody important, with a future, you know? I feel like I've got a handle on my own destiny."

"I see. You've got a future, no matter who you hurt?"

"I didn't want Elvin to die, Mr Rook. I swear it. It won't ever happen again."

"So what if Chill refuses to give Uncle Umber ninety per cent of his profits? You can swear that you won't lay a finger on him?"

"Chill's a drug-dealer, man. He knows what the risks are."

"Oh, sure he does. But that doesn't give you *carte blanche* to kill him. That's a matter for the law."

Without looking up, Tee Jay said, "Mr Rook . . . this isn't easy. I'm stuck between a rock and a hard place. I respect you, right? You're just about the only white person I ever met who understands what's happening inside of my head."

But then he raised his eyes and said, "But voodoo . . . this is such a rush. This is *empowerment.* This is black people tapping the wells of their own heritage, right? I mean you're always telling us that we ought to be true to our heritage, aren't you?"

"I'm not prejudiced against voodoo," Jim told him. "I respect voodoo just as much as Roman Catholicism, or Shinto or anything else that anybody wants to believe in. But I don't respect violence and I don't respect extortion. Most of all I don't respect murder. You should go round to see Elvin's mom and dad and try to tell *them* how empowered you are, now that you've discovered voodoo."

Tee Jay said, "We'd better get you to the nurse."

"I think I can manage on my own, thank you," Jim told him. He started to walk toward the medical room, leaving Tee Jay behind.

Tee Jay watched him for a while, and then called out, "Mr Rook! Please don't chill me out, Mr Rook! I'm doing my best here, I swear it!"

Jim stopped, but didn't turn around.

"I promise, Mr Rook, I'm going to do everything I can to make sure that nobody else gets hurt."

"What if your Uncle Umber decides to kill somebody else? Who are you going to support then? Him, or me?"

"He's blood of my blood, Mr Rook. You got to understand that."

"Exactly," said Jim, and limped off toward the medical room.

The rest of the day was quiet and anti-climactic. While the boys went to the shop for welding and auto repairs, and the rest of the girls were given a talk on home management, Jim gave Jane Firman a one-to-one lesson in word recognition, and then worked with David Littwin on his stammer.

He liked David. In spite of his speech problems, he was always enthusiastic and co-operative, and he never took offence when he was teased by the rest of the class. Jim had never believed in pretending that his students didn't have handicaps. Sooner or later they were going to have to face the world outside, and the world outside wasn't forgiving when it came to bad stammers or thick accents or slowness of thought. Jim wanted to give his students confidence without pretending that their lives were going to be easy and that they were always going to be surrounded by understanding friends and politically-correct teachers. Some day, an impatient employer was going to ask David if there was any danger of getting an answer by Christmas, and David was going to have to deal with it.

David had improved immensely since he had started in Special Class II, but Jim had no intention of making him feel that people were going to wait for ever while he s-s-s. Struggled to s-s-s. Say what he meant.

At the end of the day, there was a knock on his classroom door. It was Susan. "Listen," she said, "when I said we should keep a little distance between us, I didn't mean three thousand miles, and I didn't mean forever."

"I'm sorry," Jim said, thrusting a sheaf of essays

into his briefcase and snapping it shut. "I've been extra-specially busy today."

"You've cut your face," she said, concerned. She came forward and touched his cheek and then his nose. "How did that happen? You look like Mr Wallechinsky."

"It's nothing. A window broke."

She frowned at him. "Is something *wrong*?" she asked him.

He kept thinking of the way that she had half-closed her eyes when she had told him that she loved him; and how furiously she had kissed him, as if she wanted to eat him alive.

"Everything's fine," he said. "I've had a crappy day, is all."

He tried to leave his desk but she stayed where she was, blocking his way. "I don't want you to think that I'm angry or anything," she told him. "I'd still like to see your maps, whenever you have the time."

"Susan," he said. "I don't have any maps. Ron Philips was stirring things up between us, that's all."

"No maps?" she blinked. "What do you mean, no maps? What about Martin Frobisher's chart of the North-West Passage?"

He shook his head.

"You *invented* it?" she asked him, incredulously. "Why on earth did you invent it?"

Even as she said it, of course, she understood why; and she blushed as fiercely as a teenager. "I'm sorry," she said, "I shouldn't have asked you that. That was stupid of me. Listen – I'm making a complete fool of myself here. I'd better go."

He took hold of her wrist. "Susan . . . I don't know what's happened between us. I don't know why you said you loved me so much and then you changed your mind.

I guess women are entitled to be fickle. But I'd quite like to know what it was that put you off me so suddenly. I mean was it my breath? Did you meet Richard Gere in the supermarket the next morning? What?"

"I'm at a loss here," Susan admitted. "You seem to think that we had something going when we didn't. All that happened was, you drove me home. We talked about maps, and that was it. You bumped into a hedge and got your pants wet."

"We didn't kiss?"

"We pecked."

"We pecked but we didn't kiss? No tongues or anything?"

"*Tongues*?" she said, startled. "Jim . . . we were talking about Mercator's projection, that's all. You don't go straight from Mercator's projection to *tongues*."

Jim pressed his hand to his head. "I'm missing something here. I thought we kissed. I thought you said you loved me and we kissed."

Susan took hold of his hand. "Jim . . . I *like* you. I *admire* you. All this work you do with Special Class II. But I'm sorry . . . I never said that I loved you. And believe me, please – and don't take this wrong – we never kissed."

It suddenly came to him. The memory powder. He had tested the memory powder by imagining that Susan was head-over-heels in love with him. He remembered that now. But in spite of the fact that he could remember it, he was still totally convinced that he and Susan *had* kissed. It was the strangest feeling that he had ever had. He could still feel her lips. He could still feel the softness of her hair and her breath against his cheek. "*I fell in love with you the moment I first saw you.*" She had said it so clearly that he could imagine each word in shining fruity colour, like a roll of Life Savers.

"Jesus," he said. He was so dumbstruck.

"Listen . . ." she said. "Give it some time, then maybe we could go out for dinner together. Or maybe a picnic."

"Sure," he told her. He squeezed her hand. "I think I'd better be getting along home now. The feline formerly known as Tibbles will be wanting her supper."

"Jim," she said, as he left the classroom. He stopped, and turned.

"Nothing," she said, and let him go.

On the way back to Venice the atmosphere tightened and Jim could see snakes'-tongues of lightning flickering over the Santa Monica Mountains. By the time he was half-way home there was a deafening barrel-roll of thunder and the sidewalks were instantly spotted with rain. Soon water was cascading off the roof of his car and his windscreen wipers were flapping wildly from side to side. When he reached his apartment block he parked as close to the concrete staircase as he could and climbed out of the driver's seat with a copy of *National Geographic* on top of his head. Too bad about the fertility rituals of the Motu-speaking peoples of Papua New Guinea: they were just going to have to get wet.

He climbed the steps to his apartment. Myrlin was watching him out of his kitchen window but when Jim suddenly turned around and gave him the evil eye he promptly closed his venetian blinds.

There was a second burst of thunder as Jim opened up his front door, and the rain clattered down with even more intensity, gushing down the roof and leaping out of the gutters. Jim switched on the lights and dropped his sodden magazine into the wastepaper basket. He left the door a few inches ajar and a few seconds later his cat appeared, rubbing up against his legs and mewling for him to feel sorry for her. "All right, already," he told her.

He went through to the kitchen, opened up his freezer and took out a plateful of jambalaya that he had made for himself about two months ago. He didn't feel particularly hungry, after today, but he had a whole evening's marking in front of him and he knew that if he didn't eat properly he would end up at midnight building himself a disgusting Dagwood sandwich out of anything he could find in the icebox – pickles, gorgonzola, out-of-date prosciutto and peanut butter, and he would lie in bed in the early hours of the morning wishing he hadn't.

He slid the plate of jambalaya into the microwave and switched it to defrost. Then he popped open a can of beer, and pulled open a can of catfood. His cat came hurrying into the kitchen on speeded-up clockwork legs, and was gulping down reconstituted lumps of rabbit before he could spoon it all on to her plate. "Look at you," he told her. "You only love me for my food, and Susan doesn't love me at all."

He stood up and looked at himself in the mirror next to the phone, cautiously touching his cheek to see how much it had healed. Umber Jones's knife must have been sharper than a cut-throat razor, because the wound, although it was quarter of an inch deep, had closed together perfectly. The nick on his nose was more troublesome: it was a tiny semicircular slice close to the tip and it gaped slightly. He would have to ease off blowing his nose for a while.

Taking his can of beer, he walked through to the living-room. He picked up his remote control and switched on the television. News; baseball; *The Simpsons*; more baseball; disgusting insects in close-up, news. Lightning crackled outside his window and the television picture crackled too, and started to jump. He went over to the set and hit the top of it with the flat of his hand, but the picture continued to tremble. It was then that Jim heard his cat mewling again and he turned around to see a figure sitting on his couch. A shadowy figure, thin and bent and barely-visible; with no more substance than a silhouette cut out of a net curtain.

He stared at it, alarmed, but now that he had begun to accept the existence of wandering spirits, he wasn't as frightened as he had been when Umber Jones had first appeared. He watched it for a while, waiting to see what it would do, and then cautiously he approached it. It had none of the volcanic malevolence of Umber Jones. It sat with its head bowed and its hands in its lap, patient and quiet. He knelt down on the carpet in front of it, and then he reached out to touch it, to see if it would respond, but all that he could feel was a faint cold prickling, like dipping his fingers into a glass of tonic water.

The figure raised its head. Its face was wan and sad, its eyes concealed by dark shadows. But there was no mistaking who it was. Even after it has left its physical body for ever, a spirit can still be recognised. "Mrs Vaizey," said Jim. "Can you hear me, Mrs Vaizey?"

"I can hear you," she said. He wasn't sure if she had really spoken or not, but he could understand what she was saying.

"Mrs Vaizey . . . I'm so sorry for what happened. If I'd had any idea—"

"I knew what the risks were, Jim. And now that I'm dead, I think that you can call me Harriet, don't you?"

"Did Umber Jones catch you in his apartment?"

She nodded and said, "His smoke-spirit was out walking when it happened. His physical body was lying on the bed. His face was painted white with ash so that only his eyes looked out. His hat was propped up on the pillow beside him and he was holding his *loa* stick in his hand, just like Baron Samedi. I tried to take the *loa* stick away from him, but I was too late. His smoke-spirit returned and caught me and there was nothing I could do. He called on Ogoun Ferraille to help him, and Ogoun Ferraille forced me to eat myself."

"The pain—"

"The pain was more terrible than anything you can think of. But the mercy is that it didn't last long and now it's over. I'm never going to feel pain again."

"What's going to happen to you now?"

"I'll fade, Jim, like all spirits do, and then I'll be gone. There isn't a heaven. Beyond the light, there's just a kind of fading away, like a photograph left in the sun. One day there's nothing left but the faintest of outlines, and then there's nothing at all."

"I'm going to miss you. You know that."

"Well . . . so long as somebody still remembers me, I won't be gone for good. But you still have to find a way to deal with Umber Jones, or else he's going to plague you for the rest of your days."

"I've tried dealing with him," said Jim, turning his face so that she could see the cut on his cheek. "Look at the result. He's threatened to hurt my students if I don't do what he says."

He told her what had happened in the classroom today and she listened thoughtfully. In the end she said, "You'll have to take his *loa* stick. It's the only way. Do you think you might be able to persuade this boy Tee Jay to do it?"

"I don't think so. He's very upset about the way that his uncle killed his best friend, but he's very frightened of him. I don't think he'd want to risk his uncle's anger by messing around with something as sacred as a *loa* stick."

"Well, that doesn't surprise me. He must be a full convert to voodoo or he wouldn't be able to see his uncle's smoke-spirit. I guess *you'll* have to get it."

"You mean break into Umber Jones's apartment?"

"Either that, or do what I did, and visit it in spirit. Just make sure that he doesn't come back and catch you, the way he caught me."

"How can I do that? I don't have the first idea how to leave my body."

"It isn't difficult. You make a circle of ash and use your finger to make three signs – the moon, the sun and the wind. These will guide your spirit out of your body and guide it back again, like the markings on an airport runway. Then all you have to do is lie quietly on your couch and recite the three verses of leaving."

"I don't know the three verses of leaving. Was that all that Latin-sounding stuff you were saying?"

"You can say it in any language you like. In some languages it works much more quickly and whisks you out of your body almost at once. Creole, for example; and Yoruba, because they have very strong words for magic."

"My Yoruban is kind of rusty."

"Then say it in English. Set my spirit free . . . let it wander where it will. Let my body sleep without it. Set my spirit free . . . keep it safe from evil and darkness."

She repeated the words three times and Jim repeated them after her.

"You don't have to worry if you change them a little . . . it's your *will* that sets you free, not what you say."

"There's just one thing," said Jim. "What's it actually *like*?"

"You'll feel as if you've taken off a heavy coat which you've been wearing all your life. You'll feel so free that you won't want to come back. You'll fly. You'll flow. Once you've done it for the first time, you won't be able to wait to do it again."

Jim wasn't sure that he liked the sound of that. Up until Umber Jones had appeared on the scene, his life had been reasonably straightforward and contented. He didn't want to have his contentment disturbed by a strange craving which he could never satisfy. It would be like being an astronaut, forever yearning to go back to the moon.

"If I can fly . . . if I can flow . . . if I don't have any physical substance, how do I pick up the *loa* stick?"

"A spirit doesn't work by substance. A spirit works by will. A spirit's strength is its ability to concentrate, unhindered by flesh and blood."

Mrs Vaizey's outline began to dim. Jim said, "Listen . . . once I've got the *loa* stick, what do I do with it?"

Mrs Vaizey said something so faintly that he couldn't make out what it was. It could have been *take it* or *break it*. It could have been something quite different. She became so dim that she looked like nothing more than a faint shadow cast across the couch. Then she was gone altogether.

The feline formerly known as Tibbles gave a mystificd miaow. Jim stood up and paced around the apartment for a while, wondering what the hell he ought to do.

There was a ring at the doorbell. He answered it, keeping the door on the security-chain. It was Geraint, in a violent green-and-scarlet shirt. "Do you have my mother in there?" he demanded.

"Your mother? Of course not. What gave you that idea?"

"Myrlin said he thought he saw you talking to her."

"And how did he manage to do that? Does he have X-ray vision or something?"

"He was just walking along the balcony and he just happened to glance over at your apartment."

"Oh, just *happened*? I might have known." Jim took the chain off the door and opened it wide. "You want to come in and search the place?"

"No thanks," said Geraint uncomfortably. "But I'm getting real worried about her, you know? She never took off like this before. I've looked all over, but zip."

"I wouldn't worry. You know what she's like. Wherever she is, she's bound to be happy."

Geraint was about to leave when he wrinkled up his nose and sniffed. "You know something . . . I'm sure I can smell her perfume."

Jim knew what he meant. She had left not only the smell of her perfume behind, she had left the vibrancy of what she once was. He laid a comforting hand on Geraint's shoulder. "I'm sorry, Geraint. Wishful thinking."

Chapter Ten

He managed to eat half his jambalaya and the rest he scraped into the cat's dish. Then he took a shower and changed into a black turtleneck shirt and black pants. He found a pair of black leather driving gloves, too, that his mother had bought him for Christmas and which he had never worn. He slicked back his wet hair and looked at himself in the mirror. He might not have any burgling experience, but he certainly *looked* like a burglar.

He opened the kitchen closet and took out the blue plastic container in which he kept his motley selection of tools. He chose a long screwdriver and a thin paint-scraper. There was also a bent piece of wire with which he had once opened a college locker when a student had lost his key, and he optimistically put that into his pocket, too.

He drove to Umber Jones's apartment feeling totally unreal, as if this couldn't be him at all. He parked across the street, tucked in closely behind a carpet-delivery van. There was a dim amber light shining through the blinds in Umber Jones's upstairs window and Jim could see the silhouette of a figure moving to and fro. From this side of the street, it looked like Tee Jay.

Jim checked his watch. It was 11:11 on the nose. He settled back in his seat, preparing for a long wait. It was going to be highly risky, breaking into Umber Jones's apartment when he and Tee Jay were asleep, but he would rather do it while Umber was in his physical form than when he was in the form of The Smoke, with all the destructive strength that the *loa* could give him.

He passed the time by reciting poetry to himself. "'*But death replied: "I choose him." So he went, And there was silence in the summer night.*'"

Unexpectedly, the street door to Umber Jones's apartment opened and Tee Jay emerged. He was wearing a blue-and-white nylon windbreaker with his hands thrust into the pockets. He looked right and left and then he headed off westward, walking fast.

Five or six minutes passed and then the light in Umber Jones's window was switched off. Maybe Umber Jones had retired to bed. Jim thought that he would give him about a half-hour, and then see if he could manage to break in. There would be a few minutes of maximum danger while he tried to locate the *loa* stick, but once he had it, there would be nothing that Umber Jones could do.

He waited twenty minutes. Umber Jones's window was still in darkness. He must be asleep by now. Jim gave him another three minutes and then climbed out of his car, leaving it unlocked in case he needed to make a quick getaway. "You're mad," he told himself, matter-of-factly, as he crossed the street. "This is never going to work. He's going to wake up and he's going to cut you to bits. Not only that, you're talking to yourself."

But what was the alternative? Continuing to act as Umber Jones's 'friend' – running errands for him and helping him to extort money out of pimps and drug dealers, under constant threat of him killing his students? Or staking out Umber Jones's apartment for days on end, waiting for him to leave it as The Smoke? But supposing he returned, and caught Jim right in the act of stealing his *loa* stick, the way he had caught Mrs Vaizey? Jim didn't relish the idea of eating himself, and of ending his life as nothing but a heap of dust.

He reached Umber Jones's front door. He looked anxiously around but there was nobody in sight except for a very drunk man who looked exactly like Stan Laurel. He was leaning against a wall as if he were in love with it and occasionally bawling out random lines from *Moon River*: "*Wider than a mile . . . I'm croshin you in shtyle . . .*" The door was old and didn't fit very well. There was at least a quarter-inch gap between the frame and the door itself, and the wood looked pretty rotten. Jim took out his screwdriver and forced it into the gap, next to the lock. Then he pulled it back as hard as he could, and part of the frame splintered. Next he managed to work the screwdriver blade right into the gap until he could feel the tongue of the lock. He was just about to force it open when he suddenly became aware of a deep, thrumming sensation, as if a subway train were passing right beneath his feet. Except that here in Venice, of course, there *were* no subways.

Instinctively, he stepped away from the door. The thrumming grew louder, and as it did so it sounded more like drums beating. Furious, hectic drums. The door rattled and Jim turned around and ran. Half-way along the next block he found an empty doorway in front of an adult bookstore. He pressed himself against the security mesh, his heart beating as madly as the drums. Through the mesh, the faded picture of a plump white-fleshed girl smiled at him, her eyes encircled with thick black mascara.

After a moment or two he leaned out to see what was happening. The sidewalk was empty except for the drunk, who had managed to slide himself a few feet further away. "*Waiting . . . round the bend . . .*"

But then the air in front of Umber Jones's apartment appeared to tremble, like the hot air over a desert highway. The door opened, just a fraction, and smoke began to pour out of it. Dense, black smoke. Jim drew himself back. He knew exactly what this was. The smoke twisted and curdled and slowly rose upward; until it formed itself into the tall, dark, unmistakable figure of Umber Jones. He had emerged through an opening in the door that was no more than two inches wide.

Jim had two immediate choices. Either he could stay here and risk burgling Umber Jones's apartment, or he could follow Umber Jones wherever he was going, to see what he was planning next. It made more sense to break into his apartment. After all, once he had the *loa* stick, Umber Jones wouldn't be able to call on the spirits to give him strength; that was the way that Jim understood it, anyhow. He may still be capable of using a gun or a knife, but then so what? Jim had taught classes of fifteen-year-olds who had been capable of using guns and knives, and occasionally brought them to college, too.

Apart from that, Mrs Vaizey had died trying to bring him the *loa* stick, and he felt he had a moral duty to finish the job that had killed her. He owed her at least that much.

Umber Jones started to walk away from him, his black suit flapping like a crow's wings. He passed close to the drunk – who couldn't see him, of course, but who obviously felt him go by; like a shadow, like a dark summer draft; because he swivelled around on one leg, and stared at nothing at all.

Umber Jones crossed the street. As he did so, a taxi came speeding toward him, its flag lit up, its suspension bouncing on the patched-up roadway. It headed straight for him, its headlights shone right through his body, as if they were shining through fog. There was a moment when Jim thought that he was going to be killed, but the taxi drove right through him. The smoke that he was made of whirled and staggered, but then it blew itself back together again, and Umber Jones continued to cross to the opposite sidewalk as if he had been hit by nothing more than a sudden gust of wind.

He disappeared around the next corner. For a few long moments, Jim's courage failed him, and he stood where he was, pressed against the mesh of the adult bookstore. How could you fight a man who could leave his body and walk through the streets like smoke? But he gave himself his own answer: because you have to. Because nineteen young people are relying on you.

Because good has to overcome evil. It's the natural law.

He took two deep breaths. Then he left the bookstore and walked back to the front door of Umber Jones's apartment. He took out his screwdriver and carried on twisting at the lock. The drunk caught sight of him and began to shamble toward him. "*Waiting round the bend . . .*" he hollered. "*My huckleberry friend . . .*"

The light in Mr Pachowski's apartment was abruptly switched on, and the drapes drawn back. Mr Pachowski opened up the window and called out, "What's going on down there? Get out of here before I call the cops!"

Jim backed away from the door, lifting his hand in a conciliatory wave. "It's okay . . . I was looking for number 12002!"

"Wrong block . . . 12002 is three blocks west!"

"Great, thanks," said Jim. All the same, Mr Pachowski

stayed watching him as he walked away. He lifted his hand again. "Thanks," he repeated. "Good-night."

He crossed back over the street. The drunk came weaving after him, still singing. As Jim climbed back into his car he came up and leaned against the roof. Jim put down the window and said, "Go on, beat it. Find yourself someplace safe to sleep it off."

The drunk stared at him with eyes that refused to focus. "Tell me something," he said. "I've never been able to work it out for myself and nobody ever seems to know the answer. What the hell *is* a huckleberry friend?"

He went reeling off into the night with his arms spread wide, a scarecrow caught in a cyclone. Jim started up his engine and pulled away from the curb. He could see that Mr Pachowski was still keeping a beady eye on him. There was nothing left to do now but drive back home and work out some other way of getting his hands on Umber Jones's *loa* stick.

Or maybe there was something else that he could do. Follow Umber Jones, wherever he was going, and find out what he was up to. It could be highly dangerous, but on the other hand it might give him some valuable knowledge about Umber Jones's strengths, and maybe his weaknesses, too. There were one or two things that puzzled him about Umber Jones's behaviour. He had said that he wanted his existence to remain a secret, yet he had repeatedly appeared in a crowded classroom, where it had been almost impossible for Jim to conceal the fact that *something* strange was going on. He could have manifested himself just as easily in Jim's apartment, or in the street, and then there wouldn't have been any chance at all of Jim's students sensing his presence. There was something else, too: when Umber Jones had wanted to send Jim his instructions to talk to Chill, why had he sent Elvin, instead of visiting him in person – or at least in the form of The Smoke?

Jim drove to the corner where Umber Jones had disappeared. The street was deserted except for lines of parked cars and a man walking a brutish-looking dog. Jim turned left and drove slowly along to the next intersection, lightly drumming his fingers on the steering-wheel. He had been walking quickly, but he couldn't have gone more than four or five blocks. Jim stopped at the traffic signals – and then, when they changed to green, he turned right.

As he drove down the next block, he began to have a growing suspicion about where Umber Jones might be headed. He was now only three blocks away from Sly's bar, where Chill and his cronies hung out. Chill had told Umber Jones that he would rather see him in hell. Maybe Umber Jones had the same idea about Chill.

Jim still hadn't caught sight of Umber Jones, so he decided to risk it and drive directly to Sly's as fast as he could. He took a sharp left at the next intersection, his tyres squealing like strangled cats; and then a right. He arrived outside the bar just in time to see the dark shadowy figure of Umber Jones rounding the corner at the end of the block.

At the same time, he saw Chill and three of his minders standing on the sidewalk talking and laughing. Another minder was sitting on the hood of a green Cadillac Fleetwood, smoking a cheroot. Umber Jones approached them at unnatural speed, without once breaking his stride. His face was ghastly with ash and his eyes were scarlet, as if he had been rubbing cinders into them. He came along the sidewalk in his black suit and his black wide-brimmed hat and of course Chill and his minders couldn't see him at all. He didn't even throw a shadow.

Jim's grip tightened on his steering-wheel. He wasn't sure what he ought to do. Even if he shouted a warning to Chill and his men, they wouldn't believe him, because Umber Jones simply couldn't be seen. And it wouldn't help them, either. Umber Jones was not only invisible but untouchable. His only substance was his evil; but his power was the power of the *loas* who were helping him, Ghede and Ougon Ferraire.

Jim actually took an involuntary breath to shout, "*Look out*!" but his voice wouldn't work. All he could do was watch in horror as Umber Jones rotated his hand, revealing the knifeblade underneath.

Chill leaned back on his heels, his hands in his pockets, laughing. The minder who was standing next to him was wearing a black shirt and a white silk vest. Umber Jones came speeding right up to him and stabbed him straight in the stomach – once, twice, three times. He was even holding onto the man's right shoulder to steady himself. The man was too shocked even to shout out. He stood with his arms wide, staring down at his vest. It looked as if somebody had crushed strawberries all over it. Then – still silent – he dropped on to his knees. He coughed up a huge splatter of blood, swayed, and keeled over sideways.

The other minders spun around and around, their guns held high, trying to see who had attacked them. At first it looked as if they were blaming each other. After all, there was nobody else anywhere near them. One of them backed away, waving his automatic in all directions. Jim could hear them shouting, and for a moment it looked as if they might even start shooting. But then Chill yelled at them to stop acting like headless chickens. Appropriate, Jim thought grimly, for men being attacked by voodoo.

Chill pointed up at the opposite buildings and the

minders took off their sunglasses and peered frantically across the street, to see if their friend had been hit by a sniper. But one of them was down on one knee beside him, opening up his bloody vest, and he turned to the others and shook his head. These weren't bullet-holes: these were oval, gaping stab wounds.

All the time, Umber Jones was circling around them, his blade gleaming, his teeth gleaming, his eyes so wide and unblinking that he looked as if he were mad. He approached the minder who was kneeling over his fallen friend, bent over him, and hooked his arm around his throat. It looked as if he were holding him in a wrestling grip, but then he whipped his arm away and his knifeblade cut across the man's jugular vein and half-way through his Adam's apple. He tried to get up, but blood was pumping out of his neck so wildly that it sprayed all the way across the sidewalk and all over the windows of Chill's Cadillac.

That was enough for Chill. He shouted to his two remaining minders and they climbed into the car as if the devil was after them. And he was. Before Chill's driver could start up the engine, the black smoky shape of Uncle Umber glided over to the Cadillac and literally poured itself in through the half-open window at the back.

The Cadillac's engine whoofed into life. The tyres screamed, and smoke billowed out of the rear wheel arches. Then the car pulled away from the curb and out into the street.

It didn't get very far. It hadn't even reached the end of the block before it abruptly swerved and collided with a deafening smash into the back of a double-parked garbage truck. There was a moment's silence and then it exploded. A ball of orange fire rolled up into the night. The blazing spare tyre was hurtled thirty feet into the air and landed on top of a parked car on the opposite side of the road.

Jim thought that everybody in the car must have been killed. But suddenly the passenger door opened and Chill dropped out on to the road, the back of his hair smoking. He managed to get up onto his hands and knees and crawl away from the wreck like a beaten dog. The heat from the burning car was so intense that the soles of his yellow suede shoes momentarily burst into flame. At last he was dragged to safety by two garbage collectors, who laid him on the sidewalk and covered him with coats.

Jim stayed where he was, watching the car burn itself into a skeleton. Only he could see the ashy-faced figure in the Elmer Gantry hat who was watching the wreck, too; unmoving; but with a look of ghoulish satisfaction.

At three o'clock in the morning, Jim was awakened by a light, insistent tapping noise. He sat up in bed, suddenly alert, listening. There was a moment's pause but then he heard the tapping noise again, like somebody's fingernail against the living-room window.

He climbed out of bed. The feline formerly known as Tibbles had been curled up against his legs, and she opened one eye and gave him a look of intense irritation. He padded on bare feet across the living-room carpet. The cotton blinds were drawn down over the window, but there was a three-quarter moon tonight, and Jim could clearly see the shadow of somebody standing out on the balcony.

He stood in front of the blind for a very long time, wondering if he ought to put it up, or pretend that he was asleep and that nothing could wake him.

But then he could see the shadow raise its arm and tap at the window once again. It would probably tap all night if he didn't answer it, and he was exhausted enough already. After he had gone to bed, he had fallen asleep almost at once, but he had woken up after only ten minutes beating and flapping wildly at his bedsheet because he thought that he was on fire.

He had managed to get back to sleep shortly after two – but now he was faced with this. A shadow who stood outside his window, patiently tapping.

At last he took hold of the toggle and tugged the blind open. Standing in the moonlight was Elvin, so pale that his skin was almost luminous, his wounds looking even more than ever like the gaping mouths of dead fish. He tapped the glass yet again. He was smiling in an odd defensive way, the way that blind people smile when they think that they're approaching an unfamiliar obstacle.

Jim covered his face with his hands. He wasn't sure how much more of this he could take. But when he took his hands away Elvin was still there and he knew that he didn't have any choice but to open the door.

Elvin came shuffling into his apartment and stood staring at nothing at all.

"Hallo, Elvin," said Jim. The smell of decay was much stronger now and he thought that Elvin looked much worse. How long could Umber Jones's magic drag this poor mutilated body around, carrying his messages?

"Umber Jones wants you to go see Charles Gillespie again," said Elvin, his voice almost unintelligible. "He wants you to tell Umber Jones the same thing you told him the last time. If he still won't agree, he wants you to give him this."

He reached with a white, spongy hand into his suit and produced a chicken's wingbone tied with hair and feathers and coloured thread. It looked like a giant fishing-fly. Jim stared at it but he wouldn't touch it.

Elvin waited patiently for a moment and then laid it down on the table.

"Another voodoo curse, I suppose," said Jim.

"Another way to make Charles Gillespie see sense," Elvin replied.

He turned to go, but Jim sharply said, "Elvin!" and he stopped where he was, with his back turned. His hair was tufty with dried blood.

"Elvin – is there anything left inside you of what you used to be, before Umber Jones took control of you?"

There was an achingly long pause, and then Elvin said, "I don't understand the question."

"I just want to know if I'm talking to Elvin Clay, the real Elvin Clay, Mr and Mrs Clay's favourite boy, Elvira's brother; or whether I'm just talking to a lump of submissive meat."

"Umber Jones is my *houngan*. I do whatever Umber Jones asks me to do."

"I know you do, Elvin. But what I want to know is whether there's anything left of *you*. Any will-power. Any strength. Any mind of your own."

Elvin hesitated. Despite his revulsion, Jim put his hand on his shoulder. His flesh felt unnaturally soft beneath his suit. Jim could feel his putrescing muscles slide across his bones. Elvin bowed his head and the wounds around his neck opened up as if they were capable of speaking on their own.

Then he turned around, and his face – as hideously mutilated as it was – was filled with almost childish pleading. "Why doesn't he let me go, Mr Rook? Why doesn't he just let me die?"

"I don't know, Elvin. It seems like he needs you, the same way he needs me."

"Can't you just ask him to let me go? You don't

know what it's like, feeling yourself rot. It's like there's something gnawing inside of my guts, something that won't stop gnawing and gnawing, and I'm scared that it's maggots."

Jim swallowed, and then he managed to say, "Listen, Elvin . . . I'll do everything I can. I promise."

Elvin gave him a blind, pathetic nod. Then he turned around again and shuffled out of Jim's apartment. Jim watched him grope his way down the steps and out into the night. God alone knew where he was going, or where he stayed when Umber Jones wasn't sending him out on errands. Maybe the cemetery. Maybe some cellar. And what was going to happen to him when his body began to decompose so badly that he couldn't even walk?

He picked up the chicken-bone fetish. There was something indescribably nasty about it. It was dry and old but it had a strong, unpleasant smell that put him in mind of everything that had ever made him nauseous, from a lump of gristle to the stench of sewage. He didn't know what Chill would make of it, but it certainly frightened *him*.

He couldn't think of going back to sleep. He went into the kitchen and made himself a strong cup of coffee. He sat at the table, wearily staring at the fetish and wondering if he were ever going to be able to free himself from Umber Jones's service. He was still sitting there when he heard a sickening, regurgitating noise from the living-room. It sounded like somebody choking for breath on their deathbed.

Cautiously, he slid open the cutlery drawer and took out the largest knife he could find. Then he tiptoed out of the kitchen and stood outside the living-room door. The noise was repeated – a horrible gagging, cackling sound.

He said to himself: come on, you managed to face Elvin. You *touched* him, even. Whatever this is, this can't be worse.

He reached around the living-room door to find the light-switch. He counted to three, and then he simultaneously switched on the light and swung into the living-room with his knife held high, shouting, "*Right*!"

The feline formerly known as Tibbles looked up, startled. She had just vomited all of her supper on to the carpet. Jim stood and stared at her, his knife in his hand, and he was sorely tempted to use it. But then, well, it was his own fault for giving her jambalaya. He knew that chillis always made her sick.

He went back to the kitchen to find a bucket and a wet cloth. He had never felt so tired and dejected in his whole life.

When he came into class that morning he found his students all standing around or sitting on their desks, talking to each other. He dropped his folder with an emphatic slap, and then he said, "What's this? You've started a debating society? What's the motion for today? This house believes that all teenagers should tuck their shirts in?"

Russell Gloach came forward. He still had Twinkie filling around his mouth, and he wiped it away with the back of his hand. "No, sir. The motion is, what are we going to do about Tee Jay's Uncle Umber?"

Tee Jay was there, too, sitting at the back of the class. Jim approached him and said, "What do you think, Tee Jay? He's your uncle. What he's doing, it's all connected with your religion."

"He's gone too far," said Tee Jay. "I never knew that he was going to start wasting people."

"He's gone too far and you don't know how to stop him? You couldn't try appealing to his better nature?"

"Uncle Umber doesn't have a better nature."

Sharon said, "You can't expect Tee Jay to stand up to his uncle. He's going to get himself killed, same as Elvin."

David Littwin put in, "W-w-we've b-b. Been trying to find a w-w-way to g-get rid of him."

"Any ideas?" Jim asked them.

"We could go round to his apartment and beat the shit out of him," Mark suggested.

"What the hell good would that do?" said Ray Vito. "He hasn't done anything against the law, has he? Not that we can prove. We'll end up in the slammer ourselves, for assault and battery."

"We could wait till he leaves his body," said Titus Greenspan. "Then we could board up his front door so that he couldn't get back to it again."

Jim said, "That wouldn't work. In his smoke form, he can slide through any gap that smoke can get through."

Sharon said, "There's a voodoo ritual in one of my books. It's got all the words and everything. It's how to put a curse on somebody so that when their spirit goes out walking, it can't get back into its physical body."

"That could be useful," Jim told her. "But what we need more than anything else is Umber Jones's *loa* stick . . . the stick which he uses to call on the help of all of the lesser spirits. Without that stick, he has no power at all."

"Can't you lift it when your uncle's asleep?" Ricky asked Tee Jay.

Tee Jay shook his head. "If I could, I would. But I don't dare to touch it. It's like, sacred."

"Sacred or not, if it's the only way of stopping your uncle . . ."

"You don't understand," said Tee Jay. "It's *sacred*. It's carved out of a ghost oak which grew in a cemetery . . . a tree which was fed on dead bodies. The dead bodies belonged to Baron Samedi, and so the tree belongs to Baron Samedi – and that means that the *loa* stick belongs to Baron Samedi, too."

"Tee Jay," said Beattie. "Baron Samedi is one of those things that aren't real."

"A myth," said Seymour.

Tee Jay said, "Baron Samedi is as real as you and me, Beattie. And when I started to study voodoo, I gave my solemn oath that I would never disrespect his name or steal his property or defy his law. If I tried to take that *loa* stick away from my uncle, I would have the most powerful spirit in the whole damn Western world hunting me down. He'd have my ass. Let me tell you something, man: I'd be lucky to end up like Elvin."

There was hubbub of scepticism from the rest of the class. But Jim raised his hand for silence and said, "Listen – whatever the rest of us think about voodoo, Tee Jay's a believer and we can't ask him to compromise his beliefs. If he and his uncle were Muslims, we wouldn't expect him to disobey the will of Allah, even if it *was* a question of stopping a murderer. Plenty of people have found themselves in the same dilemma in the past, like Roman Catholic priests who hear confessions from serial killers. I think we can count ourselves fortunate that, whatever Tee Jay believes in, he's drawn the line here and said no more killing, and he's prepared to help us insofar as he doesn't commit a heresy."

Not many of his class knew what a 'heresy' was, but they got the gist. They also began to realise that Jim was making an effort to draw Tee Jay back into the family, and he was asking them not to isolate him.

Tee Jay had been attracted to voodoo because in spite of his popularity and his outward cool, he felt isolated and inferior. What was so good about being popular and cool if you were struggling to read *Green Eggs And Ham* in the remedial-teaching class of a trashy college like West Grove?

Sharon said, "Maybe Tee Jay can help us by telling us when his uncle's left his body . . . then we can go around and take the *loa* stick for ourselves."

"You won't be able to get in there," said Tee Jay. "When my uncle takes on The Smoke, he locks himself in good. He doesn't want nobody tampering with his body while he's away."

"Can't you let us in?"

"No way. He locks his room from the inside and he's also got this security bar. It would take a tank to get in there. Besides . . . that would be aiding and abetting you to steal the *loa* stick, and I'm pretty sure that Baron Samedi wouldn't take too kindly to that."

"I don't know why you ever wanted to start believing in a mean dude like Baron Samedi," said Muffy. "As if there aren't enough mean dudes in the world already."

Jim said, "If we can't physically break in and take the *loa* stick, then we'll have to break in another way. I don't know whether you're really ready for this, but since all of your lives are in danger, I think you're entitled to hear it." And as briefly and as matter-of-factly as he could, he told them what had happened to Mrs Vaizey, and all about Elvin, too.

When he had finished, the classroom was so silent that Dr Ehrlichman peered in through the window to make sure that they were still there. Jim walked up and down the aisles waiting to hear their reaction.

Jane Firman had tears in her eyes. "Is this really, really true?" she asked him.

Jim nodded.

Ricky said, "When that old woman swallowed herself . . . Jesus, you must have *barfed.*"

"I can't believe a word of it," said Rita. "This is just a test, isn't it? Just play-acting, to make us think about impossible things."

"Oh, yes?" said Jim. "And why would I want to do that?"

"To educate us, right? To stretch our imagination."

"Well, I wish it was," Jim told her. "Sharon, what do you think?"

Sharon was very subdued. "I've read about this thing of people being forced to eat themselves, yes. It's supposed to be a punishment for sticking your nose in where it's not wanted. Like treading on magic ground, or walking through a cemetery, or watching a *banda* without being invited."

"A *banda* . . . that's kind of a dance ritual to honour Baron Samedi," Tee Jay explained. "Most of the time it's pretty sexy. You know, people dancing with no clothes on."

"This eating thing, though," said Sharon. "I never knew it could really happen."

"Lots of things you don't know about," Tee Jay told her. "You keep talking about our roots and stuff . . . you don't even know the half of it."

Sharon was about to protest but Jim interrupted her. "That's why we need your help, Tee Jay. You know more about this than any of us. And even when you can't actively help, at least you can try not to obstruct us. It's the least you can do, considering what happened to Elvin."

Tee Jay flapped up his hands from his desk as if to indicate, "OK, everything's going to be cool."

Jim said, "What I propose to do is this: Tonight, if and when his Uncle Umber goes out in his Smoke form, Tee Jay can call me at home and tell me that he's gone. That's all I'm going to ask you to do, Tee Jay – nothing else – but it has to be you, because you're the only other person who can see him. As soon as I get Tee Jay's call, I'm going to try to leave my body, using the technique that Mrs Vaizey taught me. If I go immediately, there's a good chance that I can get to Uncle Umber's apartment and get hold of the *loa* stick before he returns from wherever he's been."

"What if he catches you?"

"Then I won't need to worry about dinner tonight, will I?"

Chapter Eleven

He parked a block away from Sly's and walked the rest of the way. The bullet-shaped doorman was even more hostile than he had been before. "You got your nerve, Charlie. If I was you, I'd be in Nome, Alaska, by now."

"What is this place?" Jim asked him. "The Nome, Alaska, tourist board?"

"Chill won't see you. Chill's not seeing nobody."

"Tell Chill I have something for him. A little gift from Umber Jones." Jim's heart was beating more violently than usual, but all the same there was something indescribably exciting about talking to hard men like these and knowing that he had the upper hand. For the first time in his life he understood why some men turned to crime. It was pure adrenaline. He loved the terse, euphemistic conversations that barely kept a lid on ruthless acts of violence – beatings, knee-cappings, killings. He loved the constant threat of saying the wrong thing; of showing disrespect, or weakness; or pushing his luck just a little too far.

It was almost as exciting as teaching, he thought, wryly.

The doorman talked in the phone and then he said, "Okay . . . you know where to go."

Jim went down the darkened staircase and the bouncer

frisked him and nodded him inside. The same pianist was playing selections from the Broadway musicals. The singer was gone. Jim crossed the floor through the red lights and the cigarette smoke and there was Chill sitting in his corner booth with a white turbanlike bandage on his head and both hands wrapped up like finger-puppets. He was flanked by three stone-faced minders in reflective sunglasses, one of whom kept looking at his watch as if he had an urgent appointment with the hairdresser who kept his pompadour from collapsing.

Chill said, "Sit down," and Jim sat.

There was a very long pause. Chill said, "Cigarette," and one of his minders tucked a cigarette between his lips and lit it. Chill blew out smoke then leaned back in his seat and said, at last, "This Umber Jones . . . I need to know some more."

"I'm sorry. There's nothing I can tell you. I just bring the messages."

"What I'm saying is . . . would he be interested in a little gentlemanly negotiation?"

"No."

Chill made a squeezed-up face as if he were constipated. "You see, the trouble here – the trouble we're facing here is – there's no way ninety per cent."

Jim said, "That's up to you. I think it's only fair to warn you, though, that if you don't agree to Umber Jones's terms, the consequences could be pretty apocalyptic. For you, anyway."

"Say what? Will you talk English?"

"What I'm saying, Mr Chill sir, is that you and your people had better do what Umber Jones wants you to do, otherwise you'll be in for a major-league ass-kicking."

"*Hey*!" objected one of Chill's minders, but Chill waved his finger-puppet fingers at him to keep quiet.

He leaned forward across the table and said, "So who, may I ask, is going to be giving me this major-league ass-kicking?"

Jim didn't blink. "The same people who set fire to your hair, I should imagine."

"You know who they are?" said Chill, fiercely. "Don't you think you better tell me?"

There was a moment of spring-tightening tension. Chill stared at Jim with his eyes wide and Jim stared back at him, calm and unblinking.

After a while, Jim took out the chicken-bone fetish and held it up. At first Chill didn't want to look at it but then he had to. His eyes flickered once, twice, and then he took his eyes away from Jim's and focused on the fetish with the kind of expression you would normally see on a man who has been told by his doctor that the lump on his neck is not just an ordinary lump but malignant lymphoma; and that he has less than six weeks to live.

His minders backed away – clumsy, but with obvious cowardice. They knew what the fetish was, too; and they didn't want to be too closely associated with a man who was marked for sudden death. One of them crossed himself. Another one spat and made a sign in the air. The third one shielded his eyes with his hand, so that he wouldn't even have to *look* at the fetish.

"Maybe there's some room for manoeuvre," said Chill, without much hope in his voice.

"No," said Jim.

"Hey, come on. I should meet this Umber Jones . . . maybe we can talk this whole thing out between us, man to man."

"No."

Chill flared up. "I'm trying to be reasonable here, you understand? I'm trying to make some concessions! But you have to be fair! This is my turf! I been operating here for fifteen years, man. Everybody knows the Chill. How is this Umber Jones character going to take over from me? He don't know jack."

"He doesn't have to. You're going to do all the work; and he's going to take his percentage. It's either that or more of what happened yesterday evening."

Chill banged his fist on the table and immediately regretted it: his fingers were still sore. "You can't prove to me that Umber Jones did that! There wasn't nobody there!"

Jim held up the voodoo fetish and shook it like a tiny maracas. "Oh, yes," he said. "There was somebody there. Just because you couldn't see them, that didn't mean that they weren't there. You've heard of The Smoke?"

Chill's face drained of blood, and his cheeks were almost as white as his hair. "The Smoke? Is this what you're talking about? The Smoke? That ain't possible, man. That's just a superstition."

"Oh, I see. Your minders were stabbed by a superstition, were they? Unusual way to die." He held out the fetish.

Chill couldn't take his eyes off it. It was clear that he was deeply frightened. "Take that away. I don't even want to *look* at that, man."

"It's a gift. Umber Jones is going to be seriously upset if you don't take it."

"*Take it away, you hear me*!" Chill screamed at him. "Tell him he can have what he wants! Ninety per cent, one hundred and ten per cent, whatever!"

Jim leaned forward, one hand cupped over his ear. "Did I hear that right?"

"Tell him he can have what he wants! Anything!"

Jim said nothing for a second or two, but then he

nodded, and said, "Okay. I'll tell him." He stood up and walked out of Sly's. When he passed by, everybody gave him plenty of space, staff and customers both, and even the pianist stopped playing.

He detested Umber Jones for all of his cruelty and his greed and his mumbo-jumbo, but at that moment he felt a huge surge of power. He understood why Tee Jay had felt so attracted by voodoo. It was like sex. It was like beating a man to the ground. It was liberation. It was winning. It was like having the gods on your side.

He was sitting at his kitchen table eating Chef Boy-ar-Dee Ravioli with heaps of freshly-grated parmesan cheese when the telephone rang. He lifted it off the wall and said, "Yes, what is it?"

"Mr Rook? This is Tee Jay. Uncle Umber just left the house."

"You're sure?"

"He locked himself into his room about twenty minutes ago. I kept a watch on the street and I saw his smoke-spirit heading west."

"You're sure about that?"

"Sure I'm sure. I saw him with my own eyes. Like he was floating across the street."

Jim looked at the kitchen clock. It was 22:47. The feline formerly known as Tibbles was sitting at his feet, enthusiastically licking her lips. "Listen," he said, "you'll hate ravioli. Remember what happened yesterday."

"What happened yesterday?" Tee Jay asked him.

"Forget it. I was talking to a friend of mine."

"Come on," said Tee Jay, "I don't know how long he's going to be away."

"All right," Jim told him. "But don't go counting on

anything. I never did this before, and I might not be able to do it now."

"You'll do it, Mr Rook, I'm sure of it," said Tee Jay.

Jim had already marked out a circle of ash beside the couch, with his own improvised signs for the sun and the moon and the wind. He lay down and propped a cushion under his head. He felt ridiculous, to say the least. But it had worked for Mrs Vaizey. There was no reason why it shouldn't work for him. Countless people left their physical bodies at night and wandered around the universe as smoke, or spirits, or summer draughts. There was no reason why he couldn't, too.

The feline formerly known as Tibbles watched him with narrow-eyed interest as he started to recite the words that Mrs Vaizey had taught him, as well as a few elaborations of his own. "Set my spirit free . . . let my spirit go . . . let my body sleep without it . . . let me travel where I will. Keep my body safe from evil . . . keep my body safe from darkness . . . let my spirit go . . . *let my spirit go . . .*"

He felt strangely light-headed, as if he had spent all evening in a bar, drinking one shot of whiskey after another. He looked up at the ceiling, at its waves of combed 1950s plaster, and thought, *Let my spirit go . . .* The plaster began to undulate, wave upon wave, and all the time he kept repeating to himself *let my spirit go . . .* The plaster was the sea, and the couch in which he was lying was his boat; and in his boat he rowed on waving waters, out of his present consciousness, out of his cagelike bones and his heavy, restrictive flesh; shedding the weight of his physical body; and literally rising, into the air.

He turned, as if he were swimming, and saw himself

lying on the couch, his eyes closed, his arms crossed over his chest. He approached himself and stared at himself in fear and fascination. His face looked oddly lopsided, not quite himself. Then he realised that he had never seen himself like this before, except in photographs. Most of the time he looked at himself in mirrors, in which his image was the other way around.

His cat seemed to be aware that something strange was happening, because her fur stood up, and she took three or four tentative steps away from him. She didn't look at him directly, though, which meant that cats couldn't see spirits any more than humans could.

The kitchen clock read 23:00 precisely, and he knew that he had to go. The last thing he wanted was for Umber Jones to come back and find him in his apartment.

He swam across the living-room and slid through the quarterlight, which was less than three inches open. The sensation of having no physical substance was exhilarating. Mrs Vaizey had been right: it was like suddenly shedding a heavy topcoat and finding yourself naked. He glided along the balcony, past Myrlin's apartment, and through the window he could see Myrlin peering intently at a small mirror and clipping the hairs out of his nostrils.

He carried on, down the steps and out of the apartment block, on to the street. He found that he could glide much faster than he could walk. In fact he only had to *think* that he wanted to reach the next intersection and he was almost there, like a camera-trick. He flowed through the streets of Venice, crossing streets and sliding along sidewalks. Sometimes he passed within inches of people out walking, but nobody saw him.

He knew that he could cross the street right in front of speeding vehicles without any risk of injury. The vehicles would simply pass through him, the same way that they had passed through Umber Jones's smoke. All the same, he didn't feel confident enough to chance it, and he waited at DON'T WALK signs, invisibly, like everybody else. On the corner of Mildred he was standing behind a man in a beret who was walking his poodle. The poodle could obviously sense that he was there, because it kept whining and pawing the sidewalk and anxiously looking all around it. "What's wrong, Sukie?" the man wanted to know. "You're acting like you seen a ghost."

At last Jim arrived outside Umber Jones's apartment. He rose as lightly as a tissue-paper kite until he reached the second-storey windows. In one window he could see Tee Jay, sitting on the couch watching television with the sound turned off. Every now and then Tee Jay checked his watch, and glanced toward the window. Jim's first reaction was to duck, but while Tee Jay's initiation into voodoo had made it possible for him to see The Smoke, he couldn't see Jim's spirit at all.

Jim floated along to Umber Jones's window. The drapes were partly drawn, and the room was lit with only two floating night-lights fashioned out of black wax. As he came closer, however, Jim could see Umber Jones's body lying on his bed. His face was dusted gray with ash and he was dressed in a dusty black frock-coat, complete with grey spats and black funeral shoes. His top-hat lay on the pillow beside him. In his left hand he held a chicken-bone fetish, much more elaborate than the one which he had sent to Chill, with beads and feathers and knots of fur. In his right hand he held a long cane of pale polished wood, topped with a silver skull.

The *loa* stick. As much a symbol of Umber Jones's dark authority as a bishop's crook or a king's sceptre.

Jim had been reading about *loa* sticks in Sharon's books – how they were passed from one voodoo practitioner to another, but never owned by any of them. They belonged to Baron Samedi, the lord of the cemeteries, and technically speaking they had to be returned on demand.

The window to Umber Jones's window was slightly ajar, and Jim poured through it like warm water. The air-conditioner in the bedroom had been switched off, and it was almost unbearably stuffy and hot, and the smell of incense was so strong that Jim felt as if he were suffocating. Strange, he thought, that he had no visible substance, yet he was still aware of the need to breathe. Even spirits have senses, he supposed.

He approached the bed and stood looking down at Umber Jones. Unnervingly, Umber Jones's eyes were wide open, with pupils as red as garnets. But his spirit was absent, somewhere in the night, and his eyes were sightless and unblinking.

Jim cautiously reached across his comatose body and took hold of the *loa* stick. He could feel it, but his hand passed right through it. He tried again, but again his fingers couldn't grasp it. It was exactly like trying to pick up an unwilling eel.

Then he remembered what Mrs Vaizey had told him: a spirit works by *will*, not by physical strength. A spirit's strength is in the purity of its essence, its ability to concentrate on what it wants, unhindered by flesh and blood.

Again he laid his hand on the *loa* stick, and this time he concentrated on its rising out of Umber Jones's grasp and coming with him. He stared at it harder and harder, willing it to do what he wanted. Gradually he could feel it taking on substance, smooth and hard and shiny. It still didn't feel like a real stick, at least it didn't to him: he felt that his fingers could pass right through it at any moment. But he kept on concentrating – *rise – rise – you damned stubborn piece of wood* – and inch by inch he was able to draw it out of Umber Jones's fingers.

If anybody else had been watching, they would have seen the *loa* stick sliding out of Umber Jones's hand as if by magic. They would have seen it rise into the air and float unsteadily toward the window. Jim didn't realise it, but he was using the same psychic energy that so-called poltergeists use, to fling plates and furniture around the room.

It took all of his concentration to keep a grip on the *loa* stick – or, rather, to will the *loa* stick to stay in his insubstantial hand. But once he had 'carried' it to the window, he would be able to drop it into the street below, and then all he would have to do would be to hide it close by. He could come back later in his physical form to retrieve it. He still wasn't certain what he was supposed to do with it – break it, or bury it or throw it in the ocean – and none of Sharon's books made any mention of how to deal with a stolen *loa* stick. He guessed that the best way of getting rid of it would be to burn it and scatter its ashes, the same way that he had disposed of Mrs Vaizey, God rest her.

He reached the window and manoeuvred the tip of the *loa* stick into the gap. He looked down at the sidewalk below to make sure that there was nobody around. He didn't want some passing stranger to pick up the stick and walk off with it, not knowing what it was.

As he was just about to drop it, however, he saw a dark flicker on the other side of the street. At first he thought it was nothing but the shadow from the awning of Amato's Deli. Then – to his alarm – he saw a tall black figure come striding out of the darkness, making its way directly toward the apartment's front door. Umber Jones, with his ashy face and his glistening red eyes.

He lost his concentration and the *loa* stick dropped on to the rush-mat carpeting. Panicking, he knelt down and tried to pick it up, but he was too worried about Umber Jones's smoke-spirit flowing up the stairs. He grabbed and grabbed, but his fingers went through the *loa* stick every time. From the next room, he heard voices – Tee Jay's and Umber Jones's – and he guessed that Tee Jay was trying to stall his uncle's smoke-spirit for as long as he could. But it was still no use. He couldn't even *feel* the *loa* stick now, let alone pick it up. He would just have to save himself now, before Umber Jones discovered that he was here and used the power of Ghede to make him eat himself – or punish him in some other horrible and painful way.

He was about to flow through the gap in the window when he felt a strong, calloused hand snatch at his shoulder. He was wrenched around and slapped three times across the face. The slaps were silent, but they were so hard that Jim felt as if his neck had been dislocated. He was gripped by the wrists and pulled up straight, so that he was face to face with the smoke-spirit of Umber Jones.

Umber Jones, to his surprise, was grinning.

"So . . . you found out how to leave your body and walk the way that spirits walk?" said Umber Jones. Jim tried to struggle free but Umber Jones was gripping him far too tightly. "What brought you here, to my house?" Umber Jones asked him. "Thought that you'd pay me a visit, did you? Thought that you'd be sociable?"

Jim twisted himself sideways but still Umber Jones kept an unrelenting hold on his wrists. He looked around the room – inspecting the cabinet crowded with voodoo bric-a-brac, at the tables with their charms and amulets and silver boxes. "You wouldn't have come here to *steal* something, would you, Mr Rook? I wouldn't believe that of you. I thought it was a teacher's duty to uphold our moral standards – set an example."

He gave a dry, thumping sniff. Then he said, "No . . . I don't think you came to steal anything, did you? I can't see anything missing." He was playing with Jim, taunting him. The moment he flowed into the room he must have seen that the *loa* stick was lying on the floor.

"Or . . . wait a minute, what's this?" he said, looking down by Jim's feet. "Isn't that my cane there, down on the floor? What do you think *that's* doing down there? I hope you weren't trying to make off with *that*, Jim, because that's a sacred cane. You can knock on any door with that cane and you've got the spirits with you, as many as you want. You've got Ghede and Ougon Ferraire. You've even got Vodun, if you dare."

Jim said, "You know damn well what I'm doing here. The killing has to stop."

Umber Jones tilted his head forward so that he and Jim were almost nose to nose. "The killing can never stop, Mr Rook. Not until everybody in this city pays their respects to Umber Jones. Not just their respects, neither. Their money, too, and anything else that might catch my eye."

"You're out of your mind."

"Maybe I am, Mr Rook. But you're something much, much worse. You're out of your body."

"You really think you can force every pimp and drug-dealer in Los Angeles to hand over ninety per cent of everything they make?"

"Think it? I *know* it. What did Chill say to you today? Don't tell me he's still holding out."

Jim said nothing. Umber Jones gave him a long, blood-coloured stare and then released his wrists. He leaned down and picked up his *loa* stick, sliding his hand down the length of it as if to reassure himself that it hadn't been bent or damaged. It was the *loa* stick that gave his smoke-spirit the ability to be able to intervene in the physical world – to pick up objects, to cut people, to stab them to death. He walked over to his body on the bed, opened up his own fingers, and returned the *loa* stick to its original position.

"I thought I could trust you," he said. "You don't know how much you've disappointed me. You've let your students down, too."

"Don't even think about touching my students."

Umber Jones came right up to him and towered over him. "You won't be able to stop me."

"Oh, I'll stop you. I'll find a way, believe me."

"And supposing I make you eat yourself, the way that I made your lady friend eat herself?"

Jim said, "You need me too badly. How are you going to talk to all of those drug dealers if you don't have me?"

"I can always find another friend."

"Maybe you can. But it isn't easy, finding friends, is it? Especially friends who are easy to blackmail, like me."

Umber Jones grinned at him. "You're right. But I think you need to be taught a lesson. I think you need to be given a little instruction in obedience and humility."

Jim didn't know what to say. He had never felt quite so frightened in his life. In his spirit form, outside his body, he felt naked and vulnerable, and as helpless in front of this smoke-black figure of spells and witchery as a newly-born child. He hadn't even known before Umber Jones had slapped him that spirits could even *feel* other spirits, let alone hurt them. Apart from what Mrs Vaizey had told him, and what he had read in Sharon's books and *National Geographic*, his knowledge of spirits had been limited to Jacob Marley and *Casper the Ghost*.

"What are you going to do?" he asked Umber Jones, tightly.

"You'll find out."

"You're just going to let me go?"

"As you said yourself, it isn't easy, finding friends."

"So what about this little instruction in obedience and humility?"

"You'll find out."

With that, he turned his back on Jim and went back over to the bed. He stood beside his physical body and laid his hand on its chest. He crossed himself and muttered a few incomprehensible words. His physical body began to breathe more and more deeply, its nostrils flaring, its ashy black coat-lapels rising and falling. Soon its breath was coming in huge agonised groans, like a man trapped in a submarine.

The black image of Umber Jones's smoke-spirit began to tremble. With every inward breath that his physical body took, it seemed to be pulled toward it. Then it started to fold in on itself, and become smokier and even less substantial. Right in front of Jim's eyes, Umber Jones's physical body *breathed in* his smoke-spirit, little by little, until there was nothing left beside the bed except a few dark wisps that floated and curled until they were breathed in, too.

Jim heard Umber Jones murmur something, and his fingers stirred like spiders disturbed by rain.

Now was the time to leave. Jim turned away, and flowed through the gap in the window, into the night, floating down toward the street with the lights of Venice sparkling all around him. He reached the sidewalk and looked back toward Umber Jones's bedroom window. Umber Jones was standing there, silhouetted by the dim, flickering candelight, watching him.

Jim started to make his way home, gliding from one street to the next. All he wanted now was to be back in his physical body before Umber Jones decided to teach him his lesson. It didn't look as if he was going to be forced to consume himself, thank God. But not knowing what punishment Umber Jones had in store for him was almost as chilling.

He reached his apartment block and flowed in through the window. He crossed the living-room, where the feline formerly known as Tibbles was sleeping on the floor beside the couch.

The couch itself, however, was empty. Jim's physical body had gone.

Chapter Twelve

He glided through to the bedroom. His body wasn't there, either. With rising panic, he glided through to the bathroom. The tub was empty. The shower-head dripped with its usual plangent *plink, plank, plink, plank.*

He went back to the living-room. He laid his hand on the couch but he couldn't feel any warmth. He could see, however, that the ash had been scuffed, as if somebody had stepped on it. His cat must have felt his presence, because she lifted her head and opened one eye.

What the hell was he going to do now? Was this Umber Jones's punishment, to take his physical body away and leave his spirit without anywhere to go? From what Mrs Vaizey had told him, a body and a spirit could only survive for a very limited time without each other. What if Umber Jones had taken his body away and hidden it, so that he would have to beg to have it returned?

But then again, what if his disappearance wasn't anything to do with Umber Jones? What if Myrlin had seen him lying in a coma and had him taken away by ambulance? How could he find his body then?

He circled the living-room again and again. Nobody could have seen him, but as he circled he disturbed the air. Ghosts and spirits are not completely undetectable. They raise and lower temperatures, they slow down clocks.

Their breath can always be faintly felt, or sometimes even seen, especially on a fogged-up windowpane.

He was still frantically circling when he heard a familiar tap at the living-room window. He couldn't open the door, so he flowed out through the fanlight and reassembled himself on the balcony outside. Elvin was standing by the railings, smiling at nothing at all. He was even more decomposed than he had been before. The wounds in his face were gaping open and they had started to suppurate – a thick, glistening pus that had dried around each stab-wound like the crusts around a jar of mayonnaise. Blowflies crawled in his eye-sockets, giving Jim the impression that his eyes were sparkling, and that he could see.

"I suppose you've come with another message?" said Jim.

Elvin opened and closed his mouth. His tongue was so swelled up that it was almost impossible for him to speak.

"You don't happen to know the whereabouts of my body, do you?" Jim demanded. "If this is Umber Jones's idea of a punishment, then you can tell him that I'm sorry; that I'll never touch his *loa* stick again and that I'll do whatever he wants me to do, in perpetuity, no argument. But he has to give me my body back."

"Earth to earth, ashes to ashes, dust to dust," whispered Elvin.

"What the hell are you talking about?"

A blowfly flew out of Elvin's eye-socket with a sharp, echoing buzz. "I've taken your body to the place where it belongs . . . the place where everybody's body belongs."

"What do you mean? The cemetery?"

Elvin nodded. "All bodies belong in the ground; yours as well as mine."

"My body's been *buried*? Is that what you're trying to tell me?"

"Boxed and buried, Mr Rook. But don't you worry. I said some comforting words over your grave."

Jim felt even more naked and transparent than ever. It had been wonderfully liberating, to leave his body, but now he was beginning to feel as if he had been sitting in a cold bath for far too long. If a spirit could shiver, he was shivering. He began to long for his body. He missed its warmth and its security, for all of its heaviness.

Elvin said, "Nobody will ever find you, Mr Rook. You'll have to wait for Umber Jones to dig you up again."

"And how long is that going to be?"

"A day. Two days. A month-and-a-half. Three months. Maybe never."

"But my body's not going to survive without my spirit."

"Don't worry, Mr Rook. I'm going to show you where you're buried, so that you can slip back into your skin."

"But even if I do that – how can I survive if I'm six feet under?"

"Goofer dust," said Elvin, with a smile. "I blew some goofer dust on you, while you were lying on the couch. You don't need to eat. You don't need to drink. You scarcely need to breathe. You're a zombie, Mr Rook. You'll survive for months."

Jim couldn't think of anything to say.

Elvin shuffled closer and he smelled so sickly that Jim would have retched if he had had a stomach to retch with. "Follow me," said Elvin. "It isn't far." He turned and made his way back along the balcony.

Jim hesitated for a moment, but Elvin turned around

and beckoned him. "Come on," he said. "We don't have much time. You want your body back, don't you?"

Reluctantly, Jim followed him down the steps. Instead of going out into the street, however, Elvin turned right down the narrow path to the back of the apartment block where the dumpsters were kept. The path was dark and wet from a dripping garden tap, and Elvin's feet dragged along the concrete in the same shambling gait that had characterised the zombies in *Dawn of the Dead*. God, thought Jim, talk about life imitating art, if *Dawn of the Dead* could be classified as art.

Elvin crossed the yard and then made his way through a tangle of weeds and bushes until he reached a triangular patch of waste ground between the rear of the garages and the cinderblock wall of the property next door. It was dark and shadowy here, but Jim could see that the dry, clumpy soil had been recently disturbed.

"My body's *here*?" he asked, with a feeling of dread.

"Can't you feel it, Mr Rook? Can't you sense your own flesh?"

"So what do I do now?"

"Do what spirits always do when they come back from walking about. Slide into your body, and rest."

Jim said, "Did Umber Jones *know* that I was going to leave my body tonight?"

"Umber Jones knows a lot of things, Mr Rook."

"But only my students knew what I was going to do. Nobody else. And *they* wouldn't have tipped him off."

"Well," said Elvin, "you'll have plenty of time to think about it." He wasn't being sarcastic. In some way, his thick, obstructed voice sounded almost sad, as if he desperately wished that *he* was lying in a coffin under the ground, able to rest his decaying limbs.

Jim wasn't sure what to do. He stood on the broken lumps of dug-up dirt and tried to feel where his body might be. Several minutes went by, with Elvin patiently watching him, and the night all around them busy with the sound of traffic. Then Jim became conscious of a warmth beneath his feet; a sense of wellbeing. His body was below him, he could feel it. He could almost see it in his mind's eye. He allowed himself to sink. He closed his eyes and tried to think of himself as nothing more substantial than warm water, soaking into the soil. As he sank lower and lower, he felt his spirit trickling between each individual grain, deeper and deeper. In only a few moments, he was embraced by complete darkness.

He reached the lid of his coffin. It was only a plain pine box, and he soaked through that, too, like wood stain. He flowed back into his body, into his brain. He drew on his hands like pulling on a pair of gloves. He filled out his lungs and his stomach and he stretched out his legs until he reached his toes. For a few seconds, the sense of relief was huge.

Only for a few seconds. The next thing he knew he was trapped in a dark, stifling box, his arms pinned beside him, unable to move. A wave of claustrophobia rolled over him, but he couldn't even scream. He was still paralysed by the goofer dust, his eyes wide open, his mouth wide open, but his facial muscles completely locked. Once, when he was playing football, he had dislocated his jaw, but this was a thousand times worse. He was gripped by such muscular rigidity that he couldn't even express his hysteria by panting or kicking or beating his fists. He thought he was going to die.

After a few minutes, however, he tried to persuade himself to calm down. It wasn't easy. The coffin was so tight that his nose was touching the underside of the lid. His brain was telling his heart to beat faster but his heart refused. He felt as if the frustration of being paralysed was going to explode inside him like a bomb. But then he kept trying to tell himself, *you're buried, you're paralysed, but you're not dead yet.* Stop panicking and start thinking, otherwise you'll never get out of here – not until Umber Jones deigns to dig you up, anyhow.

You know for a fact that people in Haiti have been known to survive in their coffins for several days after their 'funerals'. You can survive, too, if you try to keep your head straight. Your lungs refuse to breathe, but that's all for the best. You need to keep your metabolism down to an absolute minimum. No mental struggling, no hysteria. You practically have to flat-line.

It took him almost twenty minutes before he was able to calm himself completely. He kept having little spasms of claustrophobia which made him shudder spastically from head to foot. In the end, however, he managed to suppress his terror and to quieten his mind like a glassy pool of water. He would survive, he was sure of it. Umber Jones needed him too much to let him die. He was being punished, that was all, for trying to steal the *loa* stick. If he could accept his punishment calmly, then he would survive.

He tried to think of what he could do next. He could either lie here and wait for Umber Jones to exhume him, or else he could try to escape. The trouble was, his body was paralysed and his spirit was incapable of any greater physical activity than picking up a stick. He lay in total darkness, underneath the earth, unable to cry out, unable even to weep. He now knew what it was like to be a zombie; and why so many of them were so subservient when they were finally brought out of the ground. Either they were totally traumatised, or else they were so grateful for being rescued that they were prepared to do anything that their rescuer wanted them to do. There was nothing more terrifying, nothing more lonely, than lying alive in your own grave, waiting and hoping for the sound of a shovel.

Jim could have believed that God had forsaken him.

By ten-fifteen, Special Class II were beginning to become restless. Not in their usual way: shouting and throwing paper pellets and drumming on their desks. This time they were quiet and worried, talking to each other in low murmurs and occasionally going across to the window to see if Jim's car had appeared in the parking-lot.

Russell Gloach was eating out of a family-sized pack of nacho-flavoured tortillas. "You don't think something went wrong?" he asked. "Tee Jay's uncle sounds like one real mean dude."

Muffy looked at her watch. "Where is Tee Jay anyhow? He's just about the only person who can tell us what went down, and he's not even here."

"Something went wrong," said Russell, with tortilla crumbs dropping from his mouth. "You mark my words. Something went wrong."

"Will you stop being such a pessimist?" snapped Seymour. "Mr Rook could have been held up by anything. Traffic, who knows?"

"Did you ever know him to be late? He's never late."

"Maybe he found the stick and now he's trying to get rid of it."

"M-m-maybe w-we should c-call him at home."

"David, that's the best idea yet," said Sharon. "Does anybody know his number?"

"It's in his desk," said Ray.

"How do you know it's in his desk?"

"Because I *always* look through teachers' desks, just to see what they've confiscated. Believe me, if you want chewing gum, penknives or porno mags, there is *no* more reliable source than a teacher's desk."

They found Jim's number in the small leatherbound diary he always kept in his left-hand drawer. Sue-Robin took her mobile phone out of her Moschino bag and punched it out, noisily chewing gum as she did so. She blew a large pink bubble while she waited. The phone rang and rang but Jim didn't pick up. Eventually Sue-Robin said, "He's not answering. Something must have happened to him."

"So what do we do now?"

"Well, let's check with the office, just to make sure that he didn't come in today. Then – I don't know – maybe a couple of us ought to go round to Tee Jay's place. Maybe Tee Jay knows where he is."

Muffy went to see Sylvia, Dr Ehrlichman's secretary, but Sylvia hadn't seen Jim either. "Don't you worry, it's probably that old car of his. I'll have Dr Ehrlichman set you some work to be getting along with."

"Oh, no, no. Tell him not to bother. We've all got plenty to do."

She returned to the classroom. The rest of the students were waiting expectantly, but all she could do was to shake her head.

"That's it, then," said Sue-Robin, decisively. "Ray and Beattie, why don't you go to Tee Jay's house. Ask his mom where his uncle's place is, and then go see if you can find him."

"Do I have go with Ray?" asked Beattie, with distaste.

Ray blew her a smoochy Italianate kiss and said, "Sure you do. I'm the one with the fastest wheels."

"Fast cars are a pathetic penis-substitute," Beattie sniffed.

"Fast cars get you laid faster," Ray retaliated.

"Exactly."

They were still discussing what the rest of them should do when they heard a scratching, squeaking sound. They all fell silent and stared at each other. Then, as if they had been choreographed, they all turned their heads toward the chalkboard. A stick of chalk was hovering in the air in front of it, tapping at it again and again, like a deathly-white dragonfly.

"Oh my *God*," breathed Rita Munoz. "It must be Tee Jay's uncle again."

"Oh shit I hope not," said Seymour. "What the hell are we going to do if it is?"

The stick of chalk hesitated and then suddenly dropped to the floor, making them all jump. Then, very hesitantly, it rose up again, back up to the board. It looked as if it were being held by somebody invisible, somebody whose fingers couldn't grip properly.

"Hey, look," said John Ng. "It's making some marks. It's writing something."

With excruciating slowness, the chalk made a single vertical line. Then it moved sideways a little, and drew what looked like an Indian tepee. Then two Indian tepees.

I A AA.

"What's that supposed to mean?" frowned Titus. But then the chalk moved sideways again and wrote what looked like an 8.

"I don't get this," said Ricky. "I mean if this is like spirit communication, he'd be better off giving us one knock for certainly and two knocks for whatever."

"How do you know it's a he?" Beattie demanded.

"Well . . . it could be a woman, I admit. The message is stupid enough."

Now, however, the chalk had moved again. This time it wrote a U, and then an R, and then another vertical stroke. Whoever the writer was, he seemed to be gaining in confidence and strength as it went on. I A AA 8URIED.

"I am buried," Titus interpreted. "That's what it says. I am buried."

It went on, growing defter all the time. The class watched it, spellbound. *I am buried in back of garages at my home. Bring shovels. Jim.*

After the word *Jim* the chalk stick dropped on to the floor again, and broke. The class remained silent for a moment, then they all broke out into whoops and screams and applause. He was *here* – Jim Rook's spirit was actually here.

Sherma shushed everybody for silence, and then she went up to the front of the class, looking this way and that. "Mr Rook . . . we know you're here. That was wonderful. That was one of the most moving experiences of my entire life."

"Hey, forget about the speeches," said Ricky. "Let's go dig him up."

They all crowded toward the door, just as Dr Ehrlichman appeared with a large folder of work under his arm. They stopped, and shuffled, and coughed. Dr Ehrlichman stared at them in bewilderment, and said, "It's another half-hour before recess. Where are you all going?"

"Field trip, sir," said Russell.

"*Field* trip? I don't know anything about any field trip.

Besides, you can't possibly go on a field trip without Mr Rook."

"Oh, we're meeting Mr Rook by the beach. We have to experience the beach and then write some poems about it. You know, the little dancing waves and all that stuff."

"Yeah and the babes in their bikinis," put in Mark, cupping his hands in front of his chest, and then went "*unh*!" when Russell punched him in the back.

Dr Ehrlichman said, "I'm sorry. I haven't given Mr Rook authorisation for any field trip. Until I can discuss this matter with him in person, you'll have to consider it cancelled." He sniffed. "I've brought you some basic maths papers so that you can keep yourselves amused for the next half-hour."

"Amused?" groaned Greg. Maths, to him, was about as understandable as Sanskrit. He would labour for hours over his maths papers, only to produce answer after answer that his maths teacher said were not only wrong, but *creatively* wrong.

"We can't leave Mr Rook waiting on the beach," said Ray. "He'll be wondering what the hell happened to us."

"All right . . . in that case you and John here go to the beach and advise him of the change of plan. Be as quick as you possibly can. The rest of you . . . please sit down, and I'll hand out your papers."

There were more groans and hoots and suppressed Bronx cheers, and the class shuffled unwillingly back to their desks. From the doorway, Ray made a circle between finger and thumb, and then gave Dr Ehrlichman the finger. Behind his back, of course. He was disrespectful but he wasn't suicidal.

It took them a while to find the scrubby patch of ground

behind the garages, but when they did they knew that they had come to the right place. The soil was heaped up in big dry lumps, and the shape of a grave was unmistakable.

They had unofficially borrowed two long-handled shovels from the janitor's toolstore, but they didn't start digging right away. They stood beside the mound of soil and looked at each other uncomfortably. Back in the classroom, it had seemed like a really cool adventure, digging Mr Rook up out of the ground. But now they were actually here, standing by his grave, they were filled with trepidation. Supposing they dug him up and he was dead? Supposing he wasn't dead, but horribly mutilated? Supposing it was all a mistake and it wasn't him at all? What would they say to the police then? "Like a spirit message appeared on our chalkboard at college and told us to dig up this body."

Ray said, "Maybe we shouldn't be doing this, man."

John doubtfully prodded the soil with the tip of his shovel. "What if he's down there, and he's still alive? We can't just leave him here."

Ray bit his thumbnail. "I don't see how he *can* be alive, do you?"

"He could be. This is voodoo . . . and those voodoo guys, they can keep people alive even when they're buried."

"I don't know, man. Maybe we should call the cops instead. Like an anonymous tip-off."

John thought for a while longer. Then he reached inside his shirt and took out his necklet. He held it up to the sun and it sparkled sharply, as bright as a diamond. "I think it's going to be okay," he said. "This place has a really positive aura. There's nothing evil here . . . and nothing dead, either."

Ray said, "I'm supposed to believe some stone?"

"You saw how dark it went, when Tee Jay's uncle came into the classroom. I trust it, even if you don't."

"Okay, then, let's get digging."

Underneath them, tightly enclosed in his dark pine box, Jim heard the first chipping noises of their shovels and thought *thank God*. He was feeling exhausted, as if he had run a full Olympic marathon. It had taken all of his strength for his spirit to leave his body this morning and soak back up through the soil. He had been capable only of gliding very slowly through the streets and he had almost given up before he was even half-way to West Grove college. He had stopped underneath the freeway, feeling as if the morning breeze could simply blow him away, in transparent rags and tatters, over the ocean and into oblivion.

He had managed to summon the will-power to write his message on the chalkboard by thinking of Umber Jones, and what he had done to Elvin and to Mrs Vaizey and to *him*, too. His rage had driven him. But after that he had been close to collapse, and he could hardly remember how his spirit had managed to drag itself back to his apartment block and sink back into the soil.

The chipping noises went on and on. Now that he was so close to being released he began to experience a rising surge of black claustrophobia. He wanted to beat on the lid of his coffin. He wanted to scream out that he was here. What if they stopped digging and went away? What if it wasn't one of his students at all? What if he was dug up by some complete stranger, who thought he was dead?

What if it were Elvin, or Umber Jones?

The shovels knocked against the coffin-lid. Then he heard scraping noises as the soil was cleared away, and the muffled sound of voices. After a few more minutes the tip of a shovel was forced underneath the lid. With a sharp creak, the lid was pried off. His face was showered in soil and his eyes were assaulted with dazzling sunlight.

Ray and John, God bless them. They were kneeling down beside him now, peering at him wide-eyed. He had never realised before that Ray was trying to grow a moustache.

"Is he dead?" said Ray. "He sure *looks* dead."

John took out his necklet again. He cautiously pressed it against Jim's forehead and held it there for a while. Then he held it up and inspected it. "Clear," he said. "He looks like dead but he's still alive. Let's get him out of here before anybody sees us."

Lifting Jim out of his coffin was a struggle that was almost comical. His muscles were so rigid that his elbows wouldn't bend, so they couldn't sling his arms around their shoulders and carry him between them. Instead they had to lever him bodily out of the coffin and carry him as if he were a cigar-store Indian. Gasping with effort, they carried him round to the front of the garages where Ray had parked his Caprice. They slid him on to the back seat – and while John went to recover the shovels, Ray looked through his pockets. Billfold, college timetable, keys. He found it deeply disconcerting, the way that Jim was staring at him with those bloodshot, unblinking eyes. But he patted him on the shoulder and said, "Don't you worry, Mr Rook. We dug you up. Now we're going to fix you up."

John came back and threw the shovels into the trunk. "Where now?" he wanted to know.

"I think we'd better take him back to his own apartment; that'll be best. Then we can call the rest of the class and decide what we're going to do next."

John looked into the car, where Jim was lying stiffly across the back seat. "Do you think he can hear us?"

"I don't know. For Christ's sake, I don't even know if he's going to survive. But we have to do the best we can, right? He tried to take care of us. Now it's our turn to take care of him."

Between them, they managed to carry Jim up the steps to the balcony and drag him along to his apartment door, his shoes scraping along the concrete. They opened the door and manhandled him inside. The feline formerly known as Tibbles came mewling around their ankles as they carried him over to the couch. They laid him down flat on his back and John leaned over him and pressed his ear to his chest. "I was right. He's alive. You can just hear his heart beating."

"So what do we do now?"

"Let him rest, I guess. Whatever they've given him, it has to wear off sooner or later."

With the tips of his fingers, Ray did his best to close Jim's eyelids. He managed to shut the right eye, but the left one remained open, watching them both accusingly from under a drooping lid. At least it *looked* accusing, but in fact he was willing them to understand that he was still conscious, that he was still very much alive.

More than anything else, he was willing them to call their classmates – especially Sharon, with her knowledge of African culture and African spells. He was locked in this unrelenting physical paralysis, but he knew that there had to be a way of breaking it. After all, what did the voodoo sorcerers do, when they had to bring their zombies back to life? It was a chemical spell and there had to be a chemical antidote, even if it was made out of ground-up skulls and spiderwebs and the bitten-off heads of sacrificial chickens.

Ray said, "I'm going to call the rest of the guys, okay? We have to have a group discussion, do you know what I mean? Mr Rook isn't just *our* teacher, yours and mine. He's everybody's teacher." He paused, and then he said, "Besides, I don't know what the hell to do, do you?"

He picked up the phone and dialled West Grove Community College. "Hallo?" he said, dropping his voice an octave. "May I speak to Sue-Robin Caufield, please? It's her father. Yes, I'm afraid it's urgent. Her grandmother's suffered a very serious heart attack. Yes. She may not live the night."

While he did so, John sat down on the edge of the couch and looked at Jim with a mixture of mystification and sympathy. "Mr Rook, sir? Can you hear what I'm saying? Can you talk at all? Can you tell me how you feel?"

Jim stared at him one-eyed. He could see him and he could hear him, but he couldn't say a word because his tongue felt as if it were carved out of balsa wood and his cheek-muscles were clenched tight. He wanted his lips to move; he wanted so much to say something, but his nervous system had literally forgotten how to speak.

"We're calling the whole class together," John told him. "We're going to find Tee Jay's uncle and we're going to teach him a lesson if it's the last thing we do."

Jim lay there, rigid, one eye open and one eye closed. All he could do was wait for Umber Jones's goofer dust to wear off, or for somebody to bring him something to counteract it. If Elvin had been telling him the truth, it was quite possible that the effects would last for days, or even weeks.

Ray hung up, and came back over. He took hold of Jim's shoulder and gripped it tight. "If you can hear me, Mr Rook, everything's going to be okay. The whole class is coming over. We're going to see that Umber Jones doesn't get away with nothing no more. Nobody buries *our* teacher; *nobody*."

He picked up the feline formerly known as Tibbles and stroked his head. Jim watched him and didn't move. All of a sudden, however, Ray said, "Shit. That's it. I understand it now."

"What?" asked John.

"I understand it. *Why he stroked the cats*. In the poem, you know. Because the whole world was falling apart, all around him, and stroking the cats was like reality. You stroke a cat and it doesn't give you nothing back, so why do you enjoy it? Because people give something for nothing, sometimes; and they enjoy it."

John Ng looked very solemn. "If you say so, Ray."

The sunlight was shining through the cotton blinds, and it gave Jim's face a terrible radiance, as if he were closer to the angels than he was to earth. Inside his mind, however, he was beginning to feel a coming-together, a new sense of relaxation. He managed to open both of his eyes, and he could feel the sides of his mouth flexing a little, like a ventriloquist's dummy. He still couldn't speak and his arms and legs were still totally paralysed, but he knew now that he wasn't going to die.

He tried to say, "Thank you," and it came out as "mah-hoo". But that didn't matter. He was rapidly coming out of his paralysis. He was out of his coffin. He was back at home, with people who cared whether he lived or died, and that was one of the best curatives of all. "Mah-hoo," he repeated.

John looked up at Ray with a serious face. "What's he saying, for Christ's sake?" Ray asked him.

"He's saying 'mah-hoo'."

"Oh. Right. 'Mah-hoo'," said Ray, and knelt down beside the couch. He wiggled his fingers and said, "Hallo, Mr Rook! Can you hear me? Mah-hoo, Mr Rook! Mah-hoo!"

Chapter Thirteen

The rest of the class arrived within twenty minutes. "We didn't ask no permission," said Muffy, with bright-eyed bravado. "We just walked right out of the door. Didn't nobody ask where we was going. Didn't nobody try to stop us, neither."

"It was cool," said Russell. "We came down here in a convoy, right. Six cars and a pick-up, nose-to-tail. Cool."

They gathered round the couch where Jim was lying, and he looked up and saw all of their faces. The slow, the dyslexic, the fat, the disturbed. The children who would never be bright. The children who would never be glamorous. They were rebellious, most of the time. They bullied more successful students, and they caused disruption everywhere they went. Special Class II had always been a synonym for educational mayhem. But Jim had learned that if he showed his students that he cared about everything they tried to do, no matter how crass or clumsy it might seem to a non-remedial teacher, then his students cared, too. They couldn't spell, they couldn't add up, they couldn't draw a dog without making it look like a trash compactor. But Jim encouraged every one of their efforts – "Come on, let's not call this 'Fido'. Let's call it . . . trash compactor." In return, they were here, when he was paralysed, trying to get him back on his feet.

"Mr Rook?" said Sue-Robin, leaning over him so far that all he could see was her wide blue eyes and her warm, Babe-scented cleavage. "Are you still alive, Mr Rook?"

"Meathin," said Jim, between clenched teeth. He was trying to say "breathing", but it didn't matter. He must have been breathing to have spoken at all.

Sharon X was in the kitchen, furiously leafing through the books that she had lent him. "Here—" she said at last, lifting her hand.

"What?" said Ricky.

"It's here . . . the stuff they use to bring you back to life. It's called vive mixture."

"They got a recipe for it?" asked Russell.

"Well, it's kind of vague," said Sharon. "Something called blood root and something called betony, mixed with chicken's blood and celery."

"Sounds delicious," said Titus. "Where are you going to find that?"

"There's one of those occult herb stores two blocks down," said Muffy. "My aunt Hilda used to go there for musk oil and myrtle wood. She used to make this little fire every morning to bless her day."

"Right," said Russell, "I'll take Sharon down there right now. The rest of you . . . see what you can do to wake him up. He's starting to talk, right? Maybe you can get him to move."

Jim still lay rigid on the couch. His face was as white as a papier-mâché mask, and his eyes were circled in red. His whole system was gripped by tetrodotoxin – 160,000 times stronger than cocaine. He still had a chance of revival. In the 1880s, a Japanese gambler had been poisoned with tetrodotoxin after eating *fugu* fish and recovered in a mortuary over a week after he was declared dead. But Jim had been poisoned with *datura*, too, and *bufo marinus*. He was a classic zombie – pale, rigid and unmoving – waiting to give his gratitude to anybody who brought him back to life.

Sue-Robin stroked his forehead. "Don't you worry, Mr Rook. You're going to be fine. You're going to be back in that classroom boring our asses off with all of that poetry before you know it."

Jim's eyes flickered. He looked up at Sue-Robin's smile and thought that if any one remark could be guaranteed to bring him back to life, that was it. Sue-Robin had sat at the back of the class, dewy-eyed, while he read out *Wild Peaches* by Elinor Wylie. It had bored her ass off, had it? He wouldn't read any more poetry. She could sit in class reading *Igrat, Hell's Assassin* comics, for all he cared.

He didn't know how much time went by before Sharon returned. He saw her in the kitchen under the strong fluorescent light, her hair decorated with beads, pulping up roots and powders with the pestle-and-mortar that he usually used for crushing mustard seeds. He slept with his eyes open. He heard voices moving to and fro. The feline formerly known as Tibbles jumped on the couch next to him and purred loudly in his ear; more of a death-rattle than a purr.

Then his head was lifted by Sharon's hand and something bitter-sweet and liquid was being poured between his lips. He could feel it running down his neck and into his collar, but he didn't care. He lay back and closed his eyes. He didn't even realise how significant it was, the fact that he could close his eyes.

He slept – and as he slept, his toes relaxed, and his legs shifted sideways; and suddenly he lifted one arm and flung it across his chest. The class sat around and watched him, not saying much; passing round the beer they had found in his icebox. Sharon stood a little way away from the rest of them, very quiet, because she knew what a risk she had taken, giving Jim the the vive potion. Betony and bloodroot could have killed him, instead of bringing him back to life. Bloodroot was so dangerous that mystics always labeled it under a false name. If betony leaves were placed in a ring they were supposed to keep out all evil spirits, but betony taken as a drink could cause death by vomiting.

Hours went by. The class watched television, smoked, and read all of Jim's copies of *Playboy*.

"No wonder he's one of the those men who looks down on women," said Beatrice.

"Oh, come on," said David Littwin, "j-just b-because you d-don't have b-b-big enough t-t-t . . ."

Myrlin peered into the window to see what was going on and eighteen pairs of eyes stared back at him. He retreated into his apartment and pulled down the blinds.

David Littwin said, "Tits," and everybody turned and stared at him.

At three o'clock in the afternoon, Jim slowly sat up. "My God," he said, pressing the heels of his hands against his forehead.

"What is it?" said Sue-Robin, hurrying over to the couch and busily parking her bottom next to his.

"I'm fine," Jim told her. "I feel like I've been drinking all night, that's all." He reached around and kneaded the back of his neck. Then he stretched and tried to stand up, but he couldn't quite make it. He looked around at Special Class II and he couldn't help smiling in pride. "You made it, then. You saved me."

They all nodded wildly. "Ray and John dug you up, but we all saw the message."

Jim looked around. He still felt stiff, and oddly detached, but Sharon's elixir had definitely broken the grip of his paralysis. "I messed up," he admitted. "I managed to get out of my body and float down to Umber Jones's house, but it took me far too long to pick up the *loa* stick. I mean, when you're a spirit you don't have any hands, not in the physical sense. You have to *will* that thing into your fingers, otherwise it won't come. Same as that stick of chalk. Did you ever see that film *Ghost*, with Patrick Swayze, when he was trying to pick things up? That was exactly the same. I could only write with that stick of chalk by willpower. Nothing to do with muscular strength.

"But the trouble was, while I was trying to steal Umber Jones's *loa* stick, Umber Jones was taking my physical body right off this couch and burying me. With Elvin's assistance, of course. When I tried to come back to my body, it wasn't there."

"Hey, man, that must of freaked you out," said Ricky.

"You're right, it did. But Elvin showed me where my body was buried, and I was able to slide right back into it. Don't ask me how I did it. I just kind of soaked right into the ground. Mrs Vaizey told me that if I managed to leave my body just once, I'd always want to do it again. But after today . . . let me tell you something, no way."

"So you didn't get the *loa* stick?" said Sharon.

Jim shook his head. "We're going to have to work out another way." He looked at his watch, and said, "I'm going to have to grab some zees. If you guys want to stay here, you're welcome. Order some pizza or something. Then we'll talk about what we're going to do next."

A little after six, when they were all drinking mugs of coffee and talking about spooky encounters, Jim walked into the living-room and gave them a quick, short hand-clap to catch their attention. He had showered and changed. His hair was still wet and he was wearing his pink checkered shirt and his owlish Armani glasses. "Okay . . . I think that I'm pretty much recovered. I'm a little stiff – but then, who wouldn't be, after their own funeral? I had some dreams, but that was all. Nothing too frightening, unless you count a sexy dream about Dr Ehrlichman. Next time you see him, don't mention black stockings and garter belts, okay?"

The class laughed, but they were aware of Jim's tension, as well as his tiredness.

Much more quietly, he said, "We're dealing with some serious voodoo here. No point in trying to be sceptical. Umber Jones has *amazing* supernatural powers. He can use his *loa* stick to call on any one of two hundred different spirits. He can walk through the streets like smoke and he can kill people without them seeing who did it.

"I've been thinking about the way that he caught me last night. To begin with, I couldn't understand how he knew that I was going to be out of my body. But when I was buried in that coffin, I had plenty of time to chew it over, you know, with all of the benefit of total silence and total darkness. It's really incredible how clearly your mind can work, when you don't have any external stimuli to distract you. No airplanes passing overhead. No hookers bouncing the bedsprings in the room upstairs."

Again, the class laughed – not because he was funny, but simply because they were relieved to have somebody back in control. A class lost all of its cohesion without a teacher, no matter how laidback that teacher might be.

"Okay, informal registration," said Jim. "Is everybody here?"

"Everybody excepting for Tee Jay," said Seymour.

"Well, that's what I expected," Jim told him.

"You expected it? Why?"

Jim said, "Think about it. You all knew that I was thinking of leaving my body yesterday evening and trying to break into Umber Jones's apartment – but I was only going to do it if his smoke-spirit was out walking somewhere else. Only Tee Jay knew that his uncle had done it, and, when. So only Tee Jay knew exactly when *I* was going to leave my body to come looking for the *loa* stick. He sent Elvin here to bury my body, and that was that."

"It was a trap," said Sharon.

"That's right," Jim nodded. "It was a trap. I wanted to believe that Tee Jay wasn't totally dominated by Umber Jones. I wanted to believe that all of his interest in voodoo was a teenage fad; that one day soon, he'd get over it. But he knew what he was doing when he called me last night . . . and as much as I hate to say it, I think he knew what he was doing when Elvin was killed. It was nothing to do with a fight in the washroom. He was making a human sacrifice to Vodun."

"Jesus," said Mark.

"It says in Sharon's book that making a human sacrifice is the quickest way to have yourself accepted as a voodoo convert."

"All the same. Jesus."

"So what are we going to do now?" asked Titus, blinking behind his glasses.

"If you're willing, we'll tackle this problem together. I realised today that I can't handle it all on my own. I need my class to help me."

They glanced at each other. Jane said, "Not me. Not if it means looking for ghosts."

"Hey, come on, you can count me in," said Russell.

"Me too," said Mark.

David Littwin raised his hand and said, "You c-c-c. Can. C-c-c."

"Thanks, David," said Jim. He didn't want to be unkind, but he didn't have all night.

All but two of them wanted to join in. Jane was shy and badly dyslexic; Greg Lake had to be home early because his grandparents were visiting. Jim knew that Greg's parents were very severe: that accounted for his facial grimaces. He didn't want to give Greg any more stress in his life than he could handle.

In the end, he lifted one hand for silence, and said, "We're going to have to deal with Umber Jones on two fronts. The next time he leaves his body, a bunch of us will have to follow his smoke-spirit and keep it busy while two or three others break into his apartment and take his *loa* stick. They should also recite the chant that stops a smoke-spirit from re-entering his physical body. He won't have a *loa* stick, to call on the *loa* to help him. He won't be able to return to his body. After a while he'll simply fade away, like everybody else fades away, when they die.

"I think it would be a good idea if the group that's following the smoke-spirit is divided into two smaller groups. I can go with one group, because I can actually see him. The other group can take Mrs Vaizey's ghost-dust. If you suspect that he's anywhere near you, you can throw some dust and it should show him up.

"We have three mobile telephones between us, don't we? That's okay . . . we can all keep in touch."

"What about Tee Jay?" asked Sharon. "The way he's been talking about voodoo, he could be pretty powerful, too."

"Well, for one thing, we don't know where he is, do we? And for another thing, I may be wrong about the sacrifice, and he may not have tipped off Umber Jones that I was leaving my body. He's still our classmate, until we can prove him otherwise. Let's cross that bridge when we come to it."

They staked out Umber Jones's apartment from eight o'clock onwards. In Ray's car sat Ray and Sharon and David Littwin. In Jim's car, a few spaces behind them, sat John Ng and Beattie McCordic and Muffy Brown. Across the street, facing in the opposite direction, was Russell's Mustang Mk II, with Sue-Robin Caufield and Seymour Williams. Russell had the coffee-mug filled with ghost-dust, on strict instructions that he wasn't to eat it.

In Ray's car they all ate Big Macs with their mouths open and noisily drank strawberry milkshakes. Sharon had brought her book of voodoo ritual so that she could say the words that would prevent Umber Jones's smoke-spirit from returning to his body. They were written in a very old African language and she could barely pronounce them. She kept repeating them over and over again, until Ray said, "For Christ's sake, Sharon. You sound like you're bubbling in your bathwater."

Babai babatai m'balatai . . . hathaba m'fatha babatai . . .

Jim felt exhausted but he was determined to see this through. He sat slouched down in his seat, wearing Ray-Bans and a green West Grove baseball cap in case Umber Jones recognised him from across the street. He probably wouldn't – especially since he must still believe that Jim was six feet under, in a tight pine box, suffering a well-deserved punishment for trying to steal his *loa* stick. All the same, Jim didn't underestimate Umber Jones's cunning; nor Tee Jay's either, if Tee Jay really *had* betrayed him.

Over an hour went by and Jim was beginning to think that he ought to call it a night. He got all of his students to call their parents to tell them that they were working late on an English project, and to hold supper for them. Beattie McCordic wouldn't eat pizza or hamburgers, and much to her embarrassment her stomach began to gurgle, although John kept saying, "It's quite all right. Even your stomach has the right to express itself."

"Spare me," said Beattie.

At that moment, without any warning, the front door of Umber Jones's apartments was flung open and out strode a tall, dark man wearing a wide-brimmed Elmer Gantry hat. It certainly *looked* like Umber Jones, but was it? "You see him?" he asked Beattie. "Just across the street there . . . passing the telephone booth . . . passing the trash bin."

Beattie frowned across the street. "I don't see anybody. There's nobody there."

"Good – that's definitely him, then," said Jim. "If you could have seen him, he might have been a decoy. Let's go." Beattie gunned the engine and swerved away from the curb. Jim said, "Not too fast. He's just passing that grocery store. That's it. We don't want to get too close, just in case he gets the idea that we're following him.

He won't be too alert, though. He doesn't realise that anybody can see him."

Umber Jones reached the end of the block and crossed over without even looking at the passing traffic. A truck passed less than three inches away from him, and his smoke whirled up, but he didn't even flinch.

"Keep going, keep going, left a bit," said Jim. "He's still headed in the same direction, but I think he may take a right at Colonial."

Beattie was driving so that Jim could concentrate on their pursuit. He was an edgy passenger, but he knew that he might have to jump out at any moment and follow Umber Jones's smoke-spirit into a house or a store or a restaurant. He wanted to have a 'getaway' car ready, too, in case anything went seriously wrong. He didn't have a gun – not that a gun would have had any effect against a smoke-spirit – and he had already seen from his dealings with Umber Jones that running away was the better part of valour.

"Right," said Jim. "He's definitely turning right." He dialled Sue-Robin's number. "We're following him north-westward on Colonial. Why don't you meet up with us at Colonial and Warren?"

"Where do you think he's going?" asked John.

"I don't know . . . but wherever it is, he'll be causing mischief."

The Smoke turned left and then right again, along a street of shuttered stores and cheap hotels. Outside the Glencoe Hotel two men were talking to a girl with fluffed-up hair and a short sequin mini-dress. One of the men was dressed in a white suit and built like an oak front door. The other was thinner, with greased-back hair and sunglasses. The thin one was remonstrating with the girl about something, because he kept jabbing his finger at her and every now and then he would make a slapping gesture in the air as if he was angry enough to hit her.

"Oh God," said Jim. "Here we go again."

The Smoke-figure came sweeping down the street and as it came nearer and nearer to the hotel entrance it appeared to swell in size, until it was even larger than Mr Oak Front Door. Jim didn't see its hand twisting, but the streetlight caught the flash of its knife.

This time, he couldn't let it happen without saying a word – whether the men deserved what The Smoke intended to do to them or not. He put down the car window and shouted out, "Hey! Look out behind you!"

Immediately, the thin man in sunglasses dodged behind the girl. Chivalrous, thought Jim. Mr Oak Front Door swung around with his fist half-raised just as The Smoke glided into him and stabbed him in the side of the belly.

"What's happening?" shrieked Beattie. "Look at that man!"

Blood spattered all over Mr Oak Front Door's suit as Umber Jones stabbed him again and again. Nobody except Jim could see The Smoke. All they could see was a heavily-built man performing a jerky dance on the sidewalk, while his coat was covered in one bright red splash after another. He made one more stumbling step and then he fell face-first on to the concrete.

Umber Jones turned toward Jim's car with a hideously frightening expression on his face. His eyes burned and his cheeks were powdered with ash. For a moment Jim thought that he was going to come rushing over to attack them. His bloody knife was lifted and he even took two or three steps across the sidewalk. Then, suddenly, he stopped. Jim could almost hear him thinking aloud. If Jim had escaped from his coffin and was following him with some of his students – what were the other students doing?

He bared his teeth and screamed, "Curse you, Mr Rook! I'll kill you for this!" and he turned and went rushing back the way he had come.

"Follow him!" Jim shouted, forgetting that Beattie couldn't see him.

"Which way? Which way?"

"Back that way! Quick! He's headed back to his own apartment!"

Police sirens began to wail in the distance as Beattie performed a jerky, bouncing seven-point turn in the middle of the street. Jim picked up his mobile phone again and punched out Sue-Robin's number. There was a long burst of crackling static, but then he heard her saying, "Yes? Yes? I can't hear you, Mr Rook!"

"Can you hear me now? Good! Then head right back to Umber Jones's apartment, and step on it!"

Next he tried Ray's number, but he couldn't make any contact at all.

"Can you still see him?" Beattie asked desperately.

"It doesn't matter – he's seen us now. Just get back to his apartment as fast as you can. I'm trying to raise Ray but I can't get through."

Ray, Sharon and David were round at the back of the Dollars&Sense store, gingerly picking their way between orange-boxes and vegetable crates and stacks of sacks of potatoes. The store was still open. Through a wired-glass window they could see the back of a young man's head as he was talking on the telephone. Sharon accidentally kicked a fruit-box, and the young man turned and peered outside. There were no lights in the back yard, however, and he soon turned away again, still talking. The three of them dodged across to the black-painted fire-escape without being seen.

They climbed the fire-escape as quietly as they could. They knew that they wouldn't disturb Umber Jones's body, but Jim had warned them about Mr Pachowski, and it was quite possible that Tee Jay was there, too. When they reached the second-storey landing, Ray pointed toward Umber Jones's bedroom and whispered, "That's it. All we have to do now is break in and grab the stick."

He reached the window, and tried to lift it up.

"Is it l-l-locked?" asked David.

"Not only locked, it's been screwed down, too."

"What do we do now?"

"We use subtle Italian skills handed down from father to son for generations." With that, he took off his pointy-toed shoe, swung his arm back and smashed the whole window with it.

David said, "For C-c-c. Christ's sake, Ray!" pressing his hands to his ears. Glass pealed and tinkled into the yard below, but Ray unhurriedly put his shoe back on and gave them a shrug. "This isn't the kind of neighbourhood where anybody's going to come running at the first sound of broken glass. In fact they'll probably go running in the opposite direction."

He cleared away a few remaining splinters. On the other side of the window hung a heavy black curtain, and he had to pull that aside, too, in order to climb over the sill. He gave it three sharp tugs. And there he was, lying on his bed, with his black nightlights floating beside him – the body of Umber Jones.

"There's the stick – I can see it," hissed Sharon. "Come on, Ray, all you have to do is grab it, then I can say the words and we can get the hell out of here!"

Ray eased himself in through the window and walked across the bedroom. He looked down at Umber Jones in fascination. "Look at him, his eyes are open but he can't see me. Creepy, isn't it?"

"Just grab the stick!" Sharon urged him.

Ray put out his hand and grasped the silver skull on top of the *loa* stick. As he did so, however, the bedroom door burst open so violently that it juddered against the wall, and Tee Jay came hurtling in. He seized hold of Ray's shirt and flung him aside.

"*You dare to touch the sacred property of Baron Samedi*!" he roared. He didn't sound like Tee Jay at all. He sounded as if his voice had been composed from a hundred slowed-down screams – harsh and agonised, but totally commanding. He didn't look much like Tee Jay, either. His face was plastered white all over, except for black circles painted around his eyes and a black slit of a line painted across his lips. He was bare-chested, and his skin was decorated with scores of tiny barbed hooks, each of them tufted with red-dyed fur or clumps of chicken-feathers. He stood amidst the clouds of incense-smoke and he looked like a visitor from hell.

Ray climbed to his feet. "Listen, man," he said, "I don't want any trouble here. But we have to have that stick, man. Your uncle can't go on killing people. You know that."

Tee Jay stared at him with eyes like glistening black beetles. Then, without warning, he swung his fist and knocked Ray back against the door-jamb. Ray toppled sideways and hit his head on the edge of the table.

As Tee Jay went over to hit him again, Sharon managed to scramble in through the window. She reached out for the *loa* stick, but Tee Jay must have been able to sense her. He pivoted around and slapped her open-handed across the side of the head. She fell to the floor with her ears ringing. "Touching the *loa* stick is blasphemy!" he roared at her.

"Tee Jay!" she begged. "It's Sharon!"

He ignored her. He picked Ray up from the floor but Ray was out cold, with a swelling bruise on the side of his head. Tee Jay let him drop.

"You stay where you are," he told Sharon. "My uncle will be back here soon, and then you'll find out what we do to blasphemers."

Sharon tried to crawl back toward the window but he stepped forward and slapped her again. "Stay where you are, bitch! I've been waiting for this!"

Outside the window, David kept himself pressed against the wall, hardly daring to breathe. He couldn't even call for help, because Ray was carrying the mobile phone. He listened and waited and prayed that Tee Jay wouldn't look outside.

"It wasn't your fault," said Jim. "I shouldn't have told you to drive so fast."

They were only two blocks from Umber Jones's apartment, but the police had flagged them down for speeding, and now they were waiting with almost intolerable tenseness while a pot-bellied officer pedantically wrote out a ticket. "You just remember, little lady, ten miles on your speed puts another hundred feet on your stopping distance. There are kids around here, at this time of night; and people with too much alcohol inside them. You don't want to go killing nobody, do you, just because you're one minute late for some appointment?"

Jim was grimacing and squeezing his hands into fists. For God's sake, cut the road safety lecture and let's get out of here.

But before he tore off the ticket, the officer stepped back and walked very slowly all the way around the car, peering at the tyre-treads, checking the lights, tapping at the bodywork. Anybody would have thought that he was thinking of buying it. "All righty," he said, at last, and handed Beattie her ticket. "Just remember the golden rule."

"The golden rule?" asked Beattie, anxiously.

Come on, thought Jim. *Come on, come on, come on.*

"Better to be late in this world than early in the next."

Oh, please.

They drove slowly away, leaving the police officer standing in the street watching them go. They turned the corner, and then Beattie slammed her foot down. The rear tyres howled like slaughtered pigs, leaving twenty–foot slashes of burned rubber on the concrete.

Russell and Sue-Robin and Seymour had already arrived outside the street door that led up to Umber Jones's apartment.

"No sign of Ray and Sharon yet," said Seymour. "I just hope they've managed to grab that stick."

Russell tried the door but it was firmly locked. "Best thing we can do is stand here and wait. He may be smoke, but even smoke needs an eentsy-weentsy gap to get through."

"I'm scared," said Sue-Robin.

Russell peeled the clingfilm off the top of the coffee-mug. "There – you don't have to be scared. If he comes anywhere near, we'll be able to see him."

"And then what?"

"I don't know. Run, I guess."

Sue-Robin peered into the mug and wrinkled up her

nose. "Do you think that really works? I mean, that's just some old woman's ashes, isn't it?"

"Mr Rook seems to think that it's going to work."

He took a pinch between finger and thumb and sniffed it. "Doesn't smell like anything much."

"Oh, *gross*, Russell. You're breathing somebody in."

Russell threw the ghost dust away. As he did so, however, he was sure that he momentarily saw something in the air in front of him – something that looked like disembodied fingers. He flattened himself back against the door, and he was heavy enough to make it shudder.

"What's the matter? What's wrong?" asked Sue-Robin, in fright.

"*He's here*," said Russell, in a tiny, squeezed-up voice. "*He's here! He's standing right in front of us*!"

Sue-Robin snatched the coffee-mug and flung the ghost dust into the air. For a few terrifying seconds they saw the outline of Umber Jones, ten feet tall, with his knife raised up in the air. His teeth were clenched and his face was rigid with fury.

He vanished; but Russell rolled himself away from the door just as the shoulder of his shirt was sliced open. "Get back!" Russell yelled at Sue-Robin and Seymour. "Get the hell out of here! Run!"

The door rattled ominously; and then there was a long sucking sound, as if a current of air were streaming underneath it. Russell couldn't see it, but Umber Jones had just poured under the bottom of the door, and now he was making his way back upstairs.

Russell said, "What's Ray's number? Tell him that Umber Jones has come back!"

Sue-Robin scrabbled with her mobile phone, but even

when she managed to get Ray's number right, she heard nothing at all.

"Oh, Jesus, this is all getting out of control," said Russell.

They heard a car speeding toward them, and then a squeal of brakes. They turned around and saw that Jim had arrived, with Beattie and John.

Jim looked at Russell's shoulder. It was bleeding slightly, but the wound wasn't too deep. "What happened?" he said. "Where is he now?"

Russell nodded up toward Umber Jones's apartment. "I think we blew this one, Mr Rook. All we've managed to do is to make him pissed off. And I mean *seriously* pissed off."

An upstairs window opened and Mr Pachowski peered out. "What's going on down there? Get away from that door or I'll call for the cops!"

Jim ignored him. He gave the front door a hefty kick with his left foot, then another. The frame cracked a little but still the door wouldn't move.

"Hey! What are you doing down there?" Mr Pachowski demanded. "That's vandalism! That's criminal damage!"

"Oh shut up you old idiot!" Sue-Robin retorted.

Jim kicked the door again but still it wouldn't budge. Russell said, "Here – get out of the way. You got to leave this kind of thing to experts." He stepped back six or seven paces, and then came running at the door shoulder-first, all 300 pounds of him, and knocked it clear off its hinges and into the hallway.

"Come on," said Jim. "Let's hope to God we're not too late."

They reached the door of Umber Jones's apartment. It was an inch or two open. Maybe Tee Jay had left it like that so that his uncle's smoke-spirit could return more easily. From inside, they could see only the dimmest flicker of candlelight, and they could hear voices, too.

Jim eased the door wider. He turned around to Russell and Sue-Robin and Seymour and put his finger to his lips. "Ssh, follow me."

They crept across the darkened living-room to the bedroom. For all of his bulk, Russell was remarkably graceful. The bedroom door was wide open, and Jim could see Umber Jones's feet in their dusty black patent shoes, lying on the bed. The candles circled and dipped in their saucers, making the light swivel across the walls. He stepped closer. Through the crack at the side of the door he could see Tee Jay, standing with his back to him, tufted with feathers and fur. He could see part of Sharon's skirt, too. Ray lay sprawled in full view, his face pale, unconscious.

Jim edged just a little bit nearer, so that he could see around the doorframe. There he was, Umber Jones's smoke-spirit, standing beside the bed on which his own body lay comatose. Thank God he hadn't yet decided to breathe his smoke-spirit back in.

"We will cut them one after the other," said Umber Jones. "One hundred and twelve cuts each. A great, great sacrifice to Vodun and to Baron Samedi."

"To die for Vodun is the greatest honor of all," Tee Jay told Sharon. "It is the most painful death of all . . . so painful that you will welcome Baron Samedi when he comes for you."

"Screw you," said Sharon, although Jim could tell how frightened she was.

He glanced back at Russell and Sue-Robin and Seymour. "Russell," he whispered, close to Russell's ear. "You go barging right in and tackle Tee Jay. I'll make a grab for the *loa* stick. If I miss it, you go for it, Sue-Robin, and when you've got it, run like hell. Into the car, and away, OK – as far and as fast as you can."

"You are conscious," Umber Jones told Sharon. "We will kill you first."

Jim could see him slowly twisting his right hand and exposing his knife. Right, thought Jim. It's now or never. He touched Russell's shoulder, and said, "*Go*!" and they went.

Russell cannoned into the room and knocked Tee Jay flat to the floor with one of the greatest body-tackles that Jim had ever seen. Sharon screamed. Umber Jones whirled around, his eyes staring in surprise and fury. He slashed at Jim's face, but Jim managed to duck his head sideways.

He reached across for the *loa* stick, but Umber Jones slashed at him again and again, and cut the edge of his hand. "This time I'll kill you, my friend," he spat. "This time I'll bury you for ever."

Jim dodged toward the *loa* stick again, and again Umber Jones's smoke-spirit sliced his knife in the air from side to side. But as he did so, Sue-Robin scrambled right under the bed to the other side, reached up with one hand, and dragged the stick out of Umber Jones's grasp.

Umber Jones's smoke-spirit bellowed with rage, and sprang around after her. But Sue-Robin called, "Catch, Mr Rook!" and tossed it over to him.

Jim caught it, and threw it to Seymour. "Go, Seymour!" he shouted. Seymour immediately disappeared out of the door and ran through the living-room on to the landing, colliding as he did so with Mr Pachowski.

Umber Jones started to go after him, but Jim suddenly

thought: *if I could will myself to leave my body – if I could will my spirit to pick up solid objects – then I can will myself to stop Umber Jones.* As Umber Jones rushed toward the door, Jim went after him and punched him hard in the jaw, and then the stomach. Totally taken by surprise, Umber Jones fell back against the wall, staring at Jim in astonishment.

Jim went to hit him again, but this time his fist went through nothing more than wind. All the same – he had delayed Umber Jones for long enough. Outside in the street he could hear Seymour's tyres shrieking as he drove away.

Umber Jones stared at Jim for a long, long time, his eyes hollow with malevolence. Then he started to shuffle back toward the bed, where his physical body lay. "One day, my friend, I will find another *loa* stick, and then I will come back for you. I promise you that."

He stood beside his body and laid his hand on its chest. Then without warning, David Littwin came climbing in through the window. He ignored everybody else, and walked right up to Umber Jones's body. Sticky-outy ears, with the light shining through them. Serious expression.

"Careful, David," said Jim. Although Umber Jones's smoke-spirit no longer possessed a *loa* stick, and couldn't call on the *loas* to help him to hurt human beings, it was better to be cautious.

But David pointed his finger at Umber Jones's body and said, loudly and clearly, "*Babai babatai m'balatai . . . hathaba m'fatha habatai.*"

Umber Jones's smoke-spirit stared at him in disbelief. Then he twisted around and stared at Jim. His expression was one of utter horror. "He has hexed me! Your child has hexed me! I can never go back into my body!" He rushed from one side of the room to the other, a tornado of smoke – but only of smoke, with no power or influence at all. At last he came to rest in the far corner, shuddering with fear and desperation.

Jim walked up to him and said, "Let's hope that all the people you killed are going to be more forgiving than you ever were." With that, he twisted the knob of the air-conditioning unit under the window.

"No," whispered Umber Jones, as the motor whirred into life. "I want to keep my shape . . . I want to keep my soul." But he was helpless. The air-conditioner began to fray the edges of his coat, and then it sucked in his sleeves. Umber Jones gradually collapsed into a spiral whirl of smoke, and was drawn through the air-conditioning vents like nothing more substantial than a bad memory.

Jim went over to Russell, who was still sitting on top of Tee Jay. "Thank you, Russell, for a memorable performance. Thank *you*, Sharon, for being so knowledgeable about your own heritage. And thank *you*, Sue-Robin, for a pretty cute move."

He put his arm around David's shoulder and said, "As for you, David, you're excused speech therapy for the rest of the semester."

He met Susan as he walked across the parking lot after college. She came right up to him and kissed him on the lips. "Hi," she said. "Where are you going to take me tonight?"

"I don't know. I was thinking about a barbecue *chez* Rook. Salmon steaks and a little salad?"

"That sounds good."

They walked arm in arm toward his car. "Have you heard anything about Tee Jay yet?"

"He has to take a whole bunch of psychiatric tests. His Uncle Umber really messed him up. But, you know, give him a little time . . ."

"He really thought he was a voodoo sorcerer?"

"Oh, yes. And in a way, he was. He was young, you see, and strong. He had an aura filled with energy and life. Other spirits love that energy . . . that's why ghosts so often appear to young children, rather than old people."

"I really don't know what you're talking about."

"Well . . . it doesn't matter now," he said, opening the car door for her. Although he understood now why Umber Jones had appeared so often in his classroom. His dark and dried-up soul had reveled in all that youthfulness. He had literally devoured it, and it had made him stronger. The past feeding off the future.

That evening, as they sat by the pool, Susan snuggled up close to him. She kissed his lips and nibbled his earlobe.

"You know something," she said, "the moment I set eyes on you . . . it was love at first sight."

He smiled and kissed her back and said nothing.

"You know something else?" she said. "I had such a sneezing fit today. I think I must be allergic. It was just after lunch . . . just after you and I were talking together. I sneezed and I sneezed and I couldn't stop. I felt as if I'd been sniffing up pepper."

Jim kept on smiling at her. Not pepper, sweetheart. Memory powder. And now you remember falling in love with me; the same way that I remember falling in love with you.

The charcoal in the barbecue briefly glowed, but it was starting to die. Jim disentangled himself from Susan's arm and said, "There's something I have to do. Hold on a minute."

He left the side of the pool and walked across to the parking-lot. He opened up the trunk of his car and took out the *loa* stick.

Myrlin was walking past, and he stared at the stick and commented, "Ankle problems, Jim?"

Jim gave him the sweetest of smiles. "Nose hair problem, Myrlin?"

Myrlin looked confused and hurried off.

Jim returned to the barbecue carrying the *loa* stick. He held it up for a moment and looked at the silver skull on the top. He couldn't even guess what power this stick contained, but then he didn't really want to know. He lifted his knee, and broke it in half, and then he dropped the pieces into the barbecue charcoal.

They smoldered for a while, while Jim and Susan lay watching them. Then they suddenly flared up, and began to burn with a crackling, firecracker fierceness. Thick grey smoke poured out of the flames, and rose up into the evening sky. For a moment, Jim could have sworn that it took on the shape of Umber Jones.

He didn't see the faint outline of an old woman standing in the shadows; a faint outline with the faintest of smiles. She was smiling because her prophecy had come true, and Jim's fate had been sealed by fire.

"I love you, Mr Rook," said Susan, and kissed him again.

Jim didn't say anything, but watched the smoke drifting through the yuccas; until a cross-breeze caught it, and whirled it out of his life for ever.

TOOTH AND CLAW

TOOTH AND CLAW

The second in the new Jim Rook Series

Graham Masterton

PAN BOOKS

This edition published 1999 by Pan Books
an imprint of Macmillan Publishers Ltd,
25 Eccleston Place, London, SW1W 9NF
Associated companies throughout the world
www.macmillan.co.uk

This first world edition published in Great Britain 1997 by
SEVERN HOUSE PUBLISHERS LTD of
9-15 High Street, Sutton, Surrey SM1 1DF.
First published in the USA 1997 by
SEVERN HOUSE PUBLISHERS INC., of
595 Madison Avenue, New York, NY 10022.

British Library Cataloguing in Publication Data

Masterton, Graham, 1946-
Tooth and claw. – (Rook; bk. 2)
1. English Fiction – 20th century
1. Title
823.9'14 [F]

ISBN 0 330 396536

Typeset by Palimpsest Book Production Limited,
Polmont, Stirlingshire, Scotland.
Printed and bound in Great Britain by
Mackays of Chatham plc, Chatham, Kent

Chapter One

He came out of the kitchen to find his dead grandfather sitting in the green armchair on the other side of the room. His grandfather was wearing the same clothes that he had worn on the last day that Jim had seen him: rolled-up shirtsleeves and maroon suspenders. The early-afternoon sunlight turned his glasses into polished pennies. His tobacco-stained moustache bristled like a yard-broom.

"Hullo, Jim. How're things?"

"Grandpa?" said Jim. He was holding a can of Schlitz in one hand and a Swiss cheese sandwich in the other. His tortoiseshell cat tangled herself between his ankles and almost tripped him up.

"What's the matter, boy?" his grandfather smiled. "You look like you've seen a ghost."

Jim put down his beer and his sandwich and approached his grandfather until he was standing close enough to touch him. But he didn't touch him. He didn't know much about visitations, but he knew enough to realise that – if they made any kind of physical contact – his grandfather would instantly vanish. Visitations were nothing more than light and memory, mixed.

The sun shone across his grandfather's face, illuminating his grey-green eyes, the wrinkles of his neck, his white hair cropped as it always used to be cropped, by the barber on Main Street, in Henry Falls. He had the same dark mole on his upper lip.

"You don't need to be worried, boy. I just came to pay you a friendly visit. Thought we could talk about the old days, and maybe the new days too."

Jim pressed his hand against his chest. His mouth was as dry as a tray of cat-litter and his heart was thumping. "I never thought that I would ever see you again," he said. "Not sitting here in my apartment, anyway. Not to talk to."

"You've got the gift, Jim. You can see anybody, live'n'kicking or dead'n'gone. You know that."

"It just takes some getting used to," Jim told him. Then, "Listen . . . how about a beer?"

His grandfather ruefully shook his head. "Being here is all I can do," he admitted, "and that's not easy. Beer . . . hunh, that's a pleasure of the past."

Jim dragged across the other armchair, a dilapidated brown affair with its yellow foam stuffing trying to burst out of it wherever it was worn. "So tell me," he said. "What's it been like? Do you still see grandma? I mean, is it like heaven, or what?"

His grandfather smiled. "I guess you could say it was heaven, in a way. Every day is different. Sometimes you wake up and you're nine, and it's summertime, and the sun's shining. Other days you wake up and you're old and sick and the rain's running down the windows and you wish that you could die for a second time."

"And grandma?"

The old man shook his head. "I don't see her too much. You see, what you do when you die is pretty much try to settle up your unfinished business, the things you couldn't do when you were alive, or maybe the things you *failed* to do."

"What did you ever fail to do, grandpa?" Jim asked him. "You were the greatest grandpa that anybody could have wanted."

"That was your childish eyes, Jim. When I was nine, I failed to collect enough Ralston's boxtops for a Tom Mix six-shooter. When I was nineteen, I lost the girl I should have married to the college football hero. I was passed over for promotion three times when I worked at General Electric."

"You're trying to make yourself sound like some kind of failure. You were never a failure. I always thought you were a winner."

"You did?" asked his grandfather, querulous but obviously pleased.

"I still do. I mean, the fact that you're dead . . . what difference does that make?"

"It makes the difference that I can't touch you any more, boy. I can't hold you, the way that I'd like to. But I can do this. I can give you a warning."

"A warning?"

"It's the least that the dead can do for the living. The dead can see around the curve, so to speak – see what's coming."

"So what *is* coming, grandpa?"

His grandfather licked his lips, the way that old men do. "It's coming out of the east, whatever it is. It's dark, and it's very old, and it kind of *bristles*, if you get my meaning. More like a wild animal than a man; but cunning, like a man is, and cruel, like a man can be."

"So what the hell is it?"

"I can't see it distinctly, or else I'd be able to tell you. But I warn you, boy, it's coming real quick, and when it comes there are people who are going to be wishing that they'd never been born."

His grandfather wouldn't say any more than that – wouldn't, or couldn't. Jim asked "what?" and "when?"

and "where is it going to come from?" but his grandfather lifted his hands because he really didn't know.

They talked for a while more, as the sun gradually moved across his grandfather's shoulders. They talked about the times they used to go swimming in the waterhole close to his grandfather's house. They talked about grandfather's pride and joy, his scarlet-and-cream 1947 Pontiac Streamliner Sedan, which Jim used to polish until it looked as if it had just been driven out of the showroom. They talked about football – and then Jim suddenly checked his watch and said, "My God . . . I'm twenty minutes late. West Grove are playing Chabot this afternoon, and one of my students has made the team."

"Well, then, you'd better get going," said his grandfather. He stood up, and held out his hands as if he wanted to give Jim one last parting embrace. "I hope your boy does well."

"I'll see you again?" Jim asked him.

"I don't know . . . things aren't exactly the same after you're dead. Let's say they're less predictable." He paused, and then he said, "You won't forget my warning, will you? Keep your eyes open. Keep your ears pricked up. You might hear it before you see it."

"Goodbye, grandpa," said Jim, and he didn't make any attempt to hide the tears in his eyes.

His grandfather turned, and as he turned he vanished, as immediately as if he had walked out through the door. Jim stood where he was, staring at the place where his grandfather had been, until the feline formerly known as Tibbles jumped up on the arm of the chair next to him and rubbed his hand with her head.

"Guess you want feeding, you insatiable ball of fur," he told her. "Then I have to run. Russell's never going to forgive me if I miss his first game."

He drew up outside the college football field with an operatic chorus of tires, and his '69 Rebel SST let out an explosive double backfire. He was over twenty minutes late, but he was surprised to find that the game against Chabot hadn't even started yet, and that students and parents were impatiently milling around outside. He climbed out of his car and negotiated his way through the crowd until he found Ben Hunkus, the football coach. Ben was short and bulky, and his close-cropped head looked like one of those pieces of gristle you try to hide under your side salad. He was talking to some of his team, Russell Gloach included. The boys were all looking disappointed and bewildered, and they were still wearing jeans and T-shirts.

"What's up?" asked Jim. "You scratch the game, or what?"

Ben said, "You're not going to believe this, but we've had a vandalism situation. Someone broke into the locker rooms and tore up all of our uniforms. They even broke our goddamned *helmets*."

"You're kidding me. When did this happen?"

"We don't know. Sometime this morning, between eleven and eleven-fifteen. I'm mad. Believe me, I'm mad."

"Do you have any idea who did it?"

"What? Godzilla, by the look of it. You should see the damage."

Martin Amato, the team captain, said, "The second team are lending us their uniforms. The trouble is, most of them are back at home, in the wash, or all crumpled up in the trunks of their cars. I mean, *gross*. And it's going to take us at least another hour to get started."

Martin was tall and square-jawed and handsome. He had curly blond hair and deep brown eyes and a slow, deliberate way of talking. He was supremely dim, but he was one of the best captains that West Grove had ever had, and if the rest of his players had been as athletic as he was, they probably would have won every single game. As it was, the West Grove Community College football team had earned themselves the nickname 'The Fumblers.'

"Did anyone call the police?" asked Jim.

"Unh-hunh," said Ben. "I don't think Dr Ehrlichman is particularly enthused about having a law-enforcement scenario during a college football game."

"In that case maybe I'll go take a look at it myself. Good luck with the game, Martin, if I don't see you before. You, too, Russell."

Russell Gloach gave Jim a friendly salute. Russell was the biggest student in Special Class II, nearly 250 lbs, and he had struggled hard all summer to cut down on cakes and hamburgers to get himself fit enough to be picked for the football team. He was still too slow, but Martin had chosen him because of the sheer effort he had put into his training, and because he had the stopping capacity of a small wall.

As Jim walked up toward the college building, he almost collided with Dr Ehrlichman, the principal, who was hurrying back to his office. Dr Ehrlichman was wearing an off-white seersucker suit and he looked as flustered as the White Rabbit in *Alice*.

"Dr Ehrlichman? I've just heard what happened in the locker room."

"I'm sorry, Jim. No time. I have to take a VIP phone call."

"Ben Hunkus tells me you didn't call the cops?"

"I'd rather we carried out our own investigation first. God *knows* we've had the police around here enough times this semester. You have to think of our reputation."

"Yes, Dr Ehrlichman, I guess I do."

Jim pushed his way through the double doors that led to the boys' locker room. A few students were still standing around outside, but the locker room itself was being guarded by the college security officer, Mr Wallechinsky, in his tight brown uniform, blocking the entrance with his beefy sun-reddened arms folded.

"Mr Rook?"

"How's it going, Mr Wallechinsky? I just came to take a look."

"I warn you, Mr Rook. Your heart's going to bleed."

"Don't you have any idea how it happened?"

Mr Wallechinsky shook his head. "Up until eleven o'clock, everything was fine. By half after, somebody had managed to turn the whole damn locker room into a disaster area."

"Nobody heard anything? It must have caused a hell of a racket."

"Nobody *heard* nothing. Nobody *saw* nothing. The last person that anybody saw near the locker room was that Red Indian student of yours."

"Native American, Mr Wallechinsky, if you don't mind."

"Ah, come on, Mr Rook, what's in a name? I'm a Polack, right? You can call me a Polack if you like. There's no name never hurt me."

"All the same, Catherine White Bird is a Native American. Or a Navajo. You can call her either." He paused, and then he said, "So what was she doing here? Did you ask her?"

"Sure. She just came back to fetch Martin Amato's wallet. I guess you know that she and Martin Amato have been dating."

Jim nodded. "Sure." He always did his best to keep up with his students' love lives. It often made it easier to understand why a particular student was depressed, or dreamy, or exceptionally touchy. And he wasn't at all surprised that Catherine White Bird and Martin Amato had fallen for each other – they made a brilliantly attractive young couple. Jim could have fancied Catherine White Bird himself if he'd been fifteen years younger, and he hadn't made it a cast-iron rule never to get involved with any of his female students. Apart from calling Dr Ehrlichman a bureaucratic pinhead, that was the quickest way for any teacher to find himself looking for work.

"Catherine didn't see anything either?"

"Not a thing. And there's no way she could have done anything like this herself."

"You'd better show me," said Jim.

Mr Wallechinsky opened the door of the locker room and let Jim inside. It was gloomy, because the fluorescent strip-lights had been shattered, and there was water hissing all over the floor from three basins which had been completely wrenched away from the wall. There were grey steel lockers lying on their sides, on their backs, and all kinds of angles. But they hadn't just been pushed over: they had been bent and twisted, some of them almost in half. Three or four of them had been gouged and ripped, as if by the teeth of a mechanical excavator.

Heaps of football uniforms were strewn around everywhere, and every one of them had been torn into shreds. West Grove's bright new green-and-orange outfits had been donated by West Grove Screen & Window, at a cost of more than $3,500. Now they were reduced to slews of sodden rags. Even their shoulder armour was torn apart, and their green-and-orange helmets were split open. Jim bent down and picked up one helmet that was crushed like a trodden-on M&M. The mystery was, you couldn't crush a helmet like this with a sledgehammer, or by driving a Jeep over it.

The walls of the locker room were scarred, too. All across the far wall, the white porcelain tiles had been scratched right through to the clay. Jim walked across to the wall and ran his fingers down the grooves. There were five of them, in parallel, almost like clawmarks. Yet even a full-sized grizzly bear wasn't capable of making deep scratches on high-glazed porcelain.

Ben Hunkus came in and stood beside him. "Pretty damned tragic, isn't it?" he said.

"No question about it, I think we should call the cops," said Jim. "Whoever did this was totally berserk. Apart from that, he must have had some kind of pick or farm implement that could pierce right through the sides of these lockers. Imagine what could have happened if somebody had disturbed him."

He dropped the smashed helmet onto the floor. "What I can't understand is, why would anybody want to bust up a college locker room? I mean, what the hell *for*?"

"Maybe somebody from Chabot wanted to make sure that West Grove would lose."

"Are you kidding me? Chabot could flatten The Fumblers with shopping bags over their heads. They wouldn't have to do anything like this."

"Listen, Jim, West Grove have a pretty good chance of winning this game. Or at least of not losing by very much."

"Sure, Ben. I'm sorry. But I don't understand this at all."

While Ben tried to heave up some of the fallen lockers, Jim stood in the middle of the room looking around. He was sure that he could sense something, and he wasn't at all sure what it was. It was as strong as that feeling you get when you walk into a room crowded with unwelcoming strangers. It was a deep hostility – almost a *rage*.

"Do you feel something?" he asked Ben.

Ben was struggling, red-faced, with an overturned bench. "I feel good and mad, I can tell you that."

"I know. But can you *feel* something, here in this room?"

Ben stopped struggling and looked around. "I don't know what you mean."

"Hm. I'm not sure that I do, either. Do you want a hand with that?"

Ben didn't answer. He was too busy rattling a locker door that had been twisted into the shape of a huge grey bowtie.

He left Ben to his clearing-up and walked back down to the football field. It was a perfect October day – clear and cool, with a light breeze to make the college pennants snap. The West Grove band was playing *99 Red Balloons* for the seventh time, with all the off-key enthusiasm of a Mexican street orchestra. The cheer-leaders were strutting up and down in their short pleated skirts and waving their green-and-orange pom-poms. If there was one thing that West Grove could boast, it was the prettiest girls. Prancing in front of them was one of Jim's class, Sue-Robin Caufield, whirling her baton like a helicopter rotor. Jim gave her a smile and a wave and she gave him a winning smile in return. God, he thought, if only that girl could read and write the way she can prance.

He found Martin Amato again, down by the 20-yard line. Catherine White Bird was with him.

"Hi, Mr Rook. What do you think?"

"What do I think? I think I'm going to persuade Dr Ehrlichman to call the police. Meanwhile, tell all of your team to keep on the lookout. We could be looking for nothing more than somebody who gets a kick out of trashing locker rooms. But on the other hand there might be some psycho around who's got some kind of a grudge against you."

"A grudge? Who has a grudge against a college football team?"

"People have had stranger grudges than that," Jim told him. "There was a woman who lived next door to me who used to have a grudge against Lou Costello. She sent him hate mail till the day she died."

Catherine White Bird said, "It couldn't be a student, could it, Mr Rook?"

Catherine had only just joined Special Class II. Up until three months ago, she had lived on the Navajo reservation at Window Rock, close to the border between Arizona and New Mexico, and studied at the Navajo Community College. But her father had won a leading role in a new TV series about the Navajo police, *Blood Brothers*, and she and her two brothers had taken the opportunity to join him in Los Angeles.

Her mother had died when she was fifteen, but one of the first things that she had said when she introduced herself to the class had been, "I look just like my mother. I *am* my mother." In which case, her mother must have been very tall, over 5ft 10ins, with long black hair that fell almost as far as her waist. Catherine had high cheekbones and slanting brown eyes and full, slightly pouting lips. She was big-breasted and long-legged, and today she was wearing a blue checkered shirt and skintight jeans. Around her neck was a silver necklace with an enamel eagle on it.

Jim said, "If it *is* a student, then believe me we'll find out who it is and we'll use his guts for guitar strings."

"My grandmother had a way of finding people who caused trouble," Catherine told him. "She used to have magic bones which pointed them out."

"I don't think we're going to need any magic bones to

find this guy," said Martin. "He's probably bright green, with burst-apart clothes."

"It beats me that nobody saw anything," said Jim. "Whoever did it must have been carrying an axe or something like that. And the noise must have been awesome. All those lockers being knocked over."

"I didn't hear anything," said Catherine. "And I mean, I can practically hear the grass grow."

Russell said, "That thing that Indians do in movies, when they put their ear down to the ground and say 'heap plenty horses coming this way', can you do that?"

"Russell," Jim warned him. "I've told you before about racial stereotypes."

"I don't mind," Catherine smiled. "Just don't let my brothers hear you talking like that, that's all."

"Yes, Russell," said Martin. "You'll end up bristling with arrows."

Bristling, thought Jim. That was the word his grandfather had used. 'It's dark, and it's very old, and it kind of bristles, if you get my meaning.' The truth was, he *hadn't* got his grandfather's meaning, not really, but he hadn't been able to persuade him to elaborate any further. All he had said was 'you'll see.'

Yet there was something about what had happened today, and the strange hostile sensation that he had experienced in the locker room, that made him think again about his grandfather's warning. Maybe this dark, old, bristling menace had come around the curve quicker than he had expected.

The football game started at a quarter after three. Jim sat on the bleachers on the north side of the field with George Babouris, the physics lecturer, and Susan Randall, the head of geography. George was big and bearded and devouring Greek kebabs as if he hadn't eaten for three weeks. Susan was looking as fresh and pretty as a girl in a Norman Rockwell painting: bobbed brunette hair, rosy cheeks, and a red skinny-rib sweater and turned-up jeans. He and Susan had been having an on-off kind of relationship for the past two months. The reality was that they were completely unsuited. Susan was seriously into step aerobics, aromatherapy and ancient maps, while Jim was seriously into Chinese take-out and Bruce Willis movies. But Susan was attracted by Jim's undernourished, dishevelled looks, his scruffy dark hair and his eyes the color of green bottle-glass. She loved the way he pressed two finger-tips to his forehead and squeezed his eyes tight when he was trying to think, and he always made her laugh. She also knew that he was totally dedicated to his students. Once she had sat in back of Special Class II and listened to a tall black youth with dreadlocks reciting *Speaking of Poetry* by John Peale Bishop:

"*Traditional, with all its symbols*
ancient as the metaphors in dreams;
strange, with never before heard music; continuous
until the torches deaden at the bedroom door."

The youth himself had been awed by what he was saying, and Susan had found it hard to keep back her tears, particularly since he had started in Special Class II as one of the most aggressive and disruptive of students, with a vocabulary that was nothing but a mangled mixture of street-talk and f-words.

"'*Never before heard music*,'" the youth had said, after he had finished, pointing his finger at every member of the class, one by one. "You think what that means, '*never before heard music*.' Shit, you don't know how much I love those words."

Susan turned and laid her hand on Jim's knee. He glanced at her and gave her a tight smile.

"You're looking worried," she said.

Jim shrugged. "West Grove is losing about eight-and-a-half billion to nothing. What do you expect?"

"You're not worried about that, Jim. We usually lose by much more than that."

"I don't know . . . it's this business in the locker room. It gives me a bad feeling, that's all."

"Come on, relax. The police will find out who did it."

"I'm not so sure." He couldn't tell her that his grandfather had appeared to him today, and what his grandfather had said. She just wouldn't believe him. Christ, he could hardly believe it himself – even though he was gradually getting used to the idea that he was able to see visions and visitations that most people couldn't. At the age of ten he had almost died from pneumonia, and his near-death experience had given him the facility to see the spirits that still walk among the living, whether they came to comfort, to protect, or to seek their revenge.

"Do you *know* something about this?" asked Susan. "I get the feeling you *know* something about this."

Jim shook his head. "Just like I said, it gives me a bad feeling, that's all."

Out on the field, Russell had spent most of the game lumbering in unsuccessful pursuit of Chabot's star players. But as the game came to a close, and Chabot's captain Wayne Dooly came sprinting toward the line for a last-minute touchdown, Russell stepped out directly in front of him. Dooly was running too fast to sidestep. He tripped, missed his footing, and collided with Russell with an echoing crash of flesh and body armour. Dooly stood upright for a moment, swaying. Then – as the final whistle blew – he fell flat on his back on the turf. West Grove's supporters cheered and ran out onto the field.

They hoisted Russell up on their shoulders, although it took six of them to do it, and they paraded him around the touchline. Jim stood up and applauded. He had never seen Russell look so happy in the whole time that he had been at West Grove.

Martin came off the field and Jim and Susan went over to commiserate. "It could have been worse," Jim told him. "You did good, considering that you lost all of your uniforms."

"Sure, and considering I've got the slowest, clumsiest team in the entire history of college football. To think – perfectly innocent pigs were killed so that these idiots could kick their skins the wrong way down the field."

Catherine put her arm around him, kissed his cheek and held him close. "You're still my hero," she smiled, and blew him a kiss.

"What are you guys doing now?" Jim asked them. "I gather there's some kind of party in the gym."

"It's a Disaster Party," said Martin. "We're celebrating the longest unbroken run of defeats in community college history."

"No, we're not," said Catherine. "We're going to celebrate the very last game we lose. Next time we're going to win, aren't we? And we're going to go on winning, even if I have to use my grandmother's magic to make it happen!"

"Your grandmother sounds like quite a woman," said Jim.

"Oh, she was," said Catherine. "She could make dead cicadas dance; and she could make it rain. She could walk through a meadow and all the wild flowers would spring up after her."

Jim caught her eye for a moment and she caught his: and in that moment he knew that she wasn't telling him lies – that the stories she had told about her grandmother weren't just pretty stories, they were true. And she knew that he knew. Magic people do.

"Come on," said Martin. "I'm going to have to take a shower. Then we can get down to some serious celebrating."

"We've arranged for you to use the girls' showers," said Ben. "Mr Wallechinsky is going to be on patrol, just to make sure that you behave yourselves. Like, no using the girls' shampoo, or wearing their panties afterward. I don't want a transvestism situation here, to add to everything else."

Russell came up, red-faced and sweating, but infinitely happy. Jim gave him a high five and said, "Well done, Russell. You may have lost the game but you sure made your mark."

Russell said, "'History to the defeated, may say Alas but cannot help or pardon.'"

Jim was taken aback. "That's WH Auden. Who taught you that?"

"You did, sir."

"Did I?"

"It was one of the things that made me train for the team. It was one of the things that made me try to stop eating all the goddamned time."

Jim looked at Russell and saw him for the first time not as a fat, clowning, overweight student, but as a man. He laid his hand on Russell's armoured shoulder and nodded, and that was all he had to do. He didn't smile for very long. A black Firebird had drawn up in the visitors' parking lot, its engine burbling, and two tall young men climbed out. They came walking across the grass with all the purpose of people who have a serious score to settle.

Jim recognized them at once. They were Catherine's older brothers, Paul and Grey Cloud. They came to collect Catherine every day after college, and the only time that Jim had seen Catherine out of college, on the boardwalk at Venice Beach, her brothers had flanked her like bodyguards, conspicuously grim-faced among the smiling roller-bladers and bikini-clad cyclists. This afternoon Paul was wearing a charcoal-grey suit and a black turtle-neck, while Grey Cloud wore a black double breasted coat and jeans. Grey Cloud's hair was tied back in a long ponytail and he wore Navajo jewelry around his neck. Both of them wore impenetrable black sunglasses.

"You're late," Grey Cloud told Catherine. "Do you know what time it is?"

"The game started late," Martin put in. "Somebody vandalized our locker room."

"Excuse me, was I talking to you?" Grey Cloud retorted. Then he turned back to Catherine and said, "I specifically asked you to call if you were going to be late."

"Hey, come on, lighten up," said Martin. "She's not a twelve-year-old."

"Listen, man, stay out of this," said Paul. "This is family and it's none of your business."

"Catherine happens to be my girlfriend. I think that kind of makes it my business, don't you?"

"Catherine isn't anybody's girlfriend and especially not yours. When she does find herself a man, he's going to be Navajo."

Grey Cloud tried to take hold of Catherine's arm but Martin gripped his wrist and forced his arm behind his back. "Get off me, you bastard!" Grey Cloud shouted at him. "You get off me, or I'll kill you!"

But Martin kept hold of him and said, "You listen to me. Catherine's old enough and intelligent enough to be able to make her own decisions about where she wants to be and who she wants to see. You got that?"

Jim stepped up and separated them. "Break it up, OK?

If you want to have the second battle of the Little Big Horn, have it someplace else."

"Little Big Horn was fought by the Sioux," said Grey Cloud, in disgust.

"Yes – and the whites were massacred," added Paul.

Martin said, "You listen to me, you guys. Right now, we're having a party. Catherine's coming and if you like, you can come along too. After the party, Catherine and me are going to LA Buzz for some kick-ass chilli. After *that*, I'll bring Catherine home, safe and sound. Now, do you have any problem with that?"

"Catherine – you come home now," Grey Cloud demanded.

Catherine hesitated for a while, and then shook her head. "I want to go to the party. Come on, Grey Cloud, it's only a party."

"Father wants us all together tonight."

"Father wants us all together *every* night. I have to have some life of my own."

"With *these*?" said Grey Cloud, contemptously, looking around at Martin and Russell and Mark Foley and Rita Munoz.

"These are my friends."

"These will *never* be your friends."

Grey Cloud made another attempt to snatch her arm, but this time both Martin and Russell pushed him away. "Hear this, pal," said Russell. "You try to touch her one more time and I'll sit on your head."

"Yeah," warned Mark. "You ever hear of a tribe called the Flatheads? Well, that's what happened to them!"

"Don't you insult my culture!" Grey Cloud snapped at him, jabbing him in the chest with his finger. "My culture barely survived because of people like you!"

Jim said, "That's enough, guys. If Catherine doesn't want to go home with you, there's nothing you can do about it. So just leave the campus quietly, OK, before I have to do something I don't want to do, like call security."

Grey Cloud gave an aggressive shrug of his shoulders. He looked Martin straight in the eye and said, "I can make you one promise, my friend. If you try to take Catherine out tonight, you won't see tomorrow's sun come up."

"Are you threatening me?" grinned Martin. "Because if you are, you're crazy. I've got all these witnesses."

"I'm not threatening you," Grey Cloud replied. "I'm telling you what will happen to you, just as surely as one moon follows the next."

With that, he and Paul turned around and walked back to their car. They climbed in and drove slowly away, although they paused for a moment so that Grey Cloud could take off his sunglasses and give Martin and Catherine one last steely look.

"Pretty protective, those brothers of yours," Jim remarked.

Catherine was flushed and upset. "They're so angry all the time! They hate white culture, both of them. Especially Grey Cloud."

"Yes, I can see that by his Armani jacket and his Ray-Bans."

"Oh, it's not the accessories, Mr Rook. Navajo have always been good at adapting, at changing their ways. A long time ago they were farmers. Then they became hunters and travellers and raiders. Once they walked. Then they rode horses and carried guns. But what Paul and Grey Cloud don't like is the way that the Navajo are trying to ape white society.

"They think that too many Navajos are forgetting the old ways – forgetting what we are, forgetting what we mean. They think that we're forgetting the legends, and the stories, and the magic. They think that in ten years' time, we won't be anything more than second-class whites."

"And that's why they don't want you to go out with Martin?"

Catherine took hold of Martin's hand, and squeezed it. "They don't want me to go out with any white man. But they won't stop me, no matter what they say."

Martin said, "Listen, I don't want to cause you any trouble."

"I know that," said Catherine. "But you promised to take me to the Disaster Party, didn't you? And you promised to take me to LA Buzz? Don't tell me that you're going to be one of those white men who speaks with forked tongue."

"All right," said Jim, "I'll let you get on with your evening. Martin – too bad about the game. Maybe one day."

"Sure thing, Mr Rook," Martin told him. "And maybe, one day, Gloach will fly."

Jim and Susan went to the Disaster Party for about a half-hour, just to show willing, but Jim wasn't really in the mood for techno rock, flashing lights and noisy students, and he felt like something harder to drink than strawberry punch. "I think I'm a little too old for this," he shouted into Susan's ear. Susan nodded, although she was jiggling enthusiastically to the sound mixes of TYOUSSi and DJ Ham and he could see that she was itching to dance.

Amanda Zaparelli came up and wrapped her arms around him. "Come on, Mr Rook, let's show them what we can do!" But he managed to steer her over to Ray Vito, who had carried a torch for her ever since junior high, and he swept her away in a techno merengue that had everybody clapping and whistling.

Outside, Jim took hold of Susan's hand. The yuccas were silhouetted black and jagged against a sunset as garish as a Hawaiian shirt. "How about coming back to my place?" Jim asked her. "We could pick up some Chinese and a bottle of wine on the way. I've found this great Szechuan place where they do a stir-fried quail you could kill your mother for."

Susan shook her head. "I'm sorry, Jim. I have a whole heap of assessments to do. And we're going on a field trip Monday, to Mount Wilson. I have to get everything ready for that."

"Hey – we're not drifting apart, are we?" Jim asked her.

"I don't think so. We're just like two boats, bobbing on a pond. Sometimes we bump together and sometimes we don't."

"I know. But we haven't had a good bump in ages."

She kissed him. "I like you, Jim. In fact I think I almost love you. But I don't want to commit myself too much, not just yet."

Jim walked her over to her pink Volkswagen Beetle convertible and opened the door for her. He almost felt like proposing marriage on the spot, but he knew what her answer would be, and he preferred to keep on hoping that 'almost love' would eventually flourish into something more. He kissed her and said, "I'll call you later. Maybe you'll have changed your mind."

"I'll be up to my ears in assessments."

"Didn't you know? That's what first attracted me to you – your assessments."

"Good*night*, Jim," she said, emphatically.

Jim watched her drive away, waving to him as she went. He stood and watched her until she had rounded the curve in front of the college, and then he walked thoughtfully back to his car. Maybe he should ask his grandfather about her. Maybe the dead knew more about love than the living. It was always worth a try.

He made himself a tuna sandwich and watched sports for the rest of the evening, while the feline formerly known as Tibbles sat on the arm of the chair opposite, her eyes locked onto every tiny movement his sandwich made. When he had finished it all she gave him such a death-stare that he put her outside the front door of his apartment and told her not to come back until she stopped feeling so resentful.

He went to bed early and had a sleepless, sprawly night. He dreamed that his grandfather was walking away from him along Electric Avenue, moving in a strange, eerie glide. He kept calling his grandfather to stop.

"What do you mean it bristles?" he kept shouting. "You said that it bristles. What did you mean?"

But his grandfather wouldn't stop, and wouldn't turn around. He kept on gliding away down the street, and all the sky was luminous purple, with a bone-white sun.

He heard an alarm-bell ringing, and he thought he ought to warn Susan that something terrible was going to happen. The trouble was, he didn't know how to find out where she lived. He started to run, and then he realised that his telephone was ringing, and that he wasn't running at all, but kicking against his sheet like a small boy in a tantrum.

He sat up and dislodged the receiver. "Yes? Who is it?"

"Mr Rook? Mr Jim Rook? Sorry to disturb you, sir. This is Lieutenant Harris."

"Lieutenant Harris?" He groped for his bedside lamp. "What the hell time is it?"

"It's a little after seven-thirty, sir. I hope I didn't wake you."

"No, no. I'm always awake in the middle of the night."

"Well, it's pretty much morning now, sir. And I'm afraid I've got some real bad news for you."

Jim rubbed his eyes and pinched the bridge of his nose. "Bad? How bad?"

"Just about as bad as it can get, sir. Martin Amato was found dead on Venice Beach this morning."

Jim felt a terrible tingling surge of dread. "Dead? Martin? I can't believe it. Are you sure it's Martin?"

"His father's just identified him, I'm afraid."

"Well, what happened to him? Was it some kind of accident?"

"I don't think so, sir. It looks like he was attacked by some kind of animal. And when I say animal, I mean something very wild, and very mean, and very, very strong."

"What do you want me to do?" asked Jim.

"It'd be a help if you came down to the morgue, sir. Martin's girlfriend is here . . . Ms Catherine White Bird? She's in a real bad state and she keeps asking for you. I also think it's going to be worth your while talking to one of our counsellors – you know, so that you know how to break the news to Martin's fellow students."

"Yes," said Jim. "Yes, I'll come down right now."

He replaced the receiver and sat on the edge of the bed and he was literally shaking. Animal, Lieutenant Harris had said. Very wild, and very mean, and very, very strong. All Jim could think about were those deep scratches on the walls of the locker room, and the way that the lockers themselves had been twisted and ripped open as if by huge and powerful claws.

Chapter Two

Lieutenant Harris said, "This way," and opened the door to a small waiting-room with two beige couches, a collection of *National Geographic* magazines and a faded framed poster of an orange grove. Catherine White Bird was sitting in the far corner, her arms crossed tightly across her chest and her face rigid. She looked as if she were just about to make her first parachute jump.

Standing by the window was Henry Black Eagle, Catherine's father. He was as tall as his sons, with silvery-black hair that hung long over his shoulders. He had the same high cheekbones as Catherine, although his nose was much more hawklike and his cheeks were deeply lined. He wore a fringed black buckskin jacket and black jeans.

"Mr Black Eagle, this is Mr Rook, Catherine's tutor from West Grove," said Lieutenant Harris.

Jim held out his hand. "Of course, we've met. How are you doing, Mr Black Eagle? I watch your TV show whenever I have the chance."

He turned to Catherine and said, "How are you feeling, Catherine? Is there anything you need?"

She looked up at him with desperate eyes. "I just want Martin back, that's all. I just want you to tell me that this is all a dream."

Jim sat beside her and put a comforting arm around her. "I'm so sorry. I don't know what to say to you.

Martin is such a great guy." He didn't correct himself and say "*was.*"

Lieutenant Harris was cleaning the edge of his thumbnail with his teeth. "She says she and Martin took in a chilli at LA Buzz and then they went for a long walk on the beach. The last time she saw him was when he dropped her off home."

"So why did he go back to the beach? He lives in the opposite direction."

"Who knows? His car was parked about a half-mile away."

Jim said to Catherine, "Did Martin tell you he was going back to the beach?"

Catherine tearfully shook her head. "He kissed me goodnight and then he drove off. I can still see his face, the way he was laughing."

Her father said, "Why don't you come home now, Catherine? There's nothing more that you can do here."

"I don't want to leave Martin. I can't."

Henry Black Eagle said, "Catherine, this was a terrible thing to happen. But Martin's gone now, and nothing can ever bring him back. Besides, he could never have been yours, you know that."

Jim frowned at him. "What makes you say that?"

"Because, Mr Rook, Catherine is already spoken for. She has been pledged in marriage since she was twelve, and when the time comes she will have to honour that pledge."

"I thought that only Indians from India believed in arranged marriages."

Henry Black Eagle didn't answer. Instead, he reached out his hand and took hold of Catherine's shoulder. "Come on now, Catherine. Your brothers are waiting for you."

"Please, dad. I don't want to go. I want to stay here a little while longer."

Jim said, "Why not let her stay, Henry? Let me have a talk to her, and then I'll bring her home. I think she could use a little unburdening, if you know what I mean. Come on, now. Be a guy."

Henry Black Eagle puckered his lips so that they looked as if they been sewn together by headhunters. But then he said, "All right. So long as you bring her back no later than noon," he said, checking his gold Rolex Oyster.

"I'll be on time, honest Injun," Jim promised, and then flushed bright red when he realised what he'd said. Whatever he thought about it, Henry Black Eagle didn't reply, but nodded curtly to Lieutenant Harris and walked out of the waiting-room.

Lieutenant Harris turned back to Catherine. "Pretty serious individual, your dad. It's strange that, isn't it? On TV he always seems like such a fun guy."

"On TV he speaks from a script," said Catherine, and there was a flatness in the way she said it that made Jim think that she had often clashed with her father before, and often said those same words before.

A uniformed patrolman came in to tell Lieutenant Harris that the medical examiner wanted to talk to him, so that Jim and Catherine were left alone. Jim said, "You want to talk about what happened last night?"

"I've told you everything. We left the Disaster Party and then we drove to Venice for a chilli. Afterward we walked on the beach for a while. I've never dared to go there at night because of all the local lowlife. But with Martin I felt safe. With Martin I *always* felt safe."

"Your family didn't care for him too much."

"It wasn't Martin in particular. They've never liked *any* boy I've dated, *ever*. If they had their way, I'd go back to Arizona and do nothing but sit outside a *hogan* all day, weaving blankets."

"This guy you're supposed to be marrying . . . what's he like?"

She shook her head. "I only ever saw him once. He lives out by Fort Defiance. Dad took me to meet him on my twelfth birthday, and said 'This is the man you're going to marry.' Can you believe that? It was very dark in the trailer where we met, and all I could see was a very thin young man, naked to the waist. That's all I remember. Except that my father cut our wrists and pressed them together and said that our blood was now joined forever, no matter what happened. I think I cried. In any case my father never took me to see this man again and I kind of forgot all about it. I never thought that I really *would* have to marry him. But when we came here, and I started to date Ray, and then Martin . . . well, it's all come up to the surface again."

"You don't even know the guy's name?"

"No. And I've never wanted to know. I want to marry somebody I fall in love with. I want to marry somebody here in LA. I want some fun, you know? I don't want to spend the rest of my life sitting in some trailer park in Arizona."

Jim said, "You realise you're old enough now to do whatever you damn well like?"

"Try telling that to my dad. Try telling that to Paul, and Grey Cloud."

"You'll work it out, I'm sure of it. And if you can't work it out, come back and talk to me again. Right now you shouldn't be worrying about your family problems, anyway. You should be trying to come to terms with what's happened to Martin. It's been a hell of a shock, hasn't it, and it's going to be days before you're ready to start accepting that it's really happened. Weeks before you stop crying all the time. And *months*, believe me, before you can go through a whole day without thinking of him, even once."

Catherine's eyes welled with tears and her shoulders started to shake. "He's dead," she wept. "He's dead, and he's dead, and he's dead."

Jim held her close, and smelled the light musky perfume that she wore. He didn't particularly like it, but it was just what young girls wore, and whenever he smelled it again he would think of that bare waiting-room with its beige couches and its faded framed poster.

"You remember me talking a couple of weeks ago about Edna St Vincent Millay?" he said, in his softest voice. "She wrote a sonnet that I sent to my sister once, after her husband had died of a heart attack. It ends up:

Thus in the winter stands the lonely tree,
Nor knows what birds have vanished one by one
Yet knows its boughs more silent than before:
It cannot say what loves have come and gone;
I only know that summer sang in me
A little while, that sings in me no more."

Catherine lifted her head and looked at him, her eyelashes clotted with tears. "That's so sad," she said.

"Yes, but it tells you that you're not alone, that other people grieve too. It tells you that other people understand the pain you're suffering."

Catherine took out a balled-up tissue and wiped her eyes. "They won't let me see him. Could you ask them if I could see him, just one last time?"

"Well, I'll ask Lieutenant Harris, see what he says. I can't promise you, though."

He got up, and he was about to leave the room when the door opened and Catherine's brothers came in. They were both dressed in black T-shirts and black jeans. Grey

Cloud's was emblazoned with the initials DNA – not for dioxyribonucleic acid, but for *Dinebeiina Nahiilna Be Agaditahe*, the Navajo legal aid corps.

"What do you two want?" Jim demanded. "Don't you think you've caused enough trouble already?"

"We've come to take our sister home," said Grey Cloud, taking off his sunglasses.

"Well, you're going to have to wait," Jim told him. "We're not through here yet, and your father's given Catherine permission to stay till twelve."

"Do you have some kind of hearing impediment? I said we've come to take our sister home."

Jim stepped up to him so that their faces were only six inches apart. "You listen to me, you punk. Your sister has experienced a traumatic shock and she needs all the understanding she can get. What she doesn't need is you two swaggering in here like two medium-grilled John Travoltas and putting her through even more stress. So back off. You can wait, if you want to, and give her a ride when she's ready. Otherwise put an egg in your boot and beat it."

"You don't talk to us like that," put in Paul, jabbing his finger at Jim's chest. "This is our country, man. Not yours. You don't have the right."

"Aren't you forgetting what you said to Martin in front of half-a-dozen witnesses at yesterday's football game? I'm sure my friend Lieutenant Harris is going to be very interested in that."

"Threaten him? I didn't threaten him," Grey Cloud retorted. "I simply told him what was going to happen to him if he kept on dating Catherine. It was a prediction, *capiche*? You can't arrest anybody for making a prediction."

"Oh, no? Well, here's another prediction: if you don't back off and give Catherine the time she needs to get over this shock, your nose will be mysteriously broken before the count of ten. Besides, what the hell kind of Navajo word is '*capiche*'?"

Grey Cloud angrily clenched his fist but his brother Paul held him back. "Come on, man, this isn't worth it. We can wait for five minutes."

"Thank you," said Jim, trying not to sound sarcastic. "I'm going to talk to Lieutenant Harris and while I'm gone maybe you can find it in your hearts to be good to your sister."

"Mister, you don't know *how* good," Paul told him.

Lieutenant Harris was standing outside the morgue door, talking to Dr Whaley, the medical examiner, a balding, stoop-shouldered man with lopsided spectacles and a huge mournful nose.

"You and the rest of your faculty must be feeling pretty shaken," said Dr Whaley. "I never saw anything like this, not in thirty-two years with the coroner's office."

"Catherine wants to know if she can see him."

"I don't think that's very advisable. But you can, if you like."

Jim glanced at Lieutenant Harris, but all Lieutenant Harris did was to shrug and say, "It's up to you. You haven't had breakfast yet, have you?"

"It's just that I'd appreciate another opinion," said Dr Whaley. "And I mean *any* opinion, whether it's medical or not. I've already called Jack Skipper from the LA Zoo. He's going to come and take a look and see if he can't identify what kind of animal might have inflicted these kind of injuries. I'll tell you, it wasn't a dog, and that's for sure."

He led Jim busily into the chilly, green-tiled autopsy room, his rubbers making echoey squeaks on the floor, and Lieutenant Harris followed. There were two stainless-steel tables set side by side. One was empty. On the other lay a body, under a green hospital sheet. Dr Whaley walked around it and switched on his bright pivoting lamp.

Lieutenant Harris said, "Martin Amato was found at approximately 5 a.m. by two joggers exercising their dog on the beach. When you see his injuries you'll understand that whoever or *what*ever attacked him killed him almost instantly."

"Judging by his body temperature, he hadn't been dead for more than two hours," said Dr Whaley. He took hold of the edge of the sheet, and then he said to Jim, "Are you ready for this?"

Jim nodded, and Dr Whaley slowly drew the sheet down the whole length of Martin Amato's naked body. Or what was left of Martin Amato's naked body.

His head was unrecognizable. One side of his face had been torn completely away, exposing his teeth and part of his jawbone. Most of his scalp had been wrenched off, too, leaving a clotted red tangle of skin and hair. But it was his chest and stomach that horrified Jim the most. There were four terrible rips – three or four inches deep in places – which crossed the front of his body diagonally from his left shoulder to his right thigh. They were parallel, like a clawmark, but what kind of animal had claws that could cut through the muscle and bones of a young man's ribcage, snagging his heart and puncturing his lungs, before slicing his insides into hideously decorative ribbons? Reds, blacks, yellows and sticky beiges.

Jim stared at Martin's body for almost a minute without saying anything. Then he turned away, and he heard Dr Whaley replacing the sheet.

"Well?" asked Lieutenant Harris. "Any ideas? You ever see anything like that before?"

"I thought mountain lion at first," said Dr Whaley. "But mountain lions don't only claw their quarry, they bite them, too – and there are no teethmarks anyplace at all. What was done to that poor boy was done with no more than three extremely powerful blows – either with an animal claw or an implement that resembles an animal claw."

Lieutenant Harris said, "Besides that, how the hell could a mountain lion get to Venice Beach? We've had no reports of lions missing from zoos or private menageries or movie animal companies. And the interesting thing is that – apart from the pawprints left by the joggers' dog when it first approached the body – there were no tracks in the sand that resembled anything like the spoor of a very large lion-like animal. Only human footprints, that's all, and some bicycle tires."

"And there were no eye-witnesses that you know of?" asked Jim.

"We've already started knocking on doors, and we'll be putting out an appeal on the news – but no, not so far. The kind of people who frequent Venice Beach in the middle of the night are not normally the kind of people you might describe as concerned citizens."

Jim glanced back at Martin's body. "I think I'd like to get out of here," he said.

Lieutenant Harris took him outside, and they stood on the steps in the sunshine so that Jim could take three or four very deep breaths. "God," he said, "I hope it was quick. I hope he didn't suffer."

"Almost instantaneous," said Lieutenant Harris. "Just imagine the shock to the system. Wham. He didn't stand a chance."

"There's something I have to tell you," said Jim. "I'm not supposed to report this without going through Dr Ehrlichman, but I think the sooner you know, the better. Just before yesterday's football game against Chabot college, somebody broke into the boys' locker room at

West Grove and smashed everything to pieces. They tore washbasins away from the walls, they ripped steel lockers to pieces. What was more, they left deep scratches in the tiles – scratches that went right through the glaze into the clay. Scratches that looked like clawmarks."

"And this wasn't reported to the police?"

"Dr Ehrlichman wanted an internal inquiry first. We've had quite a bit of police trouble lately up at West Grove. Mainly minor stuff – speed, crack, petty theft. But he wasn't keen to have a black-and-white rolling up in the middle of a major football event."

"What you're trying to tell me is that the lacerations you saw on Martin Amato's body reminded you of the scratches you saw on the locker room walls?"

Jim nodded. "There's something else, too, although I don't know whether it's related. Martin's girlfriend is a full-blooded Navajo. Her two brothers came to the college yesterday and there was an argument between them. One of her brothers made a threat that if Martin didn't leave Catherine alone, he wouldn't live to see the next sunrise."

Lieutenant Harris whistled. "Who heard him say that?"

"Me . . . and maybe seven or eight other students."

"In that case, I think I'd better have a talk to these brothers of hers. Where can I find them – any idea?"

Jim heard footsteps and looked around. "Speak of the devils," he said. Walking toward them were Paul, Catherine and Grey Cloud. They came up close and then stopped.

"Sorry, but we're tired of waiting for you, Mr Shoulder-To-Cry-On," said Grey Cloud. "We're taking our sister home now."

"I told you before. Your father said she could stay."

"Sometimes our father says things that he doesn't really mean. We're going."

"Well . . . I don't think so," put in Lieutenant Harris. "I'd like to ask you two gentlemen a few questions first."

Grey Cloud gave Jim the coldest of stares. "Has somebody been talking to you, lieutenant?"

"Somebody did mention something that you said to Martin Amato at yesterday's college football game."

"I told him to stay away from our sister, yes," said Grey Cloud, without hesitation.

"And you said that if he didn't, he wouldn't see another sunrise?"

"That's correct. But it wasn't intended as a threat."

"I wouldn't call it a term of endearment."

"It wasn't. I didn't like Martin Amato at all, and I'm not going to pretend that I did. But if you warn a man not to walk across the San Diego Freeway and he insists on doing it, what do you say to him? You say the same thing: 'you won't live to see another sunrise.' That isn't a threat. It's simply a prediction."

"But why should dating your sister be such a risky enterprise? Who else was going to take objection to it, if not you?"

"Some things just can't be explained," said Grey Cloud.

"I'm sorry . . . you're going to *have* to explain them. Whatever you want to call it, you made a threat against Martin Amato's life in front of witnesses and the next morning he was found dead."

Grey Cloud said, "My brother and I were both at home last night. All night."

"Can anybody vouch for that?"

"My father and my sister."

"No other independent witnesses?"

"A friend called me from New Mexico just after 2 a.m. He forgot how late it was. His wife had just had a baby boy."

"You'll be able to give me his name, won't you?"

"For sure. And his telephone number, too. Henry Red Jacket. He called from the Wide Ruins reservation."

Lieutenant Harris jotted it down. Then he thoughtfully scratched the back of his neck. "There's still one point you haven't made clear. If you didn't have anything to do with Martin Amato's death, then who do you think did? And what made you so sure that he was going to die?"

Paul said, "Don't forget that we're Navajo, lieutenant. We can feel the rain coming days before the clouds appear. We can hear people approaching hours before they arrive."

"So? What difference does that make?"

"Martin Amato had the look of death on him yesterday, that's all. It was almost a certainty."

Lieutenant Harris pointed his pen at him, warningly. "Let me advise you, my friend. You may be able to predict all of next week's winners at Santa Rosita, but that's not going to help you in a court of law."

"You're arresting us?" asked Grey Cloud.

"No, I'm not. But I'm going to want to talk to you again. Do us both a big favor and stay at the same address until I advise you otherwise."

Catherine looked as if she were about to say something, but then Paul and Grey Cloud took her arms and hustled her down the steps to their waiting car.

"What do you make of those two?" asked Lieutenant Harris.

"I'm not sure. I guess if you want to understand them, you have to look at life from a Navajo point of view. They're trying to protect their culture. They're trying to keep their bloodline pure. That's why they don't approve of Catherine dating whites. Apparently she's already betrothed to some guy out on the Navajo reservation – has been for over five years."

"Damned pretty girl," Lieutenant Harris remarked, as he watched her being driven away. "Seems like a waste to me."

"Do you think her brothers might have killed Martin?" asked Jim.

"I'd like to think so. It would make my job a whole lot easier. They had motive, for sure. They might well have had the opportunity, too. If Grey Cloud's friend called from New Mexico at 2 a.m. and spoke for twenty minutes, he still would have had plenty of time to drive down to the beach and meet up with Martin Amato."

"Why didn't you pull them in?"

"Think about it. The real question is – *how*? Those guys are fit, and they're tough, but even they wouldn't have had the strength to rip a man's body open with one blow. Not like that. As you say, they might have had some kind of special implement – but even so . . ."

"So what are you going to do?"

"Urgent priority number one is a cup of strong black coffee. Then I'm going to do what I always do. I'm going to go plodding around looking for witnesses and circumstantial evidence and in the meantime I'm going to be keeping a close eye on those two jokers."

He laid his hand on Jim's shoulder and said, "A word to the wise . . . if I were you, I'd keep your eyes open. If they *were* the perpetrators, they're not going to be thinking it's a million laughs that you told me what they said to young Martin at the football game."

He checked his watch. "After the coffee, I'm going to take a photographer and a forensic officer and I'm going to go over to West Grove and check out that locker room. Maybe you're right. Maybe those clawmarks match."

"What if they do?"

"Then I really don't know *what* the hell we're looking for."

Jim had almost forgotten that it was Sunday. He drove back to his second-story apartment in a pink-painted block just off Electric Avenue, parked his car, and wearily climbed out. The morning was hazy and not particularly warm, but three or four residents were already sitting on the dilapidated sun-loungers by the pool, reading newspapers or knitting or listening to Sony Walkmen. Jim said hi to Miss Neagle, the middle-aged woman who had taken over old Mrs Vaizey's apartment. Miss Neagle was wearing huge dark glasses and a scarf on her head, and her big dimpled thighs bulged out beneath a 1960s-style swimsuit with brown-and-white flower patterns on it.

"Hi, Miss Neagle."

Miss Neagle lifted her sunglasses and smiled up at him. Her lipstick was so bright she looked as if she had been eating strawberry jelly. "Good morning, Mr Rook. You seem a little under the weather."

"I didn't sleep too good, that's all. Tossing and turning most of the night."

"Ha! You don't have to tell *me* about tossing and turning. I'm a martyr when it comes to tossing and turning. Sometimes I just dread the sun going down."

"How about sleeping pills?"

"No, Mr Rook. There's only one sure cure for tossing and turning."

"Oh, yes? Then why don't you try it?"

She lowered her black-blotched eyelashes coquettishly. "I would if I could, Mr Rook, believe me."

Jim suddenly realized what she was talking about, and gave her a quick, humorless smile. "Can't always have what we want, Miss Neagle."

As he walked toward the steps that led up to his apartment, he was narrowly eyed by Myrlin Buffield, from Apartment 201. Myrlin used to have a belly that hung over his shorts like a tide of slowly-melting marshmallow, but he had been working out at Gold's Gym lately and now the tide had crept back upward, giving him an extraordinary puffed-up look, as if he were constantly sucking in his breath. He still had the same slicked-back hair, though, and the same dagger earring. He was pretending to read *Men Are From Mars, Women Are From Venus.*

"Hi, Myrlin," said Jim.

"You ain't been creeping out of your apartment nights and spying on me again, have you?" Myrlin wanted to know. "I was sure I heard somebody creeping outside of my apartment last night and I was pretty damned sure that it was you."

"Sorry, Myrlin. My creeping days are over."

Myrlin was deeply suspicious of Jim, almost to the point of paranoia. Ever since old Mrs Vaizey had held a séance in Jim's apartment, and had left it thick with incense smoke, Myrlin had suspected him of being a drug addict or a dabbler in the black arts, or worse – especially since, soon after, old Mrs Vaizey had disappeared, and had never been seen again. Only Jim knew what had happened to her, and Jim was never going to tell anybody, ever.

Jim went up the steps and along the balcony until he reached his apartment. The feline formerly known as Tibbles was waiting for him outside the door with an expectant look on her face. He hadn't had time to feed her before he went out. He unlocked the door and she dashed straight into the kitchen and waited by her bowl with her tail sticking up in the air like a witch's broom.

Jim opened the icebox and was just popping open a cold can of beer when he heard a rapping at the door. It was Miss Neagle, wrapped up in a pink toweling robe. That wasn't so extraordinary: she often came up in a variety of highly informal attire to borrow coffee or sugar or orange juice. But what was extraordinary was that she was wearing a pink lobster SpaceFace hat, complete with eyes and claws. It had been a favourite of old Mrs Vaizey's.

"Hi, Miss Neagle."

"Hi yourself."

"That hat sure brings back some memories."

"I like it. I found it in my apartment when I moved in."

"Suits you. Well, it would suit anybody who wanted to walk around with a lobster on their head."

"Of course . . . that wasn't all I found."

Jim said, "Oh, no?" Then, "How about a beer?"

"A beer? I hope you know me better than that."

Jim blinked at her in surprise. Apart from exchanging a few words around the pool every day, he hardly knew her at all. "Okay, then," he said. "Whatever."

"Bourbon, straight up. No rocks."

Jim unscrewed the Wild Turkey and poured a generous measure into a highball glass with Miami Parrot Jungle printed on the side. Miss Neagle came over and took it and said, "Why don't we drink to *very* long life. With the emphasis on *very*."

"All right. *Very* long life."

Miss Neagle leaned forward and stared into Jim's eyes. "You don't recognise me, do you?"

"Sure I recognise you. You're Miss Neagle from Apartment 105."

"Yes, I am. But I'll tell you what else I found in my apartment when I first moved in, apart from this hat. I found Mrs Vaizey."

"Excuse me?"

"She was still there, Mr Rook, at least in spirit. Very faint, almost faded away. But when I was lying in bed that very first night, almost asleep, she *spoke* to me."

"She *spoke* to you? What did she say?"

"She was kind and she was sympathetic, and she gave me all kinds of encouragement. You see, I was very depressed when I first moved here. I was almost flat broke, and a man who I loved very, very dearly had just died of cancer. Sometimes I thought about ending it all. But Mrs Vaizey gave me comfort and friendship like I've never know before. She made me feel that I wasn't alone any more."

The feline formerly known as Tibbles was rubbing herself frantically against Jim's leg, desperate for food, but all Jim could do was stare at Miss Neagle with his beer half-raised to his mouth.

Miss Neagle sipped her whiskey and smiled at him. "Mrs Vaizey was about to fade away completely, the way that all spirits do, after a while. But I didn't want her to go. I loved her. I needed her. So I let her in. I don't quite know how it happened. I just sort of . . . let her in. Miss Vaizey is here inside of *me*, Jim." She tapped her forehead. "She's still here . . . she's still with us."

"I don't believe this," said Jim. "You're trying to tell me that you're Miss Neagle *and* Mrs Vaizey, both?"

"Got it in one. And it happens more often than you'd think. A spirit who isn't yet ready to fade away finds somebody who's still alive who desperately needs her. Somebody who's sick, maybe – or suicidal, like I was. Both of them benefit. The spirit gets to stay here for a whole lot longer, and her host gains all of her memories and all of her lifetime's experience."

Jim walked back into the living-room and circled Miss Neagle in deep suspicion. This was beginning to sound like some kind of very eccentric shakedown. "If this is true, that you're yourself and Mrs Vaizey both, then of course you'll know what special talent Mrs Vaizey had."

"That's right. Of course I do. She could tell people's fortunes . . . with tea-leaves, or the Tarot, or by reading palms. She was also a damned good knitter."

Jim thought: she was right, but that wasn't really much of a test. If Mrs Vaizey's son had left her lobster hat behind, he had probably left her Tarot cards and her knitting patterns, too.

"You know what her maiden name was?"

"For sure. Duncan, Alice Duncan – born January 17, 1919, in Pasadena, the second of seven children."

"And you know how she died?"

Miss Neagle nodded. "She suffered. She never told you how much she suffered, because she knew that she'd upset you. But she suffered, believe me."

"You know how, and why?"

"One night, her spirit left her body, looking for a voodoo *houngan* who was trying to take possession of one of your students. Unfortunately, the *houngan* was waiting for her."

Jim stopped pacing, and looked Miss Neagle right in the eyes. "You're in there, aren't you?" he said. "You're really in there."

"Yes," said Miss Neagle. "I'm really in here." And she lifted her hand to his cheek and touched it, very gently, not in the way that a woman like Miss Neagle normally would, but in the way that a grandmother would, or an elderly friend. Jim took hold of her hand and squeezed it. "Welcome back," he told her.

"I'm not sure you're going to say you're so happy to see me when I tell you why I'm here."

"What's the matter? Don't tell me *you've* seen something frightening coming to get me, too."

"Who else has told you?" asked Miss Neagle, in the querulous tones that Mrs Vaizey would have adopted.

Jim said, "My grandfather was here yesterday morning.

My *dead* grandfather. He told me to watch for something dark and old and *bristling*."

"Then that's much more serious than I thought."

"What? What's more serious?"

"People's relatives hardly ever make visitations from the other side unless those people are in desperate danger. I mean, why should they come back? They've had a whole lifetime of struggle and conflict, they don't want any more. But for me – no, it was your aura that worried me."

"My aura? What's wrong with my aura?"

"When you came walking around the pool just now, you had the most threatening aura I've ever seen, alive or dead. You were completely surrounded by a swirl of dark, dull colors – like – like *tentacles*, thrashing around in a muddy river – and there was a dreadful feeling of *cold*, too. That's why I came up to see you."

"So what does that mean?"

"It's very serious, Mr Rook. It means that something awful is going to happen to you – and whatever it is, it's already begun. That's why your aura has started to grow darker, the same way the sky grows darker just before a storm. It can feel the threat that's coming toward you. It can *sense* that you're soon going to die."

"I'm going to *die*? And *soon*?"

"Unless you can find a way of saving yourself, yes."

"Come on, now, what the hell is all this about? What does 'soon' mean? Sometime in the next half hour? Tomorrow? Next year? And *how* am I going to die?"

Miss Neagle shook her head. "I can't tell, not exactly, unless I read the cards."

"Listen," Jim protested, "I don't have any intention of dying. Not sooner. Not even later."

"Nobody does, Jim. *I* didn't, any more than you do now. We're all frightened of pain. We're all frightened of darkness. Why do you think I'm clinging onto this life, by staying with Valerie?"

"Valerie? Who's Valerie? Oh – I see who you mean. Miss Neagle. Yes, for sure."

Miss Neagle said, "You don't have to find out how you're going to die unless you really want to. Most people don't."

"But how can I save myself if I don't know what it is?"

"You want me to read the cards?"

"Of course I want you to read the cards. You think I want to go out, turn the corner and find myself torn to pieces by something old and cold and bristling?"

"Just because your grandfather said it was bristling, that didn't necessarily mean it was something that could tear you to pieces. It may be nothing more than a detail . . . just part of the omen, not all of it. It may be nothing more than a hairbrush, lying next to your bed when you're dying."

"Somehow I don't think so. He said '*bristling*' like he really meant it."

"All right, then," said Miss Neagle. She took a pack of cards out of her bathrobe pocket. She had obviously come prepared. "How about here, on the table?" she said, and Jim pulled out two dining-room chairs so that she could spread the cards out in front of her. Jim had never seen anything like them before. They were colored picture-cards, like the Tarot, except that the drawings they bore were even stranger, and more obscure. There were demons on stilts and dwarves with copper pans on their heads and pale, naked women with their eyes blindfolded, surrounded by huge black-beetles. There were minstrels in extraordinary heaped-up hats and sad-eyed knights carrying hideous witches on their backs. Some of the cards showed nothing but deserted landscapes, with only a shadow falling across them to indicate that somebody was just about to enter the picture.

"Pretty weird deck," Jim remarked, as he sat down beside her.

"Weird, yes, but very sensitive. You don't see many like this. They were secretly devised in the fourteenth century on the orders of Pope Urban VI – supposedly to help his cardinals to flush out an infestation of demons in hundreds of Italy's churches. Because of that it's called the Demon Tarot. The demons hid themselves in the cellars and the belfries, and only the cards could tell you where they were. Whether that's true or not, I don't know. But I've known these cards to sense that a wife was going to attack her husband with a breadknife, six hours before she actually did it. And once they warned that a little girl of six was going to die in a house-fire."

"And did she?"

Miss Neagle nodded, sadly. "Her mother wouldn't believe me. I tried to find out where she lived and take the little girl away, but by then it was too late." She paused, and then she said, "That was the last time I used this pack, until today."

"You're scaring me," said Jim, trying unsuccessfully to smile.

"I'm scaring myself," Miss Neagle told him. She shuffled the cards, tapped them three times, and then started to lay them out in an H-shaped pattern, 21 cards in all. The feline formerly known as Tibbles had been watching her closely, but now her fur rose up on end, and she let out a soft hiss of disapproval.

"One of these cards has to represent you, the significator. This one looks good – the teacher. It's the card I used to choose for young, well-educated men – especially *single*, young, well-educated men."

The card showed a man with a strange, serene look on

his face. He was wearing a long cloak that was decorated with all kinds of objects, like kettles and hourglasses and loaves of bread. A young woman was sitting in front of him, cross-legged, with a golden ear-trumpet in one ear, into which the man was pouring green oil from a green-glass bottle.

Miss Neagle placed the card face-upward in the centre of the H-pattern. Then, slowly, she turned the rest of the cards face-up, too.

"This is tomorrow," she explained, lifting up a card showing a man in a complicated black-velvet bonnet, looking out over a stormy estuary. On the man's back a shadow had fallen – a shadow like a large hand. "And this next card is the number four." Three noblemen in masks were standing in a cemetery; but almost invisible amongst the gravestones and the monuments was a grotesque grey figure with horns and a strange trumpet-like protrusion instead of a nose.

"So far this means that the next significant event in your life will not take place until four tomorrows have passed."

"So I won't be killed until Thursday? Is that it?"

"I don't know, Jim. Let's carry on."

She picked up the next card and showed it to him. A pale man was walking across a desert with the rising sun behind him. On closer inspection, Jim saw that the desert floor was composed entirely of intertwined human bones. Miss Neagle said, "Whatever is going to harm you, it's coming from the east."

"Is that good or bad?"

"It may be not significant. But all evil spirits come from the east. You should never build a house with its front door facing east."

"What's that? *Feng-shui*?"

"Not at all. It's simple survival. You don't want demons flying into your house every time you open the front door, now do you?" She leaned forward over the cards, frowning. "Now here's an odd one."

She showed Jim a very dark card, almost black. Jim held it up and his cat abruptly jumped off her chair and ran into the bedroom. Jim got the feeling she would have closed the door behind her if she could have done. He peered at the card intently, and he could just distinguish a rough, shaggy shape with two reddened eyes. More significantly, though, he could see a claw lifted into the air – a claw like a bear's claw, only bigger, with viciously hooked nails.

"Well?" he asked Miss Neagle.

"Well . . . this is what is coming after you, I presume. A beast of some kind. I don't know why it's coming after *you* in particular, but it is. Feel the card again – no, feel it. It's warm, isn't it? It's actually warm. It's charged with psychic energy. It *knows* you.".

She was right. The card *was* warm. In fact it was so warm now that he could hardly hold it. He was about to hand it back to her when it suddenly curled up and burst into flame. He dropped it into the ashtray and both of them watched as it was reduced to a curled-up wafer of black ash.

"How the hell did *that* happen?" asked Jim, flapping away the smoke.

"I told you. Psychic energy. The card acted as a cable between whatever this thing is that's coming to get you, and you yourself. And like all cables when they get overloaded with energy, it burned out."

"Well, I'm real sorry about your deck." He reached into his back jeans pocket for his wallet. "Is it worth very much?"

"They're irreplaceable. If my son had known how rare they were, he wouldn't have left them behind. But he never did like me telling fortunes."

"Oh, shit," said Jim. "I'm sorry."

Miss Neagle was gathering up the rest of the cards. "You don't have to be. I haven't lost any. That card didn't belong to this pack at all."

"I don't understand."

She laid her hand on top of his. "I've never seen it before now. It just appeared by itself. Now, is that a warning, or is that a warning?"

Jim gave her a long, grave look. Then he stared at the ashes in the ashtray. "You mean . . . ? You'd better tell me more."

Chapter Three

The cards could tell him only three ways of avoiding the 'old, cold bristling' thing that was following him. The first was to seek the advice of two friends. The second was to travel on a long journey, although they didn't say where. The third was completely cryptic. If he were going to survive, a game would have to be played, and both sides would have to admit defeat.

"A game? Do the cards say what kind of game?"

Miss Neagle shook her head. "I'm as mystified as you are. But I get the feeling that these three instructions are *progressive*, if you get my meaning. Once you've sought the advice of your friends, you'll know where you have to travel, and once you've travelled there, you'll know what kind of game has to be played, and why both sides have to lose."

Jim sat back. "You say these cards are supposed to be the best?"

"You want to try a second opinion from the regular Tarot? Or the tea-leaves, maybe? Or Sydney Omarr?" She was being sarcastic. Sydney Omarr was a professional astrologist with a 1–900 phone line.

"Unh-hunh. I think I'll stick with the Demon Tarot. At least it's offering me *some* way out. I just wish I knew which two friends it's talking about. That would be a start, at least."

"Maybe it's talking about two lecturers from college."

"Sure. And maybe it's talking about Bill and Gordon from Joe's Bar & Grill. It could be talking about anybody."

Miss Neagle put her cards away. She closed her eyes for a moment, and then she suddenly leaned forward, propping her head in her hands. "Miss Neagle – Valerie – are you okay?"

For a moment, she didn't say anything. "You want a glass of water?" he asked her. "Another shot of whiskey? How about some iced tea?"

"I'm all right," she said, at last. "It was a hell of a strain, that's all, trying to do what Alice used to be able to do."

"How's Mrs Vaizey?"

"She's okay . . . but she's exhausted, too. She found it tiring enough reading the cards when she was alive. Now she has to guide my hands and make my brain work, and I'm not a psychic sensitive, the way she was."

Jim laid a hand on her shoulder and smiled at her. "You did very well, Valerie, thank you. You don't mind if I call you Valerie?"

"Sweetheart, you can call me anything you like." She knocked back her whiskey in one gulp and prepared to go. As she went to the door, however, she said, "This thing that's supposed to be after you – this *beast*," she said. "Do you believe in that?"

"I wouldn't have done, not until this morning."

"You really think it's real?"

"Yes, I do. I don't have any idea what it is, or why it's after me – but, yes, I think that it's really real."

She kissed him, and this was definitely Miss Neagle kissing him, not Mrs Vaizey. This was the kind of half-serious kiss you got from a boozy, fortyish woman in a bar. "You're an interesting man, Jim. You don't mind if I call you Jim? One of these days you and I ought to sit down together with a bottle of wine and a plateful of spaghetti and ask each other the meaning of life."

Jim said, "Tell me one thing, before you go."

"What's that, Jim?"

"Do you argue at all? You and Mrs Vaizey, inside of your head?"

Valerie knew back her head and gave three short, barking laughs. "You *are* an interesting man, aren't you? Yes, we argue all the time. But it's a whole lot more entertaining than arguing with yourself."

Jim gave her a wave as she tottered back along the balcony in her little pink high-heeled slingbacks. Then he went back into the kitchen and opened up another beer. *Two friends*? he thought. *Which two friends*? *And where do I have to travel*?

There was one thing he knew for certain. He had to act fast, because he was now totally convinced that there was a beast looking for his blood; and that it was the same beast that had slaughtered Martin Amato on Venice Beach.

He picked up the frail fragments of ash from the ashtray, the remains of the playing-card, and sifted them through his fingers. They silkily fell back again, and formed the shape of a black, horned creature, with tiny, demonic eyes.

* * *

He arrived early for his first English tutorial on Monday morning and when his class came in he was standing at the window with his back to them, staring out at nothing at all. He hadn't slept well. He was wearing a crumpled pair of tan-coloured chinos and a green checkered shirt which looked as if he had salvaged it from the bottom of the laundry basket. His hair stuck up at the back and no amount of smoothing it down would keep it down, even with spit.

Special Class II were unusually quiet as they took their places, although he could hear the murmur of the names 'Martin' and 'Catherine' and he knew what they were all talking about. Before he turned around he waited until all the murmuring and whispering had stopped, and there was nothing but an occasional cough or the squeak of a sneaker on the composition floor.

At last he stepped up to the front of the class and looked at all of them, one after the other. Greg Lake, pulling his usual faces over in the corner. Greg suffered from a lack of co-ordination, and it was a constant effort for him to show his feelings with his facial expressions. At the moment he looked as if he were sucking on a particularly sour lemon candy.

Amanda Zaparelli, olive-skinned and sultry, with a husky smoker's voice, a liking for very strong perfume and lots of it, and a chronic inability to tell the difference between an adjective and an adverb. "You should of seen me walk into the room. I was so strutly." "Give me that quickly cigarette, will you?"

Jane Firman, pale and dyslexic and given to sudden bursts of frustrated tears. Titus Greenspan III, serious and bulgy-eyed. Titus tried harder than almost anybody else, but he always took everything too literally. If he read that 'the noon sun drilled a hole in my head' he would put up his hand and ask why the narrator hadn't dropped dead on the spot, spilling his brains all over the desert.

Sharon X, in a voluminous black djellaba-like dress which he could only presume was a Black Muslim mourning outfit. John Ng, moon-faced and serious, with a white carnation in a jelly-jar in front of him. White was the Vietnamese colour for death.

Jim looked at them all, one by one, and studied them all. They didn't have any idea how much their predicament could hurt him. Sometimes he wished for their sake that they didn't have to grow up and leave college – and, in particular, that they didn't have to leave his class. They were so characterful, so individual, so full of inflated hopes and wild ambitions. They wanted to be celebrities. They wanted to appear on TV and live in big, pink-washed houses. But he had so little time to teach them – so little time to help them overcome their turtle-slow reading speeds and their painfully limited vocabularies, not to mention their stuttering and their word-blindness and their horrifying ignorance of history or geography or world affairs.

"What's the capital of Chile?" he had asked Ricky Herman.

Mark Foley had shot up his hand and said, "I know! Con Carne!"

Jim loved them, all of them. But he hated the culture which had led them to believe that reading was unimportant, that correct spelling didn't matter, that any dumb poem which *they* wrote was just as good as any dumb poem that Marianne Moore or Robert Lowell had written. He hated it most of all because it didn't allow them the gift of expressing themselves, especially at times like these.

Very quietly, he said, "Yesterday, we all suffered a terrible shock and a loss so painful that it's difficult to put it into words. Martin Amato was found murdered on Venice Beach in the early hours of Sunday morning. He was a son, a brother and a friend. He was a civil engineering student and captain of the football team. He was twenty-one years and two months old."

Jim paced to the back of the class, where Sue-Robin Caufield was sitting. She wore a black scarf around her arm and she was biting back the tears. She and Martin had dated for a while, before Catherine came along.

"What do you say about somebody like Martin? He was reliable. He was considerate. He took himself too seriously. He wasn't a genius, but that never affected his unquestioning loyalty to his college, to his team, and to all of his friends. He was the kind of regular guy who had the potential for happiness, and self-fulfilment, and to make a lasting contribution to society.

"Now all of that has been taken away from him – and from us, too. And because of that our lives are going to be poorer, and more doubtful, and less trusting of the world we live in."

He walked up to Catherine's desk. Today she was wearing her hair tightly braided with a black ribbon, and a black dress. Her eyes looked puffy from crying.

"Are you all right?" he asked her. "You can be excused this class if you want to."

"I'm okay," she whispered, without looking up. "Please . . . I'd rather stay here."

Jim stayed beside her for a moment, watching her, and then he turned to the class at large. "Today I want you all to write me a short poem about Martin. I want you to use that poem to express in words everything you feel about him, or any other friend that you've lost."

Muffy Brown put up her hand and said, "Excuse me, Mr Rook, sir, but isn't that kind of like *cynical*? I mean Martin's been dead for no more than a day and you're turning his death into *classwork*?"

Muffy was small and pretty with a personality like a roomful of bouncing balls. Earlier this semester she had worn the most elaborate braids that Jim had ever seen, but now she had shaved her head almost bald except for a flat crewcut on top, and acquired a silver ring through her eyebrow.

Jim said, "Listen to me. If you can express your feelings about Martin's death in writing, you'll be paying him the greatest compliment you ever could. If you can put down the shock, and the anger, and the sense of unfairness . . . if you can learn to convey your grief to other people . . . not only will you be improving your communicating skills, you'll be helping yourself to come to terms with what's happened. You'll be making it clear that Martin's death touched you and affected you . . . and you'll have found a way of telling the world just how much."

He picked up one of his books and said, "After Allen Ginsberg's mother died, he wrote a long poem called *Kaddish*, which was filled with anger and bewilderment and relief, too, because his mother had been mentally sick. He used it as a way of honouring her, of remembering her – and of coming to terms with the way in which she had changed from being a pretty young girl 'sitting crossleg on the grass – her long hair wound with flowers –' to an elderly woman 'too thin, shrunk on her bones – new broken into white hair – loose dress on her skeleton – face sunk, old! withered – cheek of crone –'

"But finally, he says to her, 'There, rest. No more suffering for you. I know where you've gone, it's good.'"

He lowered the book, lowered his head. "For Martin's sake, and for your sake, too, write something that comes right out of your heart."

There was silence in the classroom. Then, almost as one, everybody brought out their pads, uncapped their pens, and began to write. Jim had never seen them so subdued. He went back to his desk, sat down, and started to write something himself. But he wasn't writing a poem about Martin's death. He was writing "2 Friends? Who? Journey? Where? Game in which both sides surrender? What?"

He sat with his head in his hands for a long time, trying to make sense of what he had written. After a while, however, he looked up. Most of the class were bent diligently over their work, although he could see that most of them had written no more than two or three lines. Still, for Special Class II, two or three lines was something of an achievement. Russell seemed to be the most inspired – or the most deeply affected – because he had already filled one sheet of paper and was on to his next, his tongue clenched between his teeth like a small boy trying to hook a maggot onto a fishing-hook.

When he looked toward Catherine, however, he saw that she wasn't writing at all. She was sitting up quite straight, her head tilted back, looking toward the ceiling. There was an extraordinary smile on her face, almost a radiance, as if she were supremely happy.

Jim watched her with gradually-increasing curiosity. She kept on looking at the ceiling, and she started to sway her head from side to side in a strange, repetitive movement that reminded him of something but he couldn't think what. *Shock*, he thought. *She's going into shock.*

Immediately, he stood up, tilting back his chair so that it fell onto the floor with a sharp, echoing clatter. The class all looked up at him, but he raised his hand and said, "Don't worry. It's okay. Just get back to your work."

He went back to Catherine's desk and stood over her. "Catherine? How are you feeling? How about going outside for a couple of minutes? Maybe you could use some air."

She didn't answer, so he cautiously reached out and touched her shoulder. "Catherine – come on, how about seeing the nurse?"

Slowly Catherine turned her head. As she did so, she closed her eyes. But when she had turned completely toward him, she abruptly opened them again. He felt a shrill sense of fright and he couldn't stop himself from taking one step away from her. Her eyes were totally expressionless, as if she didn't know who he was – or even *what* he was. He had never known anybody look at him like that before, and he couldn't even think what to say to her. What do you say to a painted portrait, when it stares at you; or a snake that stares back at you, in the reptile-house?

"It's all right, Mr Rook," she told him, in the softest of voices. "I don't need to see a nurse. I'm fine."

"All the same, maybe you'd better go home. This only happened yesterday morning. Shock can last for days or weeks or even years."

"I want to stay here," she insisted. "Please, Mr Rook, I'd prefer to stay here."

"OK, OK. But if you start to feel dizzy, or anything like that—"

"*I have to stay here*," she hissed at him. "*Don't you get it? I have to stay here*!"

"All right!" he told her, lifting both hands in instant surrender. "If you want to stay here, then stay here. That's fine by me."

Catherine continued to stare at him as he retreated along the aisle. He picked up his chair and sat down at his desk, giving her one last, long look of concern. She was still in shock, no doubt about it, but he didn't want to distress her more than she was distressed already, and he didn't want to disrupt the tutorial. He would have a quiet word with her later, when she was on her own.

He went back to his conundrum. *2 Friends? Who*? What he didn't see was the drop of blood that suddenly appeared between Catherine's tightly-pressed lips and quickly slid down her chin. It dripped onto her notepad and made a red splattery mark.

She wiped her mouth with the back of her hand. Then she lifted her head again and continued to stare at the ceiling, her eyes still expressionless, as if she were listening to a long message that came from a long, long time ago, and far, far away.

He was leaving college at four o'clock that afternoon when he saw Catherine waiting beside the parking-lot, clutching her books close to her chest, her head bowed and her long hair blowing in the warm afternoon wind. He walked up to her and said, "Waiting for your brothers?"

She nodded. This time she wouldn't even look at him.

"Come on, Catherine, you've had a hell of a rough time," he told her. "You don't have to come back to college until you feel like it. Maybe you should talk to your doctor. Or better still, you could have a word with the college counsellor. Did you ever talk to Naomi? I know she looks a little – well, *eccentric*, what with those glasses and that hedge of a hairdo, but she's a terrific listener. She's a real sane person too. Not one of these whackoes who's going to tell you that you're suffering from sublimated guilt or something."

Catherine raised her head. Her eyes were streaming with tears, so that some of the strands of her hair stuck wetly to her cheeks. "What if I *am* guilty?"

"Guilty of what? Guilty of being the last person to see Martin alive?"

"He wanted to stay with me. He wanted to sleep with me. But I said no."

"So what are trying to tell me? If you'd let him sleep with you, he wouldn't have gone back to the beach, and he wouldn't be dead?"

"I didn't know what to do. If I'd let him sleep with me, and Paul and Grey Cloud had found out—"

"Catherine, you're a big girl now. You're way past the age of consent. If you wanted to sleep with Martin, then there's nothing that Paul and Grey Cloud could have done about it."

She shook her head. She really was exceptionally pretty, especially with her hair floating across her face and her eyes glistening.

Jim said, "You can't let your brothers rule your life. All right, I know they're family. I know they think that have your best interests at heart, not to mention the racial purity of the Navajo. But look at me. I'm part German and part Scottish and part Hungarian. You may be Navajo, but first and foremost you're Catherine, your own person. Only *you* can decide what's best for you."

"That's not the point. If Paul and Grey Cloud had found out that Martin and I were sleeping together, they would have beaten up on him, I know it. Every time I've gotten friendly with anyone, they've frightened him or chased him away. Martin was the first boy who wouldn't let them push him around. If it had ever gotten really serious between us – I don't know. It all scares me. It scares me so much. That's why I didn't let Martin into the house."

Jim said, "You weren't to know what was going to happen to him. How could you? You were doing your best to protect him."

She lifted her head, her mouth tightened with grief. Jim said, "Here," and took a travel pack of Kleenex out of his coat pocket. He pulled one out and dabbed her eyes for her. It had been a long time since he had dabbed a woman's eyes.

"I killed him," she said, her voice choked with grief. "I should never have dated him. I should never have fallen in love with him."

"Come on, Catherine. You didn't kill him. It was bad luck, that's all. Everybody knows that the beach can be risky at night."

He dabbed her eyes again, and it was at this moment that he heard the throbbing of a tweaked-up V8 engine, and her brothers' black Firebird rolled into the parking-lot and stopped close beside them. Paul and Grey Cloud climbed out in their black jeans and their sunglasses, came over to Catherine and stood either side of her.

"Well, well, the Cheeryble Brothers," said Jim, referring to the irrepressibly optimistic characters in *Nicholas Nickleby*.

"The what?" asked Grey Cloud, taking off his sunglasses.

"Forget it. I don't expect you to know anything about Dickens."

"Dickens? They sound like hotels for people like you," Grey Cloud retorted.

"Well, well, a sense of humour," said Jim.

Paul came up close to him. "Catherine is coming here for the education, man. She's not coming here to look for a date. She's not here to look for any kind of counselling, either. And most of all she's not here for some kind of indoctrination into the white man's way."

"What she chooses to make of her time here is up to her, wouldn't you say?"

"No, I wouldn't say. And if I were you, I'd stick to teaching English and stay out of the rest of her life, OK?"

"Otherwise what?"

"Otherwise you remember what happened to your college football captain."

"That's a threat," said Jim.

Grey Cloud shook his head. "That isn't a threat any more than what we said to Martin Amato was a threat. That's just another prediction."

Jim took Susan out that evening to St Mark's, on Windward Avenue, for a steak dinner and an evening of live blues. He liked St Mark's because it was a friendly, jostling, casual place and dinner didn't usually cost more than $30 a head, so long as he didn't drink too much Stag's Leap chardonnay. They sat at a cramped corner table and tried to hold a conversation while King Jerry and the

Screamers gave a deafening rendition of *The House of the Rising Sun.*

Afterward, Jim drove Susan home. They sat outside her house in Jim's Rebel SST with the engine quietly burbling.

"Thanks for coming out," he told her. "I needed something like that to get my mind off Martin."

"That's OK. I enjoyed it."

He touched her shoulder. "Listen," he said, "you know what you said earlier, about boats bumping?"

She looked at him with her head slightly tilted to one side and he knew what her answer was going to be. Girls who want to bump will immediately give you a kiss: they won't look sympathetic.

"I'm sorry," she said. "It's just that – I don't know, Jim. Our relationship doesn't seem to be going anyplace."

"Where do you want it to go? Paris? Rome? Van Nuys?"

She smiled and shook her head. "It's not a question of where I want it to go. It should have a dynamic all of its own. But all we seem to be doing together is nothing very much."

Jim propped his arm on the back of his seat, and faced her directly. "So what are you saying to me? That you want to stop doing nothing very much, and do something else instead? I'm only a college teacher, Susan. My only dynamic is to turn semi-literate kids into people who can express themselves."

Susan said, "Yes. I know. And I've always admired you for what you do. But the truth is, Jim—" She paused, and then she said, "The truth is that I've forgotten why I fell in love with you."

He felt a cold snail-like sensation in his stomach. It made him feel like a teenager all over again. "Is it important that you remember *why*?" he asked her. "I mean, so long as you do?"

"That's the thing about it, Jim. I don't. Not any more."

"The other day, you said you almost did."

"Well, I've been thinking about that, and I don't think I'm being fair on you. Almost just isn't enough, is it?"

"Almost is better than nothing."

"Jim . . . I don't want to hurt you, that's all."

"You're right. Better to face up to it. We don't want to live out a lie, do we?"

"No," she said, lowering her eyes.

"Come on, we can still pass in the corridor and say 'hi' to each other. We can still watch college football games together. We can still chit-chat over cups of poisonous coffee at faculty get-togethers."

"Jim—" she said, and took hold of his hand.

He took a deep breath. "Don't worry," he said. "I'll live."

Although it suddenly occurred to him that if he didn't find the *2 Friends* within the next twenty-four hours, he would almost certainly die.

He knew that something was wrong as soon as he reached the top of the steps and started to walk along the balcony that led to his apartment. His front door was ajar, and there were hundreds of soft, crumbly fragments tumbling out of it, like snowflakes, except that they couldn't be snowflakes, with the late-evening temperature still well over 60 degrees.

He approached his front door cautiously, tightly rolling up the copy of *Esquire* that he was carrying so that he could use like a club. He listened, but he couldn't hear anything except for the occasional surge of studio laughter coming from Myrlin's television in the next door apartment, and the swooshing of traffic. Somebody was playing a guitar somewhere, and somebody else was whooping with laughter.

He reached the door and the snowflakes blew around his shoes. It was only then that he realized that they were tiny fragments of multicoloured plastic foam. He bent down and picked one up and squashed it between his fingers. It looked as if a pillow had been ripped open and emptied all over his floor.

"Pusscat?" he called, in a low, hoarse voice. He waited, but there was no response. He tried whistling, but there was still no reply. It was a damned nuisance, having a cat that refused to answer to her own name. She had suddenly stopped, about eighteen months ago, and Jim had even taken her to the vet to find out if she were deaf. The vet said, "Just cussedness, that's all."

Jim stretched out his hand and eased the front door open wide. It must have been kicked open, because the lock housing had been splintered right out the doorframe. Inside, it was almost totally dark, and he stood for a long time wondering if he dared to go in. There had been a spate of drug-connected robberies along this stretch of Electric Avenue in the past few weeks, and two innocent householders had been shot, one of them fatally.

"If you're in there, you'd better come out!" he called. "The cops are coming and I'm armed!"

Still there was no response. Jim reached around the door and felt for the light-switch. He took a deep breath, and switched it on.

At first he couldn't understand what he was looking at. Then – as he took one step into his apartment, and then another – he realised that the whole place had been torn apart, as if by a gang of enraged baboons. The snowflakes had come from his couch, which had been comprehensively gutted, right down to the springs. Polyurethane foam was scattered everywhere, ankle-deep in places. Pictures had been pulled from the walls and smashed. His television lay on one side, the screen cracked and two of the legs wrenched off. His CD collection had been pillaged, his books thrown everywhere, his venetian blinds reduced to collapsed concertinas.

It was the same in the kitchen. The refrigerator door had been pulled right off, and food strewn everywhere. A large jar of tomato-juice had been emptied across the floor like blood.

Most chilling of all, though, were the scratch-marks across the kitchen cabinets. The light oak doors had been viciously gouged by something which must have resembled a huge claw. Even the formica work-surface had been scratched – over an inch deep in places.

Jim picked up a broken picture-frame containing a photograph of his cousin Laura, with whom, when he was younger, he had fallen hopelessly in love. The glass was smashed and a claw had torn away half of Laura's face. He looked at it for a moment, and then let it drop back onto the floor. It was as if his entire life had been ripped to shreds – as if everything he had ever thought or felt or worked for had never counted for anything, and this was fate's way of showing him so.

There was worse to come. He went into the bedroom and his bed-covers had been sliced into shreds, his pillows burst apart. In the bathroom, the mirrors had all been smashed into kaleidoscopes and the washbasin pulled free from the wall – although, thankfully, the pipes hadn't been fractured.

He was just about to close the bathroom door when he noticed a reflection in the shattered mirror of his medicine cabinet. A dark reflection, on the other side of the door. At first he thought that it was just his robe, which he usually hung up there. Then he realised it was something more. His robe seemed to have a thick fur collar.

With a terrible feeling of dread, he looked around at the back of the door. His robe was there, yes. But it didn't have a fur collar. The feline formerly known as Tibbles had been hung on the same hook, right through her wide-open mouth, up through her palate and into her brain. Her eyes were wide open and glassy, and her teeth were bared in an agonized snarl.

Jim bent over the bathtub and up came half-chewed steak and string potatoes and broccoli, as well as an acid gush of bile and chardonnay.

After a few minutes of choking and gasping, he wiped his mouth on a towel and made his way back to the living-room, treading on broken glass and CDs and books. He found the telephone behind the sofa, and by some miracle it was still working. He took Lieutenant Harris's card out of his coat pocket and dialed his personal number.

He was still waiting to be put through when a figure appeared in the doorway. It was Miss Neagle, in a gauzy pink nightdress, with a ruffled collar.

"My God, Jim, what happened here? You look like you've just had your own personal earthquake."

Jim said, "Not far from it, Valerie. You know what you said about this dark thing coming to get me – this old, dark bristling thing? Well, it's almost caught up with me, believe me. If I hadn't have gone out tonight—"

Miss Neagle stepped her way carefully through the wreckage. She stood close to Jim and laid a hand on his shoulder. "I'm so sorry . . . you must be devastated."

"Devastated isn't the word for it. I'm terrified, too. And my cat – whatever it was, the damn thing killed my cat."

Miss Neagle sniffed – a long, inquiring sniff – and it sounded more like Mrs Vaizey sniffing. "I can still smell it," she said, after a while.

Jim sniffed, too, but all he could smell was Folger's coffee, spilled all over the kitchen floor. "It's left a *smell*?" he asked her.

"Not a real smell . . . it's more like a spiritual aroma. Sometimes, when I stand close to somebody who's done something really evil, I can pick up a terrible sour kind of odour, like rotting meat. Other times, I can smell when somebody's happy. It's very warm, and floral."

Jim sniffed again. "So what does this smell like?"

"It's an animal, although it isn't an animal. It has a very strong musky odour, like a bear. I can smell its aura, too. It's very fierce, almost berserk. I don't think anybody could stop it, even if they tried. It has incredible determination. It would go through brick walls to get at you, if it had to."

She paused, and frowned, and then she said, "And yet, you know – and yet –"

"And yet what?"

"I don't know. I can smell something else. A sense of *confusion*, maybe."

"It wasn't confused enough to tear up everything I own. Even my goddamn pajamas."

Miss Neagle looked at him and raised an eyebrow and now she looked just like Miss Neagle, and not at all like Mrs Vaizey. "Oh . . . I didn't know you wore *pajamas*."

Jim said grimly, "I don't, do I? Not now."

Just then, his call was connected. Lieutenant Harris sounded as if he had a headcold coming, and kept clearing his throat every few seconds. "Harris? What's the problem, Mr Rook?"

"Somebody just tore up my apartment, the same way they tore up the locker room at West Grove."

"Jesus, I'm sorry. Is there very much damage?"

"They killed my cat and they ripped up everything I

own. Furniture, books, paintings . . . there isn't anything left intact."

"Did anybody see anything?"

"It's probably just as well that they didn't. Whoever did this could rip your lungs out with one blow."

"What makes you think it was the same person that tore up the locker room?"

"I've got very similar scratches here, and clawmarks. And who the hell has the strength to pull the door off an icebox?"

"Listen," said Lieutenant Harris, "I don't want you to touch anything. I'll send a patrol car around as soon as I can, and I can get down there myself in twenty minutes. OK? But don't touch anything."

He put down the phone. Miss Neagle was prowling around the apartment, sniffing and sniffing, her arms held out almost like a ballerina. "What else can you smell?" Jim asked her.

"I smell *two* animals, not just one. I can't understand it. I can smell dog, as well as bear. Two distinctly different spiritual aromas."

"So what does that mean? That *two* animals came here and trashed my apartment, instead of one? What difference does that make?"

"It makes a whole lot of difference, Jim . . . because one animal is very strong and determined but the other feels as if it's fighting an inner battle with itself. That's all part of the *confusion* I was talking about."

"I don't follow this at all," said Jim. "I'm just going outside to wait for the cops."

But as he tried to pass, Miss Neagle clutched his arm and said, "The dog aroma comes from very far away – hundreds of miles. It must be tremendously powerful to make itself felt at such a distance. The bear is very dangerous, Mr Rook, but it's the dog you have to be wary of. The dog is going to do something really, really bad."

Jim looked around at his apartment, at his disemboweled furniture, at his shattered pictures, at his ripped-apart books. "You're telling me that this isn't really, really bad? Quite apart from the fact that I'm supposed to have less than three-and-a-half days to live."

"Something worse is going to happen, believe me."

Miss Neagle stared into his eyes and they weren't her eyes. They were pale and lucid as Mrs Vaizey's. "You don't even know what this thing can do to you, Jim. These animals can take your spirit, as well as your body. When you die, you expect to be back with your parents, don't you, and the people you always loved? You expect to be back in those old familiar places where you used to play when you were a boy? But if you give your spirit to *these* beasts, Mr Rook, you won't know anything but pain and darkness, for ever and ever. There *is* an afterlife, believe me, but if you let these beasts get hold of you, you'll wish to God that there wasn't."

Chapter Four

Jim spent the night on the couch round at George Babouris' house in the less desirable part of Westwood. George was big-bellied and black-bearded and catastrophically untidy. His living-room was strewn with cast-off sneakers and discarded sweatshirts and empty pizza boxes, as well as heaps of books and students' coursework. It looked only marginally less devastated than Jim's place.

George got up early and came padding through to the kitchen in a Homer Simpson T-shirt and a pair of baggy shorts, scratching his behind and puffing on the first cigarette of the day. Jim looked up frowzily from the couch and said, "What time is it, George, for Christ's sake?"

"Five-thirty. I always get up at five-thirty. It gives me time to have a little bit of life outside of college."

"Five-thirty is so damned early it's practically still yesterday."

"Yes, but think what you can get done. I'm writing a book at the moment. I can write two or three pages every morning before I have to start thinking about banging Newton's Law into those sloping foreheads in Applied Physics. Here, look—" he said, and passed Jim a handful of crumpled, coffee-stained paper.

Jim rubbed his eyes and peered at the title. *The Lute of Apollo: The Complete History of Bouzouki Music*. He handed it back without comment.

"You see?" said George. "I went to the library and found that nobody has ever published a definitive book on Greek café music – not even in Greece. So I thought, here's a gap in the market, I'll write one myself! I'll be famous! Maybe they'll make me President of Greece! How about some coffee?"

Jim dressed and went to college almost an hour earlier than usual because George fried himself a huge breakfast of corned beef hash which filled the whole apartment with greasy smoke, and then insisted on playing *bouzouki* music so that Jim could learn to appreciate how much it spoke of the sun, and the wine-dark sea, and a land where men were men and had seriously hairy chests and women did all the work.

Alone in his classroom, he sat in the dust-speckled morning sunshine marking essays. He had given up smoking seven years ago, but he had never felt more like a cigarette. He had asked Special Class II to write him a critical assessment of *Treasure Island*. Mark Foley had written, "Long John Silver was this cool dud with 1 leg, leder of the pirates. He wants to rip off all of the treasure but Jim Hawkins stops him. He should of kill Jim Hawkins but they had a bond, lik a father and son should of been."

Jim always found it extraordinary how his least able students were able to get right to the nub of a story. They ignored the plot and felt the pulse of it. Beattie McCordic, who always interpreted everything she read from a radical-feminist point of view, had written that 'there are no women pirates in *Treasure Island* which is ridiculous because in real life there were plenty of them and some of them were real ballbreakers.' But she went on to say 'that doesn't mean that the story is anti-feminist. The way Jim Hawkins behaves is influenced all the way through the story by his mother, who is quiet but strong and very moral. There are two main characters in this book: Long John Silver and Jim Hawkin's mother, even though she only appears right in the beginning and right at the very end.'

After two or three essays, he stopped marking, and stared out of the window. He thought of the feline formerly known as Tibbles and he felt so angry and sad that he could have cried. But while he was looking out of the window he saw a dark-blue Chevrolet Caprice turn into the parking-lot, and Lieutenant Harris climb out. Lieutenant Harris put on his dark glasses, combed his hair, straightened his coat, and walked toward the college buildings like a man who was very pleased with himself.

Two or three minutes later, there was a knock at the classroom door. "Mr Rook?" said Lieutenant Harris.

"Sure, come on in," Jim told him. "You look like the cat who got the caviar."

"Well, I thought you'd like to know that we've made a breakthrough in the Martin Amato homicide."

"That's good news. That's really good news. Did you make an arrest yet?"

Lieutenant Harris triumphantly lifted one finger. "Let me tell you something, it was classic procedural police-work. We did a house-to-house down at Venice Beach, and then we staked out the boardwalk and stopped every single cyclist and jogger and skater. We interviewed every bodybuilder on Muscle Beach and every rollerblader in the Graffiti Pit."

Jim put down his pen and waited for Lieutenant Harris to finish complimenting himself on the trouble that he had taken.

"In the end, we found two young guys from Idaho, of all places. They had hitch-hiked all the way from Boise in the hope of becoming movie extras. Saturday night they didn't have anyplace to stay so they tried to sleep on the beach. They were lying in their bedrolls when two men ran right into them."

Lieutenant Harris picked up the small plaster bust of Shakespeare on Jim's desk and peered at it closely. "Who's this? Don't tell me. That guy from *Star Trek*."

"Lieutenant," Jim said, impatiently.

"Oh, sure. Well, there was a scuffle between these two young kids from Idaho and these two guys who had run right into them. It wasn't much, and the kids wouldn't have thought anything about it, except that when the two guys had gone running off, one of them found that his hands were covered in blood. The first thing he thought was that one of the guys had stabbed him. So he went to a local bar and washed it all off, and found that he hadn't been stabbed at all. The blood must have come from the other guy."

"Suggesting what?"

"Suggesting that the other guy had either cut himself badly – or else he'd very recently cut somebody else, and gotten himself splattered in their blood."

"And?"

"And he couldn't have cut himself. The blood must have come from somebody else."

"How do you know that?"

Lieutenant Harris gave him a triumphant smile. "Because the two kids on the beach positively identified him as Catherine White Bird's brother Grey Cloud – and it didn't take much to establish that Grey Cloud didn't cut himself that night. His partner they identified as Paul – Catherine's other brother."

"You're kidding me. Those two pretend they're tough, but I don't believe they'd go that far."

"They did it, Mr Rook. That's obvious. They didn't like their sister going out with a white man, so when she refused to give him up – that was it. Tribal honour was at stake, or whatever."

"You've arrested them?"

Lieutenant Harris nodded. "Suspicion of first-degree homicide. I'll admit that I still don't know how they inflicted those wounds on Martin Amato, but they were down on the beach at the time he was killed, and Grey Cloud was covered in blood. We're running a DNA and haemotology test right now, and if that blood turns out to be Martin's . . . well, that's all folks."

"What about the locker room? What about my apartment? What about my cat?"

"In those instances, Mr Rook, I believe that we're looking for somebody else altogether."

"But the scratches match, don't they?"

"There's some superficial similarity, but we haven't finished our forensic tests yet."

"Lieutenant," Jim protested, "these incidents are all connected. That locker room was trashed by the same person who killed my cat and trashed my apartment, and the same person who killed my cat and trashed my apartment is the same person who murdered Martin Amato."

"I have a problem with that," said Lieutenant Harris.

"Problem? What problem?"

"At the time your cat was being killed and your apartment was being remodeled, Paul and Grey Cloud were having dinner at home with their father and five friends from their father's TV show."

Jim stared at him. "So what do you conclude from that?"

"I conclude that the two cases are not connected."

"What if Paul and Grey Cloud *didn't* do it? They could still be connected then."

"*Yes*, Mr Rook,' said Lieutenant Harris, with thinly-disguised impatience. "But they're not, and we're going to prove that they're not, and once we've done that, Paul and Grey Cloud are going to get what's coming to them."

The door opened and David Littwin cautiously put his head around it. "OK to come in, Mr Rook? I thought I'd come in early to finish off my poem."

"Sure, come in, David," said Jim. "Lieutenant Harris was just leaving."

"I may need to talk to you some more," said Lieutenant Harris. He was obviously upset that Jim hadn't clapped him on the back and acknowledged him as the greatest procedural detective since Maigret.

"Sure, any time," Jim told him. Lieutenant Harris hesitated by the door for a moment, and then left. Jim went back to his marking.

Sherma Feldstein had written, 'I think *Treasure Island* should be banned as the only physically-challenged person in the entire novel is presented as a villain. That is, Long John Silver, who only had one leg, not his own fault. This novel will further reinforce prejudice against the physically disadvantaged by presenting them as greedy and immoral and prepared to use their disabilities for nefarious gain.'

Jim gave her an extra point for good spelling and vocabulary, and for correctly using 'nefarious', but he simply didn't know how to mark her for suggesting that *Treasure Island* had been written as a diatribe against the disabled.

He felt the same way about Lieutenant Harris. Maybe Lieutenant Harris was right, and Martin *had* been murdered by Paul and Grey Cloud. There was strong circumstantial evidence against them, after all. But it seemed to Jim that Lieutenant Harris was doing what Sherma Feldstein was doing – closing his eyes to everything except his own prejudice.

There had been no discrimination against Long John

Silver in *Treasure Island.* In fact, he had dominated all the other characters – while Paul and Grey Cloud seemed to Jim to have a mission that white men might not fully understand, but which amounted to very much more than attacking anyone who tried to be too friendly with their sister.

When the class assembled, there were three absentees. Titus Greenspan III had another bad attack of asthma; Seymour Williams had gone to his great-aunt's funeral at Forest Lawn; and Catherine White Bird had simply failed to show. It wasn't hard to understand why.

Jim didn't tell the class that Catherine's brothers had been arrested. They would find out soon enough, and he was more interested in teaching them how to cope with their grief. Revenge could wait until later.

"You want to tell me how you got on with your poems?" he asked them. "Did you find them difficult? Did you find that they helped you to express how you feel?"

"I think it's better to smash something when you're feeling that bad," said Ray. "You know – break a window, kick in a door. It gets rid of your frustration better."

"So you felt frustrated by Martin's death?"

"Frustrated? You're kidding me, aren't you? I felt like *why*, man? The guy was so young. Like he had his whole life in front of him, and he happens to walk into some whacko who kills him. I just wish I could of been there. I just wish I could of saved him. I just wish it was Saturday afternoon again and he was still alive."

"So what did you do? Did you write a poem or did you smash something?"

"I did both. I went home and I wrecked my old Spanish guitar. I smashed it up against the wall until it was nothing more than matchwood and strings."

"And did that make you feel any better?"

Ray shrugged, and said, "Yeah. It made me feel better."

"How about your poem? Do you want to read it to us?"

Ray fastidiously picked the gum out of the side of his mouth and stuck it under his desk. He picked up a well-folded sheet of paper and cleared his throat. Usually, the rest of the class would have barracked him, but today they were silent. They knew he wasn't very articulate but they knew how he felt.

"This is called, like, *Smashed-Up Guitar:*

'I smashed up my guitar today
So that I would never have to play
Any more songs for you

I don't want to play the chords
Or even sing the words
You wouldn't hear me even if I wanted you to

You're just like my guitar
Smashed-up, that's what you are
Your only song is gone and we're all missing you.'"

"That's good, Ray," said Jim. "That's probably the best piece of work you've produced this term. You've made a really vivid analogy about your guitar being broken and silent and Martin being broken and silent, too."

Ray suddenly flushed scarlet – the first time that Jim had ever seen him embarrassed. He retrieved his gum and bent over his desk with his face covered by his hands.

"Anybody else?" asked Jim.

John Ng hesitantly put up his hand. "I've only written something very short," he said. "It's not exactly a *haiku* but I guess it's kind of like it."

"Go on, then."

"'*The grass*
Misses your tread
The sand
Misses your running shadow
But the wind
Welcomes you.'"

"Do you want to explain that a little?" asked Jim.

"Well . . . I'm just trying to say that when you leave the earth, there's another life waiting for you. Not a life that you can see, just like you can't see the wind, but just as exciting."

"So you believe in a life after death?"

"Of course, Mr Rook. The same as you do."

Russell said, "Mr Rook, sir? Do you want to hear mine? It's pretty long. Sixty-two verses. I call it *The Ballad of Martin Amato.*"

There was a quiet groan from Mark Foley. The last ballad that Russell had written was a blow-by-blow account of the plot of *Waterworld*, and it had gone on almost as long as the movie itself. But Jim said, "OK, Russell, let's hear it." He didn't think it would do the class any harm to have a little light relief.

"'*This ballad is just starting*
It's the story of a boy called Martin
Of the crop he was the cream
And he was captain of the football team.
Martin was tall with a ready smile
He was so tall that he stood out a mile
As you know his surname was Amato
Which was why he was often kidded and called Tomato.'"

Russell went on and on, and the monotony of his rhyming wasn't helped by his halting delivery. Jim found himself looking out of the window and thinking about Mrs Vaizey and the warnings that she had given him through Valerie Neagle. God, it was Tuesday morning already and he was supposed to be killed on Thursday – and he still didn't have any idea of who his '2 Friends' might be or where he was supposed to be travelling. It gave him a terrible nagging feeling of frustrated dread. Don't talk to *me* about frustration, Ray. Don't talk to *me* about smashing things up.

Russell was still droning on when there was a knock at the classroom door and Dr Ehrlichman's secretary came in. "Mr Rook? I'm sorry to interrupt your tutorial, but there's a visitor for you."

"Okay, thanks, Sylvia. Listen up, everybody. Let Russell finish reading his ballad and then I want you to read the poem on page 32 of *Gasoline* by Gregory Corso."

He left the class and walked along the corridor in the wake of Sylvia's overpowering perfume. When he reached the principal's office he found to his surprise that Henry Black Eagle was standing there, waiting for him. Henry Black Eagle's face was as serious as an axe-hacked oak.

"I don't like to disturb you, Mr Rook. But I have to ask you a very great favour."

"Well, you can *ask*," said Jim, cautiously.

"Can we talk in private?" asked Henry Black Eagle, looking over Jim's shoulder at Sylvia, who was pretending to check Dr Ehrlichman's diary while keeping one dangly earring cocked to hear what they were saying.

Jim said, "Sure . . . why don't we take a walk?" and led him out through the hallway to the front entrance. They walked out past the tennis-courts, under a hazy sun.

Their conversation was punctuated by the *plick-plack* of students playing mixed doubles.

"Lieutenant Harris told me that your sons had been arrested," said Jim.

Henry Black Eagle nodded. "The police came this morning, just after six o'clock. I've already talked to a lawyer here in Los Angeles, but I sent to the DNA for a Navajo lawyer, too."

"I gather that two hitch-hikers saw Paul and Grey Cloud on the beach just about the same time that Martin Amato was murdered."

"That's true," said Black Eagle.

"You mean they *were* there?"

"Yes, they were. But not to kill the Amato boy, believe me."

"Even though they'd already threatened him? I mean, I was a witness to that. They specifically told Martin that he wouldn't live to see another dawn."

"I know. But you misunderstood. They never had any intention of causing the Amato boy any harm."

"They had blood on them, that's what Lieutenant Harris told me."

"I know. But I can swear to you that they didn't commit any crime."

"So what *were* they doing down on the beach?"

Henry Black Eagle stopped. "They were protecting their sister, as they always do."

"Protecting her from what? From the animal that killed Martin?"

"Yes, in a way."

"So what is it, this animal? And why is it trying to hurt her?"

"This is the reason that I've come to you for help," said Henry Black Eagle. "Apart from the fact that Catherine thinks that you're a very inspirational teacher, she tells me that you have a gift. Her classmates told her that you can see things that other people can't . . . spiritual things."

"Well, that's partly true. I sometimes have – I don't know, *visions* and spiritual intuitions. But what does that have to do with this animal?"

"This animal, Mr Rook, is not a real animal. It comes from the spirit world. It is like a curse, of a kind."

"A curse," said Jim, trying not to look too unimpressed. "Do you want to tell me more?"

"I think you should talk to Paul and Grey Cloud. They are both much more involved in Navajo spiritualism than me. But you can see my problem, can't you? How can I prove that my sons didn't kill this Martin Amato boy when he was killed by something that you can't see, even if you could be persuaded to believe in it?"

"So what do you think *I* can do about it?"

"Talk to Paul and Grey Cloud, please. At least hear what they have to say. Even if you don't do it for their sake, or for my sake, at least do it for Catherine's sake. She knows that her brothers didn't murder Martin, and she doesn't want to see them go to prison for it. She also wants the beast to be sent back to the spirit world, so that it won't hurt anybody else."

"I'm going to have to think about this, Mr Black Eagle. I had a very, very bad horoscope this week, concerning beasts. Apart from that, my dead grandfather came to my apartment two days ago and sat and talked to me, as close as you are now. He warned me to watch for something old and cold and bristling, and that sounds like a beast to me."

"Please, Mr Rook. If there were any other way – if there were any other person who could help us, I wouldn't ask. But you're the only one who can see the beast. Nobody else would stand a chance."

Jim stopped and pressed two fingers to his forehead,

the way he always did when he was thinking something over. Then he said, "OK . . . I'll go talk to Paul and Grey Cloud – see what they have to say. But I can't make you any guarantees. Not until I know what this is all about."

"Let me give you something," said Henry Black Eagle. He reached into the pocket of his fringed buckskin coat and took out a thin silver whistle on a frayed cord made of twisted hair. "Here . . . it belongs to Grey Cloud, but he wouldn't have been allowed to give it to you down at the police station."

Jim took the whistle and turned it from side to side. "What is this? What does it do?"

"It works like a dog-whistle, way beyond the range of human hearing."

Jim blew it; and Henry Black Eagle was right, it was silent. But there was a man walking a Labrador bitch only fifty or sixty feet away, and the bitch took absolutely no notice, even when Jim blew it again. "So what kind of dogs does this call?" he wanted to know.

"Please . . . you'll understand more when you talk to Paul and Grey Cloud."

Jim said, "All right. But I'm not making you any promises. And I'm scared of dogs. So if this whistle calls anything more aggressive than a chihuahua, you can forget it."

"You make jokes in the face of death."

"No, I don't. Death is just about the biggest joke of all. The only trouble is, it never makes me laugh."

He arrived at police headquarters just before noon. His car let off a deafening backfire, and two policemen who were climbing out of their patrol car instinctively ducked. "Sorry," he said, with a wave of his hand.

"You want to get that muffler fixed before somebody shoots back," one of the officers warned him.

"Sorry," he repeated, and went up the steps to the front desk.

Lieutenant Harris was on the way out. He looked hot and unhappy. "Mr Rook – I really appreciate all of the assistance you've been trying to give us, but I don't think that you're going to be doing anything at all constructive by talking to those Navajo boys."

"I don't think they did it," said Jim.

"Oh. That's supposed to be constructive, is it? They made a death threat against Martin Amato in front of independent witnesses. They were seen by more independent witnesses at or near the crime scene at the time the crime was committed. They have blood on their clothes which I have learned within the past fifteen minutes is the same group as Martin Amato's, type O. And apart from that, they're uncooperative, aggressive, and their lawyer's just arrived and he looks like Sitting Bull."

"Sitting Bull was a Sioux."

"Whatever."

Jim said, "I still want to talk to them. Come on, lieutenant, the family trust me. I might be able to throw some light on what really happened."

Lieutenant Harris wiped perspiration from his forehead with the back of his hand. "OK . . . but don't take longer than ten minutes – that's if they agree to talk to you. And when you're through, don't say one single word to the Press. You got that? Not even 'no comment'. I'm not having this case prejudiced by the media, no way."

"You can trust me, lieutenant."

Lieutenant Harris was about to push his way out through the revolving doors when he stopped. "By the way, we checked the clawmarks in your apartment and measured them up against the clawmarks in the locker room. They were similar, but they didn't exactly match."

"What do you mean?"

"I mean that the damage in the locker-room was inflicted with a similar-type claw or instrument as the damage in your apartment, but there was quite a difference in measurement."

"Measurement? Like what?"

"Whatever trashed your apartment had a claw span of well over eleven inches. The widest claw span we found in the locker room was just over six."

"What about the clawmarks on Martin Amato?"

"They were different again. Eight, maybe nine inches at a stretch."

"So what conclusion do you draw from that?"

"None, so far. I'm just telling you."

"Maybe you should be looking for three different animals. Or one animal that can grow dramatically in the space of a single weekend."

Lieutenant Harris stared at him long and hard, one eye squinched up in an unconscious impersonation of *Columbo*. He didn't attempt to disguise the contempt in his voice. "Mr Rook, if you can find me any living creature whose claws grow five inches in a matter of three days, then please let me know, because I can get in touch with Ripley's Believe It Or Not. Meanwhile, if you really have to talk to those two Native Americans, why don't you see if you can't persuade them to confess that they *did* murder Martin Amato, and tell you how they did it. It would save the taxpayer money. It would save *them* money. We could go fishing instead of sitting in court. Anyhow – I have to go. Sergeant! Take Mr Rook through to see our Native American guests. Ten minutes max."

The big-bellied sergeant came forward with a long loop of keys hanging from his belt. "This way, sir," he said, with deep condescension, his moustache cropped like a brand-new nailbrush. He led Jim through a swing door, past the squadroom, and through to an interview room at the back of the building. There was a plain table scarred with cigarette burns and four plain wooden chairs. The window was covered with wire mesh.

"Just take a seat, sir," said the sergeant. "We'll bring your friends up momentarily."

Jim stood by the window and waited. Outside he could see the rear end of a squad car and the corner of a brick wall, and a narrow rectangle of intensely blue sky. He wondered what it would be like to be locked up for the rest of your life. Better to be dead. But he didn't want to think about being dead, either – not with death breathing so coldly and quickly down his neck.

The door opened and the sergeant and another officer brought in Paul and Grey Cloud, handcuffed and shackled. The sergeant told them to sit down, well away from the table. Then he said to Jim, "Remember what the lieutenant said, sir – ten minutes and no longer. No smoking, no passing of any smoking materials, foodstuffs, books, gifts or documents. No physical contact whatsoever."

"All right if I breathe a little?" asked Jim.

"That's optional," said the sergeant, and left the room, leaving the other officer standing by the door, his hands behind his back, his eyes fixed on nothing at all, slowly and irritatingly masticating a large wad of chewing-gum.

Jim sat down. "I guess you probably know that your father came to see me. He said that you needed my help."

"We wouldn't have called for you at all," said Grey Cloud, proudly lifting his head. "But Catherine insisted – and, so long as we're locked up here – there is no other way open to us. You will have to be our eyes and our ears, our legs and our voices."

"Your father mentioned some kind of animal."

"The spirit-beast, yes. The beast that nobody can see, even when it kills them."

"It's going to be hard to explain that to a jury."

"That's why we've come to you. We need you to tell people that the spirit-beast *does* exist. That's our only hope of proving that we're innocent."

"Maybe if you took a polygraph test," Paul suggested.

"Wait a minute," said Jim. "What gives you the idea that I believe you?"

"You're prepared to admit the possibility that we *might* be telling the truth," said Grey Cloud. "Otherwise you wouldn't have come."

"OK – there's an outside chance that some kind of spiritual force may have been responsible for Martin Amato's death, instead of you two. I'm probably the only person on the planet who thinks so. But I believe that the West Grove college locker room and my apartment were both trashed by the whatever it was that killed Martin, and I don't care for the way that the cops are trying to suggest that they weren't. That smells of railroading to me. But I'm going to need a whole lot more proof before I start taking lie-detector tests and standing up and swearing on the Bible that an invisible creature from the spirit world ripped Martin's lungs out, and not you. After all, you were down on the beach at the time when he was killed."

"I promise you we had nothing to do with it," said Paul. "We didn't even *see* it."

"You were covered in blood."

"It was hard not to be."

"You were right there – right after it happened?"

Paul, soberly, said, "Yes. He was still pumping it out like a gusher."

Jim ran his hand through his hair. "You've got trouble here, guys. No question about it."

"All right," put in Grey Cloud. "You saw the body. What do *you* think killed him?"

Jim hesitated. "A bear, maybe, or a mountain lion."

"It certainly wasn't done by humans, was it?"

"Not unless they had some kind of fancy claw."

"Well, sure," said Grey Cloud. "But can you imagine the strength you'd need to do something like that? And what happened to this fancy claw? Did we throw it away? Did we bury it? Is it hidden in our house?"

"OK," said Jim, "supposing you find a way of convincing me that this spirit-beast exists. What do you want me to do about it, apart from making a laughing-stock of myself in front of a court of law?"

"We want you to arrange for the curse to be lifted, so that the beast returns to where it came from."

"Oh, yes? And how can I do that?"

Grey Cloud said, "You will have to make a journey – a journey that will take you many miles in distance, and a long, long way inside your soul. You will have to learn what it is to be a Navajo. You will have to acquire the great understanding."

Seek the advice of two friends, thought Jim. Travel on a long journey. But then he said, "Don't you think one of your own kind would be better at this? A Navajo? Somebody who believes in this stuff already?"

Grey Cloud shook his head. "Too many Navajo have lost their faith. They should be looking for their spirits, but all they want is automobiles and housing developments and factories. When white men first came to our land, they defeated us not only by slaughtering us and giving us white men's diseases, but by shaking our faith in our gods. One by one, all of our deities lost their power to defend us. Even Gitche Manitou the Great Spirit was rendered powerless and silent. How could he speak to people who no longer listened? We used to hear his words in the wind, but after the white men came all we heard was train-whistles and traffic and radio shows. In the same way, where can the spirit of water survive, when the rivers are poisoned by industrial pollution? There is no place for a spirit of fire when men have atomic bombs.

"The spirits are still there, but the people are blind. Only *you* can see them."

"Well, this all sounds very mystical," said Jim, "but I'm not at all sure that I can do it. I'm not at all sure that I *want* to do it."

"I'm sorry," said Grey Cloud, "but you *have* to. You know that you do. Not just for our sake, but for yours, too. If you don't go looking for this beast – this beast is going to come looking for you. It knows that you've been protecting our sister – and, what's more, it knows that you can see it."

Jim wasn't sure that he believed any of Grey Cloud's warnings or not, but they gave him an uncomfortable feeling that he was being *watched* – or, worse than that, that something very dark and malevolent was *sniffing him out*. He glanced up at the window, but the shadow he had seen out of the corner of his eye was only the shadow of a nodding leaf.

"So where am I supposed to journey to?" he asked. "And what am I supposed to do when I arrive?"

"You have to journey to the Navajo capital of Window Rock, in Arizona. Take Catherine with you, and three other friends. My father will pay for the air fares. When you reach Window Rock, you will meet a man called John Three Names. He will take you to Fort Defiance, which we call the Meadow Between Rocks."

"Then what?"

"Then he will take you to the man that Catherine is supposed to marry."

"So Catherine's betrothal has something to do with all this?"

Grey Cloud said, "Yes. The man that Catherine is supposed to marry has gone to a wonder-worker and conjured up the spirit-beast to prevent her from forming any attachments to anyone else."

"I see."

"You don't believe us? It's true! He was so angry and jealous that he would have done anything to stop anybody else from touching her."

"Supposing I *do* believe you?" said Jim. "Why did your father promise this guy that Catherine was going to marry him in the first place? Is he rich, or what? I mean, that's not a Navajo thing, is it? Arranged marriages?"

Paul paused, and then he said, "Our father did it because our mother was dying of ovarian cancer. The man said that he knew a wonder-worker, and that the wonder-worker could intercede with the spirits to save our mother's life. All he wanted in return was to marry Catherine and breed children with her."

"And your father agreed to that? Without asking Catherine what *she* wanted?"

"He was losing his wife, Mr Rook. He was losing our mother. He was desperate."

"But your mother died anyway, didn't she?"

"Yes, she did. The spirits obviously thought that it was time for her to die. Afterward, my father went back to the man she was supposed to marry and asked if Catherine could be released from her betrothal. But the man said that a sacred promise was a sacred promise. Our father begged him, but he refused to change his mind. He said he wanted Catherine and he was going to have her, whatever it took."

Paul said, "We lit out of Window Rock overnight, leaving most of our possessions behind. Catherine didn't know why and we weren't going to tell her. We came here to Los Angeles and my father was lucky enough to get that part in *Blood Brothers*. The studio needed a full-blood Navajo and he was a full-blood Navajo, and he could act."

"But then?"

"Then we had messages that this man was going out of his mind with jealousy, and that he was going to ask the wonder-workers to put a curse on Catherine, so that no other man would ever be able to touch her. If they did – well, you saw what happened to Martin. The spirit-beast destroyed the locker-room, as a warning, and then, when he refused to be intimidated, it killed him."

Jim stood up and walked back to the window. A small puffy cloud had appeared in the rectangle of blue sky, and the squad car had gone. "This is a seriously weird story, I'll tell you that."

"Believe me, Mr Rook, this is the truth. Would we tell you a lie, when our freedom is at stake? We might even go to the gas chamber if they find us guilty."

"Think of Catherine, too," said Grey Cloud. "Think of all the other people who could get hurt."

"Yes," said Jim. "Including me."

"Will you help us?" asked Paul. Behind him, the police officer sniffed and carried on chewing his gum.

Jim said, "I don't know. You haven't told me what I'm supposed to do when I meet this spirit-man. How am I going to persuade him to give Catherine up?"

"John Three Names will explain all of that. But the main thing you have to do is make him an offer. Money, mainly. But some other promises, too."

"I'm sorry, guys. I think I need to know much more before I say yes or no."

"Mr Rook – it's far too complicated to explain right now. But I promise you – it isn't anything difficult."

"All right, maybe it's not difficult. But is it *dangerous*?"

Grey Cloud gave an evasive shrug; but Paul said, "It won't be dangerous if you remember everything that John Three Names tells you."

"I don't know," said Jim. "I'm still not sure about this."

Paul clenched his handcuffed fists and banged them on his knees. "You *must*!" he said. "*You have to*! There isn't any more time and we don't have anybody else."

"Excuse me. You may not have anybody else but I just get the feeling you're not telling me everything you know."

"There's nothing else *to* know. You go to Arizona, you talk to this guy, you make a deal with him, and that's the end of it."

"So why do I have to take three friends?"

"To take care of Catherine, that's all."

"Can't Catherine take care of herself?"

"Mostly . . . but with all this going on, we think it's a good idea for somebody to keep a close eye on her. That's why we always picked her up after college. You know, just in case."

Jim said nothing for at least a minute. The guard sneezed twice. Paul and Grey Cloud watched him with tightly-contained unease. He didn't understand this situation, not at all. But he took his grandfather's warning very seriously, and he took Mrs Vaizey's fortune-telling very seriously, and it seemed as if he were following the destiny that they both had predicted for him.

"All right," he said, at last. "Let me talk to your father again. Then I'll see what I can do."

He found Henry Black Eagle at Universal Studios, on the set of *Blood Brothers*. A small scrubby area of backlot was supposed to be the Navajo reservation in Arizona, although Jim could easily see the *Psycho* house on the horizon, and coachloads of tourists being trundled around the *Jaws* pool and through the parting of the Red Sea.

Henry was sitting in the front seat of a dusty blue-and-white police car drinking coffee from a styrofoam cup and smoking a cigarette. Jim leaned over the roof and said, "I talked to your sons. It looks like I'm going to Arizona."

Henry nodded, without looking up. "Thank you, Mr Rook. One day, you'll get your reward for this." He checked his watch, and said, "There's a flight to Albuquerque at seven tomorrow morning. I can get you a charter from Albuquerque to Gallup. John Three Names will meet you there and drive you the rest of the way."

Jim said, "There's only one thing I'm going to ask you. What kind of a character is this man who's supposed to be marrying your daughter?"

"Clever. Devious. He can twist your mind like a helter-skelter."

"How old is he? Do you know where he comes from?"

"He's as old as he looks. Where he comes from – well . . . where do any of us come from? The trees, the rocks, the dust on the ground."

"Does he have a name?" asked Jim. "It seems a little odd, flying all the way to Arizona to meet a guy and I don't even know his name."

"Well, he has several names, as many Navajo do, but most of the time they call him He Who Speaks To Animals, or Dog Brother."

"And what does he look like? I mean, how old is he? Like, what can I expect?"

"You can only expect the unexpected, Mr Rook. He's a very devious man, very unpredictable. You should take care not to upset him."

At that moment, a podgy assistant director in a sweaty green *Blood Brothers* T-shirt came waddling up and said, "Come on, Henry. We're ready to shoot the explosion scene."

"OK," said Henry, and eased himself out of the car. "How about it, Mr Rook? Do you want to watch?"

"Yes, sure. I'd love to," said Jim. He followed Henry and the assistant director to a small corner of the lot where an elderly black Lincoln Continental was already tilted into a ditch. In the driver's seat sat a dummy with a blue flowery dress and a blonde wig, slumped over the steering-wheel. Special effects technicians were still fiddling with wires and detonators, and the camera crew were standing around, switching on dazzling photo-floods and then switching them off again, smoking and drinking bottles of Evian water.

On the other side of the set, on the porch of a 'sheriff's office' that was nothing more than a front wall propped up with joists, Jim caught sight of Catherine, wearing a yellow checkered shirt and jeans, talking to a script assistant. "You brought her to work?" he asked Henry.

"What else could I do? Her brothers are in jail. Somebody has to watch over her."

"She could have come to college. We keep a pretty good eye on our students there."

Henry said, "Yes, I know," but that was all; and then the assistant director came over to put him in position.

Just before the clapper-board snapped, however, Henry turned to Jim, and the expression on his face was unlike anything that Jim had seen before. Haunted, haggard, almost pleading. Jim looked over at Catherine. She was still talking with great animation to the script assistant, flicking back her hair and moving her hands. She was just as beautiful as ever – her hair gleaming, her eyes bright. But Jim was sure that he could see a shadow around her. A dark, dim shadow – much bigger than she was – and *hunched up*, as if it were trying to hide itself within her.

The longer he looked at her, the clearer the shadow became. It followed every movement she made, but it was obviously another being altogether, a being that was imitating her, in order to stay concealed. Jim couldn't take his eyes off it.

He was standing right next to the best boy, who was wearing a *Blood Brothers* baseball cap backwards and trying to sort out a wildly frayed arrangement of multicolored electrical wires with a pair of pliers.

"Let me ask you something," he said. "That girl over there . . . the one in the yellow shirt. Can you see kind of a *shadow* all around her?"

The best boy peered at Catherine, and then looked back at Jim as if he were two fajitas short of a Mexican picnic. "Shadow?" he said, as if he didn't know what the word meant.

"It's nothing," said Jim. "Forget it." But after the best boy had gone back to his electrical spaghettini, he looked at Catherine again, and there was no doubt that there was a dingy shadow flickering over her. Even when she got up from her seat and walked across the set, the shadow followed her, like smoke, like clouds, like a black-and-white movie projected over her face.

She saw him, and waved, and he was still watching her when there was a deafening explosion, and the Lincoln blew up in a scorching ball of orange flame. The windows were shattered, the tires caught fire, and the hood was flung twenty feet up into the air. Jim turned around just in time to see Henry Black Eagle rolling away across the dust with a gun in his hand.

When he looked back, Catherine had disappeared behind the dust and the smoke and the milling crowd of extras. But he glimpsed the shadow, sliding across the front of the 'sheriff's office', and it was crouched, and angular, with a jagged, bristly outline.

Chapter Five

He met Susan in the corridor outside the geography room and asked her if she was interested in a trip to Arizona.

"Arizona? Why on earth should I want to go to Arizona?"

"I don't know. You like cacti, don't you? And the weather's pretty good."

"The weather's pretty good here. Besides, I'm right in the middle of the busiest semester I've ever had. And also, I thought that you and I were taking a raincheck."

"Well, it won't be just us. One of my students is coming along. In fact, two or three of my students may be coming along. We're visiting the Navajo reservation at Window Rock."

Susan shook her head. "I can't believe you sometimes. You are the most – I don't know. You are the most off-the-wall person I ever met. Sometimes I feel like you arrived here from another planet, and you haven't quite learned how Earth people behave."

"All the same, how about coming to Arizona?"

"No, Jim. I can't."

"I need you, Susan. I wouldn't ask you if I didn't need you. And I'm not talking about sexually. I'm talking about *needing* you, okay? Like needing your support."

"Why?" she demanded.

"Well . . . I'm taking a couple of my girl students away

with me, and I think it would be more appropriate if they had a female chaperone."

"I suppose you're taking Catherine White Bird?"

"Of course. I mean, this was what inspired the trip in the first place, her being a full-blooded Navajo and everything."

"And a very alluring full-blooded Navajo, too."

"What am I supposed to say? That she looks like the back side of a totem pole?"

"OK. Who else is going?"

"I don't know. I haven't asked them yet. But I really wanted you."

Susan said, "This won't work, Jim. You and I, we're just not suited. You say tomayto and I say tomato."

"I know that. But that's not the point. I need a clear-thinking, intelligent, responsible adult on this trip. I need a woman who can keep an eye on two or maybe three young girls in a difficult situation. I need somebody with a good grasp of ethnic cultures and the ability not to annoy me. You were the only person I could think of."

"Window Rock, you say?" she asked him.

"Window Rock . . . and maybe Fort Defiance, too. You know what the Navajo call that? 'Meadow Between Rocks.' It's going to be really, really interesting."

She looked up at him and he wished desperately that she were in love with him, but that was fate. "I don't know why I'm saying yes," she told him. "But, yes. When were you planning on going there?"

"Oh . . . there's no rush. I'll pick you up tomorrow at five o'clock."

"*Tomorrow*? I can't go tomorrow. In any case, my last lecture doesn't finish until twenty after four."

"I meant five o'clock in the morning. We're catching the first flight to Albuquerque."

Susan opened her mouth and then closed it without

saying a word. She watched Jim walking off down the corridor to his classroom and she thought to herself that she might like him more than she had ever admitted.

"I'm taking a short cultural trip to the Navajo reservation in Arizona," he announced to Special Class II. "The reason I'm doing it is to find out more about Catherine's background so that I can help her develop as an English student. Of course I've done the same for several other members of the class . . . Rita, you remember when I spent some time with your family and friends, so that I could get a better handle on Spanish culture. John . . . you kindly invited me to spend a weekend with your Vietnamese friends, and I enjoyed every minute of that, except that I was so clumsy with my chopsticks that I kept dropping *thit bo to* on my shoes.

"I can take two of you with me. One of you should be a girl, so that you can share a room with Catherine. The other – well, it doesn't matter. Girl or boy. Whoever wants to come."

Sharon X put up her hand. "Please, sir, I'd love to. I'm so interested in oppressed cultures."

"OK . . . anybody else?"

Mark Foley cautiously lifted one finger. Mark was cocky and funny, but he was one of the least academic students in the class. He was shorter and slighter than most of his contemporaries, with a pale, bruised-looking face and badly-cropped blond hair. His jeans and T-shirts were always very clean, but most of them were worn out and frayed. The sole of one of his trainers flapped when he walked.

"You, Mark? You want to come along?"

"Well, sure. I never flew before. It won't cost anything, will it?"

"No . . . Catherine's father is generously picking up

the tab. All you need is a couple of changes of clothes and a toothbrush."

"Hey – think your dad'll let you go?" asked Ricky Herman.

"I don't care what my dad says," said Mark, defiantly. "I'm going anyway."

Jim said, "If you have any problems with your father, Mark, just have him give me a call." He had dealt with Mark's father before: a real Bluto type who owned a run-down body shop in Santa Monica. He spent all day thumping second-hand Chevies into shape and all evening sluicing down jugs of draft beer at KC's Bar. He had told Jim to his face that as far as he was concerned Mark's English course was a waste of time because Mark spoke English already, didn't he? and poetry was 'all that faggot stuff'.

"Mrs Whitman will be taking over while we're gone . . . but there's a special project that I want the rest of you to do for me. I want you to find out all that you can about the Navajo people and Navajo culture, especially their religious beliefs. See if you can find out the names of their spirits and any colorful stories about them. When we come back, we'll be able to discuss what we've discovered in Arizona with what you've managed to discover here."

Ray Vito said, "Have a good time, Mr Rook. Bring us back some firewater and a couple of squaws."

"You and your racial stereotyping," Sharon protested.

"Yes, Ray – you should be ashamed of yourself," put in Ricky. "You greasy spaghetti-eating opera-loving Eyetie."

Jim stood back in amusement as the entire class started to shout racial insults at each other. Sometimes it did them good to come out with all the words that nobody was allowed to use any more. It made them realise that most racial slurs were only words, and that what really mattered was how well they got along and how much they liked each other. After a few minutes they all collapsed in laughter.

"Right, then," said Jim. "That's enough political incorrectness for one day. I'll see you Friday morning, hopefully."

He take a long last smiling look around the classroom, trying to give himself a clear picture of every face. After all, this might be the last time that he would see them.

* * *

Their flight from LAX was delayed for nearly an hour and they arrived at Albuquerque International Airport just before lunch. As they crossed the concrete apron the temperature was over 93 degrees and the wind was as dry as a whip.

All through the flight, Catherine had been unusually quiet and thoughtful. Jim caught up with her as they approached the terminal building and said, "Catherine – hey – are you all right?"

She brushed back her hair with her hand. "I think so. But frightened, I guess."

"Frightened of what? This guy you're supposed to be betrothed to? We'll sort him out."

"I'm more frightened of me."

"You? Why should you be frightened of you?"

She turned to him, and looked at him intently through her windblown hair. "I feel like there's something inside of me . . . something that's making me feel confused. Like I'm angry about something but I don't know what. I felt it the last time I dated Martin, I don't know why. But here I can feel it much more."

Jim thought of the dark, jagged shadow that had followed her at Universal Studios. "Maybe it's just your age. When you're young, you know, you *do* feel confused."

"I don't know, sir. It feels like more than that. It feels so black. It feels so *angry*. It's like a wildness in me, do you know what I mean?"

"A wildness," said Jim. "A wildness that comes out of nowhere at all?"

Catherine said, "Yes. That's it. That's exactly it."

"Let me talk to you later," said Jim. "Meanwhile, let me see if I can fix up our connecting flight."

"Hey, it's hot here," said Mark, wiping his forehead with the back of his arm. He was carrying an old grey canvas sports bag, but his Nike trainers were brand-new and shining white. When his father had heard about his trip to Arizona, he had taken him straight out and bought them for him. "I think it's a total waste of time but you ain't going to show me up by going nowhere with no flappy shoe."

Sharon was wearing a shocking-pink T-shirt and white satin shorts and she looked like an Olympic athlete. "I'm so excited," she enthused. "I mean, isn't it beautiful here? So warm!"

Susan gave her a smile. Susan, as usual, was looking very Doris Day, with a blue headband and a crisp sleeveless white blouse and a pleated skirt in yellow-spotted cotton.

"Jim?" she called. "Don't forget the infantry."

Inside the chilly air-conditioned terminal, with its highly-polished floors, Jim went to the West New Mexico chartered airline desk. An overweight woman with a huge blonde lacquered hairstyle turned around and called, "Randy! Mr Rook and party!"

Out of the back office came a wiry-looking pilot with a deep tan and a snow-white crewcut to match his snow-white shirt. "How're you doing, folks? Anybody want to use the fixings before we go? Don't like to see my passengers fidgety, that's all."

He led them back out onto the heat-baked concrete, where a twin-engined Golden Eagle was waiting to fly them to Gallup. Mark sat up front with the pilot while Jim sat next to Catherine and Sharon and Susan sat in the back. They waited their turn on the runway behind the rippling backwash of a Boeing 737 – then, when it was their turn, Randy took them up 'like a flea hopping off a dog's back'. Immediately they angled west-north-westward, with the sun filling the Golden Eagle's interior with dazzling light.

"Said you're headed up to Window Rock?" asked Randy.

"That's right," said Jim. "We're on kind of a college field-trip. We're doing a project on the Navajo way of life."

"These days, that's not much different from any other way of life," Randy remarked. "Don't be disappointed if you don't see nobody in feather headdresses and bone breastplates. Window Rock's pretty much the same as anyplace else around here. It's got motels and restaurants, and a fairground, and a bank, and a community building and an FHA housing development. They've even got their own medical college these days.

He sniffed, and then he said, "Don't forget to buy yourself a rug, though. You can't visit the Navajo reservation without coming back with a rug. Teec Nos Pos, they're the best."

Jim remembered that Catherine had given a talk in class about Navajo weaving, and told them that rugs from Two Grey Hills were easily the finest, with more than 80 wefts to the inch. But this morning she stared out of the window at the dry, wrinkled ground below them, and said nothing. Once or twice she glanced at Jim and gave him a tight, uncommunicative smile, but that was all. Jim was trying his best to make her feel protected, but he didn't really know what he was supposed to be protecting her from.

He had seen a jagged shadow around her – a shadow that nobody else could see – but he had no idea what that meant. Was she actually possessed by this smoky, bristling spirit? Or was it nothing more than an omen – a spiritual warning that the beast was hunting for her, too? The trouble with signs and messages from the other side, they were never spelled out in plain English. Everything was communicated by hints, and suggestions, and faces seen in distant windows.

"Did you ever fly before?" Randy asked Mark.

"No, sir, never. Today's my first time. I thought I was going to be biting my nails but I wasn't."

"I mean did you ever fly an airplane before? I mean, like, yourself?"

Mark violently shook his head. "No, sir! I don't even own a *car*."

"Well, you have to start sometime," said Randy. "Take hold of the controls, let's see what you can do."

"Me?" said Mark, in a very much higher voice than he'd meant to. "I can't. Supposing I crash?"

"You won't crash. You don't have the experience to crash. Come on, take hold of those controls."

Mark gripped the controls so tightly that there were white spots on his knuckles. The Golden Eagle dipped a little, and tilted to one side, and the engines gave a threatening drone. But the pilot said, "Relax, you're doing fine. Just keep her on an even keel, that's all. Like, resist the temptation to nosedive."

Gradually, Mark gained confidence, and began to fly the Golden Eagle straight and reasonably smooth, with only one or two stomach-disturbing dips and swoops. The pilot showed him how to use the pedals and how to adjust his speed. "You're a natural, boy. You should make yourself a career out of this."

Jim watched and smiled. He had never seen Mark so excited. He thought – God, if only more people took a little time with boys like Mark, and showed them what they were capable of doing, instead of always telling them that they were dumb and useless.

"What do you think, everybody?" Mark called back. "Think I'm a pretty good pilot?"

Sharon said, with a big wide grin, "You know something, Mr Rook? I've never been so scared in my whole life."

They were flying over the last slopes of the Cibola National Forest, only a little more than 10 miles away from Gallup. Jim looked down and he could see their shadow dancing through the trees. "Little more height," Randy told Mark. "That's it. Want to make sure we clear that ridge up ahead."

Mark pulled the controls back, but as he did so, the Golden Eagle's port engine let out a loud burp, and then another, and another. Randy checked his instrument panel and lifted his sunglasses so that he could see the engine nacelle more clearly. "Well," he announced, "we're not on fire, I'm very happy to say, and we've got plenty of gas. Guess we might have a fuel-line blockage."

The engine burped even more loudly, and then sputtered, and abruptly died. Susan reached forward and took hold of Jim's hand, and squeezed it hard. Jim turned around and said, "It's OK, don't worry. You too, Sharon. This kind of thing happens all the time."

Randy said, "Don't panic, folks. All we have to do is feather the prop, and land on the other engine. You can't crash one of these babies even if you wanted to."

Susan said, "I hope that's not famous last words."

Jim tried to smile at her but found that he couldn't. He

could feel his sweaty shirt clinging to his back. He had never liked small airplanes, and he had been clenching his fists and curling his toes ever since they had taken off from Albuquerque. The plane suddenly tilted to port and the starboard engine let out a low-pitched moan of protest.

Sharon moaned, too; and Mark said, "Oh, shit. Oh, shit."

"Let's keep our heads here, folks," said Randy. "We still have plenty of height and we're only five minutes away from Senator Clark's Field at Gallup. This may be a little on the rough side, but there's nothing to get hysterical about."

The plane plunged again, and then soared upward, leaving Jim's stomach about a hundred feet below. Mark sat in the co-pilot's seat grim-faced, with his hands tucked firmly into his armpits. Susan was gripping Jim's hand so tight that her fingernails were digging into his skin, and Sharon had her hands over her face, although she was peeping out from between her fingers. When he looked at Catherine, however, she was sitting calm and still, her chin slightly raised, and her eyes staring straight ahead.

"Catherine?" Jim asked her. "Catherine, are you okay?"

Catherine didn't answer, but Jim was sure that he could see that shadow around her, even though the airplane cabin was filled with sunlight. She looked almost as if she were wearing a ghostly funeral veil. She was staring straight ahead, straight at the instrument panel, and her lips were moving, as if she were whispering something.

"*Coyote . . . Coyote . . . Coyote . . .*" that was all he could catch, over and over again.

"Catherine?" he repeated.

He rcached out to touch her, but as he did so, all the indicator lights on the Golden Eagle's instrument panel winked out, and all the dial-pointers dropped back to zero. The starboard engine rumbled and shuddered and abruptly cut out. They were swallowed by an eerie quietness. All they could hear was the whistling and the buffeting of the wind.

Randy jiggled the switch to restart the starboard engine, but nothing happened. "Nothing," he said. "All the damned electrics are dead. Never known this happen, never."

"Can you glide in?" Jim asked him.

"I don't know. The way we're dropping, we won't make Senator Clark's Field."

Mark said, "Oh, shit! We're not going to die, are we?"

"Die? Hell, no!" the pilot told him. "We're going to belly-flop in somebody's alfalfa, that's all." But Jim could tell from the way he spoke that Randy's mouth was dry, and that he was just as frightened as the rest of them. They had one last ridge to clear, which meant that they would have to maintain enough height to fly over a line of tall, jagged trees. But the Golden Eagle weighed over 3½ tonnes and it felt to Jim as if it were dropping out of the sky as promptly as a grand piano. The trees rose higher and higher in front of them, and soon they were almost brushing the upper branches.

They were never going to make the ridge. They could all see it now. They were already below the level of the taller trees, and there wasn't even a gap between them which Randy might have tried to fly through.

Susan whispered, "Oh my God, Jim. Oh my God." Sharon was holding her head in her hands, and her eyes were wide with panic. Jim felt sick with fear and helplessness, and a wrenching grief, too. He had come out here to save himself, and Catherine – but now they were both going to die, and they were going to kill Susan and Mark and Sharon, too.

"You got to brace yourselves," said Randy. "With any luck, the trees'll act like a cushion."

You know they won't, thought Jim. They'll smash us to pieces, and there won't be anything left for the rescue services to pick up but arms and legs.

Jim turned to Sharon and Susan. "Take your shoes off, then heads down, hands over your neck." The Golden Eagle lurched and dropped as Randy tried one last desperate effort to gain a little more height.

Jim looked at Catherine. She was still sitting up straight, her eyes fixed on the airplane's instrument panel. The shadow around her was even more distinct now, blurry and patchy, as if he were viewing her through a black-and-white photographic negative. What was more, her eyes were totally black, with no whites showing whatsoever.

"Catherine!" he shouted at her, and gripped her wrist – but then he instantly recoiled. He hadn't felt the smooth slim wrist that he had expected. He had felt something thick and cold – something that was bristling with coarse, matted hair.

"Catherine, listen to me! It's Jim Rook! Listen!"

"Tell her to brace herself!" Randy shouted. "For Christ's sake, we're going in!"

"Catherine!" Jim yelled. "Catherine! You have to listen to me! Catherine!"

He reached across and tried to turn her face around, but as soon as he touched her cheek he shouted, "*Ah!*" and whipped his hand away. Catherine's cheek had been rough and whiskery, and he had distinctly felt *teeth*.

"Catherine, if you're in there, Catherine, try to fight it!" Jim screamed at her.

"Jim? What on earth are you doing?" said Susan. "Jim! Get your head down, you'll break your back!"

Every cockpit window seemed to be filled with nothing

but rising trees. Mark was still gibbering "shit, shit, shit," under his breath, and Sharon was praying to Allah.

Catherine can't hear me, thought Jim, desperately. She may be there but she simply can't hear me. She's an animal now, not a human being. And how can you make an animal hear you?

He suddenly patted the front of his shirt and felt the whistle that Henry Black Eagle had given him, dangling around his neck. He lifted it up and blew it. He didn't hear anything at all, and Catherine didn't respond, so he blew it again, even harder this time.

Catherine's head turned toward him with a terrifying jerk. Her black eyes glared at him with such ferocity that he flinched away. He could see the shadow around her quite distinctly now, and it was less like a shadow than a mask – a snarling animal mask, with its lips curled back in hatred.

Jim said, "*Catherine*!"

A startling look of recognition crossed her face. She said, "What? What's happening?" and even as she spoke the blackness in her eyes began to shrink. The shadow faded and suddenly flowed away, like ink washed away down a sink. She looked around her and saw the trees rearing up on every side of them, and Sharon and Susan with their heads down between their knees.

"*What's happening*?" she shrieked. "*I don't understand what's going on*! *What's happening*?"

"Get your head down!" Randy shouted at her.

But Jim said, "Catherine – you're Catherine! Catherine White Bird, that's who you are!"

Catherine stared at him for one long moment, and then she raised both hands and touched her forehead, as if she couldn't believe that this head, this hair, this face were really hers.

"You're Catherine White Bird," said Jim, and even

if they all died now, at least Catherine would die with the full knowledge of who she was, and what had happened to her.

She turned to the instrument panel, and rigidly held out her hand. "*Live*!" she demanded. "*Live*!"

Jim saw the lights snap back on again, and the indicator needles suddenly bob back up into position. But the trees were looming so close that they blocked the sunlight out of the cabin, and the Golden Eagle seemed to be dropping even faster, as if it had given up the effort to stay airborne.

"*Randy*!" Jim yelled at him. "*Randy – try the engines again*!"

Randy flicked the starter switches. Nothing.

"Keep trying, for Christ's sake!" Jim insisted.

Randy flicked them again, and then again. And then the starboard engine coughed, and the port engine coughed in sympathy, and suddenly they felt the deep, ripsaw vibration of both engines at full throttle. Randy pulled back on the controls so hard that it looked as if he were physically lifting the Golden Eagle back up into the air. Sharon screamed as branches lashed against the wings. Mark let out a long, eerie-sounding moan of sheer terror.

Jim thought, "*Please, God*", and held Catherine's hand, and now it was smooth and small, the way it should have been, and she interlaced her fingers with his, and whispered, "Gitehe Manitou, save us."

The Golden Eagle burst through the top of the treeline, its propellors spraying leaves and branches in all directions. It continued to climb over the lower slopes of the Cibola Forest, higher and higher, rising to such an altitude that they could see the sun shining across twenty miles of forest and desert, with the Zuni Mountains rising behind them now in a faint purplish heat-haze.

"Well, I don't know what in hell happened back there," said Randy. "But today I can truly tell you that I believe in God. Or Allah," he added, turning to Sharon. "Or Gitche Manitou, whatever."

Mark said, "Whew."

"Is that all?" Randy ribbed him. "Just 'whew'?"

"Yeah, 'whew.' I thought I'd crapped myself but I haven't."

"I guess that's one small mercy," said Randy, and tilted the Golden Eagle toward Gallup.

John Three Names was waiting for them on the hot, sun-glaring airfield. He was a small, dapper Navajo in a brown coat, beige slacks, and a brown wide-brimmed hat with feathers in it. He had one of those crinkled, soft-skinned Native American faces that always reminded Jim of a parcel wrapped in secondhand brown paper. But his eyes were bright and hard, and he spoke in quick, clipped sentences, and there was nothing soft or secondhand about his ideas.

"Hi, I'm John Three Names," he said, grasping Jim's hand. "I gather you had some trouble getting here. They had two firetrucks and an ambulance standing by."

"Well, let's say we've had something of a scare," Jim told him. He turned around and looked at Catherine, who was helping Sharon with her bags. "I'd like to think that it's over, but somehow I don't think that it is."

"I have a car outside," said John Three Names. "Or maybe you'd like to rest up here for a while."

"I think we can go on," said Jim. "How's everybody feeling?"

"Let's go on," said Catherine. "The sooner we get there, the better."

Jim said, "You're sure?" but she reached out and touched his hand, very lightly, and he knew that she wanted nothing more than to get this journey over with. She hadn't thanked him for what he had done in the airplane, but then she didn't need to. Only she and Jim had shared that moment when she had realised who she really was, and that shared understanding was better than thanks. Jim felt very close to her, just then, and as she followed John Three Names, with her long hair shining in the afternoon sun, he could almost have loved her.

"Don't let Dr Ehrlichman see you looking at your students like that," said Susan.

"Like what? I've been worried about her, that's all."

"As you said yourself, she doesn't look like the back of a totem-pole."

"Susan—"

She linked arms with him. "We're alive, that's all that matters. I really thought that we were going to die back there. I suddenly realised how unprepared I was."

She stopped, and lifted her head, and kissed him. Mark and Sharon were walking close behind them and Mark wolf-whistled.

Jim said, "Do you mind? Even faculty members are allowed to make discreet demonstrations of mutual affection."

John Three Names had a blue Ford Galaxy parked outside the airfield, with seats enough for all of them. "I borrowed this from the Navajo Community College. You must drop in and see it, Mr Rook. I think you'll be impressed."

"How come they call you John Three Names?" asked Mark, as they drove away.

"Because I have three names, of course."

"Really? What are they?"

"'John', 'Three' and 'Names.'"

Mark frowned at him for a long time. "You're putting me on, aren't you?"

John Three Names looked at him and laughed. He said, "Nobody laughs louder than a Navajo, when he's tricked a white man." Jim smiled and sat back and tried to enjoy the drive to Window Rock. Once or twice he took out the whistle that Henry Black Eagle had given him and turned it around in his fingers. It had saved him, he understood that. It had saved all six of them. But he still didn't really know why, or how. Catherine didn't seem to have the shadow around her any more, but what were the chances that it might come back? And what might it try to do to them next time? He lifted the whistle to his lips and he was about to blow it when he saw Catherine looking at him with her fingertip raised to her lips.

He said, "What?"

"Better not to disturb him again," she warned.

"Him? Who's him?"

Catherine lifted her hands so that they were covering her face, but opened her fingers so that her eyes could look out. Jim couldn't understand what she meant, but it had a very sinister effect, like a mask, or somebody who was spying on the world from somewhere else.

He lowered the whistle and dropped it back into his shirt. Obviously there were times when it was going to help them, and other times when it was going to bring them trouble.

Susan reached across and held Jim's hand. It could have been a gesture of revived affection, or it simply could have been a way of confirming that they were all still alive. There was one thing that Jim knew for sure – he wasn't going to *fly* back to Albuquerque, not with Catherine, anyway.

John Three Names said, "Any of you ever visited the Navajo Nation before? I think you're going to find it quite an eye-opener. I've lived here for the past twenty-five years and I've seen some changes here, I can tell you.

We still have far too many people on welfare, but we've kept up to date with the modern world in most ways. To me, the most important thing is that we've kept our native language and our national identity. It's just a pity that so much magic has gone out of the land."

They arrived in Window Rock at mid-afternoon, under a flawless blue sky. It was a small Arizona town much like any other, with stores and gas stations and office-buildings. John Three Names had booked them into the Navajo Nation Inn, $73 the night. A calm, handsome woman in a blue dress showed them to their rooms – plain, but sunny, and decorated with *yei* rugs with stylized figures on them. A boy of about five followed them a few paces behind, frowning with shyness and curiosity. John Three Names stopped, and went back to the boy. He held up both hands, which were empty, but then he rubbed them together, and produced a quarter out of thin air. He gave it to the boy and said, "Don't spend it all on candy."

Sharon and Catherine were sharing a bright, big room with a view of the pool. Jim touched Sharon's shoulder as she carried her bag through the door, and said, "Don't forget, will you? Keep your eye on her . . . and if you see anything that worries you—"

"I'll look after her, Mr Rook," Sharon reassured him. "She comes from an ethnic minority that's even more minorer than mine."

Jim and Susan had adjacent rooms with a connecting door. Susan rattled the handle to make sure it was locked. "You know, just in case you start sleepwalking."

"What if I'm awake?"

"If you're awake, you die." She didn't realize how prophetic that was.

John Three Names followed Jim into his room. Jim slid open the patio door and stepped out onto a small terracotta-tiled balcony with a table and chairs. In the distance, the vermilion mountains were washed out with heat. A lizard baked in the dust beyond the balcony, but didn't stir.

"Like the room?" asked John Three Names.

"It's fine, thanks."

"Tell me what really happened on the airplane."

Jim looked at him. "What do you mean?"

"It wasn't just instrument failure, was it?"

"Oh, no? What makes you think that?"

"When we were driving here, I could see you in my rear-view mirror. I saw you take out the whistle. I saw Catherine White Bird caution you not to blow it. Then I saw her cover her face."

"So what did that tell you?"

"It told me that you had probably blown the whistle before, for some reason, and that you were puzzled about the effect it had produced. So maybe you wanted to try it again, to see what would happen this time. But Catherine White Bird said no, you would disturb him – and when you asked who *him* was, she covered her face.

"You know why she did that? She didn't want to speak his name, in case it was carried to him on the wind, and he knew that she was coming closer. But that whistle has only one purpose, to call the spirit called Coyote. And to do *this* –" and here he covered his face in the same way that Catherine had done "– is to warn people that Coyote isn't far away, and that he's listening out for you."

Jim said, "I think you'd better explain this from the bottom up."

John Three Names came and stood next to him. "In days gone by, before the white men came, when you could see spirits by broad daylight, Coyote was the greatest mischief-maker of all the Navajo demons. A killer, a trickster, a raper of women, and a thief. When it came to the grand assembly of all the supernatural beings, the gods would sit facing the south and the demons and other malevolent spirits would sit facing the north. But Coyote was so deceitful that none of the other spirits would allow him to sit close, and he stood by the door, ready to run away before the others ganged up on him.

"Coyote did everything perversely. He profaned against the sacred rites. He tipped his arrows with grey feathers, which is a recognized sign of bad luck. The month of October, which is the month of mishaps and mistakes, was dedicated to him. When the night sky was created, he was given a handful of stars to put in their places, but he was too irresponsible to do it properly, and so he flung them up all in one mass, and created the Milky Way.

"Whenever games were played, Coyote would set one side against the other, and then run off with the prize."

Jim said, "This is all myth, surely. I mean, it's a story – the same kind of story that the Greeks and the Romans used to tell. Zeus hurling his thunderbolts, Neptune with his trident – and Apollo riding his fiery chariot through the sky."

"Not quite," said John Three Names. "There are no records of anybody ever having *seen* Zeus, in the flesh. But Coyote was spotted by Navajo hunters as late as 1861. They turned back from the hunting-ground, of course, because if you ever saw Coyote it meant unhappiness and death. It's all recorded on blankets, if you want to see them."

"I'll take your word for it," said Jim. "I was always a slow reader when it came to blankets."

"The days of the gods and the demons began to die in 1864, after the Navajos had persisted in raiding their neighboring tribes, the Hopi and the Zuni. Colonel Kit Carson went on what you might call a search-and-destroy mission to rout out the last of the Navajo. Carson laid waste their crops and killed their livestock. Then he made eight thousand of them walk three hundred miles from Fort Defiance to Fort Sumner on the Pecos River. Many died. The rest he kept prisoner for four years until the Navajo finally agreed to sign a treaty.

"It was during this time that the Navajos' faith in their spirits was so badly shaken, and their spirits – well, what can spirits do when nobody believes in them any longer? They don't die, they're immortal, but they melt away. The earth gods sank into the ground, and if you go out into the desert you can still see the hills where they did it. The wind gods blew away across the mountains, and caused tornadoes. The river gods ran away to the ocean, although once in a while they come back to flood the Mississipi to remind us of the powers they used to have.

"But mostly the gods were not believed in, so they went their way. There was only one exception – Coyote. When the white men came, and the days of myth and legend were all over, he was wily enough to find a way to live in the open, so that humans would believe in him, and spirits, too. He mated with a human woman, who gave birth to a child that was human and Coyote, both. And this boy gave birth to another child, and so on, from one generation to the next. What this means is that Coyote is still with us today, Mr Rook, and he's very much alive."

"This isn't easy to believe," said Jim.

"Why shouldn't it be? You've seen Coyote's mischief with your own eyes. Henry Black Eagle told me what happened at your college; and he also told me that your apartment had been torn apart, and your cat killed."

"So explain it to me. Why is he doing it, and how?"

"The why is simple. The man that Catherine was supposed to marry went to a wonder-worker and asked him to summon up Coyote's powers, so that Coyote would bring Catherine back to him – and if she fell in love with any other man, to kill him."

"Like a hex, you mean?"

"You could call it that. Except that this hex has taken the shape of a beast, which watches Catherine day and night."

"I think I've already seen it a couple of times," said Jim. "It's like kind of a shadow that seems to follow Catherine around."

John Three Names said, "You're the only man who ever has – and that's why Henry Black Eagle and his family asked you to come here. If you can persuade this man to release Catherine from her promise, the beast will have to leave her – and only you can be sure that it really does."

"Do you *know* this man that Catherine's supposed to have married?" Jim asked him.

"I've seen him once or twice, but I've spoken to him only once. He lives in a trailer up at Meadow Between Rocks. Most of the time he keeps himself to himself, and everybody respects his privacy and leaves him alone. He's supposed to have quite a ferocious temper on him, although I've never seen any of that."

"Does he have a name?"

"Several. But most people call him Dog Brother."

Jim sat down on the end of the bed. "The question is, John, what am I going to offer this – Dog Brother to give up Catherine? She's a beautiful girl. If I had the choice, *I* wouldn't give her up."

"Henry Black Eagle has some property up by Shiprock, as well as stocks and bonds. You're authorized to offer these to Dog Brother in exchange for releasing Catherine from her promise, plus a quarter of a million dollars in cash."

"What if he's not interested?"

"Then we will have to try another way. We will have to find the wonder-worker who conjured up Coyote's curse and see if we can make a bargain with him."

"And supposing *he* doesn't want to play ball, either?"

"I think we should cross that canyon when we come to it."

"What about this Coyote character? If he's half-human, then he must be findable."

John Three Names shook his head. "You wouldn't want to try that, Jim."

"I don't know. Maybe he's more human than you think. Come on, John, how can this be real? A demon who lives for ever by mating with human women?"

John Three Names laid a hand on his shoulder. "How about a drink? I'll bet you could use one, after that journey."

The bar was deserted except for three iron-haired Navajos in ponytails and business suits talking about industrial leases in Tuba City. Jim ordered a beer and John Three Names asked for a Bloody Mary ("I didn't have time for lunch, and this is as good as.") In the background, Nat King Cole sang *Ramblin' Rose*.

John Three Names guided Jim over to a table by the window. "I like to see what's coming and what's going, especially at times like these." He parted the venetian blinds with two fingers and peered out into the glaring street.

"In the original Navajo legend," he said, "Coyote lusted after a very beautiful girl. She had two brothers who tried to protect her. The girl was strong-willed as well as beautiful, and Coyote struggled for months to seduce her, to take over her soul. She hated him at first, and put him through all kinds of tests – literally making him die for her. But each time he died, he buried a flint next to his body so that he could dig himself up again. In the end, he was so persistent that she couldn't resist him any longer, and she allowed him past the hem of her skirt.

"Under Coyote's influence, she became a creature which we call the Changing Bear Maiden, joining Coyote in all of his evil-doing. The stories say that she took a particular pleasure out of snapping men's necks with her jaws, and ripping their chests open with her claws."

"She had only one vulnerability – she couldn't change into a bear when anybody was watching her, so her family protected her by making sure that they kept a guard on her day and night."

"Sounds familiar," said Jim.

"It's a legend. How much of it you care to believe – well, that's entirely up to you."

"What's your part in all this?" Jim asked him.

"I'm an interested party, that's all – apart from being a friend of Henry Black Eagle. I work as a freelance for the Navajo newspaper *Diné Baa-Hané*. A demon hunter by night and a mild-mannered reporter by day."

At that moment, Susan came into the bar, followed by Catherine and Sharon and Mark. "I thought I'd find you two in here," said Susan. "I could murder a Bloody Mary."

Jim moved around so that Susan could sit next to him. Catherine sat opposite, and gave him an odd, worried look, as if she had something on her mind but didn't quite know how to start talking about it.

"What happens next?" asked Susan.

"We'll go up to the Meadow Between Rocks at first light tomorrow," said John Three Names. "We're lucky. They're holding a first laugh rite there for one of my nephews. That's something you don't get to see very often."

"A first laugh rite?"

"When a child first laughs, around its fortieth day, he joins the human race, and he will make a covenant with the laughter gods which will be sealed with salt. There will be prayers and a big celebration. Meanwhile I suggest you all get some rest. You haven't had an easy journey, and there will be much more difficult times ahead of us."

"I'm going out to catch some rays," said Mark.

"Don't burn," Susan told him.

Catherine stayed where she was. John Three Names asked her if she wanted a Coke, but she shook her head. "Something's happening to me," she said. "Something's happening to me and I don't know what it is."

"Go on," said Jim.

"It's just that I keep having these nightmares, only they're not nightmares. They happen during the day."

"What kind of nightmares?"

"They're just like a flash in my head. Flash, and they're gone. But since we've come here to Window Rock I've had three or four of them already."

"Are they all the same?"

"I keep imagining that I'm running very fast. Not running away from anything. I'm not frightened. In fact it's the opposite – I'm chasing something, or somebody. I want to jump on them and attack them. I want to hear them screaming. I'm strong. I can't believe how strong I am. I could tear somebody's arm off just like that.

Tears suddenly welled up in her eyes. "You just talked about a child laughing and joining the human race. I don't know, I have such a terrible feeling. I feel like I'm leaving it."

Chapter Six

During the night, Jim was woken up by the sound of his own heart beating. He placed his hand over his chest, but then he realised that it wasn't his heart beating at all – it was drumming. He sat up in bed and he could hear it quite distinctly – a slow, persistent *throb-THROB-THROB-throb, throb-THROB-THROB-throb*. He listened for a while, frowning into the darkness. Jesus, it sounded like *Drums Along The Mohawk.* He swung his legs out of bed and walked to the patio window, pulling up his newly-bought pajama pants. He slid the window back and stepped out barefoot onto the tiled floor, which was still warm from yesterday's sunshine.

In the near distance he could see a fire glowing, its sparks whirling into the darkness. Up above him, the whole sky was crowded with stars. He hadn't seen stars like this since he was a boy, and his father had taken him fishing off the coast of Santa Barbara. He felt a strange emotional surge – a mixture of nostalgia for days gone by, and regret that he never saw the stars any longer, not like this.

He climbed over the railing that surrounded his patio and dropped heavily down onto the dusty, prickly ground. He heard something scurry in the darkness, and a lizard flickered over his foot. He was beginning to regret that he hadn't put on his sneakers. There were rattlesnakes here, too, and scorpions.

But the drumming went on, resonant and repetitive. *Throb-THROB-THROB-throb*, echoing and flat. Jim looked around. He was amazed that it hadn't woken anybody else – but then again, maybe it had, and they had recognised it for what it was, and ignored it. He hesitated for almost a whole minute, wondering whether he ought to go back to bed and forget about it. But then he saw a dark figure rise from the ground, just in front of the fire, and begin to sway from side to side. It looked as if the figure was wearing an odd, bulky headdress, with horns or ears, and dangling necklaces.

What was more, on the far side of the fire, Jim was sure that he could make out a black, bulky shape. It didn't seem to be illuminated by the flames: it was more like a shadow, except that it couldn't be a shadow, because there was nothing to cast it. He saw two red sparks that might have been sparks, or might have been blood-red eyes. A cool wind blew against his bare back and brought goosebumps all the way up to his hairline. There was something there, he was sure of it. *Something cold. Something old. Something bristling.*

He made his way cautiously toward the fire, trying to step over rocks and dried-up weed and prickly vegetation. He could see now that it was the figure with the headdress that was beating the drum. It was a naked man, his body shining with sweat. He was grasping a tall decorated drum between his thighs and banging it with the edge of his hands. The fire had burned low now: it was nothing much more than a heap of glowing ashes, but it gave off so much heat that the air above it was rippling and distorted. Jim stopped, and shaded his eyes with both hands, but it was impossible for him to tell if the shadow was really there, or whether it was nothing more than a mirage produced by the heat. All the time the drum kept beating *throb-THROB-THROB-throb*, and now Jim could hear the man chanting, too, although he couldn't understand any of the words.

He thought: this isn't getting me anyplace at all. This is probably some kind of Navajo ceremony. Paying homage to the night sky. Thanking the moon for coming up and going down again. Who knew? He felt embarrassed because he was intruding; and he felt slightly paranoid because he kept looking at every slow-dancing shadow around the fire and imagining that it was more than just a shadow. It was the Changing Bear Maiden, with her claws and her teeth, ready to snap men's necks.

He turned back toward the Inn, but as he did so, he saw Sharon rush out onto his patio. "Mr Rook!" she called out, and she was obviously distressed. "Mr Rook? Where are you?"

The man standing by the fire turned around, his pelts and necklaces swinging. Abruptly, the drumming stopped. Jim called out, "Here, Sharon! I'm just over here!"

"It's Catherine, Mr Rook! She's gone missing!"

Jim glanced toward the fire. The man in the head-dress was still staring in his direction, his drum stilled. The heat from the fire was deflected by the wind, and for one split-second Jim was sure that he saw a huge, sloping-shouldered figure, as black as the sky between the stars – just like a bear only three times larger. But then the wind blew up a cloud of smoke and ashes, and the figure vanished.

Jim walked back to the patio, his feet bruised and scratched. Sharon was wearing a voluminous pink T-shirt with a picture of the Care Bears on it. Her hair was thicketed with pink plastic rollers. "I woke up to go to the bathroom, Mr Rook, and Catherine was gone! She was only wearing a nightshirt and she didn't take no clothes with her. I was looking for her along the corridor when I heard that drumming and I was frightened."

"It's OK," said Jim. Behind him, the drummer was still silent, and the fire was beginning to die down. "I don't know what's going on, but the best thing you can do is get yourself back to bed. Catherine's been pretty disturbed since she came back here. Maybe she's gone for a walk to think things over."

Sharon nodded toward the fire, and the silhouetted man with the drum. "What is that, Mr Rook? What's going on here? Is that guy wearing any *clothes*?"

"Erm, no. It doesn't look as if he is. But, you know, this isn't Santa Monica. I guess they do things a little differently here."

"And where were *you* going?" Sharon frowned. "You're not even wearing any shoes."

"I was . . . well, I guess I was going to investigate."

Sharon gave him a narrow-eyed look. "There's something weird about this trip, Mr Rook? I mean, this isn't like your usual college cultural trip. So far I've been scared out of my brain in an airplane and now it's all drums and fires and people shouting in the middle of the night, and nobody's even *mentioned* anything cultural."

"Oh, it's cultural, all right," Jim told her. "I'm just worried that it may be a little *too* cultural."

"What do you mean?"

"Well," said Jim, "the truth is, we're not really here on a field trip. We're here mostly for Catherine's sake. When she was fifteen she was promised in marriage to a Navajo guy called Dog Brother, but now she doesn't want to marry him. I came to Window Rock to see if there's any way to break their engagement. I needed you guys along to keep her company."

Sharon stared at him, distinctly unimpressed. "This Dog Breath, he still wants to marry her?"

"*Brother*, not Breath. But yes, so far as I know, he still wants to marry her."

"But why did she have to come back at all? Why not write him a 'Dear Dog Breath' letter, and forget about it? And why did you have to come? Couldn't her father have brought her?"

"I had to come because of Martin, and what happened in the locker room. I had to come because my home was wrecked and my cat was killed."

"Hunh? I don't get it."

"Sharon, this Dog Brother is a very jealous guy, by all accounts, and he's worked some kind of spell on Catherine. If any guy gets too close to her, Dog Brother makes sure that he suffers. Anything that means anything to him gets destroyed. In Martin's case – well, he was destroyed, too."

"I thought Catherine's brothers did all that. They're in jail for it, aren't they?"

"There's some circumstantial evidence that suggests they might have killed Martin, for sure. But for all of the vandalism and killing my cat they have pretty unshakeable alibis. They claim that everything was done by some kind of a *force* – a force which Dog Brother conjured up when Catherine ran off to LA. It's all to do with Native American magic. I don't even understand it myself. But it looks like the only way to face up to this force is to come here and talk to this Dog Brother face to face."

"When you say 'force,' do you mean like that voodoo guy you had to hunt down?"

"I guess something like that. It's invisible. Nobody else can see it except me."

"Why didn't you tell us before we came out here? Don't you trust us?"

"Of course I trust you. That's the whole reason I wanted you to come. It's just that I didn't know what I was dealing with. The logical explanation is that Catherine's brothers *were* responsible. But I've been seeing things and feeling feelings that make me think that maybe they're telling the truth. Or part of the truth, anyhow."

"What feelings? What things?"

"Nothing specific . . . shadows where shadows shouldn't be. A kind of tension in the air. Maybe I'm just being paranoid."

"Well, next time you see something like that, maybe you'd like to let the rest of us know."

"Sure, I promise," said Jim, trying to be reassuring. "Now, we can talk about this later. Why don't you go back to your room and wait to see if Catherine comes back. I'll go take a look around the grounds and see if I can find her. I doubt she's gone far."

"Just remember – *trust*," said Sharon. Jim gave her a high five and she went back to her bedroom.

Jim started to walk cautiously back toward the fire. He hadn't gone far, however, when he heard Susan's voice calling, off to the right. "Catherine! Sharon! Where are you?"

"Oh, God, that's all I need," said Jim. "Susan! Sharon's fine! She's gone back to her room! I'm just looking for Catherine!"

He couldn't see Susan at first, but then she appeared out of the smoke, halfway between the Inn and the fire. She was wrapped in a light white towelling robe, and she was carrying a flashlight. "Jim?" she said. "Is that you? I've been looking for Catherine and Sharon! Their beds are empty!"

"For Christ's sake, Susan—" Jim began, but he was interrupted by the sharp bang of a hand on a drum. The fire had almost completely died down now, so it was difficult to see the man's figure, except for his dangling headdress and the curve of his glistening chest. But then he banged his drum again, quicker and harder, until he was beating out a fast, insanely complicated rhythm and his hands were a blur. Susan, confused, stopped where she was for a moment. "Jim?" she called out. "Do you have Sharon with you? Where's Catherine?"

She was still more than a hundred feet away. And it was then that Jim saw the black shadow detach itself from the other side of the fire and come rushing toward her, quite silently, with no other trace of its passing than a light whirl of dust and a few small clattering rocks. Susan was standing quite still now, obliviously waving. Yet the darkness was approaching her with all the speed of a charging bull. Weirdly, though, it was totally silent.

"Susan!" Jim shouted. "Susan – watch out!"

He sprinted toward her as fast as he could. He hadn't run like this since he was at high school, when he had almost won the 200m against the school's best athlete, Eddie LaFrance. He could see Eddie's grinning, self-satisfied face even now. Jim had burst his heart trying to win that race and he hadn't been able to believe it when he came second. He had done the unforgivable, and started to cry.

That was why he was running so furiously now. He couldn't fail a second time.

"Susan!" he gasped. "Susan, watch out! On your right, Susan! It's there, on your right-hand side!"

Susan stopped, perplexed. She looked to her right but it was obvious that she couldn't see anything at all. "*Just believe me*!" Jim screamed at her. "*Just get down*!"

The beast was big – much bigger than Jim had imagined. Its shoulders were hunched, its claws were lifted in terrifying curves, already tinged red by the fire. But its speed frightened Jim the most. He was running so fast toward Susan that he was almost flying. His feet skipped from rock to rock and he leaped over bushes like a hurdler.

Yet the huge black shadowy thing was bearing down on Susan and he knew that it was going to be touch-and-go to stop it.

The worst thing was that only *he* could see it. Susan stayed where she was, turning around and around, looking for something which was totally invisible.

Jim reached Susan and flung himself at her in a football-tackle. Astonished, frightened, she stepped back, and he hit the ground with a bruising impact and rolled over into a thicket of thorns. He twisted his head around in time to see the beast almost on top of her, its fur bristling, its eyes smouldering like coke-cinders. Jim could *smell* it: the cold, old bear smell – rank with blood and urine and decaying pelts. He could smell it and he could see it, yet Susan was standing right beneath it, her hands perched on her hips, saying, "Jim – for God's sake – do you mind telling me what's—"

Jim screamed, "*Get down*!" at her, but she was still looking at him in annoyance when a huge claw swept right under her chin and knocked her head right off her body, skying it right up into the night, right up against the stars, with blood spraying behind it like a comet's tail.

For a moment, her body remained where it was, still standing, headless, with her carotid artery pumping out geysers of blood. Her towelling robe turned from white to crimson right in front of Jim's eyes. Then the beast dug its claws into her again, and literally tore her apart – ribcage, pelvis, arms and legs. The crackling of bones was so loud that Jim pressed his hands over his ears, and closed his eyes. He opened them again to see what was left of her collapsing onto the dirt, like a broken bird's nest, rags and sticks and branches.

He looked up at the beast. For a moment, he thought that it was going to strike him down, too. It stood over him for a moment, blotting out the night sky. Jim lowered his head and closed his eyes and he was sick to his stomach. But then he heard the drums start up again – *throb-THROB-THROB-throb – throb-THROB-THROB-throb*. He looked up, and saw the beast turn its head. Then its outline appeared to waver, and soften, and one by one he saw the stars begin to shine through its bristling fur. The drum persisted – *throb – THROB – THROB – throb* – and the beast began to move away, or perhaps to *melt* away, disappearing into the darkness in the direction of the fire.

Jim was sure that he saw it cross in front of the fire, because the fire momentarily dimmed, but then it vanished altogether, and all he could see was the man and his drum and the hot, dying embers, and all he could hear was Sharon calling him.

"Mr Rook? Mr Rook? I heard somebody shouting. What's happening, Mr Rook?"

Jim climbed to his feet. He was bruised and shocked and hyperventilating. Thank God it's dark, he thought, and she can't see Susan's body. Thank God I can't, either.

"It's OK, Sharon," he told her. "I was just trying to find Catherine, that's all. She hasn't come back yet, has she?"

"Not yet, Mr Rook. Maybe I should help you look."

"No, no. Go back to your room. Please. You'll be doing me a favour."

Sharon waited on the patio a little while longer, straining her eyes out into the night, but then she reluctantly went back inside. It was just after three o'clock. Jim walked back to thc place where Susan's body had fallen. Then he walked over to the fire, and the man with the drum.

The fire may have been low, but it gave off so much

heat that Jim couldn't stand very close. The man had stopped playing now, and was crouched next to it, completely covered from head to foot in a grey-and-white Navajo blanket.

"Who are you?" Jim demanded. "What's been going on here? Do you know what's happened? A woman's been killed." His voice was trembling like a loose bandsaw.

The man reached into a leather pouch and tossed a handful of powder onto the fire. It briefly sparkled, and gave off the smell of dried herbs, along with another smell, less definable, more like memories. Jim saw himself playing in a wood beside a lake, and then he didn't.

"I'm going to have to call the police," he said.

The man threw another handful of powder onto the fire. Then he tightened up his leather pouch, and stood up, winding the blanket around him so that he looked like a pilgrim, or a monk. It was John Three Names. His face was impassive. His eyes gave nothing away.

"You've killed my friend," Jim insisted. He was very close to tears. "She's – you took her head off – and then you just – *snapped* her."

"I didn't do that," said John Three Names. He walked past Jim to a smooth flat rock, where he had left his clothes. Unabashed, he took off the blanket and proceeded to dress himself in a checkered shirt and jeans, with a bolo necktie.

Jim said, "That thing was here. That beast. What did you do, conjure it up?"

"I didn't see anything, Jim. The only person who can see that creature is you."

"So how do you think that Susan was torn to pieces? It took her head off, John, right in front of me!"

John said, "I'm sorry. I saw her go down, and I'm deeply sorry. But that's all I can say. This is a struggle, and when you have struggles, people get hurt. Particularly when you start struggling with powers that you don't really understand."

"I'm still calling the police. I came here as a favour. Now my girlfriend is dead. Jesus, what's the matter with you? What the hell do you have to be so calm about?" He was almost screaming.

John Three Names said, "I'm not calm, Jim. I'm not calm at all. I'm as shaken as you are. But that beast is going to go on killing people until Dog Brother can be talked into letting Catherine go, and calling it off. And only you can do that."

"I'm calling the police."

"Oh, yes? And what are you going to say to them?"

"I'm going to tell them the truth, what else?"

"The truth? An invisible beast came along and took your girlfriend's head off? I saw you run up to her. I saw her fall. But as far as I'm concerned, there was no invisible beast. So what conclusion do you think the police are going to draw from that?"

"It ripped her to pieces. I couldn't have done that!"

John Three Names shrugged. "They're still going to hold you under suspicion, aren't they? They're Navajo, Jim, the cops around here, and they're always very intolerant with whites. After all, they have plenty to be intolerant about."

Jim looked around in desperation. "You didn't see *anything*? You didn't see the shadow? It was here, by the fire, while you were drumming."

John Three Names touched one eyelid with his fingertip. "I don't have the eyes to see such things, Jim. Most of the time, I'm glad that I don't."

"So what were you doing here, lighting this fire and beating that goddamned drum?"

"I was making a prayer to my ancestors. I was asking them to help us when we go to see Dog Brother tomorrow, so that we should be successful, and that Dog Brother should let Catherine go."

"So why do you think that the beast showed up?"

"Perhaps to show me that tomorrow's confrontation will not be easy, and that we still have much to fear."

"There won't be any confrontation tomorrow. After tonight, I quit."

John Three Names looked taken aback. "How can you quit, when you are the only person who can make sure that the beast who killed your girlfriend is sent back to the world in which it belongs? How can you quit, when so many others might die?"

Jim looked back in the direction of Susan's body. "How do you expect me to go on with this, after what's happened tonight?"

John Three Names took hold of his arm. "Jim, you have to go on. You don't have any choice. Destiny only goes forward. It can never go back. The door behind you is closed. The door ahead of you may be difficult to open, but it is the only way out."

"So what can I do with Susan's body?" asked Jim. "It'll be dawn soon."

John Three Names nodded toward the fire. "It's very hot now, Jim. We can cremate her."

Jim took a deep breath. Hiding a body was illegal, and deeply incriminating, if it were ever found. But shocked as he was, he knew that there wasn't a court in the country that would believe that Susan had been killed by an invisible spirit-beast – not until he could prove that it existed, if he ever could. He said, "All right, then. But I'm going to need your blanket, to wrap her up in."

"This is a Ganado," said John Three Names, clutching it tight.

"I don't care if it's the Turin Shroud. I need it."

John Three Names reluctantly handed over his rug.

Jim trailed it over to Susan's remains, and laid it on the dirt beside her. He reached out once to touch her, and found that he couldn't. But then he quickly tugged at her bloodsoaked bathrobe and rolled her onto the rug. The noise of bones and sloppy viscera almost made him sick – but what was worse was that, headless, she *sighed* as he rolled her over – a faint, regretful sigh.

"Just a little air left in her lungs," said John Three Names, pragmatically.

Jim wrapped up the blanket and John Three Names helped him to carry it over to the fire. It swung heavily, like somebody in a hammock. They raked back the embers with sticks and lowered the blanket right into the hottest part. Jim's eyes watered, not only from heat. The blanket scorched and flared and there was a choking smell of burned wool.

"We have to find her head," said John Three Names, grimly.

Jim said, "I don't know. I don't think I can." He was so overwhelmed by grief and shock that he could hardly stay standing.

John Three Names gripped his wrists. "You have to. What do you think you're going to do – leave her head here for the dogs to find?"

They spent the next twenty minutes bent double, peering into the darkness for any sign of Susan's head. The sky began to lighten and the stars began to fade away. The noise of cicadas was almost overwhelming. At last, his back aching, Jim looked up. Along the back perimeter of the Inn there was a corrugated-iron fence, with a top that had been cut into serrated spikes. Three-quarters of the way along it, he saw a pale, cross face. For a split-second he thought that a woman was watching him, over the top of the fence, and he half-lifted his hand to wave at her. Then he realized that he was looking at Susan's head.

It had fallen with appalling neatness and landed on top of the fence, and it was still frowning at him in the same way that she had frowned at him before she died.

He said, "John," in a hollow voice, and approached the fence with knees like water. As he came closer, he realized that her head was nearly seven feet off the ground. Her eyes were open, and if he hadn't known that the rest of her body was burning in the pit behind him, he could have easily believed that she was still alive.

He couldn't touch the head himself, and he had to turn away as John Three Names used a dry stick to dislodge it. All the same, he heard it thud to the ground. John Three Names picked it up by its blood-matted hair and carried it over to the fire. Jim couldn't look. He stayed where he was, gasping for breath, with tears running down his cheeks.

After a while, however, John Three Names called him, and he managed to compose himself enough to rejoin him beside the embers. John Three Names said, "We'll have to let this burn itself out . . . then I'll come and cover it with dirt. I asked the Inn management if I could light a ceremonial fire here tonight . . . there's no reason for them to get suspicious about it."

"But what happens when Susan doesn't appear for breakfast?"

"You'll just have to persuade your students that she was taken sick in the night, and decided to go back home. I'll take her clothes and her suitcase and keep them hidden."

"But if anybody finds out what we've done, they're going to think that *we* killed her."

"Exactly," said John Three Names. "Just as the police in Los Angeles think that Paul and Grey Cloud killed Martin Amato."

"So what the hell are we going to do?"

"We're going to have to do what we always intended to do . . . what you came here to do. We're going to have to talk to Dog Brother and see if he'll be prepared to let Catherine go."

"That still won't prove our innocence."

"It'll prevent any more killings. And maybe we can discover a way of *proving* what Dog Brother did."

Jim looked down at the fire. It was still very hot, but it was much more ashy now, and the early morning breeze blew some of the ashes across the ground, so that they clung in the thorn-bushes. He said a quiet prayer for Susan's soul, and hoped that wherever she was, she could find it in her heart to forgive him.

It was then that he heard Sharon calling him again, "She's back, Mr Rook! Catherine just came back!"

While John Three Names continued to rake over the ashes, Jim returned to to his room and quickly dressed in jeans and a blue checkered shirt. His fingers were trembling so much that he could hardly fasten his buttons. Then he went across to the girls' room and knocked on the door. Sharon opened up immediately. Jim walked in and found Catherine sitting on the end of her bed in a green nightshirt, thirstily drinking from a can of Coke. He looked down at her feet and they were dusty with ashes.

"Do you want to tell me where you've been?" he demanded. "We've all been worried about you." He paused, and then he said, "Ms Randall's been so worried it's brought on her asthma, and she may have to fly back home."

Catherine looked up at him and there was the strangest expression on her face. Dark, suspicious, almost creepy. "Asthma?" she said.

"That's right. She suffers very badly when she's stressed."

"You mean she has difficulty breathing?"

"Yes."

Catherine lowered her head again and Jim had a suspicion that she hiding a smile.

"You still haven't told me where you've been," he insisted.

"I couldn't sleep, that's all. I went for a walk."

"That wasn't particularly wise, was it, under the circumstances?"

"Sometimes wisdom is a matter of opinion," said Catherine. "You told us that yourself."

Jim hated it when his students quoted his own words back at him, particularly when he didn't agree with what he said. He opened his mouth but then he closed it again without saying anything. He had intended to ask Catherine if she had heard the drumming outside, and if she had seen the fire. But he decided it would be better to hold his tongue, just for the moment. If Catherine were involved in Susan's death in any way, then she knew about it already. If she weren't, then it was better that she didn't know anything about it.

Mark appeared, his hair all scruffed up, wearing a T-shirt and droopy shorts. "What's going on?" he wanted know. "I keep hearing people shouting and doors banging and stuff. Any chance of getting some sleep?"

Jim took his arm. "I'm sorry, Mark. Catherine went for a walk and I guess we all got a little over-excited."

"OK, then," said Mark, "but keep the noise down, hunh? I was having this terrific dream that I was the drummer for REM."

Jim met John Three Names in the corridor and took him back to his room. Susan's door was locked, and the interconnecting door was still locked, too, but Susan had left her sliding patio door slightly ajar. They climbed over the railings that separated the two patios, and let themselves in.

Jim immediately went to the closet and took down Susan's dresses. They smelled of her perfume and he had to bite his lip to stop himself from bursting into tears. He took down her case, opened it up, and quickly packed. John Three Names came out of the bathroom with her toothbrush and her toiletries.

"Is that everything?" said Jim. "Look under the bed, in case she's left anything there."

John Three Names ducked down and came back up with a pair of flowery cotton mules and a dog-eared copy of *The San Andreas Fault*.

"Geography teacher," said Jim, flicking through the book. "She's a geography teacher."

John Three Names picked up the case. "OK," he said, "I'll take this back to my house. Why don't you go back to bed for a couple of hours? Even if you don't sleep it'll give you a chance to settle your nerves. I'll meet you back here at eight thirty, say."

Jim said, "It's unbelievable. You didn't see that thing at all? Not even a shadow of it?"

John Three Names shook his head. "I only saw your girlfriend die . . . and I know that you couldn't have done it, not like that."

"It was . . . *huge*," said Jim. "It was *black*, and *tall*, like a bear. And *fast*. Susan didn't stand a chance."

"You mustn't blame yourself. There was nothing you could have done to stop it."

"I shouldn't have asked Susan to come to Arizona in the first place."

"Jim . . . life is always dangerous. She might have stayed in Los Angeles and died in a traffic accident. Only Gitche Manitou knows the ways that we're going to walk."

Jim couldn't think of anything else to say. He looked around Susan's empty room, and then he opened the door. He checked that there was nobody in the corridor, and then he beckoned John Three Names to follow him out.

"Eight thirty," he said, and went back into his own room. He went to the bathroom, switched on the light, and stared at himself in the mirror. There were two ashy smudges on his cheeks, but apart from that he looked completely normal, as if nothing exceptional had happened at all. Behind him, through the patio windows, he could still see the smoke rising from the fire, and it was almost impossible to believe that it was Susan's funeral pyre, and that he would never, ever see her again. Just at the moment he was beyond tears.

He tried to watch some television, but all he could find was *The Prisoner of Zenda* in black-and-white, and a Mexican program about the Day of the Dead. He switched the television off and closed his eyes. Almost immediately, he opened them again. Under his eyelids, he had seen the dark, bristling beast rushing toward him, its claws upraised.

He thought: it's Thursday already, the day I'm supposed to die. He lay back, staring at the ceiling, with a sweaty sensation of dread. He couldn't begin to imagine what it must be like, to have your head ripped off, or your body slashed open. You must feel something, surely, if only for an instant. Weren't there stories of people's eyes moving, after their heads had been cut off – staring in horror at their own severed neck?

He climbed off the bed and went to the mini-bar. He poured two miniatures of bourbon into one glass and drank both of them, straight down. He coughed, and wiped his eyes. He was shaking so much that he dropped the glass onto the floor.

At a quarter past eight he went to the girls' room and knocked. After a while, Sharon answered it. "Just thought I'd give you a wake-up call," he said. "John Three Names is picking us up in forty-five minutes."

"How's Ms Randall?" asked Sharon. "Did she get over her asthma?"

"Her asthma? No – no she didn't. It got worse. Terrible. She could hardly breathe. I sent her back to Albuquerque. She's going to have some treatment there, and then she's going to fly back to LA."

"That's too bad," said Catherine, sitting up in bed and swinging her hair behind her.

Jim said, "Yes. But anyhow, I'll see you after breakfast."

He closed the door. He didn't know what to make of Catherine at the moment. She seemed to be changing. When she had first arrived at West Grove, she had always been open and friendly. She had been first in class to put up her hand and ask questions, and she had never been afraid of expressing her feelings. She had loved the poetry of Delmore Schwartz, and recited in class: '*The heavy bear who goes with me, A manifold honey to smear his face, Clumsy and lumbering here and there, The central ton of every place.*' At the time, he hadn't thought anything much of it, but after what had happened tonight, it seemed to have a new and threatening significance.

Here, on her own territory, Catherine had become remote and prickly, and had withdrawn deeply into herself. This morning he hadn't seen any sign of the shadow over her, but her tension was almost visible, like the heat waves that had risen from John Three Names' fire.

Mark came up to him, wearing a baggy faded pair of plaid Bermuda shorts and a Delco/Bose T-shirt, which his father had probably been given for free. "Hey, Mr Rook.

I want to thank you for this. This is the best time I ever had in my life."

"I hope so, Mark."

"You seem like you're down, Mr Rook, if you don't mind my saying so."

"Well, it's Susan – Ms Randall. She had an asthma attack and she had to go on back home."

Mark said, "You like her, don't you, Mr Rook? I've seen you looking at her. You really like her."

It was the hardest thing in the world for Jim to smile, but he put his arm around Mark's shoulders and said, "Yes, I really like her."

They walked together to the Inn's cafeteria. There was a pungent smell of fresh coffee and muffins, and a severe-looking Navajo woman in a long print dress was serving out platefuls of bacon and eggs and pancakes. Jim and Mark sat down by the window. Outside, Jim could see a hazy spiral of smoke still drifting upward, and he thought to himself, that's the last of Susan's spirit, rising into the sky.

Mark was fiddling with the sugar and the Sweet'n'Lo. "You know something, Mr Rook, before I met you, I never knew half of the feelings that I had inside me. You know what I mean? I always thought that poetry sucked. But the way you teach it, it's like you can understand what it means. It's like your own feelings, put down on paper. And there's something else you showed me, too. There's a whole wide world outside of Santa Monica. I mean not just Arizona, but all of those places that people write about, like France, and Russia, and who knows where.

"Like, if you live on this planet, you have to know where you live, because once you know where you live, you know who you are."

He paused, and then he said, "You're friends with Ms

Randall. Do you think she could maybe take a little time to teach me some geography? You know, just to *orient* myself."

The severe-looking Navajo woman had arrived at Jim's elbow. "Coffee?" she demanded. "Juice?"

Jim looked at Mark and said, "I'll talk to Ms Randall about it when we get back to LA, OK? I'm sure she wouldn't mind." The words felt like ashes in his mouth, Susan's ashes.

He sat and sipped a cup of black coffee while Mark enthusiastically dug into a plateful of eggs and bacon and hash browns. He didn't look out of the window again. He didn't want to see the smoke. He didn't want to think that he would never see Susan again, as long as he lived.

The morning was glaring and dusty as they drove across the high plateau toward Fort Defiance. John Three Names did most of the talking, telling them all about the history and the culture of the Navajo people.

"The Navajo weren't a 'tribe' as such, back in the old days. The basic unit of economic support was the biological family – a man, his wife and their unmarried children. Each family lived in its own fork-stick house, or *hogan*.

"You'd see a few *hogans* loosely grouped together, because some of their daily tasks needed more than the members of one family could manage. Quite a few of the men used to have more than one wife, or else they'd marry sisters."

"I can't see any Navajo wanting to marry *my* sisters," put in Mark. "They never stop talking about lipstick and clothes and boys and who's cool and who's a dweeb."

John Three Names said, "A Navajo husband would

have great authority over his wives. If they displeased him, he would thrash them."

"Is that a violation of women's rights, or what?" said Sharon. "If my boyfriend ever tried that, I'd break his arms."

"You're not in Los Angeles any longer," John Three Names reminded her. "This is a people who go back thousands of years, before white men or black men were even dreamed of. This is a land that used to be a land of great magic. Most of that magic has gone now, but not all."

With that, he gave Jim a meaningful glance.

Sharon was chatty and inquisitive all the way. Mark came up with one or two subliminal jokes. But Catherine remained silent, staring out at the reddish-colored mountains.

"Are you all right?" Jim asked her.

She gave him a quick, humourless smile. "I think so. I just want today to be over."

Not too damn soon, thought Jim. This could be my very last day on earth.

They reached a trailer park with a wooden sign over the entrance that read *Meadow Between Rocks Homes*. John Three Names turned into it, and drove slowly past the trailers that lined the main strip on either side. Most trailers had their own small gardens, with herbs and vegetables and flowers. Small children ran around everywhere, chased by yapping brindled dogs. As they passed, a woman lifted her washing to the line that was tied to the side of her trailer, and her eyes caught Jim's with such steady familiarity that he felt as if she had been expecting him.

About two-thirds of the way along the main strip, John Three Names drew the Galaxy to a stop outside one of the larger trailers. There were seven or eight cars and trucks parked outside it already, and a small crowd of people gathered around it. Young families in freshly-washed jeans and plaid shirts – older men and women in traditional costumes. A barbecue had been set up behind the trailer, as well as two long trestle tables.

As they climbed out of the Galaxy, John Three Names was approached by a tall, smiling man carrying a small baby in his arms. "Jim," said John Three Names, "I want you to meet my cousin Dan. And this little fellow here is the reason for all of today's celebrations."

"I'm real glad you could make it," said Dan, ushering them up the steps and into the trailer. Although it was quite large, it was already crowded with neighbors and friends and relatives. Dan's wife Minnie passed them cans of beer and they all stood jostling each other in the kitchen section.

"Tell me about the first laugh ceremony," said Jim, tickling the baby under the chin. The baby chuckled and wildly pedalled his arms and legs.

Dan smiled. "When he made man, the Great Spirit gave man two gifts, life and laughter. Animals have life, but no animal laughs. Laughter is what makes man human. Laughter is what makes man closer to the Great Spirit. Every day that a man fails to laugh, he takes one day's journey further away from his spiritual birthplace.

"Today we celebrate my son's arrival in the human race, and his joining together with the spirits."

John Three Names said, "Unfortunately, Dan, we won't be able to stay for very long."

"After you've driven so far? You can't be serious!"

"Actually, we came here on other business," said John Three Names, pressing himself back against the kitchen cabinet as a very generously-proportioned woman in a fringed buckskin dress pushed her way past him. "We came to see Dog Brother."

"Dog Brother? What business do you have with Dog Brother?"

"Family business."

"Not to do with—?" said Dan, nodding his head toward Catherine.

John Three Names nodded. "He refuses to let her go. He says that a bargain was struck, and a bargain must be honoured."

"I warned Henry at the time," said Dan. "I warned him but he wouldn't listen. He was crazy with worry for his wife. He said, 'Don't worry, when the time comes for Catherine to go to him, I'll take her away, and Dog Brother will never find her.' I told him that Dog Brother would always find her, wherever she went.

"Henry didn't seem to understand that Dog Brother himself could have given his wife the cancer."

"Excuse me," said Jim. "You may be able to give people the 'flu but you can't give them *cancer*."

Dan looked at him as if he had just said something spectacularly stupid. "This is Dog Brother we're talking about here."

"So? He's only a man."

"*You're* going to see him, too? A white man?"

"Sure. That's why I'm here. Henry asked me to try to buy him off. A hefty payment in stocks and bonds in place of Catherine."

Dan shook his head and kept on shaking it. "Are you crazy? Do you think he'll really give up Catherine in return for money? You don't know what kind of individual you're dealing with here."

John Three Names laid a hand on Dan's shoulder. "Come on, Dan. Let's not get alarmist here. Most of what people say about Dog Brother is superstition, hearsay. He's just an ordinary guy."

"So why do people go to him when they want somebody cured of cancer?"

"Dan – everything's going to be fine. Everything's going to work out. We'll go see Dog Brother, and then maybe we'll be back in time for the prayers."

"You'll need them, believe me," Dan told him.

Chapter Seven

Toward the end of the main strip, the trailers began to look shabbier and more weatherbeaten. Some had half-collapsed verandahs built onto them. Others had scabby tarpaper roofs. In place of the meticulously-tended vegetable beds there was nothing but scrub-grass and dust and all of that indescribable detritus that seems to collect around trailer-parks as if they were some kind of Sargasso Sea of useless junk. Heavy, rusty objects that had no apparent purpose whatsoever. Car seats, right in the middle of nowhere at all. Heaps of worn-out tyres.

The neat lines of trailers began to straggle, and then there were long gaps in between them. Outside one of them, its windows bedecked with filthy net curtains, a handpainted sign said, *Keep Away. Owner Has Gun & Itchy Trigger Finger*. A dog was tearing at a dead buzzard.

At the very end of the strip, parked askew to all the rest of the homes, was a large black-painted trailer with blacked-out windows. The heat shuddered from its roof, distorting the distant vermilion mountains behind it. There were empty cans and automobile parts strewn all around it, as well as a stack of what looked like old newspapers gummed together with some black substance like tar. Whatever it was, a host of flies were crawling all over it.

Not far away, an old blue Buick Electra was shaded

under a single tree, while high above, two buzzards lazily circled in the flawless sky.

John Three Names stopped the Galaxy at a respectful distance. Immediately, two black Dobermanns got up from the grass in which they had been lying and pricked up their ears. Jim was relieved to see that they were both chained to one of the trailer's rear wheels.

"This is where Dog Brother lives," said John Three Names. "From now on, we should take this very, very easy."

"What do we do if he's not home?" asked Mark.

"Oh, he'll be home. He's *always* home."

Jim said, "OK, then. Let's screw our courage to the sticking-place."

"Let's screw what?" frowned Mark.

"Shakespeare, Mark. *Macbeth.* You should have read it."

"I did. I remember 'out damned spot.' The first time I read it I thought he meant, like, zit."

Sharon clucked her disapproval. "I'll tell you something, Foley. I used to think that I was stupid till I met you. Then I graduated to genius overnight."

John Three Names said, "I'd better go first, then you and Catherine can follow. But don't worry: Dog Brother isn't especially prejudiced against whites. He hates everybody equally."

"What shall we do?" asked Sharon.

"Just stay in the car for a while, if you don't mind. You can leave the motor running to keep the air con on."

"Hmph," said Sharon. She was very strong-willed and she didn't like being left out of the action, whatever it was.

John Three Names led the way across the dust toward the trailer. The Dobermanns twitched and quivered and strained at their chains. They looked as if they were ready to rush over and take a leg apiece, but they didn't bark. John Three Names climbed the steps to the trailer's door. There was a knocker on it, with a face like a snarling wolf. John Three Names gave three cautious knocks, and then waited.

Jim shaded his eyes. "It's odd how Dog Brother's trailer is set at an angle from all the others," he remarked.

Catherine said, "His door faces east, where the demons come from."

"I thought that Native Americans avoided doing that."

"Dog Brother is different, Mr Rook. Dog Brother positively welcomes them."

After a while, John Three Names knocked again. There was a long paused, and then the trailer door swung open, on its own. Inside, Jim could see nothing but pitch-blackness. No sign of Dog Brother. No sign of anything at all. He suddenly began to feel alarmed, and he could sense his pulse-rate quickening. Just remember what the Indians used to say, he told himself. "Today will be a good day to die."

John Three Names peered inside the trailer, then turned back and beckoned Jim and Catherine to come closer. "It's OK, I guess."

Catherine suddenly snatched hold of Jim's hand. She was startlingly cold, and she was trembling. He looked at her and her face was as white as paper.

"Listen," he said, "you don't have to go through with this if you don't want to. Nobody's going to force you, least of all me. All we're going to do is see if we can't persuade this Dog Brother guy to forget your father's promise."

"I don't know – I don't know if I can do this," Catherine gasped. "I don't know if I can face him. I want to see him. I really want to see him. Don't you understand me, I'm *burning* to see him – but I don't know – I'm afraid of him

– I'm so afraid of him, Mr Rook – and I'm so afraid of myself."

Jim put his arm around her. "Do you want to turn around and go back to LA? I don't mind. I don't know what will happen if you do. I guess this whole problem is going to stay unresolved, and your brothers are going to stay in prison. But you have to think about *you*. Otherwise, the way I see it, this whole mess is going to go on being a mess, and more people are going to get hurt."

Catherine stared at him. "Ms Randall – did *she* get hurt?"

"What makes you say that? She had asthma, that's all."

"No she didn't. She got hurt, didn't she? She got hurt!"

"Catherine—"

"You can't say she didn't because I saw it! I'm sure that I saw it! I saw her fall to the ground!"

John Three Names called, "Are you coming or not? He's waiting for you."

"So what do you think?" Jim asked Catherine. "Are you coming inside or not?"

Catherine's eyes were filled with tears. "I saw her fall and it was all my fault. I saw her fall and I was glad that she fell, I don't know why."

Her confusion was almost total. Her eyes were unfocused, and her movements were abrupt and jerky. What was more, Jim was sure that he could see the shadow beginning to form around her – dim, blotchy traces of darkness that clung in the air like bloodclots.

"Jim!" called John Three Names.

"Catherine, you can say no if you want to," Jim repeated. "Just say the word, and we're out of here."

"I can't," she said, and her voice was suddenly deep and harsh. "A promise is a promise. An oath is an oath."

With that, she began to walk stiffly toward the trailer. Jim called, "Catherine!" but she mounted the steps and disappeared into the darkness. John Three Names beckoned Jim yet again, and said, "Come on, Jim. This is the only way."

Jim looked back at the Galaxy, where Sharon and Mark were waiting for him. Then he took a deep breath and walked up to the trailer. "It's all right, Jim," said John Three Names, holding out his hand. "He's agreed to talk to you, even if you are white."

Jim peered into the darkness. An odd smell was wafting out of the trailer. It reminded Jim of stale sweat and dogs, but there was another fragrance mixed up in it, too – a fragrance like burning leaves, and woods, and long fall days, and *leather* for some reason, the smell of a leather watchstrap that you've worn too long.

"Go ahead," said John Three Names, and Jim took a step into the darkness. It was a heavy black sheet, hung over the doorway so that the light couldn't penetrate. Inside, the trailer was painted as black as it was on the outside, with black-upholstered furniture, and it was lit only by tiny lamps with bulbs no bigger than beads.

Catherine was already seated on one of the couches, her hands held across her chest in her familiar 'parachute-jump' position, her hair shining in the lamplight. She was facing a tall, thin man who was sitting cross-legged in a large antique chair with faded, gilded arms, and a seat that must once have been the finest midnight-black velvet, but which was now reduced to a faded collection of grey strings.

The man was naked to the waist, and his body was very lean and muscular, with no excess fat at all. Both of his nipples were pierced and hung with various beads and bird's-wings. He had long black hair that draped over his shoulders. His eyes were concealed behind small spectacles with yellow lenses. His face was hard and angled and vulpine, as if his great-great-grandfather might have been a wolf, but he was handsome, too, in a very primitive way. He wore a tight pair of black leather britches, half-unlaced at the front.

"Jim . . . this is Dog Brother," said John Three Names. "Dog Brother . . . this is Jim Rook."

"You are the one who sees?" asked Dog Brother. He spoke slowly and harshly, as if he weren't used to making much conversation.

"I guess you could call me that," said Jim. "And you . . . you're the one who puts hexes on people?"

"Jim—" John cautioned him.

"No, no. That's the whole reason I'm here," said Jim. "I've come here to prevent any further killings by this spirit-beast of yours."

Dog Brother lifted his right hand. On the palm of it was tattooed a picture of the dark, bear-like creature that had attacked Susan back at Window Rock. "You are a wise man, for a white. Not many Navajos still believe in spirit-beasts these days, let alone whites."

"I believe in it because I've seen it."

"You've actually seen it with your own eyes? Do you want to tell me what it looks like?"

"Like many bears, with claws. And with eyes like coals from a furnace."

"You *have* seen it, haven't you?" said Dog Brother, with a smile that revealed crowded, pointed teeth. "I never thought that anybody ever would. Well . . . you can go back to your lodges now and tell them that it was all a bad dream. Tell them it's over, and that the Changing Bear Maiden will never trouble them again. Unless, of course, it chooses to. But then you can never tell with the Changing Bear Maiden. She's always so spontaneous."

He laughed, a crackling laugh like dry twigs breaking.

In the dim light, Jim could see Catherine sitting hunched on the sofa, her hands lying in her lap, upturned. Next to her sat John Three Names, conspiciously tense. He kept drumming his fingers on his knees and shuffling his feet. If a ticker-tape had come out of his brain, it would have, read, 'Come on, come on. Let's get going. For Christ's sake, Jim, let's cut the niceties and get the hell out of here.'

Jim leaned forward so that he was looking directly into Dog Brother's glasses. "Let's cut straight to the chase, shall we? Henry Black Eagle has authorized me to make you an offer of stocks, bonds and ready cash. All you have to do is name your price."

Dog Brother stared back at him for a long, long time without saying anything. Then, as if had just woken from a coma, said, "Price? What are you talking about, price?"

Jim reached into his pocket and took out his organizer. In it, he had clearly written a list of all of Henry's stocks, bonds and insurance investments. He had also jotted down that in the last resort, Henry would give him a percentage share in his next contract with Fox TV, and a percentage share in all of his royalties, 'in perpetuity and for ever,' as they like to say in Hollywood contracts.

"Henry can raise $950,0000. Just say the word, and it's all yours. No more living in a trailer, hunh? You'll be able to build your own house for this, with pool."

"Is this some kind of . . . *dowry*?" asked Dog Brother.

"No, no. I don't think you get it. Henry is offering you this $950,000 so that you won't chase after Catherine any longer."

"I won't chase after her. I promise. Why should I need to? She'll be here, sitting by my side."

Jim took off his reading-glasses and tucked them into his shirt-pocket. "Dog Brother, we're talking at cross-purposes here. Henry Black Eagle is offering you this money to set Catherine free – to tear up your marriage agreement. The money isn't a dowry, sir. It's a form of compensation. A goodwill gesture, if you like."

Dog Brother turned to John and snapped, "You told me this white man was bringing Catherine White Bird back to me."

"Well, he is, and he has."

"Excuse me," said Jim. "You're not thinking of taking both of them, are you? The girl *and* the money? Because I'm afraid that this is a 'tick one box only' situation. Either you get to keep Catherine, who has made it perfectly clear to me over the past few days that she wouldn't live back on the reservation if you gave her all the peanuts in Georgia. Or, you can take the money. But not both."

"No," said Dog Brother.

"No, what? No, you're quite aware that you can't have both? Or, no, you don't want the money but you do want the girl? Or, no, you want the money but you do—"

"Enough!" said Dog Brother. "You've done well to bring me back this woman. Now you can go."

He climbed out of his chair and took hold of Catherine by the wrist. "You see this scar?" he said. "That was where our blood was mingled when she was fifteen years old. She belonged to me from that day onward. You can't change that with money."

"Mr Dog Brother," said Jim. "I know that you feel that Catherine belongs to you, but the fact is that in the eyes of the law your betrothal doesn't mean squat."

"Take it easy, Jim—" John Three Names cautioned him.

"What do you mean, 'take it easy'?" Jim demanded. "Are you part of this, too?"

"We couldn't fight it, Jim. You've seen it for yourself. After your college boy died, and Paul and Grey Cloud were accused of killing him – Henry knew that he didn't have any choice."

"You mean that he didn't send me here to bargain at all? All he wanted me to do was to take Catherine back to this feather-nippled yahoo?"

"Jim! They couldn't risk any more killing!"

"Then why didn't they come back here and turn this creep over to the cops?"

"Because who would believe them? Even the Navajo cops wouldn't believe them."

Dog Brother was still holding onto Catherine's arm, still grinning widely. His teeth looked as if he could take a bite out of a three-inch mahogany tabletop. "John Three Names is right. Nobody would believe that you had seen the Changing Bear Maiden. You would be locked up by the same people you had asked for help, and they would throw away the key."

Jim said, "You refuse the money?"

"I would be happy with the money, if Henry Black Eagle wishes to give it to me."

"But you're not letting Catherine go free?"

"Absolutely not. She's going to be my wife. She's going to bear my children. She's going to feed me and bathe me and worship me. She's going to lick the sweat from between my toes."

Catherine was staring at him. There was a turmoil of darkness around her. John Three Names obviously couldn't see it, but Jim could, and the way in which Dog Brother was taunting her made Jim wonder if *he* could, too – or maybe *sense* it, at the very least.

"I don't want to marry you!" Catherine retorted. "I won't ever marry you!"

"Of course you'll marry me. You'll grow to love me so much that you'll cry every time I'm out of your sight."

"I won't! I hate you!" The darkness began to leap and dance with a life of its own, and to coagulate around her shoulders in hunched, shadowy knots.

Jim said, "Come on, Dog Brother, let her go."

"You!" said Dog Brother, contemptuously. "You've been warned, haven't you? This is your day to die!"

"I've heard enough of that for one week," Jim told him. He was angry now – angry and tired and frustrated. "All you have to do is let her go and then we can negotiate this situation like reasonable men."

"You think you were sent here to *negotiate*?" Dog Brother sneered at him. "You were sent here for two reasons only – to bring Catherine White Bird back to me, and to see that the Changing Bear Maiden returns to the great outside, where she came from, because you're the only one who can. That was the one single condition that Henry Black Eagle asked for, before he returned his beautiful daughter, and who was I to refuse him? A promise is a promise."

Jim said, "John, is this true?"

John Three Names nodded. "I'm sorry, Jim. I didn't like deceiving you, believe me, but there was no other way. Dog Brother and Catherine are supposed to be exchange their marriage-promises – and when they do, you're supposed to witness the spirit-beast disappearing back to the spirit-world."

"Oh, I see. Then you've been telling me lies right from the start."

Dog Brother smiled. "They weren't exactly lies, Mr Rook. They were just a way of getting you out here, and to make sure that Catherine got here, too. You've seen the beast. You've seen what it can do. Even *I* can't control it sometimes."

"Oh, I've seen it, thanks, and I've seen what it can do. It killed a promising young student. It wrecked my apartment and killed my cat. It turned the West Grove locker room into a disaster area. And yesterday it killed – a woman I was very fond of."

"So you'd like to see it go for good?" said John Three Names.

"Are you kidding me?"

"Then let's see Dog Brother and Catherine married, and that'll be the end of it."

"And what about Paul and Grey Cloud?"

"You can go back to LA and testify to what you saw."

"Oh, sure, and a jury's going to believe me?"

"You can take a polygraph test."

"Inadmissible as evidence. You know that."

"But what if somebody else were killed in exactly the same way, hundreds of miles distant, while Paul and Grey Cloud were still in custody?"

Jim stared at him. "You're talking about *Susan*?"

"Too badly burned, I'm afraid. You see, Susan was a necessary sacrifice to Coyote. You don't walk on the master's territory without paying him homage."

"You mean that Susan was a *burnt offering*?"

John Three Names shrugged. "That was why I built the fire. I expected her to come out looking for Catherine, but I didn't expect *you*. All the same, you were quite a help. Pity about the blanket."

"You mean you summoned up that beast? You did it on purpose? Just so that Susan could be murdered and burned?"

Dog Brother said, "Coyote always appreciates the smell of human flesh, burned in his honor. It makes him more amenable to the human race. In the old days, they burned virgins, and buffalo, and they burned them alive."

"Just a minute," said Jim. "If you're not talking about Susan being killed in exactly the same way, who *are* you talking about?"

Dog Brother said, "You brought some friends with you, didn't you, just like Henry Black Eagle asked you to?"

"Hey – wait a minute," said Jim. "Nobody touches one hair of those students' heads. You talk about promises? I made three promises when I agreed to come here. I promised Henry Black Eagle that I would try to negotiate Catherine's release from her marriage vows. I promised my students that I would take care of them. And I promised myself that I wasn't going to die. Not today."

"Pretty hard promises to keep," said Dog Brother, slowly approaching him, until Jim could see every blackhead in every pore of his nose. "I'm taking Catherine, don't you have any doubt about that; and I'm going to give Henry Black Eagle all the evidence he needs to free his sons from prison; and if you raise any objection whatsoever, then so help me I'll hunt you down for the rest of your life, and destroy everything that means anything to you, and kill anybody you love. That's what it means to die, my friend. That's what it *really* means to die. That's what the white men did to us, not so very long ago. Destroyed our houses and burned our crops and killed our cattle. Our women and children starved and what did you care? You spat on our graves.

"Today, you die," Dog Brother repeated. "Tomorrow, you die. Every day for the rest of your life, you die."

Jim stared back at him and thought, Christ, what am I going to do? He looked across at John Three Names, who held his gaze for only a moment before he uncomfortably looked away. Then he looked at Catherine, whose expression was a tangle of confusion and fright.

"All right, then," he said. "I guess if it's Catherine you want, you can have her. What can I do?"

Dog Brother slowly grinned. "That's good. I like a realist. Now, which of your students can we have, or shall we take them both?"

Jim was appalled at Dog Brother's cold-bloodedness.

How can I possibly sacrifice one of my class? And even if I could, which one would it be? Sharon, who had a future ahead of her as a social worker or even a local politician for black causes; or Mark, who would probably end up just like his father, beating automobile panels, but whose humour and poetic insight would break the mould of his father's ignorance, and make sure that *his* son had a chance?

"Maybe I should ask them to toss a coin," he said. "They don't need to know what it's for."

Dog Brother seemed to like that. "I knew that you were an intelligent man, when I first saw you. Henry Black Eagle chose wisely."

"Catherine?" said Jim. He tried to catch her full attention – tried to appeal to Catherine White Bird, instead of the shadowy shape that was forming all around her. "Catherine, I'm sorry. You see what kind of position I'm in."

Catherine said, "I – I don't know what you mean. What are you trying to say to me?"

"I'm trying to tell you that you have to marry Dog Brother. I don't have any choice."

He stepped up close to her and took hold of her hand. Already he could feel the prickle of harsh, invisible hair, like static electricity.

He leaned forward as if to kiss her cheek. "I'm going to grab your hand real tight," he murmured. "When I do that, *run*, you understand?"

He stood up straight. There was nothing in her face to tell him if she had understood him or not – just the same bewilderment, the same fear.

"Okay, then," he said to Dog Brother. "I guess I'll go out and ask my students to decide which of them is going to live and which of them is going to go the Happy Hunting Ground."

John Three Names said, "I guess I'll be going, too. I've seen enough blood for one week, believe me."

He turned, and Dog Brother stepped back to let him pass, and at that moment Jim pushed Dog Brother flat in the chest, so that he lost his balance and fell back against the armchair. John Three Names turned back again, but Jim shouldered him roughly out of the way. He gripped Catherine's hand and shouted, "*Now*!"

He tried to pull at her hand, but as he did so Dog Brother let out a high, unearthly shriek. Catherine's hand seemed to explode inside his. One second her fingers were slim and smooth – the next he was holding a gigantic, bristly claw. He cried out, "*Ahh*!" and whipped his hand away. There was no longer a slight, long-haired girl behind him, but a bulky bearlike shadow that reached almost to the trailer's ceiling. It had tiny eyes that glared red like the perforations in a furnace-door, and claws that literally clattered as it lifted them up.

Jim dropped to the floor, shielding his face with his arm. As he did so, one claw whisked past him, so close that it tore the skin along his knuckles. It struck the side of the trailer with a thunderous crash, breaking a Formica cabinet in half and puncturing the aluminum wall, so that five jagged stars of daylight suddenly burst through.

"*Catherine*!" Jim yelled at it. But the beast lurched forward yet again, so that the whole trailer shook. It swung at Jim again and again, but Jim rolled away across the floor and slid beneath one of the couches. He heard Dog Brother howling and whooping, and singing some kind of high-pitched, repetitive chant. "*Aheeiioo – ahane – aheeiioo – saabate –*"

The beast lashed out in all directions, its claws tearing through upholstery, metal and laminate. The noise was ear-splitting, and it didn't stop. It felt to Jim as if a bomb had detonated in slow-motion. The foam seating over his head was torn apart; the flooring was ripped up; glasses smashed; furniture was wrenched limb-from-limb. The air was filled with a blizzard of broken china and shreds of upholstery, and with every blow the Changing Bear Maiden ripped her way through the sides of the trailer, so that sunlight came criss-crossing in from every direction.

The trailer's framework began to give way. The walls were all battered and dented, and even ripped open, in places. The entire structure tilted, and suddenly its wheels collapsed, which threw Dog Brother back onto the floor, hitting his head against the television stand. John Three Names had been struggling to reach the door, and had to cling onto the drapes to prevent himself from tumbling backward. Jim – under the couch – was forced into an awkward corner, his legs doubled-up. He managed to push his back against the side of the trailer and force himself free, just as the Changing Bear Maiden's claw detonated through the cushions on top of him and slammed through the wall with all the force of a fork-lift truck.

Jim knew that he had to make a run for it. He might not survive, but anything was better than waiting here to have his head torn off, the way that Susan had. He took a deep breath, counted to three, and then he jack-knifed out from under the couch, rolled across the floor, and grabbed hold of the first support that he could find – which turned out to be John Three Names' ankle. John Three Names, panicking, screamed, "Let go of me! Let go of me!" He tried to kick Jim's hand away, but Jim wouldn't let go. He dragged himself forward until he and John Three Names were lying side by side.

"Do you know what you've done?" Jim yelled at him. "You've killed two innocent people, just because you were too frightened to stand up to some sly, treacherous, out-of-date demon! Did you really think that I was going to allow you to kill any more?"

John Three Names struggled to get himself free. "What do you white men know? This whole country is Navajo country and always will be! We're waiting for the time, that's all! We're taking care of our spirits, we're bringing them all back out of hiding, one by one, we're reviving the old beliefs, and we're waiting for the time! Let me tell you something, Mr Rook – it won't be long now before every white community between here and Los Angeles is populated by nothing but corpses. Blowfly heaven, that's what it'll be."

The floor shook beneath them. Jim glanced up. The Changing Bear Maiden was looming over them, cold and dark. Its stiff fur bristled and its eyes burned red and it uttered a sound in its throat like men being strangled. It lashed out at Jim, ripping his shirt and tearing his shoulder open. He felt blood springing wet down his back. John Three Names struggled with him and kicked him and tried to lift him up from the floor, so that the beast's next blow would hit him in the head. Jim tipped himself backward and rolled John Three Names over on top of him. John Three Names gripped his wrists and tried to wrestle him over again. Jim felt his sweat dripping on his face and the smell of stale coffee on his breath.

"We were supposed to forget, were we?" he roared. "We were supposed to forget about what you did to us? All those women and children who died here at Fort Defiance?" His anger was so intense that he seemed to have forgotten all about the spirit-beast that was shaking the trailer all around them.

Over his shoulder Jim saw a paw lifted – a shaggy black paw with claws that caught the criss-cross sunlight. Even though John Three Names was shouting at him and struggling with him, he tried to push him sideways, out of the way. But there was a *whakkk*! and a sharp gristly noise like somebody twisting the leg off a raw chicken, and Jim was suddenly spattered with warm blood. John Three Names fell off him, clutching the side of his head. "My ear! It's taken my ear off!"

The trailer seemed to blow up. The beast tore down its ceiling and ripped away its walls. Torn fragments of aluminum hurtled everywhere, along with a billowing cloud of foam and feathers and shredded sheets. Dog Brother, unconscious, was showered in rice and flour and dried fettucine.

John Three Names tried to climb to his feet, his face streaked with blood. He reached for a wall that was no longer there, and teetered. At that moment the Changing Bear Maiden gripped him in both of its claws, and lifted him high over its head. John Three Names screamed. His legs bicycled. The beast's claws had penetrated his ribcage on both sides, deep into his lungs and his liver.

"No!" he screeched out. "No! I served you! I saved you!"

But then the beast pulled its claws wide apart, and with a loud crackling noise it tore open his body from his neck to his crotch, and then violently shook him, so that he was emptied out all over the floor of the trailer, heart and lungs and stomach and intestines, in a sloppy, splattering heap. The beast then dropped his gutted, flaccid body, all arms and legs like a marionette, and turned toward Jim.

Jim was already running. As soon as the beast had caught hold of John Three Names, he had scrambled toward the door, dropped to the ground, and headed for the Galaxy where Sharon and Mark were waiting.

It was hot, and he was badly shocked. He could hear his shoes chuffing in the dust and it sounded as if somebody were two steps behind him. Sharon was out of the vehicle already, staring in shock at the wildly-exploding trailer.

Mark was sitting in the back seat, punching wildly at John Three Names' mobile phone.

"Sharon! Get back in!" Jim shouted at her, as he ran toward her.

"What? What about Catherine?"

"*Get back in*!"

He looked back over his shoulder and the spirit-beast was already running toward him, in the heavy, sinister lope of a grizzly bear. It was enormous, almost three times the size of a real bear, and its claws made a clashing noise on the ground as it ran, like somebody sharpening carving-knives.

"Sharon, for Christ's sake! Get back in!"

He reached the Galaxy and pushed Sharon back into her seat. He climbed behind the wheel, slammed the door and gunned the engine.

"But Catherine!" Sharon shrieked at him. "What about Catherine?"

Jim violently reversed the Galaxy and swung it around so that it was facing back toward the trailer-park. "Catherine isn't Catherine," he told her. "Not any more, anyway."

"But she's there!" said Sharon, taking hold of his arm and shaking it. "Look, Mr Rook, she's there!"

Jim kept his foot down and the Galaxy slithered in the dust. Jim looked up in the rear-view mirror and he could see Catherine running after them, her hair swinging as she ran. But when he twisted around in his seat, all he could see was the huge dark shadow of the Changing Bear Maiden, relentlessly trying to catch up.

"Mr Rook, stop!" begged Sharon. "You're leaving Catherine behind!"

Jim jammed on the brakes. "Sharon, it isn't Catherine. It's something else. It may look like Catherine to you, but to me it looks like something else altogether."

"I called the cops," said Mark, hopefully, holding up

the mobile telephone. "They said they'd try to get here in a half-hour, if they could."

Catherine was still running toward them. In his mirror, Jim could see that her expression was fixed, her eyes were glazed. She was running like somebody who was determined to catch up with them, no matter what.

"Hold tight," he said, and stepped on the gas. The Galaxy's tyres slewed sideways on the dirt, and then they were speeding away. At that moment, however, they felt a catastrophic bang at the back of the vehicle, and the rear window shattered inward. Then they heard a hideous scraping, followed by a jarring, wrenching sound, and Jim felt the Galaxy's steering wheel twitch in his hands as if it had a mind of its own.

"What's happening?" said Sharon, in terror.

Jim looked back and saw the Changing Bear Maiden running after them, faster and faster. It lunged at the back of the Galaxy and tore off the rear door panel, which bounced away over the dusty ground. Then it smashed the brake lights and pulled off more of the trim. Fragments of red plastic were scattered all over the ground.

"It's *Catherine*," said Mark. "What the hell is she doing? She's tearing the whole damn car to pieces!"

"It's just like I said, Mark," Jim told him. "It isn't Catherine, not at the moment. It's kind of a beast. The same beast that killed Martin Amato. The same beast that wrecked the locker rooms."

"What are you telling us?" said Sharon. "You're trying to say that *Catherine* killed Martin? You're trying to say that *Catherine* did all of that damage?"

Jim turned around and saw the beast running up closer. It collided with their rear bumper with a heavy thump and he had to swerve wildly from side to side. They were speeding down the main strip between the trailers now, and there were children and dogs scampering everywhere.

Yet he didn't dare to slow down. The back of the Galaxy was already battered and torn and scored with scratch-marks, and he knew that if he stopped now, the beast would hurtle through the back window into the passenger compartment and tear them into pieces before they had time to open the doors.

"*Mr Rook*!" screamed Sharon.

Ahead of them, an old Navajo woman was crossing the main strip with a Zimmer frame. She was accompanied by a little girl of no more than six or seven, who was smiling to her and chatting to her and offering her wildflowers.

Jim saw them like a photograph – utterly clear, utterly detailed. He was already hitting 70 mph and he had no chance of stopping before he hit them. He just had time to shout "Hold tight!" before he swerved off the main strip and crashed through somebody's picket fence, mowed down their garden planted with beans and squash and pumpkins, collided with a water-butt, tore up another length of fence like a giant zip-fastener, skidded around the back of another trailer straight through a line of freshly-hung washing, and then bounced back onto the main strip.

He drove out of the trailer-park, hung a howling right turn, and sped back toward Window Rock with his foot flat against the floor.

He checked his rear-view mirror. Catherine wasn't running after them any longer. She standing outside the trailer-park watching them speed away. He turned his head around and she was still Catherine. The beast had vanished. He had an almost irresistible urge to U-turn and go back to her. Christ, he was her teacher, he felt responsible for her. He couldn't imagine what she was going through, what fears she was feeling. But he did know that until she was released from Dog

Brother's influence, she was capable of killing all of them.

"You're just going to *leave* her here?" asked Mark.

"I don't have any choice. This man she's supposed to be marrying has put a spell on her, for want of a better word. Back then, when she was running after us, you saw Catherine but I saw a huge black beast."

Mark turned around and looked back along the road, just in time to see Catherine turning back toward the trailer-park. "A beast. It's hard to believe it."

"Look at the damage she did to the van. If she wasn't possessed by this *thing*, whatever it is, she couldn't even have dented it."

"Come on, Mark," said Sharon. "You know that Mr Rook can see things like spirits and ghosts and all."

"Yeah, but a *beast*, man – in broad daylight! Wish I'd seen it!"

Jim said, "Listen," and told them the legend of the Changing Bear Maiden, the way that John Three Names had told it to him. What he didn't say was that John Three Names was dead; or that Susan had been killed, too, and burned as an offering to Coyote.

They reached Window Rock and drew up outside the Navajo Nation Inn. "What are we going to do now?" asked Sharon.

"We're going to pack our bags and get the hell out of here, that's what."

"What's Catherine's old man going to say when you come back without her?" asked Mark.

"I'm very much looking forward to finding out."

"Wait up a minute. You mean – he didn't *expect* her to come back?"

"I don't think he expected any of us to come back. Only me, so that I could confirm that the beast was gone for good. And I doubted if I would have lasted long, after that."

"I don't get it. We were all supposed to die, *all* of us?"

Jim nodded. "Henry Black Eagle took his family to California to duck out of his promise to give Catherine to Dog Brother. But he underestimated how powerful the magic was, and how far it could reach. After Martin was killed, and Paul and Grey Cloud were arrested for murder, he realized that he had to honour his promise. He wanted us killed by the Changing Bear Maiden so that he would have evidence that his sons couldn't possibly have murdered Martin. Which, of course, they didn't. They went down on the beach that night to try to find Catherine before she hurt anybody."

Sharon pushed the revolving glass door into the reception area. "It seems terrible, leaving Catherine behind like that. I mean whatever she's turned into now, she was always such a totally sweet person."

"Sharon, there's nothing else we can do right now. If we go near her, she'll rip our heads off. And I'm beginning to think that Dog Brother doesn't have the slightest intention of sending the Changing Bear Maiden back into limbo, or wherever. I think he likes her fine the way she is."

Jim rented a Pontiac station-wagon and they drove all the way from Window Rock to Gallup, where they stopped for cheeseburgers; and then 138 mph nonstop to Albuquerque. They arrived in time for an American Airlines flight direct to Los Angeles and they took off into the sun. Sharon and Mark slept for most of the flight. Jim was exhausted but he was still suffering badly from shock and he didn't want to close his eyes for fear of what he might see.

He took out the silver whistle that Henry Black Eagle had given him. He wasn't tempted to blow it, but he wondered exactly what it was for. Catherine had warned him that it would alert Dog Brother and give away their location, but Jim didn't really see the point of a whistle that did nothing more than that. It had snapped Catherine out of her Changing Bear Maiden trance when their airplane had been nosediving into the Cibola Forest, but Jim couldn't understand how. He had quite a list of questions for Henry Black Eagle when they returned to Los Angeles.

He drove both Mark and Sharon home, and by now it was dark. "Listen," he said, "I think it would be better if you didn't tell your parents what happened at Fort Defiance. They're bound to want a police investigation, and if there's one situation that the police won't be able to handle, it's this. I'm thinking of Catherine, more than anbody else. If the police find her and she goes berserk the way she did at the trailer-park . . . well, you can use your imagination."

"We'll see you tomorrow in class, Mr Rook," said Sharon, and she unexpectedly gave him a kiss on the cheek. "Thanks for getting us out of trouble."

"I shouldn't have gotten you *into* trouble to start with."

"Hey, what's life without a few scares?" said Mark. "I had the best time ever. Better than sitting on your duff watching TV, anyhow."

"You didn't think that when we was headed for those trees," Sharon retorted.

"I didn't crap myself, did I?"

"If you had, I would have been the first one out of there, with or without a parachute."

"Listen," said Jim, "you don't have to show up for

college tomorrow if you don't want to. Maybe you could use the rest."

"Try and stop us, Mr Rook. Just try and stop us."

Chapter Eight

He drove to George Babouris' house and found George sitting on the porch strumming his bouzouki. "Jim – you're back already! How about a glass of retsina? You should listen to this song I've composed. It's called *How We Danced In Aspropirgos*."

"Catchy title," said Jim. "Is it OK if I stay here tonight? The super is supposed to be clearing up my apartment, but I'm not sure that I can face going back there, not till tomorrow."

"Of course you can stay. Are you hungry? I made stuffed peppers yesterday, all they need is a couple of minutes in the microwave."

"That's all right, George. I think I just need a drink."

George led the way inside. To be fair, he seemed to have tidied the place up since Jim had last stayed there. The goldfish were still swimming through a dense turquoise murk, and there was a pair of discarded socks on the back of the couch, but George had thrown out most of his waste paper and empty beer cans and there was even a bowl of oranges on the table.

"Don't tell me you're in love," said Jim.

"Well, not exactly," George confessed. "But I've met this woman and we've been getting along pretty well. I think you know her, as a matter of fact. Well, you *would* know her. She lives in the same apartment block as you do."

"Go on," said Jim, suspiciously, setting down his bag.

"You left my number with your super, right, in case he had any questions? So he called and said that he couldn't replace the kitchen cabinets with exactly the same doors, but would these other doors be OK? So I went around there and they were fine, the doors I mean. They were just like your old ones only better quality. Except that I met your neighbour from downstairs. The woman."

"You mean Miss *Neagle*?"

"That's it. Valerie! And I can tell you something, Jim, two people never got on better than Valerie and me. The spontaneity! It was great! And she's crazy for Greek café music!"

"Well, George. I hardly know what to say. I'm very happy for you – both of you."

"I'm going round to see her later this evening. Say – why don't you join me? You could see how your apartment's coming along."

"I don't know. I don't want to get in the way."

George opened the fridge and took out two cans of Pabst. "You won't. So how was Indian country? Did you manage to get everything sorted out?"

"To tell you the truth, George, it was a disaster."

"Hey – how come? I thought you were looking forward to it. Acting as a marriage guidance counsellor to Native Americans. Smoking peace-pipes. Dancing round the totem-pole."

"Henry Black Eagle was lying to me all along. He didn't want me to take Catherine back to the reservation to break off her engagement. He simply wanted me to chaperone her, to make sure that she returned there safe, and married this guy.

"He made a deal with a devil, George, and then he found he couldn't go back on it."

"When you say '*devil*'—?"

"I mean exactly that. Devil, or demon, or evil spirit, or whatever you want to call it. The man that Catherine is supposed to be marrying has some way of invoking the worst of all the Navajo spirits, called Coyote. His name's Dog Brother. He can turn people into beasts."

"He can turn people into *beasts*?" George repeated, raising one black bushy eyebrow.

"I know it doesn't sound very believable, but there are dozens of mythological stories from all kinds of cultures about demons turning men and women into animals. In Ireland, there's a jealous fairy who turned men into dogs. In Africa, there's a demon who makes women into monkeys. I don't know whether any of these myths have any basis in fact, but here in America there's a spirit who can turn a young girl like Catherine into a huge black creature like a bear. It was Catherine who wrecked the locker rooms. It was Catherine who trashed my apartment. It was Catherine who murdered Martin Amato. Worse than that, she's killed two other people, too."

"I'm finding this difficult," said George. "Who?"

"John Three Names, the Navajo guide who took us out to meet Catherine's prospective husband. She tore him apart." He hesitated, and he found that he could hardly speak. "The other was Susan."

"Susan? Susan Randall? You're kidding me!"

Jim's eyes were suddenly blurred with tears. This was the first time that he had allowed himself to show his emotions since Susan had been killed. "The beast just went for her, George. It took off her head. It ripped her apart. I was shouting at her to warn her but I couldn't do anything."

"So what – so where did this happen?"

"Window Rock . . . in back of our hotel. We burned her body on a fire."

George pressed his beer-can against his forehead. "Jesus Christ, Jim. Catherine turned into a beast and killed Susan and then you burned Susan on a fire?"

Jim took off his glasses and said, "I swear to God, George. It's true. All of it. It's true. You only have to ask Sharon and Mark."

"And what about this John Three Names?"

"It happened in Dog Brother's trailer. I was trying to get her out of there. She just – well, one second she was a pretty girl and the next second she was a raging black creature who could tear holes in steel."

"Jesus Christ, Jim. What are you going to do?"

"There's only one thing I *can* do. I have a responsibility to Catherine, for what I did, taking her back to the reservation. All right, I was deceived, I didn't know what I was getting her into. But she's an innocent party in all of this, George, and I helped to take her back to a life she doesn't want and a man she doesn't love."

"But she *killed* Susan."

"Not her, George. The Changing Bear Maiden – the beast – that's what killed Susan."

"What are you going to tell Dr Ehrlichman? What are you going to tell Susan's family? You think they're going to believe you? Like, I know you, and I trust you, but even I'm not sure if I believe you."

"What I tell people is going to have to wait. Right now there's only one way to see justice for Susan and to save Catherine from a whole lifetime of living on the reservation with this Dog Brother character – and that's to exorcize her, or whatever the hell you're supposed to do when somebody's possessed with a ten-foot invisible creature with claws like goddamned scimitars."

George said, "You're upset, you know. I wouldn't go so far as to say deranged. But you should think about this in the morning."

"I can't stop thinking about it now."

"Well, let's go around to see Valerie and see if the sight of your newly-decorated apartment can take your mind off it."

Jim took hold of George's hand, and gripped it tight, and George was vaguely embarrassed. "You know something, George. I never saw anything like this before. I've seen ghosts, and spirits, and I've seen a man leave his body and walk through the city for hours on end, with cars passing right through his body like he wasn't even there. But this – no, this is different. This isn't just a spiritual parlour-trick. This is a force that comes right out of the air we breathe and the ground we tread on. This is serious power, George. This is real Native American magic."

George clapped him on the back. "I'll say one thing for you, Jim. You never do things by halves. When you go bananas, you go *seriously* bananas. Did you try Prozac yet?"

"Don't you think I have enough ups in my life?"

"Right now, probably yes."

"Just let me ask you something. Even if you don't believe a single word I've said, will you accept that I'm sincere?"

"Sure, yes, I believe you're sincere."

"Then support me, help me. Even if you think I've lost the plot."

Quite unexpectedly, George put his arms around him and hugged him. His belly was enormous. His beard scratched, and he smelled of kebabs and Sure deodorant. "Don't you worry, Jim. Whatever gibberish you talk, George is right behind you."

They drove to Electric Avenue in George's huge old Silverado pick-up. For Jim, it was very strange going back there, after the feline formerly known as Tibbles had been killed, and his apartment had been wrecked. He felt as if this wasn't his home any more, and in a sense it wouldn't be, ever again. Once you've been burgled, once you've been vandalized, your home loses its sense of safety, and adding more locks makes it feel even less secure.

"Go take a look at your apartment, then come on down," George told him. "They're doing a great job for you. You'll like it."

Jim climbed the steps to the second-story landing and walked along to his front door. He saw a blind twitch just opposite, and he knew that it was Myrlin spying on him, to make sure that he wasn't spying on *him*. He hesitated for a moment and then he inserted the key into the lock. There was a strong smell of fresh paint and carpentry. He switched on the lights and saw that George was right: the walls had been newly decorated in a color that Jim could only describe as "faded camel". All of the gouges in the plaster had been smoothed over and the kitchen cabinet doors replaced.

Underneath a large dusty sheet of heavy-duty plastic all of his possessions were heaped: his books, his pictures, his CDs, even one of his cardigans. He felt as if he were walking into the apartment of somebody who had recently died.

He turned to leave when he saw his grandfather standing by the window. He looked very much older tonight, his shoulders hunched, his hands deep in his pockets. Jim approached him and said, "Grandpa? What did you come back for? Are you all right?"

"All right? No, I don't think I am," said his grandfather.

"Then what's wrong? Tell me. My friend said that relatives don't come back unless it's something serious."

"How does your friend know that?"

"Because she's dead, just like you. Her name's Alice Vaizey and – well, you probably won't believe this, but she talks to me through the woman who took over her apartment when she died."

"Why shouldn't I believe it? It's the kind of thing that happens all the time. The dead, clinging onto the living."

"So what's wrong?" asked Jim. He was so tempted to touch his grandfather – just to take hold of his hand, and feel those dry old fingers and those veins like wriggling roots. Just to feel that soft, well-shaved cheek. He could even smell his grandfather's hairdressing lotion, and his tobacco.

"That thing I warned you about – it came, didn't it?" said his grandfather. "That old, cold bristling thing."

Jim nodded. "It came all right. Look around you. They've just finished cleaning up the mess."

"This isn't the only mess, is it, Jim?"

"No, grandpa, it isn't. There was a woman that I was in love with. Susan Randall. The thing killed her, too."

His grandfather sucked at his false teeth. "I've seen Susan: that's why I came."

"You've *seen* her? Like, where?"

"Jim, there isn't any *where* when you're dead. One minute bells are ringing and you're looking out over these wet, tiled rooftops. Next minute you're riding the Eighth Avenue Local. Then, before you know it, you're walking by the shore at Hilton Head, tossing sticks for your dog."

"How was she?" Jim wanted to know. "Come on, grandpa. I tried to save her. I hope she knows that."

"She didn't know anything much. She was very shocked, as folks usually are when their bodies have been beheaded. It takes them quite a while to get over the way they died. But she said one thing to me, and she meant it, Jim. She said, 'Tell Jim to go as far away from West Grove College as he can. Tell him to go to Europe. Tell him to go to Japan. Tell him to go anyplace that beast can't reach him, because it will.'

Jim said, "Do you think you might see her again? Do you think you might pass on a message?"

His grandfather gave him a quick, impatient look. "I'm not a go-between, Jim. I'm not some kind of spiritual mail-carrier."

"All the same, do you think you could tell her that I love her, and that I won't stop loving her? Do you think you could tell her that I'm going to make sure that she gets justice?"

"Justice doesn't mean too much to the dead, Jim. Justice is only for the living."

"All the same, can you tell her?"

His grandfather shrugged. "I guess I could try. No guarantees, though."

At that moment there was a knock at the door and Miss Neagle came in, dressed in a black ruffled negligee and strappy high-heeled slippers. "Jim?" she said. "George and I were wondering if you'd like to come down and join us for a drink. He said you had a *very* interesting time in Arizona."

She suddenly stopped and blinked and stared at Jim's grandfather. "Oh—" she said. "I'm sorry. I didn't realise you had company."

Startled, Jim said, "You can *see* him?"

"Of course. He keeps flickering in and out of focus like an old TV, but I can see him, for sure."

"Who are you to call me an old TV?" Jim's grandfather demanded.

"Mrs Alice Vaizey, I think, grandpa," said Jim. He turned to Miss Neagle and said, "Right?"

Miss Neagle smiled. "That's right. I couldn't see him, not on my own, but Mrs Vaizey can. That's why he's so flickery."

"What's going on here?" asked Jim's grandfather, suspiciously. "Is this the friend you were telling me about? The one who's dead?"

"That's right, grandpa. Miss Neagle here took over her apartment, and her spirit, too."

Jim's grandfather slowly approached Miss Neagle and stood right in front of her. He lifted his left hand and held it an inch or so away from her forehead. It was obvious that he wanted to touch her, but he couldn't. "I can see her," he said. "I can actually see her. It's like there are two women standing here, one inside the other."

Without any warning, tears formed in Miss Neagle's eyes and ran down her cheeks. "Do you know something?" she said, "That's the first time that anybody's seen me, since I died. I was beginning to think that I was invisible to everyone, even to other spirits."

"Well, now, you shouldn't have to worry about that," Jim's grandfather comforted her. "*I* can see you . . . I can see you as clear as daylight."

"So what do I look like?" asked Miss Neagle, in the same coquettish way that Mrs Vaizey would have said it.

"You're slim, very slim, like a dancer. Not like this lady at all. And you're a very handsome woman indeed."

"Well, you're very complimentary," said Miss Neagle. "And even if we never meet again—"

Jim's grandfather smiled at her, and blew her a kiss. Jim said, "I don't believe this, grandpa. You come here to give me a warning and you end up flirting with the spirit of the woman who used to live downstairs."

"Jim, that's not flirting. When people die they need comfort – more comfort than they ever needed when they were alive. It's bad enough for a woman to grow old and lose her looks, so that nobody notices her any more. What do you think it's like when you die, and you can't get any kind of response from anybody? You're nothing; you're invisible. You think that's good for your morale? You don't know how lucky I am that I have a grandson who can actually see me."

He suddenly looked more serious. "Listen, Jim, this thing wants your blood and you're going to have to do one of two things. Either you're going to have to pack your bags and go someplace where it can't follow you; or else you're going to have to find a way of beating it."

Miss Neagle said, "Today was the day you were supposed to die, Jim; and you're not dead yet, are you? So if I were you I'd have courage."

"I'm as good as dead," Jim told her. "So long as that thing is still in this world, it's going to be coming after me."

"Then go," said his grandfather. "It's the only answer. Go."

Jim suddenly realized why his grandfather had said that he was a failure. He *was* a failure. Whenever any kind of challenge appeared on the horizon, his answer had always been to turn on his heel and walk very quickly in the opposite direction. Jim wasn't like that. Jim was his mother's son, and his mother had always stood up for herself. She had refused to help his father when he had started up his marine insurance business, and taught herself to play the piano instead. "If you don't get rich on your own, then you don't deserve to be rich. But you do, and you will, and if I don't learn to play the piano, what will all your rich friends listen to, when we we entertain them at dinner?"

Jim said, "No, grandpa. I'm going to stay. The Native Americans are always talking about tribal honor. Catherine's my student. She belongs to Special Class II. That's enough of a tribe for me to feel honourable about."

His grandfather looked at him for a long time, and then nodded. "That's bravely spoken, Jim. It looks like all I can do is to wish you all the luck in this world; and a hundred times more in the next."

"Goodbye, grandpa," said Jim. "I won't forget this, I promise you."

His grandfather went to the open door and stepped out into the darkness. Jim followed him and watched him walking along the balcony. His image seemed gradually to fade, so that by the time he reached the steps the streetlights were shining right through him. He stopped, turned, and looked back at Jim, and gave him a wave. He hadn't even taken one step downward before he vanished, and there was nothing in the night but streetlights and automobile horns and somebody laughing.

"Jim," said Miss Neagle. "Come down for a beer."

"I don't think so, Valerie. I'm tired enough already."

"But George can't dance any of those Greek dances by himself."

"All right," Jim acquiesced. He guessed that anything would be better than lying on George's couch listening to the icebox rattling all night – unable to sleep, and thinking about Susan's head flying off.

Miss Neagle entwined her arm around his. "I was never sure about Greeks, you know. But then I met George, and I thought to myself, 'What was good enough for Jackie must be good enough for me.' You don't happen to know the Greek for 'I love your beard,' do you?''

* * *

Before he went back to college the next morning he called Susan's brother Bruce, who was a screenwriter who lived in Sherman Oaks.

"Susan's staying in Arizona for a few more days."

"Oh, yes?"

"Well, I thought I'd better tell you, just in case you were worried."

"Why should I be worried? She's a grown-up now, the last time I looked."

"OK, then. But I thought I'd better tell you, that's all."

There was a pause. Then, "There's nothing *wrong*, is there?"

"Wrong, what do you mean?"

"Well, Susan and me, we hardly ever speak to each other. We have a very different view of life, if you understand me. She thinks I'm a trashy materialist and I think she should try sailing round the world with one of her antique maps and see where *that* gets her."

"Oh. Well, OK."

He drove to college feeling strange, mainly because everything looked so normal and familiar. The morning smog hadn't yet cleared and the day had a soft, blurry appearance, like an Impressionist painting. He parked in the faculty parking-lot and waited for his car to backfire, which it didn't. He climbed out, and he had almost reached the main entrance when it let off a tremendous detonation that echoed all around the buildings.

Everybody in the staff room was eager to find out all about his trip to the reservations, but he found it very hard to talk about it. He kept repeating, "Sure, it was great. Fascinating. Susan loved it so much she decided to stay out there for a few more days."

Richard Bercovici, the social studies lecturer, came up smelling strongly of pipe-tobacco. "What was your view of Navajo alcoholism? From what I've read, drunkenness is the blight of the reservations."

Jim said, "I think, Richard – if you saw what I saw, you'd need a drink, too."

At last, however, it was time for his first class, and

he walked with some relief along the corridor to Special Class II. Almost the whole class were already there, except for Jane Firman, who always had difficult periods, and Jim was sensitive enough not to ask where she was. Sue-Robin was finishing off painting her nails in pearlized pink and Sherma was noisily rustling a large brown grocery bag.

"Sherma? Any chance of hearing ourselves think?"

"I'm sorry, Mr Rook. I'm supposed to be baking applesauce cookies with Mrs Evers afterward and I think I forgot my raisins."

Mark was sitting behind David Littwin, looking uncharacteristically pale and subdued – much to the frustration of his best friend Ricky, who kept trying to tell him stupid jokes. "'Doctor, I keep thinking I'm a spaniel.' 'Well, just get up on the couch.' 'I can't. I'm not allowed.'" Sharon was wearing a tight black dress with jet necklaces and black ribbons in her hair. When Jim came in, they both looked at him with the intensity of people who had shared a traumatic experience, and needed very badly to talk about it.

Jim said, "You'll be pleased to hear that our short field trip to Arizona was extremely arduous and that you didn't miss much except some spectacularly breathtaking scenery and some spectacularly disgusting food. We did however learn quite a lot about Navajo mythology and I'm very keen to discover what you were able to find out from your resources here.

"Unfortunately, Catherine White Bird decided to stay on for a while to – well, to visit some people she knew. So we're missing her input, which is a pity. And we're also missing Ms Randall, who wanted to stay for a while, too, so that she could—"

He hesitated, and saw Mark and Sharon looking at him and frowning. He hated lying – especially to his class –

but he knew that there was no alternative, not until the Changing Bear Maiden had been exorcized for good.

"– so that she could look for some historical maps, you know what she is about maps."

Beattie McCordic put up her hand and said, "How did you find, like, the way that Navajo women are as opposed to the men? Do you think they're as equal as we are – you knew, here in California – or not so equal?"

"Nobody's as equal as you are, Beattie!" said Seymour Williams.

"Good literary reference," said Jim. "What's it from, Seymour?"

"What?" asked Seymour, in bewilderment.

"George Orwell's *Animal Farm*. 'All animals are equal but some animals are more equal than others.'"

"Oh, right," said Seymour, with a grin, and the whole class hooted in derision.

"Anyway, to answer your question, Beattie, from what I've seen the Navajo woman has a very different standing within her family to that of women in other parts of the country. Navajo men still seem to think that they're the undisputed head of the household. That's a traditional, historical view. But the reality is that there's so much unemployment that it's the women who hold the family unit together – the women who have the strength – the women who make the really fundamental day-to-day decisions."

Mark said, "That may be, but you have to admit that it's pretty tough trying to be a great warrior and hunter and everything when there's nobody to fight and nothing to hunt. I mean, what are you going to do, maraud the 7-Eleven?"

"But let's go back a bit and talk about their history and their mythology," said Jim. "Some of them say that it's the collapse of their magic that led to their present plight.

Did anybody manage to find out anything about Navajo legends?"

Sue-Robin said, "I found about a giant demon called Big Monster. He was half as tall as the tallest fir tree, and had an ugly face with blue and black stripes. He wore a suit of armour made from flint stones knitted together with all the guts and the sinews of the people that he killed."

"That's disgusting," said Amanda.

"It's all right," Jim told her. "It's only a story." Thinking, as he said it, of the way that John Three Names' body had been pulled apart, and all his insides emptied onto the floor.

Sue-Robin said, "Big Monster was finally caught by two brave gods called the Twins. They tried to sneak up behind him while he was drinking a large lake, but he saw them reflected in the last drops of water. He shot two enormous arrows at them, but they caught hold of a rainbow and used it as a shield. Big Monster ran after them, but just as he was about to catch up with them, a bolt of lightning struck him dead. The Twins cut off his head and threw it to the east. It took root in the ground, and it's still there today, called Cabezon Peak."

"I found out about Big Monster, too," said Titus, putting up his hand. "There's a web site all about Native American mythology. It said that Big Monster wouldn't have been killed by the lightning, but another demon had cut off all his hair, which left his head unprotected. The other demon was called . . . I wrote it down here someplace . . . Coyote."

Jim felt the back of his neck prickle, as if an insect were crawling down it. "Coyote, huh? Did anybody else find out about Coyote?"

"Hey, I did," said John Ng. "To me, he was one of the most interesting of all the Native American spirits, because there are spirits just like him in Japan and

Vietnam. He was very cunning and tricky, you know? And he really liked human women. He was always chasing after them and trying to get up their skirts. I found this Navajo song that goes: '*One day walking through a mountain pass, Coyote met a young woman. What have you in your pack, she said. Fish eggs. Can I have some? If you close your eyes and hold up your dress. She did as she was told. Higher, said Coyote and stepped out of his britches. Stand still so I can reach the place. I can't there is something crawling between my legs. Don't worry it's a bee, I'll get it. The woman dropped her dress. You weren't fast enough. It stung me.*'"

"Typical male," put in Beattie. "Even when you're demons you can't keep your things to yourselves."

Ricky Herman said, "Play another tune, Beattie." But Jim interrupted and said, "Go on, John. What else did you find out about Coyote?"

"Well, he was different from all the other spirits because he had power over death. This happened because he loved this one woman so much that he agreed to die for her. The only thing was, he buried his lungs, his heart, his blood and his breath deep in the ground, so that he could dig them up again. He died four times for this woman and each time he came back to life again. So in the end the spirits of the underworld said that he would never have to return."

"Presumably, then, he's still alive today?"

"If you believe in spirits, I guess he is. But it says in *Navajo Legends* that he only managed to survive when the white men came by mating with a human woman. Every generation that goes by, he picks the most beautiful Navajo woman that he can find, and gives her a son; and that son is him, too, so that when he dies he's still alive, if you get what I mean.

"In the old days he was so frightening to look at that he

used to wear a coyote skin on his back to disguise himself, which is why he was nicknamed Coyote. His real Navajo name is First One To Use Words For Force. These days, he looks like any ordinary man, except that he has to wear yellow glasses so that people can't see that he has yellow eyes like a dog."

Jim had a sudden flash of Dog Brother, sitting in his trailer. The feathers, the leather pants, the yellow spectacles. John Three Names had lied to him, because he must have known that he wouldn't have taken Catherine to see him if he had suspected the truth.

Dog Brother wasn't a man at all. Or rather, he was only half human. He hadn't needed to find a wonder-worker to put a hex on Catherine. He hadn't needed to call on Coyote. Dog Brother was *Coyote.*

Jim suddenly realised that John had stopped talking and was looking at him expectantly.

"Go on, John. I'm listening. You've done really well."

John said, "Coyote is supposed to choose his wives on their fifteenth birthday. He cuts his hand and he cuts her hand, and they exchange blood."

"Doesn't he know about HIV?" asked Seymour.

"It's a *legend*, for crying out loud," said Ray. "Legends don't get sick."

"Superman gets sick when he's exposed to Kryptonite," Ricky objected.

"Yeah, but Superman is a comic character, not a legend. Besides, he wouldn't get HIV because he isn't gay."

"He *looks* gay."

"So do you but I don't make a class discussion out of it."

"That's enough," said Jim. "John – you finish telling us what you've found out."

"Once Coyote's blood is flowing inside the woman's

veins, he can control her with magic, wherever she goes, even if she tries to run away from him."

"What did I tell you?" said Beattie. "Typical domineering male behavior."

Jim walked slowly and thoughtfully to the back of the class. "You've done very well. That's all very interesting research. I wonder, though – even though Coyote was apparently exempt from death – did anyone find out if it was possible to get rid of him? Banish him, maybe, to a place where he couldn't escape? Or rob him of some of his magical strength, the way that he cut Big Monster's hair and robbed him of his?"

"*Navajo Legends* says that in the old days, wonder-workers used to call Coyote with a whistle, and they would make bargains with him to defeat any opposing tribes. It says here, 'In 1837 a Navajo wonder-worker whistled up Coyote and agreed to give him five virgins in exchange for invincible strength against the Hopi. The next day the Navajo attacked the village of Oraibi, which had a claim to being the oldest continuously populated community in America, and they wiped out almost everybody living there.'"

He ran his finger down the page, and then he said, "It looks like the only way to deal with Coyote would be to have him killed by one of his fellow-spirits . . . and men dig up his heart before he could, and hide it where he could never find it."

Beattie said, "Mr Rook? I found out about a woman who turned herself into one of those big furry animals that live in the forest." Beattie suffered from anomia, which meant that she had difficulty in remembering what things were called.

"You're talking about the Bear Maiden," said John. "She was the one that Coyote was really in love with."

Jim said, "I don't think we need to discuss Navajo

legends any more for today. After this week I'm all Navajoed out. But next week I'd like you all to write a modern-day story based on an old Native American myth. Bring it up to date, so to speak."

"Oh, I see," said Beattie. "Just when we get to women demons we have to stop."

The students gathered up their books and papers and noisily left the class. Jim went back to his desk and looked through his schedule for the rest of the mouth. He was still bent over it when Mark and Sharon came up to him. Both of them looked serious.

"Hi, you two. I think I know what you're going to say."

Sharon said, "What's the story, Mr Rook? Did Ms Randall really have an asthma attack, like you told us back in Arizona, or is she still on the reservation, looking for old maps? Or is it neither?"

"I owe you both an apology," said Jim. "You know how I usually feel about telling the truth. But back there in Window Rock I didn't want to upset you more than I had to."

"What happened?" asked Mark. "Ms Randall's OK, isn't she?"

"I'm going to have to ask you guys to keep this to yourselves, for the same reason I kept it from you. This business with Catherine isn't finished yet, and unless I have freedom of movement I'm not going to be able to help her.

He paused, and then he said, "Ms Randall was involved in an accident. I'm afraid she was killed."

"She's *dead*?" said Sharon, shocked.

"What kind of an accident?" asked Mark.

Jim gave them a small, helpless shrug. "It was something to do with Catherine, but right now I can't really explain it. As soon as I can, though, you'll get the whole story. I promise."

"But you told everybody that she was still back in Arizona – even Dr Ehrlichman."

"I know, and when the time comes, I'm going to have to apologize to them, too."

"Jeez," said Mark. "I just can't believe that she's dead. I can still see her face."

Jim laid a hand on his shoulder. "Believe me, Mark, so can I."

Jim was packing up at the end of the day when Dr Ehrlichman came into his classroom. "I'm glad you had an interesting trip, Jim. I have to admit that I wasn't sure about your ethnic adventures to start with. I didn't really see their relevance to remedial English studies. But I've heard some approving noises from the board of education, and I gather that your test results have been improving."

"Communication is communication," said Jim. "I just believe that if everybody in my class can understand each other's background, and what makes them think the way they do, then they're going to be much better at explaining their own background, and their own ideas."

"Well, that's good. That's very good. It seems like *The Los Angeles Times* may even be interested in running a piece about it."

"I think my students could do without that sort of publicity," said Jim. "Between these four walls they don't mind admitting their shortcomings, but they don't want the whole world to be told that they're slow."

"A story like that would do the college good, you know . . . especially after last week's tragedy."

"Well, we'll see. I'll think about it over the weekend."

"We're going to see you tomorrow afternoon, I hope?"

"What for?"

"The game against Azusa tomorrow. Ben Thunkus thinks we have a better-than-even chance of winning."

"You're still going to play? After what happened to Martin?"

Dr Ehrlichman dry-washed his hands with a particularly unpleasant squeak. "I talked to his parents. They're all for it. I talked to the team. They all want to play this game as a tribute to everything that Martin did for them."

"OK . . . if that's the way they feel."

"It is, Jim. It is. And it's the way *I* feel, too. This college has had a very shaky semester, very shaky. I'd like to see us back on track again. Remember the West Grove motto – 'Achievement Through Enjoyment.'"

"I think the student version is 'Getting It All By Having A Ball,'" said Jim.

Dr Ehrlichman said, "I didn't know that, and I wish I didn't know it now."

"I'll see you at the game," Jim told him.

Chapter Nine

Early that evening he drove over to see Henry Black Eagle. A pretty young Hispanic woman was standing on his doorstep, busily polishing his brass doorplate.

"Mr Black Eagle at home?" asked Jim.

"No, *senor*. But you can find him at the Cafe del Rey."

"You seen him today?"

"Sure. He wasn't working today. He said they were shooting around him."

"What kind of mood was he in? Can you tell me that?"

"*Que*?"

"Well, was he happy, cheerful, humming songs? Or was he sad and depressed?"

"He was very itchy."

"He was *itchy*? You mean like scratching himself all the time?"

"No, no, itchy like he was waiting for something. Every time the telephone rings he goes voom! to answer it."

"Voom," Jim repeated, thoughtfully. "OK, that's helpful. Thank you."

He climbed back into his car and drove toward the ocean. It was an hour before sunset and the streets were striped with marmalade light. He turned into Admiralty Way and drove toward the marina with the warm sea air blowing in his hair. If he hadn't been so worried it would have been a perfect evening.

He found Henry Black Eagle sitting at the cafe's dining bar, where singles can look out over the yachts jostling at anchor in the marina and eat in peace. He was halfway through a steak and a fennel salad, with a large glass of red wine. Jim approached him from behind and slipped onto the empty stool next to him.

"How's the steak, Mr Black Eagle? Bloody enough for your taste? Or do you prefer something more like a burnt offering?"

Henry Black Eagle jerked back, his eyes wide with shock.

"Oh, excuse me," said Jim, "did I surprise you?"

"What are you doing here?" asked Henry Black Eagle. Then he looked around the busy cafe as if he were searching for somebody. "Where's Catherine?"

"You want to know what I'm doing here?" Jim told him. "I'm here to settle a score, that's what I'm doing here. As for Catherine – well, mission accomplished, for the most part. I managed to get her to Fort Defiance trailer park and hand her over to her prospective husband, which was exactly what you wanted me to do, wasn't it? The only trouble was, it all got a little messy."

"Messy? What are you talking about?"

"Hasn't your friend John Three Names called you and told you? Well, I'm not totally surprised. Right now, John Three Names looks like that steak probably looks like, inside of your stomach."

"John Three Names is dead?"

"That's right. And so is Susan Randall, who came with me to help look after your daughter."

"How about your students?"

"Oh, thanks for your consideration. They're fit and

well, no thanks to you, or to the Changing Bear Maiden, or to First One To Use Words For Force."

"Listen," said Henry Black Eagle, pushing his plate away. "I didn't have any choice. If I hadn't sent Catherine back to Coyote, she would have gone on killing. What was I supposed to do?"

"Sending Catherine back to Coyote was one thing. But you sacrificed the life of a completely innocent woman and you were quite prepared to sacrifice the lives of two completely innocent young people, just to get your sons out of jail."

"That wasn't the only reason, Mr Rook. Coyote knew how much you cared for that woman, and he knew what those students meant to you. He wanted to show you that if you ever set yourself against him, or tried to take Catherine away from him, you would be as good as dead."

"Then he wasn't going to kill *me*?"

"It depends on your definition of death, Mr Rook. He would have killed everybody that you love and destroyed everything that you cherish. That's his way."

"But what for? What the hell have I ever done to him?"

"You're a white man, Mr Rook. That alone would be quite enough. But more than that, he knows that you have the gift of sight. He would have sensed it from the moment you first came near Catherine. His blood runs in her veins, remember."

"And?"

Henry Black Eagle lowered his eyes for a moment and then looked up again and gave Jim a narrow, piercing look. "And he's just a little bit afraid of you, that's what."

"What can I possibly do to him, when he's got the kind of magic that can turn your daughter into a beast like the Changing Bear Maiden?"

"He remembers what the white men did to all of the other spirits, Mr Rook. He's alone now, the last spirit who can actually walk on the earth. Maybe 'afraid' is an exaggeration, but he's certainly wary of you. He thinks you must be in contact with the white man's spirits, and he doesn't want to risk offending a demon who might be stronger than him."

Jim looked at Henry Black Eagle for a while and didn't know whether to feel disgusted or sympathetic. In the end, he said, "What are you going to do now?"

"What *can* I do? You've found me out, and I can't even begin to tell you how ashamed I am, how guilty I feel. I will have the death of your woman on my mind for the rest of my life; and the deaths of my sons, too, if the courts find them guilty. If I had known when my wife was dying that this was what would happen if I made a bargain with Coyote, then I would have preferred to have done nothing, and let her die."

"I may have found you out, but there's nothing I can do about it," said Jim. "You haven't broken any laws, have you, except the laws of common humanity."

"My head is bowed," said Henry Black Eagle.

"Well, maybe you can unbow it by helping me to get your daughter back. I think we owe her that much, don't we?"

"It's impossible. Coyote will only transform her into the Changing Bear Maiden again and again, and each time it happens to her, the beast grows larger and the transformation lasts longer. In the end, she will be a beast for ever, and she will have to roam the reservations every night looking for men to kill. Can you imagine what a nightmare that would be? And every fresh killing would be on my conscience, too.

"If we leave her alone, Mr Rook, Coyote will take the curse off her and treat her well. She will be treated with great respect by everybody on the reservation. She will lead a much better life than most Navajo women."

"Mr Black Eagle, that's not the life she wants to lead. We owe it to her to get her away from him."

"It's impossible," Henry Black Eagle repeated. "And who knows what revenge Coyote would take?"

"God almighty," said Jim, "no wonder the Indians lost the West."

"Mr Rook – if I knew how to get my daughter back – if I thought that there was a way to make some kind of amends for what I've done—"

"There is. You can arrange for you and me to fly back out to the reservation tomorrow and we can beard this Coyote character in his den."

"To do *what*? You don't have any idea how powerful he is."

"The legend says that you can keep him under control by having him killed by another spirit and then taking his heart and hiding it from him. You must know some wonder-workers who could conjure up another spirit, surely."

"Grey Cloud does. But even if you could find a wonder-worker who was prepared to do it, you wouldn't find another spirit that would kill Coyote for nothing. Spirits always demand a payment."

"Then maybe a human could kill him. Maybe *we* could kill him."

"I'm sorry, Mr Rook, we wouldn't stand a chance in hell. Nobody challenges Coyote unless they're dead drunk or tired of living."

"I can find a way, I'm sure of it."

Henry Black Eagle lifted his hand to call for the check. After he had paid, he said, "Okay, Mr Rook, I'll arrange two flights tomorrow afternoon. If I can't stop you from going, then the least I can do is go with you. Maybe if the Changing Bear Maiden kills both of us, the police will let Paul and Grey Cloud go free."

Jim scribbled George Babouris' number on a paper coaster. "You can call me here before twelve. After that, you can catch me at college. There's a football game tomorrow afternoon."

Henry Black Eagle stood up and held out his hand. "I don't know what to say to you, Mr Rook. I don't expect you to forgive me. All I ask is that you try to understand."

"Well, there is one thing," said Jim. He lifted the silver whistle out from under his shirt. "What exactly does this thing do?"

"It attracts Coyote's attention. All the old wonder-workers used one, when they wanted to summon him up from the underworld. It's set at the same pitch as a bat's squeak, and in the days before he became half-human, Coyote used to have a taste for bats."

"Let me tell you – we were flying from Albuquerque to Gallup when the airplane lost all of its power. No engines, no electrics at all. Catherine was staring at the controls and I could see the beast's shadow around her. It was a miracle that we didn't nosedive into the forest. But I blew the whistle and it seemed like she woke up, and we got all of our power back. If we'd have hit those trees we would have been dead for sure."

They left the cafe and walked out onto the sidewalk. The sun was melting into the ocean, and a chilly wind was beginning to blow. Waste paper tumbled between the gliding wheels of the day's last rollerbladers, and the sun caught the spokes of a passing bicycle. Henry Black Eagle looked thoughtful.

"What you've said . . . that's very strange. Coyote would have done everything he could to make sure that Catherine reached him safely. He wouldn't have wanted her to crash the plane like that. He didn't want any of you dead until you had reached Window Rock, and he didn't want *you* dead at all.

They walked a little further and then Henry Black Eagle said, "You know, it seems to me that someplace inside of her, Catherine knew what was going to happen to you. After all, she had Coyote's own blood in her veins. She knew what was going to happen to you and she knew that it would be far more terrible than dying quickly in a plane crash. So she used Coyote's own powers to shut down the plane's electrics. He can do that, you know. In the old days, when the white men first set up their telegraph lines, he could silence them just by staring at them, the same way that some men can silence a dog with just a look."

"So when I blew the whistle—"

"That's right. You alerted Coyote, and when he realised what was happening, he stopped her."

"But that means that Catherine has some kind of will of her own, even when she's turning into the Changing Bear Maiden."

"Perhaps. But even if she has, I doubt if Coyote will let her exercise it ever again. Remember what I said. The more times she changes, the more of a beast she becomes."

Jim reached his car. "Call me tomorrow," he said, and Henry Black Eagle nodded. Jim glanced at him in his rear-view mirror as he drove away. He decided that he didn't feel any sympathy for him, not after what he had done, but he did think that he looked like the loneliest man on God's earth.

Jim slept badly that night. He kept dreaming about the thin man with the yellow glasses, and his dream was filled with a stomach-dissolving sense of dread. He thought that he woke up, and looked across the room, and saw a figure in a charred, smoking blanket sitting on the armchair opposite. He thought, God, it's Susan, she isn't dead after all, and he climbed off the couch and approached her. But the blanket-figure didn't move, and he was too frightened to open it to see what was inside it. He reached out his hand but then he woke up and realised that this was a dream, too. He was soaking with sweat and he was shaking.

Over breakfast, George looked at him through the haze of frying bacon and said, "You're looking rough, Jim. After everything's that happened, you ought to take a break, you know that."

"I'm probably going back to Arizona tonight."

"Really? What the hell for?"

"Well, let's just say that I've got some unfinished business."

George sat down opposite and began to fork up mouthfuls of bacon and runny fried eggs. "Don't do anything stupid, Jim. I know you. You've got kamikaze written all over you."

"Oh, and you don't think that a 4,000-calorie breakfast is suicidal?"

"Jim – I have to keep my strength up. That Valerie, I'll tell you. She's a very demanding woman."

"You haven't—?"

"She kept me dancing till ten after two. Polka, foxtrot, waltz, shimmy, shake, Charleston, twist, frug, locomotion, turkey trot, you name it."

"You enjoyed it, didn't you?"

"Sure I enjoyed it. And let me tell you something else. I think I'm in love."

Jim left him to his bacon and eggs and drove to the college. After last night's dreams he wanted to take another look through the book that John Ng had been reading – *Navajo Legends*. He needed to know as much as he could about Coyote's possible weaknesses – his vanities, his petty jealousies, the way he played tricks. He was convinced that the only way to beat a deceiver was to out-deceive him.

The college campus was almost deserted this morning, apart from three or four students who were hanging up the bunting for this afternoon's game. West Grove had a long-standing grudge against Azusa Commmunity College, mostly because Azusa had never beaten them by less than 38 to 7. Jim looked up as he crossed toward the college building. The sky was strange, with heavily-building clouds. He had a feeling that something threatening was in the air.

He walked along the wax-polished corridor toward Special Class II. Mr Wallechinsky, the security guard, was just coming out of Sue Randall's room, and locking the door behind him.

"Ah – Mr Rook! Any idea when Ms Randall's coming back? She borrowed a projector from the science department and I know they're pretty keen to have it returned."

"I think she's going to be a few more days yet, Mr Wallechinsky. Why don't you just give it back to them?"

"Sure thing."

Jim unlocked his classroom and opened the door. Immediately, he stopped dead. The room had been totally wrecked. All of the desks had been toppled over, and some of them had been completely dismembered. Personal computers lay everywhere, their screens smashed, their keyboards ripped apart, their printers crushed. The portraits of Shakespeare and Mark Twain and Walt Whitman had been pulled from the walls and torn apart. The fluorescent lights dangled down from the ceiling. Jim's own desk had been tipped on one side and its contents strewn all over the floor.

Worst of all, though, were the marks on the walls. There were criss-cross gouges everywhere, like the gouges of giant claws. Whole furrows of plaster had been dragged out, in deep parallel stripes, and one clawmark went right through the frame of the blackboard, and across its surface – not just scratching it but cutting it almost through to the wall behind.

Jim took two or three steps into the room, and sniffed, the way that Mrs Vaizey would have sniffed. He could pick it up now. Animal – or maybe two different animals. The heavy funky smell of bear, and the sharper, rancid odour of wild dog. He picked up a first edition, his own, of John Peale Bishop's *Green Fruit.* His father had given it to him when he had graduated. Now its spine was broken and half of its pages fell out onto the floor.

She's here, he thought to himself. It had never occurred to him that she might follow him back to Los Angeles, but she obviously had. She's here, and she's making sure that I suffer.

He heaved his desk back onto its feet. For some reason, it had never occurred to him that the Changing Bear Maiden might come after him. No wonder his grandfather had been warned him to go away – as quick as he could and as far as he could. Coyote was obviously not willing to forgive and forget, even though he had now had his bride-to-be, and he had no reason to suspect that Jim would try to set her free. Although maybe he did. Maybe he had sniffed out in Jim that burning sense of consideration that had made him want to teach a remedial class in the first place. Maybe he knew that Jim would never let Catherine go.

Jim started picking up chairs and desks, one by one. The floor was strewn with ripped-up poems and essays and broken glass. God knows it was hard enough for most of these students to write one coherent sentence. Now most of their semester's laborious work had been thrown all over the floor. Jim picked up Mark Foley's essay on Rip van Winkle: 'Rip van Winkle let his childrin run wile they never wore no shos and his suns pants was alus fallin down.' When he thought of the essays that Mark was capable of writing now, only a few months later, it really hurt him that somebody could have treated his first efforts with such disrespect. He picked up another sheet and it was Mark's latest piece of work on Walt Whitman: "Walt Whitman was gay. He kissd dyin soldiers durin the Cival War which was part human but it exited him too. Still he loved his mother and was never rude about women. He rote about 'a merry housefull of young ladies' and 'I never saw so many fine-looking grey hair'd women . . . such as no time or land but ours could show.'"

Mark's spelling was still erratic, but his ability to read and to *comment* on what he had read had increased enormously. Henry Black Eagle had been right: Coyote knew how to attack his enemies where it hurt. He knew what they valued the most, and he had no compunction about destroying it.

He was still picking up papers and books and pieces of broken glass when Mr Wallechinsky came in. "What the hell happened here?" he demanded.

"Our vandal came back," said Jim.

"Look at the state of this place. I don't believe it. I only looked in here about an hour ago."

"And you didn't hear anything, and you didn't see anybody?"

"Only that big fat student of yours – what's his name, Gloach?"

"Russell Gloach, that's right. And I'd prefer it if you

didn't call him big and fat. Think of some other way to describe him. Like, think of his hair."

"OK, I saw that big fat crewcut student of yours. He was in here maybe fifteen minutes ago."

"Anybody else?"

"I don't know. Let me see . . . there were two or three of them wandering in and out. That Indian girl, she was one of them."

"Catherine White Bird? Catherine White Bird was here?"

"I saw her with my own eyes, walking down the corridor. She was brushing her hair."

"Do you have any idea where she went afterward?"

"How should I know? Wherever it was, though, she wasn't in any kind of a hurry."

She's back, thought Jim. And now she's come to get me.

"OK, Mr Wallechinsky," he said. "Take it easy. Let's lock this room up for now."

"You don't want me to clean it up?"

"No, I want you to leave it just the way it is. After the game this afternoon I'm going to call the cops, and I don't want any of this evidence swept up or tampered with."

"In that case, maybe you should stop tidying it up yourself, Mr Rook. I bet by now you've left so many fingerprints they're going to be able to prove that *you* did it."

Jim dropped Mark's essay on Whitman onto the floor. "You're right," he said. "But there's something I *am* going to tidy up."

He went back outside and walked around the buildings, but there was no sign of Catherine anywhere. He went down to the football field. Greg Lake was there, sitting on the bleachers talking to Sherri Hakamoto.

"Hi, Mr Rook. Looking forward to the game this afternoon?"

Jim shaded his eyes with his hand and peered all the way around the field.

"You seen Catherine today?"

Greg's face went through a complicated series of contortions before finally deciding to look mildly puzzled. "Catherine? No. I thought she was still in Arizona."

"Well, so did I, Greg, but apparently not. By the way, I'm going to have to ask you to stay out of the home room today. There's been some more vandalism."

"Hey, none of my stuff's been damaged, has it? I left all my project in there."

"I don't know. You'll have the chance to look later. But meanwhile, keep an eye out for Catherine, will you?"

"Okay, Mr Rook."

Jim borrowed Mr Wallechinsky's spare set of keys and spent the next twenty minutes combing the college grounds. Because it was Saturday, many of the buildings were locked, but he checked the art studio, the design block and the gym complex. He even searched the girls' locker-rooms (making sure he shouted "halloo!" loudly before he went in). He opened Catherine White Bird's locker but there was nothing inside it to suggest that she was back. Books, magazines, T-shirts, cosmetics – as well as cut-out pictures of fashion models and moody-looking young rock stars. Kurt Cobain grinned from beside her mirror, and Jim thought, if you think that what happened to *you* was bad . . . wait till you see what the Changing Bear Maiden can do.

In the end, he had to give it up. He gave Mr Wallechinsky's keys back and went to the faculty lounge and picked up the phone. He waited and waited and at last Henry Black Eagle answered.

"Mr Black Eagle? Jim Rook. No, it doesn't matter that you haven't booked the tickets yet. No, I'm glad that you didn't. We don't need to go to Arizona. Catherine's here."

"What do you mean?" asked Henry Black Eagle, in a chilled voice.

"Catherine's here. My classroom's wrecked, the same way the locker room and my apartment were. Our security man told me that he saw her in the corridor."

"But don't you see – now that's he got her – Coyote wouldn't let Catherine out of his sight."

"I don't understand."

"It's simple, Mr Rook. If Catherine's here, then Coyote must be here, too."

"I hope you're kidding me."

"No, Mr Rook. I've told you how possessive he is."

"So what do you think he wants?"

"I think, Mr Rook, that you must have left him feeling very angry. Coyote likes to think of himself as the trickster, not the tricked. He might be wary of you, as I said, but it looks as if he's come to show you who's boss."

"I don't understand it. Why should he bother? I'm only one white man."

"He's seen how much you care for your students, Mr Rook. Maybe he knows that you're not going to rest until you get Catherine away from him."

Jim thought: that can't be the whole story. Even if I came after Catherine, Coyote could set the Changing Bear Maiden on me, or use all kinds of magic to kill me before I could get anywhere near him. He doesn't have anything to fear from me, not really. So why has he come all this way to hunt me down?

And then it occurred to him. Maybe he *does* have something to fear – something that he knows about but I don't. Maybe I *can* kill him, after all.

It must be something to do with the fact that I can see spirits. Not only white man's spirits, but Native American spirits, too.

"Are you still there?" Henry Black Eagle asked him, impatiently.

"Yes, yes, I'm still here. Listen, I'll tell you what I want you to do for me. Go see Paul and Grey Cloud and ask them which Native American spirit is Coyote's deadliest enemy. Ask them which spirit could be most easily persuaded to kill him."

"There are many. I don't know them all."

"Well, go ask your sons. Then come up to the college, and make it as quick as you can."

"But Mr Rook—"

"No buts, Mr Black Eagle. You owe me. And more than that, you owe your daughter, too. This could be the only way of saving her."

The Azusa team and their supporters arrived in a procession of coaches and people carriers just after twelve. Dr Ehrlichman had arranged a cookout under the trees on the north side of the college, and the air was already pungent with the smell of mesquite. Jim circled the school grounds, his coat slung over his shoulder, looking from right to left for any sign of Catherine or Coyote. If they were still around, they were keeping themselves well out of the way, but Jim was sure that he could sense their presence. He kept seeing furtive movements behind the trees, and flickering shadows where no shadows ought to be cast. He felt a prickling sensation in his skin, too, and thought of *Macbeth*: '*By the pricking of my thumbs, Something wicked this way comes.*'

He walked between the wooden picnic tables where the West Grove team were eating their lunch. Mitch Magro, the new captain, was trying to work the Fumblers up into a serious fighting mood. "We owe this to Martin, OK? He didn't die so that we could lose to Azusa. He trained us, didn't he? He really inspired us. So we're going to go out there this afternoon and we're going to beat the living crap out of those guys.

"If we catch it, we run with it. If it hurts, we think how bad Martin got hurt. If we feel like giving up, we don't. I'm going to tell you this: I would rather die than lose this game, and I want you all to feel the same way."

Russell Gloach was sitting a little way apart from the others, cutting up a bunless hamburger into very small pieces.

"How's the struggle going, Russell?" Jim asked him.

"Oh, great. I love these diet burgers. It's just that I could eat about four hundred of them."

"Come on, Russell. You're doing good."

"I'm weak, Mr Rook, I promise you. I'm so goddamned weak I can hardly stand up, let alone play football. I haven't had a Twinkie since two weeks Tuesday. I can't remember what peanut butter tastes like."

"Listen, Russell," said Jim. "Something pretty weird is happening here today. Catherine's back."

"What's weird about that?"

"Well, she's not exactly herself. She's having some kind of a breakdown. The point is, if you see her, I want you to make sure that you grab hold of her and send somebody off to find me."

"Grab hold of her? Supposing she doesn't want to be grabbed hold of? Especially by me. Why don't you get Brad Kaiser instead?"

"Grab hold of her all the same. And for God's sake don't let her go."

Russell said, "You're right. This *is* weird. Do you want to tell me what's going down here, or what?"

"I'm not at all sure," Jim told him. "But I'm worried that it's something real bad."

"It's not like that voodoo business, is it? I mean that scared me. I had nightmares about that for weeks."

"I don't know. But if I can depend on you to grab Catherine if you see her, and to tell me if anything really bizarre happens—"

"Sure thing, Mr Rook. I'll do it. You don't have to worry about me."

It was then that Jim looked up and saw a figure silhouetted between the trees. The air was hazy with barbecue-smoke, and a lot of students and parents were coming and going, right across his field of sight. He looked again, and frowned, because the woman had disappeared, but all the same he said, "Excuse me," to Russell, left the table, and began walking right toward the trees. He stopped, and looked around. He caught the faintest smile of white musk on the wind, as well as that tingle of psychic electricity. He thought he could hear a hand-slapped drumbeat, too: one beat, then a pause, then another beat.

He went back to the table. Russell had already finished his hamburger and was writing down how many calories he had consumed on his diet chart.

"They tell us to be totally honest – just like this was confession or something."

"What happens if you secretly eat a whole pack of Reece's Pieces? What happens then?"

Russell flushed. It was obvious to Jim that he *had* eaten a whole pack of Reece's Pieces, or something similar, and kept it all to himself.

"You jog five times round the football field and hope you've burned it all off, that's all. These diets, these days they're very forgiving."

"OK . . . but just remember this. Forgiving is not a mood I want to see from you this afternoon. I want you to go out there and kill those guys. You're a battering-ram, Russell. I want you to batter. I want people in twenty years to say, 'Do you remember that Saturday? That was the Saturday that Russell Gloach single-handedly road-rollered Azusa into the turf. He was great. He was like a one-man elephant stampede.' "

"You watch me," grinned Russell.

But Jim said, "Something else may happen, too. Something totally unexpected. And if that happens, I want you to be ready for that, too."

"Something unexpected? Like what?"

"Like – I don't know. As bad as that voodoo thing, maybe worse."

Russell suddenly looked serious. "You mean this, don't you, Mr Rook?"

"Yes, Russell, I do. Today isn't going to be a normal day, believe me. Look at those clouds, over in the east. The wind has changed around. Whatever happens this afternoon, remember your class, remember your friends, and do whatever you think is right."

"I'm not sure I get it, Mr Rook."

"You'll get it when the time comes, believe me."

"OK, Mr Rook." He stared down sadly at his empty plate. "Do you know what I used to have for breakfast, only six weeks ago? Two peanut butter and jelly sandwiches, with crispy bacon and french-fried potatoes."

"That's what killed Elvis," said Jim.

"Oh, sure, I know that. I wouldn't go so far as that. I made sure I had a tomato and a lettuce-leaf with it."

By three o'clock, when the game was due to kick off,

the sky had become completely overcast. In the distance, over the Santa Monica mountains, lightning was flashing behind the clouds like a curtained-off photo-booth. The West Grove college band was playing *Pasadena* as if they were anxious to get it over with, and their pom-pom girls were leaping and strutting. There was a strong smell of electricity in the air.

Jim sat on the bleachers at the south end of the field and kept on checking his watch. Henry Black Eagle hadn't turned up yet, but he tried to tell himself not to be so anxious. There was no sign of Coyote or Catherine, and for all he knew they had decided that it was enough to vandalize Jim's classroom, without causing any further damage. But he didn't want to bet on it.

Just as West Grove kicked off, George Babouris arrived, with Valerie Neagle. George was wearing a purple windbreaker that was two sizes too tight for him and Valerie Neagle was dressed in a leopard-print dress with a *décolletage* that was two inches too low for her age. As the crowd stood up and applauded, Jim manoeuvered his way next to Valerie and said, "Hi. You're looking very striking."

"Why, thank you," said Valerie, and printed a big red kiss on his right cheek. "I always knew you had taste."

"Listen," said Jim, "this isn't really the time and the place, but I wondered if I could talk to Mrs Vaizey?"

Valerie blinked her mascara-speckled eyelashes at him. "You want to talk to Mrs Vaizey? What about?"

"Something's going to happen here today . . . something bad. I need Mrs Vaizey to talk to the spirit world for me."

Valerie's next words were drowned in a roar of applause as Azusa scored their first goal. George covered his face with his hands and Ray Vito, who was sitting three rows behind them, let out a long string of Italian expletives, many of them involving mothers and hunchbacks and paraplegics.

"What did you say?" asked Jim.

"I said that Mrs Vaizey has left me. She decided that it was time for her to fade away."

"*Now*? She decided to fade away *now*?"

Valerie shrugged. "I couldn't stop her, Jim. She said she'd clung on long enough, and it was all becoming too tiring for her."

"But *now*? Just when I really need her?"

"I'm sorry, Jim. She was talking to your grandfather, and they both faded away together."

Jim said, "I don't believe this. They both warned me that I was in danger. They both predicted that I was going to be killed. And now they've gone, and left me to face up to this situation on my own."

"Mrs Vaizey left a message for you."

"Oh, yes? What was it? 'Rest in peace'?"

"No. She said that you really didn't need her any longer. You had powers enough of your own. She said that you ought to have faith in yourself, and what you can do."

"That's terrific. The trouble is, I don't *know* what I can do. I was very much hoping that Mrs Vaizey could tell me."

"Well, search me," said Valerie. "That's all she said. Then she just . . . melted away, you know? I had the sweetest sensation – the sweetest, most blissful sensation – and she was gone."

"We've scored!" George bellowed, so close to Jim's ear that it almost burst his eardrum. "Magro's scored! Did you see that run! That boy's a genius!"

Jim took hold of Valerie's hand and kissed her.

"Thanks, Valerie. If you ever feel Mrs Vaizey again, you can tell her how much I miss her."

He sat down again. The afternoon was even darker now, and the clouds began to trail across the sky like sheets soaked in Indian ink. George said, "Hope it doesn't rain. I've left my sandals out in the yard."

"Your sandals?"

"They're Greek. I bought them in Agnos Ioannis. They're great so long as you never get them wet. Otherwise they curl up like dried fish."

While George was talking, Jim looked across the football field, past the ducking, tackling, helmeted players – past the crowd of supporters from Azusa, waving Azusa Community College pennants and banners. Standing at the very top of the bleachers on the opposite end of the field were two dark figures, almost silhouetted against the threatening sky. Catherine White Bird, her long hair flying loose, in a big-shouldered black leather coat; and Dog Brother, in a long grey poncho, his eyes concealed by yellow-tinted glasses. Coyote, the First One To Use Words For Force, here at West Grove Community College.

Jim said, "You'll have to excuse me, George," and pushed his way along the row of cheering West Grove students until he reached the aisle. He kept his eyes on Dog Brother and Catherine as he circled the football field. He wasn't sure whether they had seen him or not, but the likely betting was that they had.

"Hi, Mr Rook!" said Sue-Robin Caufield, as she jiggled her pom-poms by the touchline. "Isn't this a great game? Isn't that Azusa full-back just swoony? I think I'm going to the wrong college. For boys, anyway," she quickly corrected herself. "Not for education."

Jim gave her a smile and a nod, although he hardly heard her. One of Azusa's guards had ducked through the West Grove defence for a touchdown, and suddenly everybody was on their feet. For a moment he lost sight of Dog Brother and Catherine, and he had to keep jumping up to see if he could catch sight of them. But then a last ray of sunshine reflected like a heliograph from from Dog Brother's yellow glasses, and he located them again. He didn't quite know what he was going to do when he reached them, but they were dangerous, both of them, and he didn't want them here at West Grove, threatening his students.

He had almost reached the other end of the field when he felt a tremendous slap on the back. He turned around and instinctively lifted his arm to protect himself, but it was only Ben Hunkus, the football coach. "What a game, Jim! I got a feeling in my water we're going to win this one! Pass it, Beidermeyer, for Christ's sake, you're not married to the damn thing!"

"Ben, I want you to keep your eyes open," said Jim. "The person who killed Martin is here."

"You know who it is? I thought it was them Indian boys."

"No, it wasn't. But I can't explain who really did it, not just yet."

"Just give me the name, Jim, and I'll have my boys pile on top of him, until you can call the cops."

"Not as easy as that, Ben. All you can for now is to watch out for anything unusual."

"OK, Jim. Whatever you say."

Jim had reached the bleachers where Dog Brother and Catherine were sitting. As he climbed the aisle, however, West Grove were awarded another four downs, with only 15 yards to go to the Azusa goal line. The crowd stood up in unison, and started cheering and whistling and chanting, and in the confusion he lost sight of Dog Brother and Catherine for a second time.

He picked the row in which he guessed they were standing, and elbowed his way along it. "Pardon me, excuse me. Sorry. Pardon me. Sorry."

When he reached the place where he had last seen them, however, they were gone. He desperately looked all around him. He caught the arm of a large man with a golfing hat on backward, so that his hair sprouted out of the front. "Pardon me, sir. Did you see two people standing here a moment ago? A girl in a black coat and a man with a pair of yellow sunglasses."

The man turned around and looked behind him as if he expected them to be hiding behind his enormous rump. Then he looked back at Jim and dumbly shook his head.

Jim pushed his way further along the row. Azusa had regained control of the ball and the excitement had subsided. As everybody sat down again, Jim was able to see all around the field. He couldn't understand how Dog Brother and Catherine could have escaped without his seeing them.

Well, he thought, there's one sure-fire way to find out where they are.

He lifted the whistle from around his neck and blew it. The large man in the golfing hat stared at him in dull curiosity. He waited, his eyes scanning the field and the college grounds beyond. Nothing – no sign of Dog Brother or Catherine anywhere. He blew the whistle again, and then again.

It was then that Dog Brother raised both his arms and Jim caught sight of them, although he couldn't believe where they were. They were standing on the opposite side of the field, only a few rows away from the place where Jim had been talking to George Babouris. It was impossible. Nobody could have made their way all around the field in only a few seconds, not even an Olympic runner. Yet there they were, and now they knew for sure that he was here, and that he was watching them.

At that moment, Jim began to understand the immense occult power of what he was up against, and for the first time in a long time he felt profoundly afraid.

Chapter Ten

He climbed down from the bleachers and walked toward the college buildings. The sky was completely dark now, and a strong wind was buffeting the bushes. He wasn't at all sure what he was going to do. He couldn't call the police, because he couldn't prove that Dog Brother and Catherine had done anything wrong. And now that Mrs Vaizey had faded away, he couldn't even call on his only adviser from the spirit world.

He had almost reached the main entrance when Henry Black Eagle appeared from the direction of the parking-lot, dressed in his black fringed buckskin jacket and wearing a headband. He was carrying a small rolled-up parcel of buffalo-hide, tied tightly with waxed cords and decorated with faded old feathers.

"I managed to talk to Paul and Grey Cloud," he said. "They're both very worried that Coyote has come here. He's very vengeful, you know, and they think that he intends to kill many people to show you that he is greater than all of your white man's spirits."

"Did they give you any ideas how to stop him?"

"They say the same as all of the legends. Coyote must be killed by one of his own kind, and his heart must be taken away from him. The only spirit who hates Coyote more than he fears him is the Rain Spirit. The story says that Coyote tricked his daughter into having sex with him, and that after she had done so, she died of shame, because she was supposed to be keeping herself pure for a noble hunter called Deer Slayer."

"So how do we go about enlisting the help of this Rain Spirit?"

Henry Black Eagle lifted the buffalo-hide bundle. "In here, there are sacred bones which Grey Cloud brought back from the Wide Ruins reservation. They were used to call the Rain Spirit in times of drought. This time we shall have to ask him to do us another kind of favour."

"Won't he want something in return?"

Henry Black Eagle said, "Yes. He will want a gift. What do you think you could offer him?"

"It depends what kind of gift he likes. I mean, what do you give to a Rain Spirit who's probably got everything?"

"You could give him your gift of supernatural vision."

"He'd really take it?"

"Why not? It's a gift like any other. One man gave his singing voice to the Buffalo Spirit, in exchange for bringing his family plenty to eat."

Jim frowned. When he first discovered that he could see spirits, he would have given his vision away to anybody who could have taken it, and been glad to be rid of it. But now it seemed so natural and normal that it would be like having one eye taken out. All the same, a man could still see with one eye, and what was important was saving Catherine and ridding the world of Coyote.

"All right," he said. "He can have my vision, if he wants it. I don't really have anything else."

"You're lucky you have that," Henry Black Eagle told him. "Sometimes a spirit will ask for a hand or a foot, or even a man's virility."

"The vision, OK? He can have the vision."

"Then we must hurry," said Henry Black Eagle. "Have you seen Coyote and Catherine here already?"

"The last time I saw them was in the crowd. I tried to go after them, but when I got to where they were standing, they were way over on the opposite side of the field."

"What would you have done, even if you *had* caught up with them?"

Jim shrugged. "I don't know. I hadn't really thought it through."

"With Coyote, you *must*. He is too cunning to be faced head-on. Now, let's get under those cedars, and see what we can do to call up the Rain Spirit."

There was more cheering from the football field as Russell Gloach caught a perfect 20-yard pass from Micky McGuiver.

"Run with it, Russell!" the captain was screaming. "Get those goddamned legs moving!"

Jim didn't try to see what was happening. He could imagine Russell lumbering along at his usual elephantine pace, and knew that he would be lucky to cover more than a yard before the Azusa quarter-backs brought him down. He followed Henry Black Eagle to the three tall cedars which stood on a rise at the north-west corner of the college. Underneath their overhanging branches it was quiet and dark and sheltered from the wind.

Henry Black Eagle sat cross-legged on the ground and untied the buffalo-hide parcel. Jim stood beside him and watched. "I'm not a wonder-worker myself," said Henry Black Eagle, "so I will have to rely on *your* spiritual gifts to contact the Rain Spirit. All I can do is to perform the ritual."

He rolled the hide out flat. Inside were five yellowed bones, which looked to Jim like old human arm-bones. The ends of each of them were tied with hanks of hair and faded red ribbons. Henry Black Eagle picked up two of them and tapped them together, in a quick, hesitant rhythm.

"Sit in front of me," he instructed Jim. "Empty your mind of any thoughts about Coyote and Catherine. Empty your mind of any thoughts about yourself – any fears, any questions, any doubts. Your mind should become as dark and as empty as the universe beyond the stars, where there are no more stars, only blackness, and that is where the Great Old Ones live, far beyond the reach of men."

Jim eased himself cross-legged onto the dry turf. He hadn't sat like this since he had last eaten at Koto, the Japanese restaurant, and then he had spent the rest of the evening walking like Groucho Marx. Henry Black Eagle tapped the bones again, and then again, and each time the rhythm because faster and more frenzied. He began to hum, and then to sing, both in Navajo and in English.

"*The Rain Spirit walks in the west . . . He lives on top of the highest mountains, wrapped in clouds for a cloak . . . He carries water in his cloak and spreads it on the dry ground . . . He is generous and just, the protector of all life . . . We ask him now to appear so that we may honour him, and to ask of him a special favor . . .*"

This went on and on, in a monotonous warbling sing-song. Jim didn't need to make much of an effort to empty his mind – Henry Black Eagle's singing was so hypnotic that it emptied it for him. He kept his eyes open, but he could feel all conscious thought sliding out of his head. Soon there was nothing but blackness and emptiness.

"*Rise now, O Rain Spirit and lend us your strength . . . Rise up, so that we may see you . . . Throw back your cloak of clouds and stand in front of us, so that we can witness your return . . . Rise up, Rain Spirit*! *Rise up*! *Rise up*!"

Henry Black Eagle was chanting this so loudly that two passing students stopped to give Jim and him the most peculiar looks. But they had hardly turned away when there was a blinding flash of lightning and a deafening crack, and the cedar tree under which they were sitting was split halfway down its trunk, and instantly burst into flames.

"Henry! For God's sake, let's get out of here!" Jim shouted, trying to untangle his legs.

But Henry Black Eagle stayed where he was, tapping and tapping the bones, murmuring and singing, while sparks drifted down all around him, and the cedar tree crackled and spat.

Several people started running toward them. It was then, however, that Henry Black Eagle lifted the bones right over his head and let out a howl like a triumphant animal.

"*Let us see you, O Rain Spirit! Let us see you! Rise up and be our guardian! Rise up and be our protector!*"

As he clacked the bones together one last time, the ground shook with the reverberation of a massive peal of thunder, like all the kettle-drums of all the orchestras in the world, all rolling at once. Even before the first helpers could reach them, rain came blasting out of the sky in a vicious, slanting torrent that almost stopped them in their tracks. The rain drowned the fire in the cedar tree and came rattling down through the branches. Jim looked down toward the football field, and he could see some people running for cover and others holding coats or newspapers over their heads. The game, however, was still going on. West Grove and Azusa were battling for their honour, and neither team was going to let a rainstorm put them off. West Grove were looking for their first victory this season, and Azusa were determined not to be beaten by the Fumblers at any cost. Swathes of rain trailed across the football field like soaking-wet net curtains, and in only a few minutes the grass was half-flooded. The players dodged and kicked and scrimmaged in showers of spray, with rain dripping from their helmets and water spraying from their boots.

Jim yelled at Henry Black Eagle, "What the hell's going on? There's plenty of rain, but where's the Rain Spirit?"

"Believe!" Henry Black Eagle shouted back at him. "You have to believe!"

The rain was so heavy now that Jim could barely see the football field. It spouted off the college guttering and filled up the rosebeds beside the main entrance, until muddy water started to pour over the top of the brickwork and run down the path toward the parking-lot. Many parents and supporters had convertibles, and they had all rushed to the parking-lot to put up their tops.

Another devastating crack of lightning jumped across the sky, and then the ground shook again.

"*Believe*!" screamed Henry Black Eagle. "*You have to believe*!"

Jim stood up and walked out from under the cedar tree. He was instantly soaked in freezing rain – his coat hanging from him, his hair plastered flat against his forehead. There *is* a Rain Spirit, he said to himself. There *is* a Rain Spirit and I believe in him. I have the gift. I have the vision. I believe in him and I can see him. I believe in him and—

I can see him!

There, in the pouring rain, right in front of him, Jim could make out the watery outlines of a tall creature – almost like a man, yet not a man at all. It had a proud, remote face, as colourless as rain, and a body swathed in tumbling, smoking cloud.

Jim felt its power – cold and sharp and stinging like the rain itself. He had never believed that such spirits existed – that the elements themselves were controlled by living, thinking beings. But here in front of him was the proof, its watery features wavering and pale and distorted, a face from the times when America was being created out of rock and wind and water.

He dropped to his knees on the grass. He felt exhausted and humble. He felt as if everything he had ever taken for granted had been swept away, like the mud and the leaves that were being swept away by the Rain Spirit's storm.

Henry Black Eagle came up and laid a hand on his shoulder. "You can see him, can't you?" he said.

Jim nodded. "He's there. He's just like the rain."

"You don't know how much I envy you," said Henry Black Eagle. "To see what a spirit can do, that's one thing. Rain, thunder, lightning, that's impressive enough. But to see a spirit's face—"

"What do we do now?" Jim asked him. "How do we get him to kill Coyote?"

"We ask. That's the only way."

Henry Black Eagle knelt down beside him and raised both hands. "O great spirit," he said, "we have been wronged by the First One To Use Words For Force. He is here today, with my daughter, Catherine White Bird, whose hand he wants to take in marriage. He has deceived me in the same way that he deceived you, O spirit. For my sake, and for my daughter's sake, I beg you to kill him for me, and take away his heart."

Jim kept his eyes on the Rain Spirit but he didn't see any response. The spirit continued to drift in the rain, its cloud-cloak billowing and fuming. Sometimes it was almost impossible to see if there was anything there at all.

"Please, great spirit. I abase myself in front of you." And with that, Henry Black Eagle laid himself flat on the ground, his arms outstretched, while the rain continued to pour down on top of him.

A black senior called Mo Sharp came up to Jim, his

college T-shirt soaking. Mo was academically slow, but he was almost a genius at cabinet-making. "You okay, Mr Rook?" he asked, looking down suspiciously at Henry Black Eagle.

"Sure, Mo, everything's cool. You get back down there and cheer us on."

"Never saw it rain like this before, Mr Rook."

"No, well, neither did I. Maybe you should start building us an Ark."

Another crackle of lightning lit up the falling rain like a strobe light. Mo scampered off and Jim turned back to the Rain Spirit. It looked to Jim as if he were fading, as if his cloud-cloak were breaking into fragments.

"You have to help us!" he shouted. "You can't leave us to fight Coyote alone! You have to help us! I've got the gift of vision! You can have that, if you kill Coyote for us!"

Jim heard a blur of words in his mind. It was like somebody with a very deep voice whispering very close to his ear. Henry Black Eagle lifted himself from the ground, and said, "Thank you, great spirit. Thank you."

"What?" Jim wanted to know.

"The Rain Spirit has agreed to do it. He will kill Coyote for us. All he wants in return is your gift of vision and one of my fingers."

"You're kidding me. One of your *fingers*?"

"Mr Rook – it will be a very small price to pay to get my daughter back."

"But you can't let it take one of your fingers!"

Henry Black Eagle lifted up his right hand. "It already has," he said. His middle finger was missing, except for a quarter-inch stump of broken bone. Blood was pouring down the back of his hand and into his sleeve.

Jim touched his forehead. "He hasn't taken my vision yet, has he?"

"Not until he has killed Coyote. He wants you to see him doing it."

Jim heard more blurred words. Henry Black Eagle dragged a handkerchief out of his pocket and wrapped it around his hand. "We should follow him," he said. "He is going to find Coyote and rip his heart out."

The blurry Rain Spirit turned around and began to move down the slope toward the football field. The rain was still driving down just as fiercely as before, and Jim found it difficult to follow it. It kept fading away, and then reappearing, no more substantial than a drift of smoke from a garden fire.

They followed it all the way around the back of the bleachers, until it reached the far side of the field. There – almost alone at the very top – stood Dog Brother, his hair streaked with rain, and Catherine, with her collar turned up. Jim walked up the rows of bleachers and stood in front of them, with rain pouring from his chin like a faucet.

"So – what do you want?" asked Dog Brother. "Haven't you caused me enough trouble?"

"I've come for Catherine," said Jim. "If you let Catherine go, then maybe I'll let you go."

"I came here to kill you," said Dog Brother. Droplets of water quivered on his yellow-lensed spectacles. "I came here to destroy everything you touch and everybody you love. Your class of young people are going to die first. Then I'm going to kill anyone who ever meant anything to you, *ever*. Remember your cousin Laura, whom you loved so much? You remember that poem you wrote her, *My Golden Girl*, and she couldn't even read? You'll know what's happened to Laura in the next few days, when your mother's sister calls you up and tells you that she's dead."

"What are you trying to do to me?" Jim yelled at him.

Dog Brother grinned. "Nothing that you white people didn't do to me. You killed my people, and when you killed my people, you killed me. Well, now it's *your* turn to find out what it's like."

Jim turned to Catherine. Her long hair was dripping in the rain and she looked extremely pale. "Catherine," he appealed. "Are you just going to stand by and see innocent people killed?"

"And not just any innocent people," smiled Dog Brother. "Your fellow-students, Catherine. Your precious Special Class II, where you've been learning to forget the Navajo way and the Navajo beliefs – where you've been learning to forget *me*."

"If you harm any one of my students—" Jim began, but Dog Brother raised his hand. It was a long, narrow hand – more like a claw than a hand, with a thin, hairy wrist. Dog Brother said, "I'm going to slaughter them all, Mr Rook. David and Sharon and Muffy and Mark. There's going to be so much blood, you'll think that you're drowning in it."

"Catherine," said Jim. "Catherine, please. Think what you're doing. Those are your friends he's talking about. He wants to murder all of your friends."

Catherine turned her face away but Jim could have sworn that he saw a flicker of response.

"Catherine," he repeated. "Listen to me, Catherine."

"You can't stop me," said Dog Brother. "Your spirits are all much weaker than mine."

Jim took three steps back down the bleachers. Thunder bellowed directly overhead, which made him feel as if the sky were falling in. "*My* spirits may be weaker than yours, Coyote. But *yours* aren't. I summon you, great spirit, to rise up and see what Coyote has become. And I bid you destroy him – extinguish his breath, tear out his lungs, pull out his heart."

A father with a gingery moustache turned round to Jim and said, "Excuse me, mister. There are kids here. You two guys want to say things like that, take your argument someplace else."

"Yes, sorry," said Jim. But then he flung his arms wide and shouted, "*Great spirit, come and kill Coyote! Great spirit, come and tear out his heart*!"

"Jesus," said the father with the gingery moustache. "The principal's going to hear about this."

But at that moment, a sharp gust of rain snapped across the bleachers, and Jim saw the Rain Spirit climbing up the aisle, its watery face grim with the look of revenge. In one hand it carried a huge and complicated spear, with water continuously pouring from its tip, and raindrops falling from its shaft.

"*Your time has come, Coyote*," said the Rain Spirit, somewhere inside of Jim's head. "*And this isn't a good day to die*."

"Wait," said Dog Brother, raising his hand. "Can't you allow me one last wish before you kill me?" Catherine clung close to his arm, and even though Jim said, "Catherine! *Catherine*!" again and again, she wouldn't look at him.

The Rain Spirit said, "*Why should I grant you any last wishes, after what you did to my daughter*?"

"I simply want to choose the way I die," said Dog Brother. He was still grinning. All around them, the few spectators who had braved the rain were cheering West Grove toward another touchdown. "Go West Grove! Go West Grove!"

"*You may die any way you wish*," said the Rain Spirit. "*Choose, but be quick, My spear is growing impatient for your heart*."

"You're the spirit of storms – kill me by lightning! Let me hold up your spear and take the full force of your anger! I'm half a spirit, but I'm half a man, and that will kill me as quickly as snuffing out a torch."

The Rain Spirit hesitated for a moment. "Don't listen to him," said Jim. "Just stab him, and take out his heart."

"*If an enemy asks to die in a particular way, then it is shameful not to grant him his wish.*"

"You're going to give him your spear? That's good thinking!"

"*I am water, my friend. I am nothing but rain. My own spear cannot harm me.*"

"Well go on, then. Do it. But do it now. And you – Dog Brother – you make sure that Catherine stands well away from you."

"Do you think I would harm the most beautiful girl I have ever known?"

"Just make sure she stays clear, you got it?"

The Rain Spirit tossed his spear to Dog Brother. Nobody but Jim could see any of these things. They couldn't see the Rain Spirit, in his tumbling cloak of clouds. They couldn't see why Dog Brother suddenly lifted his hand as if he were catching something. But Jim could see him standing on the top row of the bleachers with the Rain Spirit's spear held high in his right hand, pointing up at the hurrying black clouds.

"I'm ready," said Dog Brother. He took off his yellow spectacles and revealed eyes that were yellow, too.

The Rain Spirit lifted one finger to the skies. There was a moment's pause, while the rain continued to lash down all around them. Then a leader-stroke of lightning came forking out of the clouds, heading right down toward them. Jim stepped back, and pushed back the father with the gingery moustache.

"Who are you shoving, buddy?" the father demanded, just as the blinding bolt of lightning hit the tip of the Rain Spirit's spear. How Dog Brother had the split-second timing to do it, Jim would never know. But he threw the spear back at the Rain Spirit, and the Rain Spirit instinctively caught it – right at the instant when the lightning's return stroke hit it, with more than a quarter of a million volts.

Jim saw the Rain Spirit's expression for only a fraction of a second – an agonized mask. Then it exploded into steam, like the ear-splitting blast from a locomotive. Scores of people turned around to see what had happened, but all they saw was the last stray fragments of steam drifting away.

It kept on raining, however, as if the skies were in mourning for the loss of their spirit, the one who had guided them for century after century, even when the white men came.

Dog Brother replaced his spectacles and said to Jim, "No spirit can touch me. No man can kill me. Now I'm going to show you what Coyote can do to you, if you make him angry."

He turned to Catherine and laid a hand on her shoulder. "*No*," said Henry Black Eagle. "Leave her alone."

"She isn't yours any longer, old man," said Dog Brother. "She's mine, and she's going to stay mine. Catherine, let's see what pain you can inflict on Mr Rook's team here. You told me they've never won a game. Well, let's see how badly they can lose this one."

"*Catherine, no*!" Jim shouted at her. But already he could see the shadows forming around her head, her shoulders hunching, her eyes beginning to shrink and smoulder scarlet.

"*No*!" he said, and tried to grab hold of her arms, but they were already thick and hairy and she pushed him aside.

Henry Black Eagle couldn't see Catherine's transformation, but he knew what was happening to her. He climbed up the bleachers to Dog Brother and tried to seize hold of his coat. "You can't do this! She's a child! She can't change when people are watching her! Leave her alone!"

"When I'm here, she can change whenever I want her to. And I want her to." With that, Dog Brother grasped hold of Henry Black Eagle's lapels, and head-butted him, so that he fell backward and tumbled halfway down the aisle. There were screams and shouts and George Babouris called up to Jim, "What the hell's going on, Jim? What's happening?"

"Call an ambulance! Call the cops!" Jim told him. "Stop the game! Get everybody out of here!"

"I just want to know what's happening!"

"Do it, George, that's all I ask! Just do it!"

Dog Brother came down the bleachers, took hold of Jim's shoulder, and slapped him across the face. Jim tried to punch him back, but Dog Brother slapped him again.

Behind him, Catherine had grown taller and darker and now she was *bristling*, just the way that Jim's grandfather had predicted. Her claws were like black crescent moons, and she had rows and rows of hideously hooked teeth.

Dog Brother said, "This is my revenge, white man. This is what happens to people who try to cross me. Catherine White Bird is mine. She was always mine, and she always will be, even when she has given me the child I need, and she becomes nothing more than a beast."

George had gone down to the field waving his arms to stop the game. Ben Hunkus was shouting at him and so was the Azusa coach. The players were standing around in muddy bewilderment. The crowd had shrunk away from Dog Brother and Jim, but they would have shrunk away even further if they could have seen the beast that Catherine was gradually becoming.

"I'm going to murder your children now," said Dog

Brother. "I'm going to murder your children just as the white men murdered our children."

He waved his hand, and the Changing Bear Maiden began to descend the steps. All that anybody else could see was Catherine – walking stiffly perhaps, with her shoulders hunched. But Jim could see a huge black shadow-creature with claws and teeth – a creature that could slaughter every young man on the football field and tear their bodies into shreds.

"*Catherine*!" he roared. "*Catherine, listen to me*!"

Dog Brother kept hold of him, but grinned at him even wider. "It's no use, Mr Rook. It's time for the bloodshed."

"Catherine," Jim repeated. "Catherine, this creature isn't you. It's only an illusion. Magic, trickery, that's all it is. You're still inside there, Catherine, someplace. Catherine White Bird, who's free. Catherine White Bird, who wants a life of her own."

"You can't stop her, Mr Rook," smiled Dog Brother. "Why don't you sit down and enjoy the spectacle, mmh? It's going to be better than the Roman games."

"Catherine," Jim pleaded. "You never wanted to go back to the reservations, did you? You never wanted to be Dog Brother's bride? Come on, Catherine, listen to me. You have to break free. You have to be *you*!

He paused for breath, and then he recited,

'Thus in the winter stands the lonely tree
It cannot say what loves have come and gone;
I only know that summer sang in me
A little while, that sings in me no more.'

The shadowy spirit-beast hesitated. It turned its head toward Jim and there was a look of hurt in its eyes, a look of deepest hurt.

"Go!" Dog Brother commanded it. "Go and rip their

lungs out! Go bite off their heads! Come on, heads! I want to see some heads!"

But the Changing Bear Maiden stayed where she was; and then she turned, and came back toward Dog Brother and towered over him, her fur streaked with rain.

"Kill," said Dog Brother, unconvincingly. But the Changing Bear Maiden loomed over him and wouldn't move.

"*Kill*!" Dog Brother screamed at her. "*Kill the bastards before I kill you*!"

Without warning, the Changing Bear Maiden slammed her claws into Dog Brother's shoulder. He let out a high-pitched shriek and tried to wrestle himself away. But the Changing Bear Maiden lifted him completely off the bleachers until his feet were kicking in the air like a hanged man.

"*Let me go*!" he shouted. "*Let me go*!"

But he was half a man, as well as half a spirit, and he didn't have the strength to tear himself free. And even though it needed one of his own kind to kill him, she was the same – half-beast, half-spirit – and that was what he had forgotten.

She let out a roar that made Jim's skin prickle all the way down his back. Then she ripped open his chest with a single catastrophic blow, tearing through skin and muscle and ribs, and she dragged out his living heart. She held it up in one bloodstained claw, and roared again.

Jim heard more screams all around him. To the horrified crowd, it must have looked as if Catherine had pulled out Dog Brother's heart. There was blood spraying everywhere, and Dog Brother staggered and slipped and fell on the bleachers, clutching his chest, coughing and gasping.

He held up his hand toward the Changing Bear Maiden, to give him back his heart, but she took one step backward and downward, and then another, and with every step the shadows around her the bristles began to fade, and the shadows melted more. The claws shrank and the eyes stopped glowing. By the seventh step, she was Catherine again, her face white with shock, still holding Dog Brother's heart, but Catherine again.

Dog Brother heaved himself up and grasped hold of the metal handrail. "Catherine," he said, "give me back my heart."

Catherine stood with his heart held up in the air. Blood and rain were running down her sleeve. She turned to Jim and looked at him in desperation.

"I love you, Catherine," said Dog Brother. "Please, give me back my heart."

Jim mouthed one word. "*Don't.*"

Dog Brother came down the steps, one by one. His bloody hands slid down the handrail, inch by inch. "Please, Catherine, I'm begging you."

Catherine took another step back and Dog Brother lunged at her, but he lost his footing and tumbled at her feet. He lay sprawled across the bleachers, one foot shuddering. Then he lay still. Blood ran down the steps onto the grass below. Henry Black Eagle went across and put his arm around Catherine's shoulders and held her tight. "I'm sorry," he said. "You don't know how sorry I am."

"Is he dead?" asked Catherine.

"He's half-human but he's half-spirit, too. He can survive for quite a time without a heart."

"He *looks* dead."

Jim looked around the football field. The spectators were all standing in the rain staring at them, confused and frightened. He could sirens in the distance. On the field itself, the players stood like statues. Dog Brother lay on the steps, broken and silent, with the rain soaking his coat and his blood dripping from the bleachers onto the ground below.

"Come on," Jim told Catherine, holding out his hand. "You'd better give me that."

At that moment, however, Dog Brother lashed out and caught hold of Catherine's ankle. She stumbled, colliding against her father, who stumbled too. Dog Brother struggled up onto his feet and seized hold of her arm, trying to snatch his heart away from her.

"*Catherine*!" shouted Jim, and held both hands up, even higher. He didn't realise that Catherine had thrown him the heart until it came flying toward him, spraying blood like a pinwheel. He caught it and it landed in his hands with a sharp flap, with its protruding arteries still attached. Cupping it closely, he jumped and bounded down the wet bleachers, trying to avoid the dumbfounded spectators, some of whom caught at his coat in a half-hearted attempt to stop him, simply because they didn't understand what was happening.

Dog Brother came leaping after him, and both of them slithered and tripped on the wet woodwork, although Jim managed to keep his balance until he reached the field. He cannoned his way through a crowd of milling spectators, and then he ran up the field as fast as he could, dodging in between the players. The rain lashed his face like a bucketful of cold salt, and his shoes splashed in the puddles.

He thought he was clear. He thought he *must* be clear. But then he glanced back over his shoulder and saw that Dog Brother was only five or six yards behind him, and closing. His chest was hanging open. His lungs were blown up like bloody balloons. Yet he kept on running and his yellow eyes were glaring with hatred. Jim suddenly realised that he didn't have the speed or the stamina to get away.

"Mo!" he shouted, to one of West Grove's tackles, Mo Newton. "Mo, take this and run with it!"

He threw the heart to Mo and Mo caught it before he realized what it was.

"What the hell is *this*, man? This is gross!"

"*Run with it*!" Jim yelled at him.

Mo started to run and Mo was fast, but Dog Brother was faster, even with his body ripped open. He swerved past Jim and just had time to say, "Bastard!" before he was running through the rain after Mo. Like Jim, Mo must have thought that he was clear, and by the time he reached the 20-yard line he started to ease off. But then Dog Brother lashed at his football shirt, and tore the back of it wide open, and Mo realised that he didn't have a chance of getting away. He called, "Ron!" and threw the heart to Ron Hubbard, one of their half-backs, who caught it one-handed and started running back toward the Azusa goal with it.

All around the field, the crowd watched it disbelief as Dog Brother came running after Ron Hubbard, gaining on him yard after yard. He was half-human, and he couldn't survive for very long without a heart, but he was running for his own survival, and that made all the difference. Ron Hubbard threw the heart to Keith Altham, the quarter-back, who passed it on almost immediately to Denzil Green, another tackle. Denzil was quick-footed and liked to play football for laughs, and he danced and skipped in front of Dog Brother, holding up his heart like a football trophy, and then twirling around just out of his reach.

But then Dog Brother caught hold of his helmet and wrenched it around, and all Denzil could do was hurl the heart wildly in any direction. The only player anywhere near was Russell Gloach, who caught it neatly, stared at it in complete disgust, but then went lumbering off up the field, his big legs working and his boots kicking up spray.

"*Run, Russell!*" Jim bellowed at him. "*For God's sake, run!*"

Russell kept up his heavy, measured jog; and all the time Dog Brother was catching up with him, his coat-tails flying, his teeth gritted, his face a mask of complete hatred. He was only three yards behind Russell when Russell looked around and saw him coming.

It was a transformation. Russell arched back his head, filled out his chest, and began to run faster. Dog Brother lashed out at him, but missed him, and Russell ran faster still. The rain gradually began to clear as he sped through the puddles, past the 35-yard line, past the 50-yard line, kicking up fountains of spray. Everybody cheered and whistled and clapped, even though most of them didn't understand what was happening, and didn't realise that Dog Brother's chest was gaping open.

Dog Brother lost his footing by the 50-yard line, and tripped, and fell to his knees. Russell ran all the way to the goal line and performed a little triumphant ballet of his own. The clouds had almost passed over now, and the air was warm and steamy. Jim walked over to Dog Brother and stood beside him. Dog Brother was close to collapse. He took off his yellow spectacles and wiped them, and then he looked up at Jim and there was an expression on his face which wasn't hatred, or anger. It was more like resignation.

"Well, white man, it seems like you've beaten me, after all."

Jim said nothing. Three policemen were approaching, across the grass, and he lifted his hand to warn them to keep their distance.

"Maybe I should have realised that times have changed," said Dog Brother. He spat a string of blood onto the ground.

"Maybe I should have realised that the world doesn't have a place for creatures like me any longer."

"You want me to feel sympathetic? Because of you, an innocent young boy was murdered, and I lost a woman I loved – and whatever I think about John Three Names, he didn't deserve to die, either."

"If I could have my heart back—" said Dog Brother.

"I'm not giving you your heart back. Your days on this earth are over, Coyote."

"But you forget. I have power over death. Lives are taken away – yes. But lives can be given back again, can't they?"

"What are you talking about?"

"I'm talking about a deal, white man. I'm talking about getting my heart back."

"You mean you can bring these people back to life? What are you talking about? The woman I loved, she had her head taken off, and then her body was burned. She was a sacrifice to you."

"What's a sacrifice? A gift, that's all. And gifts can always be returned."

"I don't believe you."

Dog Brother lowered his head, and coughed more blood. "That's your privilege. But wouldn't it be wonderul if it *were* true?"

Jim was silent for a very long time. He looked around the field and saw the spectators all anxiously milling around. He saw the teams watching him in bewilderment. He saw the clouds blowing away and the sun coming out.

"If I give you back your heart," he said, "you have to promise me one thing. You have to promise to leave Catherine White Bird alone, for ever. You have to go back to Fort Defiance, and if you want a bride, you have to find yourself a Navajo girl who really wants to marry you.

"If I even smell you anywhere near Catherine White Bird again, then by God I'll come after you and you'll wish that you were never even thought of."

Dog Brother nodded. "Don't worry, Mr Rook. I won't touch her again."

Jim beckoned to Russell and Russell brought the heart over. "You deserve a medal," said Jim, and gave Russell an affectionate cuff. Then he handed the heart to Dog Brother, who looked at it for a moment, and then took it, and stowed it into his chest like a man putting his wallet away. He passed his hand down the front of his body and his bones knitted together with an odd creaking sound, and his skin mended itself over his wound like melting wax.

He stood up. "Perhaps I should have realised that times have changed," he said, almost regretfully. "So many of us died, but that was a long time ago now, the way you humans look at things, at least. Maybe it's time to forget."

He lifted up the whistle that was hanging around Jim's neck. "If you ever feel the need for some spiritual reinforcements, why don't you whistle?"

At that moment, Catherine White Bird came up, closely followed by Henry Black Eagle. "I don't know how to thank you," she said.

"You can start by forgiving your father," Jim told her. "And then you can get the best English grades ever."

He turned around to talk to Dog Brother, but Dog Brother had vanished. He hadn't even left any footprints. The sun shone on the wet football field and there was a sharp smell of ozone. The game had been played in which both sides had lost; and his encounter with Coyote was over.

Catherine took hold of his hand and walked back to the college with him. She was wet and her hair was straggly but she was still very beautiful. "Do you ever date your students?" she asked him, squeezing his hand. He smiled at her and squeezed her hand back. "No," he said. "Never."

Later that evening, in the West Grove mortuary, the body of Martin Amato, the football captain, suddenly twitched and stirred. In another mortuary, in Window Rock, Arizona, the body of John Three Names, the Navajo journalist, uttered a low, vibrant moan.

And behind the Navajo Nation Inn, the wind started to blow like a small tornado, and blue lights started to flicker. Dust and ashes were blown up into the air.

Then, slowly, a woman's hand appeared out of the ground.